A Daughter's Destiny

Rosie Goodwin is the million-copy bestselling author of more than thirty-five novels. She is the first author in the world to be allowed to follow three of Catherine Cookson's trilogies with her own sequels. Having worked in the social services sector for many years, then fostered a number of children, she is now a full-time novelist. She is one of the top 50 most borrowed authors from UK libraries. Rosie lives in Nuneaton, the setting for many of her books, with her husband and their beloved dogs.

Rosie GOODWIN

A Daughter's Destiny

ZAFFRE

First published in the UK in 2022 by
ZAFFRE
An imprint of Bonnier Books UK
4th Floor, Victoria House, Bloomsbury Square, London, England, WC1B 4DA
Owned by Bonnier Books
Sveavägen 56, Stockholm, Sweden

A CIP catalogue record for this book is
available from the British Library.

ISBN: 978–1–83877–356–4

Also available as an ebook and an audiobook

1 3 5 7 9 10 8 6 4 2

Typeset by IDSUK (Data Connection) Ltd
Printed and bound in Great Britain by Clays Ltd, Elcograf S.p.A.

Zaffre is an imprint of Bonnier Books UK
www.bonnierbooks.co.uk

This book is for David Codd, a very brave man and a true gentleman, and Penny his wife, who have been behind me every step of the way since my very first publication. Thank you my dear friends xx

Chapter One

March 1875

'Is the meal not to your liking, Gerald?'

Glancing up from his untouched plate, Gerald Winter nodded. 'It's quite delicious, Dorcas, but I find I don't have much of an appetite this evening, my dear.'

'Again!' His wife sniffed her disapproval as she dabbed at her lips with a snow-white napkin while her two daughters glanced anxiously at each other. It looked like they were set for another uncomfortable evening, but they were getting used to it now. Since the month before when their father had lowered the housekeeping money, their parents seemed to be constantly squabbling and their father had become unusually quiet, often locking himself away in his office for hours.

At that moment Hetty, their maid, appeared to clear the main course pots from the table, returning a short time later with the dessert, which she lay in the centre of the crisp white cloth. It was a large apple pie with a golden crust and beside it she placed a jug of fresh whipped cream.

At sixteen, Abigail was the younger of the two girls, and she licked her lips in anticipation.

Her mother eyed it with distaste. 'I can't believe we have to resort to such *common* meals,' Dorcas said huffily. 'Was it *really* necessary to cut the housekeeping down, Gerald?'

'I wouldn't have done it if it wasn't.'

Emerald, his nineteen-year-old daughter, gave him a sympathetic smile. If asked, she would have been forced to admit that she had always been far closer to her father than her mother, who, unfortunately, was a terrible snob. It upset her to see him looking so worried and haggard but there was nothing she could do about it apart from hope things improved. He had admitted some months before that his business – a brickworks in the nearby parish of Stockingford – was struggling, and Emmy – as he affectionately called her – was not surprised. Her mother was very demanding and expected the very best of everything and more than once recently Emmy had heard her father ask her to curb her spending as it was eating up any profit they made. Yet only that afternoon she had decided that the drawing room really *must* be redecorated, even though it had only been done less than two years ago, and she had sat poring over a book of wallpaper samples that cost more per roll than most people would earn in a week.

She mentioned it now to her husband, and Emmy saw him visibly flinch, although he said not a word.

'Mrs Henderson-Ward had her room done in paper from this particular book,' she gushed. 'And it really does look quite regal. I particularly like the silk patterns, although they do tend to be a little more expensive. What do you think, dear?' Suddenly Dorcas was all smiles again but her husband merely shook his head and, rising from the table, he left the room.

'Really!' Dorcas tutted her disapproval. 'Your father's manners are quite appalling lately. He didn't even ask to be excused.'

Quite suddenly Emmy's appetite had vanished too, although Abigail more than made up for it and had second helpings. The two girls took after their father in looks with brunette hair that shone like polished conkers and deep-green eyes, but there any resemblance ended for they were like chalk and cheese in nature. Emmy, who was the tallest and the slimmest of the two, tended to be the more quiet, studious one, while Abigail was more like her mother: petite and quite demanding. She attended a private school in Coventry. The same one that Emmy had attended until she had reached the age of eighteen. Sometimes Emmy almost wished she was back there, for ever since she had finished school her mother had done nothing but parade what she considered to be eligible suitors for her daughter's hand in marriage under her nose, each one a little bit richer than the last.

Now, Emmy sat impatiently waiting for the meal to be over, and when it was, she immediately excused herself and went in search of her father.

'I reckon he's in his study, miss,' Hetty informed her in the hallway, and smiling her thanks, Emmy headed in that direction.

Tapping at the door, she went in and found him seated at the imposing polished mahogany desk in front of the large window that overlooked the sweeping lawns surrounding the house. His head was in his hands, but when he saw Emmy standing there he sighed with relief.

'Ah, it's you, my lovely.' He held his hand out to her. 'For a terrible moment I thought it was your mother come to tell me that she needed new furniture to go with the new wallpaper.'

'No, Papa. It's only me.' She gave his hand a gentle squeeze. 'Is there anything I can do for you?'

'Huh! I doubt there is anything *anyone* could do for me at this moment,' he said bitterly. Then instantly regretting his words he gave her an apologetic smile. 'I'm afraid I have been rather a fool, my darling . . . I should have curbed your mother's spending habits many years ago, but because she always reminded me that she had married beneath her class I always felt that I owed it to her to pander to her every whim. But whatever happens, I want you to always remember that you are one of the best things that has ever happened to me. I can remember the day you were born as if it was yesterday.' His eyes grew moist as his mind drifted back in time. 'You were *such* a beautiful baby. Even at birth your eyes had a hint of green in them, which was why I persuaded your mother to call you Emerald. She was a much gentler, less demanding person back in those days,' he said regretfully. Then with a shake of his head he pulled his thoughts back to the present to say urgently, 'Promise me you will marry for love.'

Emmy chuckled. 'Don't worry, Papa, I will. I have no intention of marrying the man of my mother's choice.'

'Good.' He rose from his seat and as his arms closed around her, much as they had when she was a little girl, she nestled contentedly into his chest. She had always run to her father for comfort as a child, because her mother had usually been too afraid of her messing up one of her expensive gowns.

They stood like that for precious moments until he gently held her away from him and stared at her as if he were trying to memorise every feature of her face, before saying softly, 'As much as I would love to spend the evening talking to you, my dear, I really must finish these accounts for the brickyard.'

'Of course, Papa.' Emmy kissed his cheek and wished him goodnight and left feeling vaguely uneasy. The feeling stayed with her for the rest of the night, and even when she retired to bed, her father's drawn face haunted her, so it was a long time before she fell asleep.

'Is Papa not joining us for breakfast?' Abigail asked the next morning as she helped herself to another slice of bacon from the covered silver salvers on the sideboard in the dining room.

'I have no idea.' Emmy glanced towards the door. It was usual for her mother to take breakfast in bed but it was very rare that her father didn't eat with them. 'Perhaps he had to be in work early?'

'Mmm.' Abigail bit into a thick juicy sausage with relish. 'Well, I intend to make a complete pig of myself until I have to go back to school after Easter. As you will remember, the food there is *so* unappetising.' She sighed dramatically. 'In fact, it's a wonder I haven't already wasted away.'

Emmy laughed and they enjoyed the rest of their breakfast in companionable silence.

Later that morning their mother ordered the carriage and went visiting friends, leaving the two girls to their own devices.

Emmy opted to go for a long walk in the countryside that surrounded their beautiful home while Abigail chose to stay in and read a book.

When their mother returned, they all gathered in the dining room for lunch and they were just finishing it when Hetty appeared. 'Mr Pembroke is here asking to see the master, ma'am. What shall I tell him?'

Dorcas rose from the table. 'But my husband should be at the works,' she said with a frown. 'Show him into the drawing room.'

'Yes, ma'am.' Hetty bobbed her knee and rushed off to do as she was told, while Dorcas swept after her.

She found Mr Pembroke, the bookkeeper at the brickworks, standing in front of the marble fireplace she had had shipped from France, nervously rolling the brim of his hat around.

'Mr Pembroke. I'm a little confused. Hetty tells me that you wish to see my husband but I believed he was already at the works?'

He shook his head, his face grave. 'He hasn't been there at all today, ma'am,' he answered respectfully. 'And I don't know what to do. He promised me that he would give me the money to pay the suppliers this morning and I'm afraid they are not prepared to wait any longer. Without fresh supplies I shall have no choice but to shut the business down until the outstanding debts are settled.'

'*Outstanding debts*?' Dorcas looked horrified. 'What are you talking about, man? Ours is a thriving business!'

'It *was* a thriving business,' he gulped. 'But I'm afraid it hasn't been classed as such for some time now and people are baying for the money they are owed.'

Dorcas tutted with annoyance. This man clearly didn't know what he was talking about. And where was Gerald? Blast the man.

'Tell me how much you need and I shall go to the bank and get the money for you immediately,' she told him imperiously.

He withdrew a piece of paper from his pocket and handed it to her and when she saw the amount written on it her face paled, although she otherwise remained calm.

'You may go now,' she said dismissively, drawing herself up to her full height. 'And I shall bring the money to you later this afternoon.'

'Much obliged, ma'am.' He gave a little bow and scurried from the room like a frightened rabbit as Dorcas hurried away to order the carriage to be brought round to the front of the house for her.

An hour later she swept into the bank in Nuneaton in a beautiful dark-blue velvet two-piece costume with a matching hat trimmed with white feathers, and demanded to see the bank manager immediately.

Within minutes he had ushered her into his office and, after shaking her hand, he offered her a seat.

'I am so glad you've come, Mrs Winter,' he began. 'I asked your husband to call in some weeks ago.'

'*Really?* And why would you do that?'

'To discuss his, er . . . situation.'

'*What* situation?'

He swallowed, making his Adam's apple bob up and down in his throat, before saying cautiously, 'About the bank loan he took out some time ago to keep his business afloat. He hasn't made any of the repayments. And so it is with deep regret that I have to inform you we now have no other option but to foreclose on the loan.'

Dorcas gasped and her hand flew to her mouth. 'B-but there must be some mistake,' she croaked.

He shook his head and took a file from his desk drawer. Opening it, he circled a large number before pushing the paper towards her. 'This is the amount outstanding.'

Her eyes popped as she stared at the staggering amount on the paper, then on legs that had suddenly turned to jelly, she rose, telling him, 'I'm sure there must be some way we can settle this matter, Mr Davidson. I shall go and see our solicitor immediately. Good day to you, sir.' She took the folder containing the unpaid bills and, cheeks burning with humiliation, sailed from the room with what dignity she could muster.

One thing was for sure, Gerald was going to have some explaining to do when she got her hands on him, but first she would seek their solicitor's advice.

Chapter Two

It was almost two hours later when Dorcas returned home, her face puce with rage.

Hetty hurried into the hall to take her hat and coat, smiling cheerily, but her smile vanished after taking a glance at her mistress. 'Good afternoon, ma'am.'

'Has the master returned?' Ignoring the girl's shocked expression Dorcas almost threw her outer garments at her.

'I, er . . . haven't seen him, ma'am.' Hetty was nervous now.

'Then I must assume that he hasn't come out of his room today, and I'm not surprised.'

Without another word, Dorcas stormed up the stairs, her starched petticoats rustling, and threw her husband's door open – she had insisted on separate bedrooms since the birth of Abigail. The bed was neatly made and she frowned before crossing to the wardrobe in his dressing room. Flinging the door open she glanced at the neat row of clothes hanging there, seeing at a glance that a few items were missing. It was then that her eyes came to rest on an envelope with her name on it propped up against his cologne on the dressing table, and a feeling of dread flooded through her as she lifted it with suddenly shaking fingers.

She slit the envelope with her thumb, a habit that she normally hated, and began to read.

Dear Dorcas,

   I can only apologise for the financial mess I am leaving you in. I have been trying to tell you for some time that the business is in trouble but I could never bring myself to admit it and always felt a failure if I couldn't meet your demands. I am placing no blame for the situation I find myself in on you. I should have been strong enough to be completely honest with you long before now. I am hoping that Bernard will be able to help you out of this whole sorry mess – he does have shares in the business after all, so it will be in his interest to do so. Perhaps your parents were right, and I was not good enough for you. But have no fear, you will not see me again. I have known for a while that your feelings for me have died but I pray that you and our daughters will have a happy life.

   Forgive me,
   Your husband,
   Gerald.

With a cry of rage, Dorcas screwed the letter up and flung it across the room. What did he mean, she would not see him again? And did he *really* think that she would swallow her pride and approach her brother Bernard, for help? But then she remembered the pile of unpaid bills she had left with Mr Lansdown, the solicitor, and the enormous figure on the slip of paper that Mr Pembroke had handed her and she lifted the crumpled letter and smoothed it out. For now, all she could do was wait for the solicitor to call on her, hopefully with a solution to their problems. If he couldn't help, she really didn't know what she would do. Fortunately, she wouldn't have to wait long. Mr Lansdown had promised that he would give the matter his urgent attention and would call to see her later that afternoon, and suddenly she knew that waiting for him to arrive would seem endless.

'Mama is in a bad mood today, isn't she?' Abigail remarked to Emmy as she leafed through a magazine containing all the latest London fashions. She prided herself on being one of the best-dressed girls at the private school she attended. 'I only said hello to her when she got home earlier from wherever she had been, and she almost snapped my head off.' She pouted. She was good at doing that if something upset her or she didn't get her own way.

Emmy smiled. 'Everyone is entitled to their off days. I think I'll go for another walk. It's too nice to stay indoors. Would you like to come?'

'Not likely!' Abigail shook her head. Walking was too much like hard work to her mind. And so Emmy put on her warm coat and bonnet and set off.

Astley House, their home, was situated on the outskirts of Nuneaton between the small hamlet of Astley and Galley Common, and Emmy loved living there. She knew the area like the back of her hand. The house was a large, rambling gentleman's residence that her mother had completely redesigned and refurbished over the years, surrounded by three acres of immaculately landscaped gardens. The gardener had been out and scythed the lawn that day and it stretched ahead of her as smooth as a bowling green. Primroses, daffodils and crocuses were peeping tentatively through the earth amongst the hedgerows that surrounded the property, and on the trees that lined the long drive, soft green leaves were beginning to unfurl after the long, hard winter.

She was fascinated with the history of the place and as a child had loved it when her father told her stories of their village. Once upon a time the village had been a Saxon settlement surrounded by dense woodland but most of that had been cut down and was now farmland where sheep and cattle grazed. The village also boasted a castle – once the home of Lady Jane Grey's mother – close to St Mary the Virgin Church, which the family attended every Sunday. Even now she was older, Emmy still liked to try to picture the village as it would have been back in Lady Jane's day. She often wondered if the unfortunate girl had ever trod the very same paths that she did. How different things must have been back then.

She was soon glad of her warm coat for it was a typical March day, windy and a little cold and she had been walking for no more than a few minutes when it started to drizzle. Without thinking, her footsteps turned in the direction of Astley Castle and soon she entered the beautiful little church that stood next to it where she could shelter from the rain and sit quietly and think. She always felt a sense of peace in there and after settling into one of the pews, she sat for a while admiring the stained-glass windows.

I wonder what put Mama in a bad mood? she pondered. Had her father upset her by refusing to pay for yet more wallpaper for the drawing room? She sighed. She knew all too well that her mother could be very challenging, and she had noticed for some time that her father hadn't seemed himself. His usual cheery disposition was absent and only the night before she had also noticed that he had lost weight. *Perhaps I should try and talk to him to find out what's wrong?* she thought. Rising from her seat, she curtsied towards the brass crucifix on the altar and headed for the door. The rain was drumming on the roof and coming down in torrents and she realised that for now at least she would have to abandon her walk. So she pulled the hood of her cloak up, lowered her head and hurried for home, splashing through the puddles and soaking the bottom of her gown and her little black buttoned boots in her haste.

The second she entered the house she sensed that something was wrong and her feeling was proved to be right when Abigail appeared from the door of the day room wringing her hands, as nervous as a kitten.

'Come in here,' she whispered, grabbing Emmy's hand and dragging her into the room.

Emmy was very aware that her clothes were dripping all over her mother's highly prized Turkish carpets and she shook Abigail's hand off. 'Whatever it is, can't it wait?' she asked irritably. 'Can't you see I'm soaked through? I'll go and get changed and then you can tell me what's wrong.'

But Abigail shook her head and grasped her arm again. 'It's Papa,' she said as tears began to slide down her cheeks. 'Mama says some of his clothes have gone from his room and no one has seen him today. He's taken Major from the stables and just gone off by the look of things. What do you think might have happened?'

Emmy's mouth dropped open in shock. 'But why ever would he do that?'

Abigail shook her head. 'I have no idea, but Mama is in a terrible state and has locked herself in her room. She won't talk to anyone and I think she's been crying. She said Mr Lansdown, Papa's solicitor, would be coming to see her later this afternoon and she would speak to us then.'

'I see.' Emmy chewed on her lip for a moment before turning to the door again. 'Then all we can do is wait to see what's going on,' she answered calmly, although her heart was pounding with fear, and with that she hurried away to get out of her wet clothes, a feeling of dread hanging over her.

The light was fading when Mr Lansdown's carriage clattered down the drive late that afternoon. After finally leaving the bedroom, Dorcas had shut herself in the drawing room all afternoon and anxiety had her pacing up and down like a caged animal. She knew that she would have to talk to the girls soon and give them the awful news, but she needed to hear the full extent of their problems from Lansdown first.

'Ah, Mr Lansdown.' Dorcas crossed the room and shook his hand when Hetty showed him in. 'Do take a seat. Hetty, could you bring some tea in?'

'Yes, ma'am.' Hetty bobbed her knee and shot off as Mr Lansdown came to stand in front of the fire.

'You and I have known each other for a long time, Dorcas,' he said quietly. 'And because there is no easy way to tell you this I'm just going to come out with it. I'm afraid you are almost penniless.'

'Don't be ridiculous,' she snapped. 'Even if Gerald had drained what money we had in the bank I still have the house and it's worth a great deal of money. I shall mortgage it and pay off his debts and his loans if need be then we can keep the business running.'

He shook his head, his face grave, and his next words made her hand fly to her throat. 'I'm afraid that won't be possible. You see, Gerald has already remortgaged the house.'

Her head wagged from side to side in denial as she tried to take in what he was saying. 'Then what am I to do?' Her voice came out as a squeak and she had to blink furiously to stop her tears from falling.

Mr Lansdown sighed. There had been a time many years ago when he had had a soft spot for Dorcas himself, but then she had met Gerald and they had fallen in love. At the time he had been heartbroken, but after seeing the life she had led Gerald into, he had realised over the years that in fact he'd had a lucky escape, but that didn't stop him from feeling sorry for her now.

'Unless you can raise a great deal of money, I'm afraid the house and the business will have to be sold,' he told her gently.

Again, she shook her head. '*No!* I shall ask my brother for help rather than that if it's the only way.'

His eyes were sad as he told her, 'But we are talking about many thousands of pounds. Do you think Bernard could help that much?'

'I don't know.' She sat down heavily on the nearest chair as Hetty wheeled the tea trolley into the room and for

15

a while they were silent as the maid strained the tea into delicate china cups and saucers.

It was only when Hetty had gone that Dorcas croaked, 'How much exactly do I need to get us out of trouble?'

He placed a piece of paper with an amount written on it in front of her and as she stared down at it her face turned ashen.

'Dear God . . . That much?'

'I'm afraid so.' He sipped at his tea as she sat staring sightlessly out of the window. Once he had finished he stood and bowed. 'I shall leave you now, but as soon as you have spoken with your brother and decided what you wish to do, come and see me. And remember, Dorcas, I shall do all I possibly can to help.'

'Er . . . yes, yes . . . thank you.'

She was vaguely aware of him leaving the room and of the sound of his carriage pulling away down the drive just as Abigail burst through the door with Emmy trailing behind, somewhat more tentatively.

'So, will you tell us what's wrong *now*, Mama?' Abigail asked peevishly. 'You've hardly spoken to us all day and we want to know what's going on. And where is Papa? He's usually home from work by now.'

Pulling herself together with an enormous effort, Dorcas rose and headed for the door. 'I have to go and see your Uncle Bernard but I shall speak to you when I get back,' she told the girls quietly.

As the door closed behind her mother, Abigail stamped her foot. 'I might as well still be at school for all the notice Mama has taken of me today,' she said with a pout, and throwing herself on to a sofa, she went into a sulk, while Emmy gazed worriedly towards the window.

Something was terribly wrong, she could feel it, but until her mother chose to tell them what it was, they would have to try and be patient.

Chapter Three

As the carriage turned into the long drive that led to Crossroads Farm, not far from her own home in Astley, Dorcas clenched her teeth. Her family had lived there for three generations and following the death of her father the farm had passed to her brother, Bernard. Dorcas had always considered it unfair. Admittedly Bernard was her senior by five years, but after the death of their mother when she was still in her teens, Dorcas had taken over the role of lady of the house. Because of this she'd felt that when her father died, the farm should have been left to them jointly, but because Bernard was male and the oldest child, he had inherited everything.

From that moment on they had never seen eye to eye and a year later when he married Sybil quite suddenly things had gone from bad to worse and it had become all too apparent that there was no room for two mistresses at Crossroads, so soon after, she had married Gerald. Back then, he had been working hard to build his business and had been handsome and kind. She had never considered that he was her equal but at the time she had thought anything was better than having to spend another day in what Bernard considered was very much *his* home. Admittedly her father had included a clause in his will stating that Dorcas should have a home there for as long as she wished, but once Bernard became the master it had become unbearable.

In truth, her marriage to Gerald had turned out far better than she had hoped. He was clearly besotted with her and had worked tirelessly to meet her many demands, until now that was. For the first time she wondered if she had been wrong to deny him her bed after the birth of Abi. She knew how much she had hurt him but even so, to go off and leave them all like that . . . As the carriage rattled down the drive, she blinked back tears of humiliation. To think that it had come to this and she was having to go cap in hand to her brother . . . But what alternative did she have? She ground her teeth as rage spread through her like iced water. It would be God help Gerald when he chose to put in an appearance again, but for now she would have to swallow her pride and throw herself on Bernard's mercy. No doubt he would gloat. He had always told her that she had married beneath herself but she was sure he wouldn't allow her to become a laughing stock. As the large farmhouse came into view, she frowned. Over the years Bernard had extended it and now it looked more like a mini mansion than a farm.

Unlike her father, who had never been afraid to turn his hand to anything, Bernard was a gentleman farmer who oversaw the work on his land rather than get his own hands dirty. He had an under-manager who handled some of the running of his estate so it was no wonder that at forty-five years of age Bernard had developed a paunch and looked years older than he was. *But I mustn't think of that now*, she

19

told herself as she dabbed at her eyes and sat upright. *I must try to be reasonable.*

The instant the groom drew the horses to a halt he jumped down and helped her from the carriage. Without a word of thanks, Dorcas climbed the steps to the stout oak door and yanked the bell pull to one side. The door was opened almost immediately by a young maid in a starched white apron and mop cap, and without waiting to be invited, Dorcas sailed past her and told her imperiously, 'Inform my brother that I am here to see him.'

'I'm afraid the family are having dinner, ma'am,' the girl told her nervously.

Dorcas glared at her as she drew off her gloves and without another word the girl scuttled off only to return a moment later to tell her, 'The master says you're to wait in the drawing room, ma'am.'

Gritting her teeth, Dorcas followed the girl and once in the drawing room she glanced around. The room was expensively if somewhat plainly furnished; Sybil had never been one for frills and furbelows, but the quality of every piece jumped out at her. The mahogany sideboard that stood against one wall was so highly polished that she could see her face in it and comfortable leather wing chairs stood either side of a roaring fire. The carpets were fringed and colourful but apart from the cut-glass decanters and goblets that stood on another table there were very few ornaments, unlike her own home where every surface was covered with costly trinkets. After a while she glanced at the heavy grand-father clock that stood in one corner and tutted. It was ter-rible of her brother to keep her waiting like this. He could at least have invited her to join the family, but then she supposed she should have expected no more. It had been some time since she had last seen him and they were hardly close.

At last the door opened and Bernard appeared. He was tall and his once thick dark hair was now receding and was specked with grey. But his dark eyes, so like her own, were curious as he looked towards her. He was dressed fashionably in a dark frock coat under which he wore a smart embroidered waistcoat and a silk cravat.

He nodded at her. 'So, to what do I owe the honour of this visit?' There was a hint of sarcasm in his voice as he crossed to the decanters and poured himself a brandy and Dorcas had to swallow the hasty retort that sprang to her lips. She was annoyed that he hadn't offered her a drink too but it wouldn't do to upset him right now.

'I, er . . .'

Before she could say any more, the door opened and Sybil appeared and Dorcas's heart sank even further. She and her sister-in-law had never seen eye to eye and she would have preferred to speak to Bernard alone, but it couldn't be helped.

Sybil was dressed in a good quality gown but it was a drab grey colour and her once fair hair was pulled into a tight bun at the nape of her neck, which did nothing to flatter her plain features whatsoever. Dorcas had always wondered what Bernard had ever seen in her and had assumed that it was the large dowry she had brought to the marriage that had been the attraction. She had heard rumours that Bernard had a mistress who he had set up in a little cottage on the outskirts of Nuneaton. She had no doubt the rumours were true; Bernard was a vain, bombastic man who liked his own way. It had never occurred to her that the reason they didn't get along was because they were too much alike. However, despite Bernard's flaws, the marriage seemed to be standing the test of time and Sybil had presented him with two sons.

'Good evening,' Sybil said formally as if she were greeting a stranger. There was no welcoming smile and Dorcas's spirits sank even lower. 'May I offer you tea or coffee? Or perhaps you would prefer a glass of sherry?'

'No, I . . . thank you. It was a word with my brother I wanted.'

As Sybil inclined her head and sank into one of the wing chairs with her hands folded primly in her lap, Dorcas gulped. It looked like she was going to just have to come out with it in front of both of them, so she took a deep breath and began tentatively. 'The thing is . . . I find myself in a bit of trouble . . . Well . . . quite a lot of trouble actually, and I've come to ask if you might help me out . . . Only temporarily, of course,' she added hastily as she saw Bernard's frown deepen. Just then the door opened and to make matters even worse Bernard's two sons entered the room. Jasper, the younger of the two at eighteen, was the spitting image of his father in looks and in nature, while Jake, who was now twenty-one, was milder mannered, fair-haired with grey eyes and favoured his mother in looks.

'Hello, Aunt Dorcas.' Jake immediately held his hand out in greeting while his brother merely eyed her curiously. 'How are you and the family? It's been a while since we saw you last.'

'Er . . . we are all well, thank you,' his aunt muttered politely.

Sybil glared at Jake, she had never made a secret of the fact that Jasper was the favourite.

The situation was becoming worse by the minute until Dorcas feared that she wouldn't be able to bring herself to speak in front of them all. 'Bernard . . .' She gulped and licked her dry lips. 'I was wondering . . . would it be possible to have a word in private? It's quite a delicate matter I wish you speak to you about.' Every instinct she had was telling her to just lift her skirts and get out of there but she couldn't afford to and so she tried not to notice Sybil's pursed lips.

Bernard sighed heavily. 'I suppose so; we'll go into my study.' Lifting his drink, he marched from the room, and after inclining her head to Sybil and the two young men, Dorcas scuttled after him.

'So, what is it that's so private you couldn't speak of it in front of the family?' Bernard asked sternly once they were in the privacy of his study.

'I . . . Well, the thing is . . . I find myself in difficulties. Financial difficulties, that is.'

Bernard frowned as he swirled the amber liquid in his glass and stared at his sister's flushed face. 'But I thought Gerald's business was doing well. Isn't this something *he* should be sorting out?'

'He . . . he's gone,' she said quietly, bowing her head in shame and silently cursing her husband for leaving her and her daughters in such dire straits. There had been a time when he would never have contemplated doing such a thing, but then, she realised with a little shock, somewhere along the line they had grown apart. 'And so it seems that the mess is left for me to sort out,' she went on in a shaky voice. 'It appears that the business has been in trouble for some time. I didn't know until the manager came to see me today, so I went to the bank and discovered just how bad things are. I have spoken to our solicitor and he has told me that if the debts aren't cleared, I shall have to sell the house to pay them.'

'And how much money are we speaking of? Hundreds?'

When Dorcas shook her head, his frown deepened. 'Thousands?'

She fumbled in her bag and when she pushed a piece of paper with the amount they needed across his desk to him, he gasped. '*Surely* you can't expect me to loan you this amount?'

Dorcas began to cry but it didn't soften him in the least and he began to pace up and down the room. Eventually he turned to her and shook his head. 'It appears to me that the solicitor was right. You will have to sell everything. But where has Gerald gone?'

'I don't know; he just left a note saying he was sorry and disappeared. And if I do what you suggest, what will become of me and the girls? Where will we live? We'll be penniless.'

Bernard's first instinct was to tell her that this wasn't his problem, but then he thought of what people would say if he was to turn his back on his sister and he thumped the table. 'The bloody *fool*!' he ground out through clenched teeth. 'Didn't I tell you not to marry him?'

Dorcas bit her lip. He was speaking to her as if she were an errant child but she was in no position to retaliate so she remained silent.

Eventually he paused in his pacing to say, 'Before I make a decision on what is to be done I would like your permission to speak to the manager at the works and your solicitor tomorrow.'

She nodded; there was nothing else she could do and sensing that for now he had nothing more to say to her she turned for the door. 'And you will speak to me again tomorrow?'

He gave a curt nod and with her cheeks burning with shame and humiliation, Dorcas went out to the carriage.

'So *now* will you tell us what's wrong, Mama?' Abigail asked sulkily the second her mother set foot in the house again. She knew it must be something serious; her father hadn't come home for dinner and her mother hadn't eaten all day as far as she knew.

'I'm afraid you will have to be patient for a little longer,' Dorcas told her wearily.

Abigail pouted. 'But *why?*' she pressed. 'And where is Papa? He's never this late home normally.'

'I doubt your father will be home this evening,' Dorcas said as she handed her hat and gloves to Hetty who looked almost as concerned as her daughters. And with that she made for the stairs leaving Emerald and Abigail to stare at each other worriedly.

Dorcas was not at breakfast or lunch the following day but confined herself to her room, and when Emmy went to tap on her bedroom door to see if she was all right, she was sent away.

'I'm afraid it must be something serious,' she told Abigail.

Her sister frowned. 'It had better be. Mama was supposed to be taking me to a fitting for my new gown in Nuneaton this afternoon. Now I've missed the appointment it's doubtful it will be ready in time for me to take it back to school.'

Emmy couldn't help but smile. Trust Abigail to think only of herself. She could be incredibly selfish at times but Emmy loved her all the same. At the moment she was more worried about her father, though. She couldn't ever remember him not coming home of an evening and she had a bad feeling in the pit of her stomach.

It was late in the afternoon when her uncle arrived and after showing him into the drawing room, Emmy hurried upstairs to inform her mother that he was there. Dorcas's bedroom door was firmly locked but she told her daughter that she would be down presently. When she finally appeared on the staircase, Emmy was shocked at the sight of her. Her mother's eyes were red-rimmed and she was so pale that she looked like a ghost. She was still wearing the gown she had worn the day before and had clearly slept in it as it was crumpled, and her hair was unbrushed and straggling from its pins. She looked nothing at all like the confident, arrogant woman Emmy knew and her sense of foreboding deepened.

Once downstairs, Dorcas took a deep breath then entered the drawing room where she found Bernard with his back to the fire and a grave expression on his face.

'Well . . . did you speak to them?' she asked instantly.

'Yes, Dorcas, I did and I'm afraid things are even worse than you realise.' He stared at her intently for a moment before going on, 'There is no way I can help you out of this financially and so it seems that you will have to accept Mr Lansdown's advice and sell the house – sell everything, actually – and if that isn't enough to cover the debts, I shall have to help out with what is left owing. I cannot believe that you have been foolish enough to let it get to this stage!'

'I didn't know about the debts,' she objected hotly.

He smirked. 'Quite! No doubt you were too busy spending money to worry about how Gerald earned it.'

Panic gripped Dorcas and she began to pace up and down. 'But I *can't* sell the house,' she whimpered pathetically. 'We shall be a laughing stock. And where shall we live? How will I pay for Abigail's school fees?' A thought occurred to her then and she rounded on him. 'Father made a clause in his will that I would have a home at Crossroads Farm for as long as I needed it.' There was a note of panic in her voice now and had Gerald been there at that moment she would happily have wrung his neck for putting her in such a position.

'I'm quite aware of that,' he answered coldly. 'I have no intention of seeing you on the streets.'

'Well, it would be Emerald and me there for most of the time,' she pointed out. 'Abigail is away at school for much of the year and next year we were planning to send her to a finishing school for young ladies in France.'

He laughed aloud as he raised his eyebrows. 'You can't seriously expect me to fund her schooling?' He snorted with derision. 'No, I'm afraid Abigail's school days are well and truly over.'

Colour flooded into Dorcas's cheeks as she clenched her fists. 'But . . . but . . . she'll be *horrified*!'

He shrugged. 'Unfortunately, it can't be helped. There will be no money for anything but essentials for you and the girls in the foreseeable future. We might be able to sneak enough furniture out of here to furnish the cottage for you before the bailiffs come in if we're quick.'

'What do you mean? Furnish *what* cottage? Surely we shall be living in the farm with you and Sybil?'

'I don't think you need me to tell you that that wouldn't work in a month of Sundays. You and Sybil would be at each other's throats in no time. No, we've talked about it and decided that you and the girls can move into one of the empty farm labourers' cottages on the estate.'

'A *farm labourer's* cottage?' Dorcas looked so horrified that she seemed in danger of bursting a blood vessel.

He nodded. 'Yes. Admittedly it's a little run down as it's been standing empty for some time now, but I'll get some of my men to fix the roof and then I'm sure you and the girls can make it habitable.'

With her head in a spin, Dorcas dropped heavily on to a chair feeling as if she were caught in the grip of a nightmare.

'But in Father's will he stipulated that I should have a home with you for as long as I liked,' she choked out indignantly.

'And that is exactly what I'm offering you. A cottage on the estate. Take it or leave it. Meanwhile I shall need to see Mr Lansdown again to set the wheels in motion for selling the house and the business.' He made a little bow and grim-faced he left the room, banging the door resoundingly behind him.

28

Chapter Four

Bernard had been gone for no more than a few seconds when the door banged open again and Abigail appeared followed more slowly by Emmy.

'What's wrong with Uncle Bernard?' Abigail questioned peevishly. She was still seething because she had missed her appointment with the seamstress. 'He just strode past us in the hallway without even acknowledging us.'

Dorcas took a deep breath. At that moment all she wanted to do was run away and hide to lick her wounded pride but she supposed the girls would have to be told what was happening sooner or later so she may as well get it over with.

'Sit down. I need to speak to you both.'

The girls took a seat on the small sofa opposite their mother and waited as Dorcas licked her lips. 'I-I'm afraid I have very bad news for you,' she began and Emmy instantly looked panic-stricken.

'Is it something to do with Papa? Has something happened to him?' she gasped worriedly.

'*Huh!* It's something to do with him all right, although as far as I know he's well.' Dorcas glared at the girl. 'If you must know, he's left us! In the lurch, as it happens.'

Both girls frowned with confusion but it was Abigail who asked, 'What do you mean, Mama?'

'I mean the business is in terrible trouble and your father owes money everywhere. We are going to have to sell everything we own, including the house, to try to cover his debts.'

'What? But where shall we live?'

Dorcas had never made a secret of the fact that Abigail was her favourite child. It was probably because she was the prettier of the two, Emmy had always thought. She had a dimpled smile and an extrovert personality that could charm the birds off the trees. But tonight, Dorcas was too shocked and upset to give either of her daughters much time.

'I have been discussing that with your uncle,' she informed them, deliberately not mentioning the labourer's cottage just yet. 'And I shall know a little more about what's happening when he has seen the solicitor again tomorrow.'

'Perhaps things won't be as bad as you fear,' Emmy said hopefully. In truth she was more concerned about her father's whereabouts than losing the house but she didn't dare say that.

'I assure you they *are!*' Dorcas almost snapped her head off. She had always envied the closeness her firstborn and her husband shared.

Abigail started to cry. 'Does this mean we won't have time to get to the seamstress again tomorrow?' she asked dejectedly. 'I was hoping to have my new gown finished for when I went back to school.'

'You won't be *having* a new gown and you won't be going back to school either,' her mother informed her abruptly as she dabbed ineffectively at the tears that were streaming down her cheeks.

'*What?*' The colour drained out of Abigail's face. 'But I . . . I *must* finish the year. And what about going on to a finishing school?'

Dorcas shook her head. 'I have a very small inheritance left to me by my grandmother, which thankfully I insisted should be kept separate from everything else. We should be able to live frugally on that for a while but when that's gone . . .'

As her voice trailed away, Abigail began to wail and Emmy glared at her. How could she think of new gowns and finishing schools at a time like this? she wondered. Personally, she was far more concerned about where their father was, although she bit her cheek to stop herself from blurting it out.

'May I get you anything, Mama?' Emmy enquired. Her mother seemed to have aged ten years in as many hours.

Dorcas was gazing vacantly towards the window but she glanced at Emmy and shook her head. 'Er, no thank you. Now if you don't mind, I'd like a little time to myself to gather my thoughts.'

Emmy nodded and grasping Abi's arm she almost hauled her out of the room, closing the door behind them. Once in the hallway Abi shook her off and stamped her daintily shod foot.

'How could Papa *do* this to us?' she wailed. 'Do you think this means we shall have to go and live with Uncle Bernard?' She shook her head at the thought and grimaced. 'And Aunt Sybil – she's never liked me, you know! I heard her once telling Papa she thought I was flighty and spoilt!'

Emmy secretly agreed with her aunt on that score but she wisely didn't admit it. Instead, she asked, 'Don't you think we should be more worried about where Papa is? He must have been in a terrible state of mind to clear off like that.'

Abi ground her teeth. 'He can go to the devil for all I care!' she spat. 'How could he just walk away like that leaving Mama to clear his mess up? And what will happen to my pony if we have to leave here?'

Once again Abi's thoughts and concerns were all for herself and Emmy felt the beginning of a headache start to throb behind her eyes as she imagined her father somewhere all alone and heartbroken.

'Excuse me, I think I'm going to go for a lie-down,' she told her sister as she headed for the stairs. 'I need a little time to think.' And with that she went on her way, leaving Abi to rant as she paced up and down the highly polished tiles on the hallway floor.

The following morning, although Abi helped herself to a little of everything laid out for them on the sideboard in the dining room, Emmy found that when she tried to eat, the food just seemed to lodge in her throat. She had tossed and turned all night worrying about her father and wondering how she might find him. So much so that at one point in the early hours she had seriously considered saddling her own pony and going to look for him. But then common sense had kicked in and she had realised how fruitless that would be. Her father could be anywhere by now and it would have been like looking for a needle in a haystack, so she had lain in bed restlessly watching the dawn break through her bedroom window.

'I think Papa could come back today now that he's had time to consider what a mess he's left us in,' Abi stated optimistically as she speared a juicy sausage.

Emmy shook her head. 'I doubt it. If things are as bad as Mama said then he's probably too ashamed to face us.'

Abi sniffed disdainfully. 'Huh! And so he should be.'

Emmy scraped her chair away from the table, her temper rising. 'Did you ever consider that you might have contributed to Papa's problems, when you were demanding new gowns,' she said angrily. '*Or* when you insisted that your pony was too small for you so you needed another one. *Or* what the price of your school fees might be.'

Abi tossed her head. 'He should have said if we couldn't afford those things!'

'Oh yes, and risk one of your tantrums!' Hands on hips, Emmy glared at her and Abi was so shocked that she temporarily fell silent. She could count on one hand the number of times Emmy had lost her temper with her in her whole life but she certainly looked angry now and her eyes were flashing. 'You're just . . . just *utterly* selfish,' Emmy finished and she stormed from the room in a swish of skirts, leaving her sister to stare after her open-mouthed.

Emmy slammed out of the room so abruptly that she almost collided with Hetty who had just come into the hall armed with beeswax polish to start polishing the banister rails.

'Are you all right, miss?' Her voice was full of concern as she saw the tears in Emmy's eyes.

'Oh, Hetty, I wish I could answer yes but I'm not! Nothing is!' Emmy sobbed and, lifting her skirts, she raced up the stairs in a most unladylike manner.

Hetty chewed on her lip for a moment then placing the polish down on a small console table she quietly followed the young miss up the stairs. Since going to work there when she was just thirteen, Hetty had always adored Emmy. She never talked down to her like Miss Abigail did and Hetty was concerned about her.

She tapped tentatively on Emmy's bedroom door; she knew she would cop it if Mrs Parrot the housekeeper caught her skiving but she couldn't bear to see Emmy upset.

'C-come in,' a choky voice said, and Hetty quietly opened the door and stepped inside to find Miss Emmy sprawled across the bed crying her heart out.

'Is there anythin' I can get fer yer, miss?'

Emmy glanced up into Hetty's concerned face and managed a wavery smile. 'Not unless you can wave a magic wand and put everything right.' Sitting up, Emmy swiped the tears from her cheeks with the back of her hand and took a deep breath. 'I'm sorry, Hetty. I'm not usually given to bouts of weeping, but . . .' She frowned. Should she tell Hetty what had happened or would it be best to keep the news to herself? she wondered. But then common sense told her that everyone would know soon and she trusted Hetty, so she patted the bed at the side of her and Hetty crossed to plonk herself down.

Once Hetty knew what had occurred she looked horrified. 'So, will we all lose our jobs when the house is sold?' she asked in a small voice. Her mother relied on the wages that Hetty gave her since her father had died the year before.

Emmy shrugged, looking thoroughly miserable. 'I don't know what will happen yet but I assume so,' she admitted, adding quickly, 'Although I shall do all I can to persuade Mama to keep you on.'

'And where will you live?'

'With Uncle Bernard and Aunt Sybil at Crossroads Farm, I presume, but I'm not sure yet,' Emmy admitted. 'We'll know more when Uncle Bernard comes back today. But will you keep what I've told you to yourself for now, please, Hetty?'

'Of course,' Hetty promised. 'But I'd best get back to work, else Mrs Parrot will 'ave me guts fer garters if she finds I ain't doin' me job.' She gave Emmy's hand an affectionate squeeze and hurried away, hoping that she hadn't already been missed.

It was late afternoon before Bernard appeared looking pale and grim-faced. Hetty showed him into the drawing room and rushed away to fetch the mistress, who joined him minutes later, telling Hetty, 'Fetch a tray of tea immediately.' There was no please or thank you but then Hetty had long since stopped expecting any.

'Well?' Dorcas wrung her hands as she stared at him expectantly as if she were somehow hoping that he had managed to make the whole nightmare situation go away.

He joined his hands behind his back and told her gravely, 'It appears that there is nothing to be done. The situation is so bad, in fact, that after speaking to Mr Lansdown I have had to ask Mr Davidson to lay off the workers immediately. There isn't even enough money to pay their wages. I will, of course, pay them the money they are owed up to now but I can't afford any more than that, so I've instructed

Mr Lansdown to put the house and the business up for sale as soon as possible. Meanwhile he will be arranging for bailiffs to come in and see what there is of worth in the house so I suggest you decide what you wish to take with you and have it removed, otherwise they could be seized and sold off too.'

Dorcas's head wagged from side to side in shocked denial. 'But what is to become of me and the girls?' she wailed.

He took a deep breath. 'I'm sure you will be quite comfortable in the cottage I told you about and of course I won't see any of you starve, although the girls are quite old enough now to seek positions.'

'*Positions?* But they have been brought up as young ladies. What could they possibly do?'

'Become a governess or a nanny?' He sighed. 'I'm sure we'll think of something and you do still have the small inheritance that our grandmother left to you, I presume?' When she nodded he tapped his fingers on the table. 'Good, good, that should keep you for some time if you live frugally. But now I really must go; I have my own farm to run without having to worry about your business as well,' he ended abruptly. 'I shall set some of my men on to repairing the cottage immediately and hopefully it will be ready for you to move into next week. Good day.'

After he'd gone, Dorcas sat in a daze. It was as if all her worst nightmares had come true and now, somehow, she was going to have to come to terms with it. She would have to speak to the staff too. If there was no money to pay the staff at the brickworks there would be no money to pay the household staff either.

The girls joined her within minutes of their uncle leaving and it was Emmy who asked, 'So what is happening, Mama?'

'It's very bad news, I'm afraid, Emerald.' Her mother never shortened her name. 'Even worse than we feared, and so I wish you to ask Hetty to get all the staff together tomorrow morning. I just can't bring myself to speak to them this evening. We will be losing the house and the business as your uncle predicted, and there is no money to pay the staff, so I have no choice but to let them go. We will then be going to live at Crossroads Farm, probably within the next week before the bailiffs come in.'

'Ugh!' Abi grimaced. 'How will we *bear* living with Aunt Sybil?'

'We won't exactly be living *with* her,' Dorcas informed her in a small voice. 'Your uncle is having a cottage on the estate prepared for us . . . we shall live there.'

'In a *cottage*?' Abi gasped incredulously. 'But we *can't* do that . . . everyone will laugh at us and who will cook and clean for us?'

'According to your uncle we shall be doing most of our own cooking and cleaning,' her mother told her and Abi began to cry. 'Although I may be able to keep just Hetty on to help if she is prepared to work for less than she's getting now.'

'*Us!* Cook and clean? But I don't know how!'

'Then we shall have to learn, shan't we? If Hetty agrees to come with us we can't expect her to do everything,' Emmy said, ever the practical one. 'And at least we'll have a roof over our heads, which is more than can be said for some poor blighters!' She was heartbroken at the thought of the staff losing their jobs. How would they manage?

'Emmy – mind your language *please!*' Dorcas snapped. 'We haven't even moved yet and you're talking like one of the peasants already!'

Choking back a sob, Dorcas lifted her skirts and raced towards the stairs. Abi and Emmy watched her go with their mouths hanging open. It seemed that the times ahead were going to be very dark indeed.

Chapter Five

'What's happenin' then, miss?' Hetty asked tentatively later that evening after tapping on Emmy's bedroom door. 'The mistress 'as asked me to get all the staff gathered together in the hallway tomorrow mornin' at ten.'

Emmy stared at her with tears in her eyes. 'I'm afraid we're going to have to let all of the staff go, Hetty,' she said sorrowfully. 'My uncle has promised to pay the wages that have been earned up to now but beyond that . . .' She spread her hands in a helpless gesture. 'But at least Mama has agreed to keep you on . . . if you'll take a slight cut in wages, that is, and if you want to come?'

Hetty's vigorous nod was her answer and Emmy was grateful for that at least. 'Good. The bailiffs will be coming in very shortly, apparently, and Uncle Bernard has told Mama to put aside anything she wants to take. We're to live in a cottage on his estate, it seems, so we won't be able to take any of the big furniture. Just necessities like beds, a sofa, pots and pans, I should think.'

'We can do better than that,' Hetty declared comfortingly. 'The mistress has some very expensive trinkets in her china cabinets. I can filch some of them away an' you'll get a good price for 'em, I've no doubt.'

'But isn't that dishonest?' Emmy asked worriedly.

Hetty laughed and gave her a wink. 'The bailiffs won't miss what they don't set eyes on, so leave it wi' me.'

'But I'd have no idea where to sell them,' Emmy said falteringly.

Hetty chuckled. 'You needn't worry about that. Me brother will know where to get the best price an' in your position you can't afford to be too honest. Now try an' get some sleep, you look all in.'

'I am.' Emmy swiped her hand across her weary eyes. 'The trouble is, every time I try to rest, I start worrying about where my father might be and if he's all right. He must have been in a terrible frame of mind to disappear like that. You don't think he'll do anything silly, do you, Hetty?'

Hetty shook her head as she lifted the untouched tray of food she had brought up to Emmy earlier. 'No, he'll come through all right. I feel sorry fer him in a way. He were so mild-mannered but he didn't seem to be able to say no to your mama's demands. That's probably what's brought all this about if truth be told.' Then realising that she might have said too much she added hurriedly, 'Not that it's any o' my business o' course, miss.'

'It's all right, you're probably right.' Emmy sighed as she sank down on to the side of the bed and Hetty headed for the door. 'Goodnight, Hetty. I'll see you in the morning.' And then she was alone and she allowed the tears to fall again.

'The servants are all assembled, ma'am,' Mrs Parrot informed Dorcas the following morning.

With a nod at her two daughters, Dorcas Winter rose from her seat, straightened her back and followed the housekeeper into the hallway with her hands clasped primly at her waist.

'I am very sorry, but because of unforeseen circumstances I have no option but to inform you all that your services will no longer be needed as of today. All of the wages owed will be paid but I would ask that each of you vacate the premises by tomorrow morning.'

A murmur of dismay rippled through the assembled crowd but Dorcas merely turned and strode back into the drawing room.

'Well, that's great,' the gardener grumbled. 'What the 'ell is goin' on, eh, fer her to just sack us all like that?'

'It's appalling,' Mrs Parrot joined in, and as the kitchen maid began to wail she rounded on her furiously. 'And you can just stop that row, Nell. We're all in the same position, you know. I would have expected at least a month's notice.'

Back in the drawing room, Emmy sighed as she heard the disgruntled comments coming from the staff in the hallway and her heart went out to each of them.

'Poor things . . . I hope they find new posts,' she said sadly.

'*Poor things!* Why, it's *us* you should feel sorry for,' her mother scolded. 'I just hope wherever he is your father gets his comeuppance for leaving us all in this mess.'

Emmy bit back the hasty retort that sprang to her lips. There was no point in causing even more unpleasantness, and anyway, her uncle would be calling shortly with the money to pay the staff's wages and she had promised she would help him do it. She doubted Mrs Parrot would do it now that she had been dismissed.

She found the woman in her private sitting room, already in the process of packing her clothes.

'Ah, Miss Emmy.' Removing the chatelaine that contained the keys to the different rooms in the house she laid it on the table. 'You'll be needing these,' she said stiffly. 'And you will find the ledger containing the household accounts and staff wages owing in that cupboard over there.'

'Thank you, and I'm so sorry this has happened,' Emmy told her sincerely. 'But you really don't have to rush away. Mama said no one need leave till tomorrow morning.'

Mrs Parrot inclined her head. 'Thank you, but if it's all the same to you I shall leave as soon as I have been paid.'

'Where will you go?'

The woman shrugged. 'I have a sister who lives in Lincolnshire. I shall go and stay with her while I seek a new position. I wonder, do you think your mother would do me a reference?'

'I certainly can,' Emmy offered. 'In fact, I shall do one immediately and you may take it with you. And once again, I'm so sorry.'

Seeing the girl's genuine distress, Edith Parrot softened a little and pausing in her packing she asked, 'Will you and the family be all right, Miss Emerald?'

'We'll survive no doubt.' Emmy gave a wry smile. 'Although we're going to have to get used to an enormous life change. We'll be living in a cottage on my uncle's farm.'

'Oh dear. I can't see your mother liking that,' Mrs Parrot replied. She better than anyone knew what an enormous snob Dorcas Winter was, but then she supposed that once she had

42

left it was no business of hers what became of them, so she got on with what she was doing.

Mrs Parrot left later that afternoon after Emmy, under her uncle's watchful eye, had paid her. The staff then trooped in one at a time to be paid their dues and by teatime most of them were packing to leave too.

'My groom will be coming to fetch the carriage and horses later this evening,' her uncle informed her. 'And you and Abigail can ride your ponies over to my stables.'

'Yes, Uncle,' Emmy answered meekly. and it was in that moment that she truly understood that life as she had known it would never be the same again.

'First thing in the morning some of my men will be bringing the large cart over to collect what furniture you wish to take with you so I suggest you all come to the farm tonight and I'll show you the cottage. You'll know then what it will accommodate. I shall send the carriage for you at seven o'clock.'

Once again Emmy merely nodded as her uncle rose to leave. As soon as he'd gone she went to tell her mother what he'd said, but Dorcas shook her head as she looked around her magnificent drawing room. 'I have no wish to see it,' she said sharply. 'You and Abi can go, and take Hetty with you. She'll have a better idea of what will fit.'

And so at seven o'clock prompt, the carriage arrived and when Emmy, Abi and Hetty went to get inside they found their cousin Jasper waiting for them.

'You needn't smirk,' Abi growled as she saw him grin. 'But for the grace of God it could have been you finding yourself in our predicament!'

43

He looked at her fine gown, which was totally inappropriate for where they were going, and laughed. 'I don't think so, cousin dear. My father would never be so reckless with his money.'

His cruel words spurred Emmy to respond, 'And how would *you* know what led Papa to lose everything? Something must have gone wrong with the business.'

He shrugged, but seeing that Emmy was angry, he wisely remained silent.

Once they had reached the drive that led to the farm, the carriage veered off and travelled some way across rough ground before the driver slowed the horses to a halt.

'I'm afraid I can't take the carriage no further, Mr Chetwynd, sir,' he told Jasper, respectfully touching his cap. 'I wouldn't want it to overturn.'

'It looks like we'll be walking from here then,' Jasper told the young ladies, and jumping down from the carriage he helped Abi and Emmy to alight, although Emmy noticed he didn't offer to assist Hetty. Like his mother, Jasper believed that servants were far beneath him.

'Oh really,' Abi groaned as she shook out the skirts of her pale-blue muslin gown. 'I hope it isn't too far. I only got this gown a few weeks ago.'

'It's only about half a mile,' Jasper responded. 'In fact, you can just see the roof over there, look.'

They set off and as the cottage came into sight, Abi gasped with horror. 'But that can't be where we are expected to live, surely?'

The cottage was surrounded by a small copse. It was clear that someone had been doing repairs to the roof by the amount of broken tiles that had been thrown against the rickety picket fence that surrounded it, and someone had scythed down the majority of the overgrown weeds in the garden. They now stood in a large pile to one side of the door, ready to be burnt. The windows were so grimy that it was impossible to see through them and the paint was peeling from the front door.

'You should think yourself lucky. This is one of the biggest cottages on the estate,' Jasper told her, clearly enjoying himself. 'The gamekeeper used to live here but he bought a small house in Bedworth a few years ago and travels into work now. The cottage has stood empty ever since he left so I can't say what it will be like inside.'

If the outside was anything to go by, Emmy had a pretty good idea and her heart sank. But she remained silent as they walked up the path to the front door.

'Here we are then, welcome to your new home.' Jasper grinned as he threw the door open with a flourish and they stepped in. It was very dark and gloomy inside and festoons of cobwebs hung like dirty lace from the rafters and the quarry tiles on the floor were so dirty it was impossible to see what colour they were.

Abi began to whimper with distress. 'B-but we can't *possibly* live here. It's nothing more than a hovel,' she said between sobs.

It was Hetty who tried to lighten the mood. 'It ain't that bad, Miss Abigail. Come on, let's 'ave a good look around.'

The room they were in was clearly a sitting room-cum-kitchen and a large blackleaded range stood against one wall beside an inglenook fireplace. On another wall was a large pot sink attached to a long wooden draining board with a pump above it.

'Look,' Hetty whooped. 'We've even got a pump, so there must be a well outside.' She tried it out and after a time was rewarded when a gush of brackish water streamed out of it. 'That's only cos it ain't been used for a while,' she assured her young mistresses. 'Once it's been cleaned out the water will be lovely, you'll see.' She crossed the room and threw open another door and exclaimed with delight. 'An' look 'ere. There's a nice little parlour. Now let's go an' 'ave a look upstairs, eh?'

After climbing the rather rickety staircase that led directly up from one corner of the kitchen, they found themselves on a small landing with a door on either side of it. 'There yer go,' Hetty said with a smile. 'There's a room fer the mistress and you two can share the other one.'

'*Share!*' Abi looked horrified. 'But I've always had my own room ever since I left the nursery!'

'Hm, but beggars can't be choosers,' Jasper pointed out, obviously enjoying her discomfort immensely. 'And I think it was jolly good of my father to offer you a roof over your heads in the circumstances.'

'Oh, shut up!' Abi glared at him before pointing to what amounted to no more than a ladder further along the landing that led up into the roof space. 'And what's up there?'

'I'll go up an' take a look, miss,' Hetty volunteered, gathering her dull skirt into a bundle and showing her ankles in a most unladylike way. 'Though I doubt I'll be able to see much wi'out a light if it's up in the eaves.' She disappeared from sight and when she reappeared a few minutes later, looking grubby, she grinned. 'It's another room, an' that'll do nicely fer somewhere fer me to sleep. It's got a slopin' roof but I should be able to get a bed up there at least.'

Abi shuddered in disgust. 'Ugh. I bet the whole place is crawling with spiders and it's filthy,' she complained.

'There's nowt that a bit o' soap an' water an' a lot of elbow grease won't fix,' Hetty assured her. 'I reckon it'll be smashin' once it's 'ad a good clean an' got some decent bits o' furniture in. I'll come an' make a start on it first thing in the mornin'. Yer won't know the place by the time I've done.'

Unable to bear the indignity of the situation she found herself in, Abigail suddenly flounced about and headed for the door, declaring, 'I can't stand this a moment longer; I'm leaving!'

Jasper was leaning against the wall with his arms crossed and a smirk on his face and he grinned as she pushed past him and stormed down the stairs. 'Don't you want a lift back home? Oh, sorry, I forgot this soon *will* be your home.'

She gave him a final glare and was lost to sight. Hetty chewed on her lip worriedly. Emerald seemed to be a lot more accepting of what was happening, probably because she was far more worried about her father than herself, Hetty thought, but she dreaded to think how the mistress and the other young miss were going to cope. Still, what was done was done and now they were all just going to have to try to make the best of it.

Chapter Six

When Hetty and Emmy got home they found the house in chaos. Dorcas was in the sitting room weeping loudly having just said goodbye to her lady's maid and the first words she uttered when Emmy joined her were, 'How am I supposed to cope without Miss Oliver? Who will look after my wardrobe and dress my hair? And who will draw my bath for me?'

Emmy sighed. 'I'm afraid you'll have to manage the best you can, Mama,' she said wearily. 'I'm sure you are more than capable of dressing yourself and doing your own hair. And as for drawing your bath, well . . . from now on bathing will be done in a tin bath in front of the fire in the kitchen.'

'*A tin bath!*' Dorcas clutched at her throat. 'You mean there isn't even an inside bathroom in the godforsaken place?'

Emmy shook her head. There was no point in lying. 'It's a cottage, Mama,' she pointed out patiently as she took the pin from her bonnet. 'But it's not so bad. Or at least it won't be when we have some of our own things around us and Hetty and I have given it a good clean.'

'Ah, I'd quite forgotten about Hetty.' Dorcas looked slightly mollified. 'I'm sure she could take on some of Miss Oliver's duties.'

Emmy took a deep breath, trying to contain her anger. 'I'm afraid that won't be possible. Hetty will be doing most of the cleaning and cooking as well as the laundry. She certainly won't have time to pander to you. We are all going to have to pull together if we're to make the place liveable.'

Dorcas stared at her in stunned disbelief. 'But I wouldn't know how to tackle household chores. I wasn't brought up to do mundane work and neither were you and Abigail.'

'Then we're going to have to learn, aren't we?' Emmy was almost at the end of her tether. 'You surely can't expect Hetty to do everything!' And with that she turned on her heel and marched out of the room leaving her mother staring after her in disbelief.

There were many tears the following morning when Emmy said goodbye to the rest of the staff. Some of them had been there for years and she had grown fond of them, especially Mrs Pierce, the cook.

'I'm so sorry,' Emmy told her as tears rolled down her cheeks.

The woman gave her a gentle hug. 'Don't you get worryin' about me, pet. I've been thinkin' it were time I retired for a while now an' this has just made the decision for me . . . but I hope you'll all be all right. An' your dad, God bless 'im, he's a good man. Just remember, it's allus darkest before dawn.' She gave Emmy a peck on the cheek and went on her way.

Dorcas was still in bed, unable to face anyone, and Emmy supposed that she would be trying to come to terms with the fact that the husband who she had thought loved her, had walked out on her. But surely her mother realised that it was just as bad for all of them? That she and Abi were hurting and missing him too?

'Psst . . . Miss Emmy.'

Emmy's sorry thoughts were interrupted as she turned to see Hetty beckoning to her from the doorway of the drawing room.

'I've taken a few choice bits from the china cabinets,' Hetty informed her in a whisper when she joined her. 'An' I've spread the rest out so they won't be missed. We'll take 'em with us an' hide 'em at the cottage.' She would have said more but Abigail breezed in at that moment and gazed from one to the other of them.

'What's going on now then?'

'Nothing at all,' Emmy assured her hastily. 'Hetty was just saying we should be going to make a start on the cleaning at the cottage shortly. Are you coming to help?'

Abigail sneered. '*Me!* No, certainly not. Let *her* do it, she's the servant.'

Emmy's eyes flashed as she glared at her. 'Please yourself then! But I'll tell you now, if you want a clean bedroom to sleep in, you'd better make your mind up to pull your weight because I shan't be cleaning your half of it.'

'It's all right, miss, I'll do it,' Hetty interrupted hastily. Things were bad enough without the sisters being at each other's throats. 'Let Miss Abigail stay here to cook dinner.'

'*Cook dinner!*' Abi's eyes were almost starting from her head. 'But I've never cooked in my life!'

'There's a first time for everything,' Emmy answered coldly and went off to find her oldest clothes to wear for cleaning.

Soon she and Hetty set off, loaded down with cleaning materials and a mop and bucket. They were out of breath by the time they reached the farm where they saw Jasper leaning on the garden gate with a grin on his face.

'I could have taken you for a servant, Emmy,' he goaded but she merely smiled, determined not to rise to the bait. She had never got on particularly well with Jasper, although she had all the time in the world for Jake.

'Needs must,' she said brightly as she and Hetty sailed past him.

As he watched her go Jasper couldn't help but admire her spirit. She was easy on the eye too, he realised with a little jolt. He'd never taken that much notice before.

'Stuck up little devil,' Hetty muttered once they were out of earshot, then she blushed. 'Sorry, miss. I shouldn't say such things about yer cousin.'

'Why not? You were only telling the truth.' Emmy smiled at her. 'I've never found Jasper easy to get on with, although I like Jake. In fact, I almost feel sorry for him at times. Aunt Sybil and Uncle Bernard never seem to have any time for him whereas Jasper has been the golden child since the day he was born.'

'It's per'aps cos Jasper is the youngest,' Hetty commented and Emmy nodded in agreement. The cleaning things they were carrying seemed to be getting heavier by the minute and they fell silent until the cottage came into sight. It looked very forlorn and neglected with the bright March sun shining down on it.

Seeing her young mistress's glum expression, Hetty told her, 'Don't get frettin', miss. We'll have it lookin' like a little palace in no time.' She pushed the small gate open and they went down the weed-strewn path to the front door.

Once inside they stood looking around for a moment before Hetty took charge. 'Right, let's start by gettin' the range lit fer some hot water. We'll tackle the dirty winders first an' let some light in then we'll throw out everythin' we don't want an' make a start on gettin' the floors clean.'

Emmy only wished that she could feel as optimistic as Hetty sounded. All she could do was head outside to fetch some wood for the fire and then roll her sleeves up ready to get stuck in.

By lunchtime they were making some progress. Anything they couldn't use had been carried outside and piled up ready for a bonfire and now the windows were gleaming, the place did indeed look a little brighter.

Hetty had been down on her hands and knees scrubbing the tiles on the floor and Emmy had swept all the floors and scoured the deep stone sink until it shone.

'I think we should stop for something to eat,' Emmy suggested. She had packed them some bread and cheese and so they both went out into the garden to eat it. While they were sitting there Jake appeared armed with a spade and fork.

'I thought I'd come along and see if I could make a start on tidying the garden,' he told them kindly and Emmy was so touched that a lump formed in her throat. 'Mind you, I'm not sure if I'll do more harm than good. I never seem to know which are flowers and which are weeds.'

Hetty giggled. 'Well, lookin' at the state o' this jungle, sir, anythin' will be an improvement,' she assured him.

Emmy nodded in agreement. 'Yes, it will, Jake. Thank you. We'll be grateful for any help we can get.'

The afternoon was darkening by the time Hetty said, 'I reckon we should call it a day now, miss. I should be gettin' back to get us all an' evenin' meal. I doubt Miss Abigail will have prepared anythin'.'

They placed all the cleaning things neatly in a corner and when they stepped outside they were impressed to find themselves standing on a weed-free path. Jake had fixed the gate so that it now opened and shut properly and with the path clean and swept it was looking tidier already. He was now busily digging away in the garden and when he turned to look at them Emmy smiled for the first time in days to see the state he was in.

'Oh dear, I don't think your mother will be very pleased if you turn up for dinner looking like that,' she warned.

Jake shrugged and chuckled. 'I doubt she'd even notice if I didn't turn up at all as long as Jasper was there,' he said, but there was no envy in his voice. He had accepted his place in the family a long time ago.

They walked back together as far as the farm where Emmy thanked him again for all his hard work. As Emmy and Hetty were about to set off again, he asked tentatively, 'No news of Uncle Gerald yet, then?'

Emmy's face fell as she shook her head. 'Not a word. I just pray he's safe wherever he is. He must have been in a terrible state mentally to go off as he did.'

Jake nodded in agreement. 'Yes, he probably was, but I'm sure he'll be all right,' he said encouragingly.

It was strangely quiet as they entered the grounds of Astley House. Usually, the gardener or one of the grooms would be pottering about but this late afternoon it was deserted and it brought home to Emmy the fact that they wouldn't be there for much longer.

'It's going to be so hard to leave here,' she told Hetty in a choky voice. 'I've never lived anywhere else.'

'Ah, that's as maybe but it's just an 'ouse after all,' Hetty said stoically. 'A home is where yer make it an' we'll have the cottage lookin' like the bee's knees in no time, just you see.'

Emmy could have kissed the girl for being so optimistic but her mood plunged further when they entered the house to find Abigail having a tantrum.

'Where have you been?' she shouted at Hetty as she stamped her foot. 'Mother and I haven't eaten all day and I can't find my blue gown.'

Hetty shrugged. 'Your blue gown is probably in the laundry room. If it ain't been washed you'll 'ave to do it yerself. An' if you ain't eaten that's your fault an' all, miss. I can't be in two places at once an' as yer well know, me an' Miss Emmy have been over at the cottage tryin' to get it fit fer you to move into. Furthermore, I were never employed as a cook!'

'*Why* . . . how *dare* you talk to me like that,' Abigail spluttered. 'For two pins I'd sack you!'

'Then go a'ead, but who'll do yer cleanin' fer yer then?' Hetty answered cheekily.

Abigail's mouth clamped shut and turning on her heel she stamped away, her satin skirts swirling about her.

Hetty grinned at Emmy. 'Right, that's shut her up . . . for a while anyway, so if you'll excuse me, miss, I'll go an' start the evenin' meal. I've a feelin' none of us'll eat tonight if I don't. Tell the mistress it'll be ready in about two hours.'

Emmy grinned. She'd enjoyed seeing Abi being put in her place. 'I will, and thank you, Hetty. For all you're doing, I mean.'

Hetty patted her arm and pottered off to the kitchen as Emmy went to find her mother to tell her of the progress they'd made on the cottage – not that she thought she'd be that much interested.

Chapter Seven

It was now eight days since Gerald had disappeared and still there had been no word from him. Emmy's eyes were dark from lack of sleep and worry, and her hands, which had never done manual work before, were red and chapped. The day before, Bernard had called to see Dorcas to inform her that they must leave the house within three days for the bailiffs would be coming then to take a full inventory of the house's contents. Dorcas had wailed and cried but Bernard hadn't flinched. He had never had a lot of time for his brother-in-law, thinking him far too soft-hearted, but he had even less time for his sister who had been spoilt shamelessly by their parents from the day she drew breath.

'I shall send a couple of my men round with a cart tomorrow to transfer what you wish to take with you to the cottage,' he had told her unfeelingly, and without waiting for a reply he had left, feeling he had done his duty.

And so Emmy, Abi and their mother had started going from room to room looking for suitable furniture to take to the cottage.

'I *must* have the mahogany sideboard,' Dorcas said in the dining room the next morning. 'It's so handy to put all the food on when we entertain.'

Emmy's eyes stretched wide as she stared at the enormous piece. 'But we don't even have a dining room in the cottage,' she pointed out. 'There's just a kitchen-cum-living room and a small parlour. We would never even get that through the door!'

'Oh dear.' Dorcas clutched her throat as if she couldn't breathe, sure that she was trapped in some sort of a nightmare. 'Then what about my escritoire? I had that shipped over from France shortly after your father and I were married and I've always been so fond of it.'

Emmy eyed it doubtfully. She really didn't think there would be much need for it any more, but seeing as it was only small, she supposed they could find a corner for it, although she would much rather have taken something a little more practical.

'Very well.' She nodded to one of the men her uncle had sent to help with the furniture removals and he stepped forward and lifted it as if it weighed no more than a feather.

'We ought to be getting the beds out next,' Emmy said practically. 'Although we won't be able to take the four-posters – we'd never get them through the cottage door. I'm afraid we'll have to take some of the beds from the servants' quarters. They're so much smaller.'

Now it was Abi's turn to look horrified. 'You *surely* can't expect us to sleep in beds that the servants have slept in,' she gasped.

'Well, it's either that or sleep on a mattress on the floor,' Emmy snapped and Abi promptly burst into tears.

Emmy let out a deep breath. This was turning out to be even harder than she had thought it would be and they had barely started yet.

It was Hetty who stepped in quickly to say, 'But you *can* take all your nice beddin' an' linen, miss. I'll start to pack it up now, shall I?'

Emmy flashed her a grateful smile as Hetty hurried away to make a start on it.

Within an hour the cart was fully loaded and Emmy went with the driver to show the men where to put things in the cottage. In fairness, it was looking much better now. Jake had done a grand job of clearing all the weeds from the front garden and with the tulips and daffodils now on show and the windows sparkling in the sunshine it looked quite pretty. Hetty had been there until late the evening before blackleading the grate, and with smoke lazily drifting up into the blue sky it felt warm when they entered. Hetty had also spent hours cutting down some curtains she had found in the attic at Astley House to fit the cottage windows, although she hadn't had time to hang them as yet.

Truthfully Emmy didn't know how they would have coped without her. She had worked tirelessly, even cooking the meals when she got back at night, although she must have been extremely tired. Now she got the men to place the large dresser they had brought from the kitchen against one wall in the cottage kitchen, then while they carried the beds in, she began to unpack the china and put it on the shelves. Her mother had insisted they should bring all the best gilt-edged china and it looked slightly out of place in the humbler abode but Emmy supposed it didn't matter if it made her mother feel a little more at home. She was just finishing that job when Jake strode in and he noticed instantly that Emmy looked worn out.

'Where are Hetty and Abi?' he asked, glancing around.

Emmy snorted as she swiped a stray lock of hair from her face. 'Hetty is busy packing back at the house and Abi is having a full-blown tantrum,' she informed him with a sigh.

'And your mother?'

Emmy shrugged. 'Doing nothing to help as usual.'

'Right, then it's up to us to get this place sorted,' Jake said kindly, removing his jacket and rolling his sleeves up. 'Now tell me what room you want these boxes in.'

The men had already unloaded the first lot from the cart and had gone back to the house to collect some more. While they were gone Jake and Emmy carried all the boxes into the right rooms. Jake then found a hammer and began to fix some nails into the back of the bedroom doors where the women could hang some of their clothes.

'Not quite the expensive armoires Abi is used to,' he commented and Emmy grinned.

'She'll just have to get used to it then, won't she?' she replied.

Soon there was nothing more they could do until the men returned with the next load so they went out into the garden and sat down on the bench Jake had found beneath a tangle of undergrowth.

'Unfortunately, I have to return to medical school in a couple of days,' he told her regretfully. 'I wish I could have been around a bit longer to help you settle in.'

'You've done more than enough already,' Emmy assured him. 'You must be coming close to the end of your course now?'

He nodded. 'Yes, it's my final year, unless I decide to stay on longer to train as a surgeon, but I'm not planning to.' His desire to become a doctor had been a bone of contention between him and his father. His father had hoped that as Jake was the oldest, he would train to take over the running of the farm one day – Jasper certainly didn't show any interest in doing so, or doing anything else for that matter – but Jake was set on becoming a doctor.

'You wouldn't believe the sights I've seen,' he told her. 'As part of my practical training I worked at the poor hospital in London for a few months last year and that decided me on what I want to do. The poverty there is unbelievable. Why this'– he spread his hands – 'would be like a palace to some of the poor beggars there. They die like flies in slums because they can't afford to call a doctor, and they're the people I want to help.'

'I think that's a really admirable thing to do,' Emmy said. 'And I'm glad you stuck to your guns. I shall have to think of something I can do now too. I thought perhaps I could try for the post of a governess or a home tutor.'

'But surely you'll stay here with your mother?' Jake raised his eyebrow.

She shook her head. 'No, Mama will have a small amount to live on but it won't run to keeping me and Abi, especially not in the style Abi is used to. As soon as I'm happy that Mama has settled in, I shall start to look around for a post.'

The sound of the cart rattling along the uneven lane leading to the cottage brought an end to the conversation and soon they were busy unloading it again. Hetty had sent drawers for the bedrooms, a small table and four wooden chairs for the kitchen as well as a gilt-legged sofa for in front of the inglenook fireplace.

'I bet Mama insisted that should come,' Emmy commented wryly as the men carried it inside. It looked completely incongruous in the small kitchen-cum-sitting room but Emmy put it in position just the same. Dorcas had also sent a number of fancy gilt-framed mirrors and oil paintings, and after glancing at each other and grinning, Jake fetched the hammer and nails and began to hang them on the walls. Next, Emmy hung the heavy velvet curtains that Hetty had painstakingly altered at the windows, and suddenly the place was looking quite cosy. The next job was making the beds up with clean sheets and blankets and by the time they'd finished, they were both exhausted.

'I think that's enough for today,' Emmy said wearily as she wiped the sweat from her brow on the sleeve of her dress. 'Once again, thank you so much for all your help, Jake. I wouldn't have got half as much done on my own.'

They walked back to the farm side by side where they parted and Emmy went on her way to Astley House.

She entered the hall to the sound of shouting and, hurrying into the drawing room, she found Abi and Hetty in the middle of a heated row.

'Sorry, miss,' Hetty apologised the second she set eyes on Emmy. 'All I did was ask her to pack the clothes she wanted to take with her and she laid into me.' Hetty looked exhausted. 'The trouble is, I can't do everythin', as I've just pointed out!'

'Why not – you're the servant, aren't you?' Abi said rudely.

'Aye, I am,' Hetty shot back. 'But I'm not bloody superhuman an' I've been on me feet since the crack o' dawn same as yer sister has while you've been sat on yer fat idle arse!'

Abi gasped as she clutched at her throat. 'Why . . . how *dare* you speak to me like that, you . . . you little *guttersnipe!*' she shrilled.

'Abi, that's *quite* enough!' It was Emmy's time to shout now. 'I will *not* have you speaking to Hetty like that, do you hear me?'

Abi sniffed and lowered her head but there was no apology forthcoming, although she did at least shut up – for now at least.

'Right . . . I suggest you go and do as Hetty suggested and don't forget we have limited space in the cottage.'

With a defiant toss of her head, Abi gave Hetty one last glare and flounced from the room as Emmy apologised for her sister's behaviour.

'It's all right, miss.' Hetty sighed wearily. 'This ain't easy fer none of you but it seems to me you're the one havin' to organise everythin.'

'But I've had your help and Jake's. I couldn't have done it on my own,' Emmy pointed out, noting how tired Hetty looked. 'And someone has to do it.' She dreaded to think what would have happened if she and Hetty hadn't got stuck in, the clock was ticking and tomorrow they would have to move out whether the cottage was ready or not, which spurred her on to keep going. Deep down she just wanted to lie down and cry or spend every minute of the day looking for her father but she knew that wouldn't have been practical.

'Well, there's a cottage pie in the oven,' Hetty informed her. 'So let's call it a day for now and get something to eat, eh? I dare say you've had nothing.'

It was only then that Emmy realised how hungry she was and while Hetty went to fetch the meal, she quickly laid out the plates and the cutlery in the dining room.

'Cottage pie,' her mother remarked scathingly some minutes later when they all sat down to dinner.

'Yes, cottage pie and very nice it looks too,' Emmy said sharply as she served it up. 'And we can thank Hetty for it. If it wasn't for her, we'd probably be sitting down to bread and cheese.'

Her mother sniffed. She was used to at least three far grander courses but she ate everything on her plate just the same.

'There will be four of us sitting down to eat after today,' Emmy pointed out. 'Once we're at the cottage we can hardly eat without Hetty joining us, especially as she will no doubt have cooked it.'

Dorcas looked horrified at the very idea but seeing the fierce look on her daughter's face she wisely said nothing. Instead, she took a scrap of lace handkerchief and began to sniffle into it again. 'I still can't believe we're going to be reduced to living in a labourer's cottage,' she whimpered. 'And at my brother's mercy.'

'But you won't be.' Emmy had already heard quite enough and her patience was growing thin. 'As Uncle Bernard pointed out, we'll have to find jobs once we've settled in. Your inheritance won't be enough to keep us all.'

Abi opened her mouth to protest but she too quickly clamped it shut again as she saw the murderous look on Emmy's face. Instead she and her mother watched in silence as Emmy loaded the dirty pots on to a tray and carried them away to the kitchen.

She's got another think coming if she thinks I'm going to go out to work, Abi silently fumed, and excusing herself she went off to sulk for what would be the last night in her own bedroom. After this evening she and Emmy would be forced to share a room and it didn't bear thinking about.

Chapter Eight

'Is the last load ready?' Jake asked early the next morning when he and some of Bernard's workmen arrived with the cart.

Emmy nodded. 'Yes, it's all piled in the hall.' She had stayed up late the night before collecting together everything her mother had insisted they take, and she was so tired she didn't feel as if she had been to bed.

As Jake glanced down at the fine Turkish rugs rolled up on the hall floor ready to be loaded on to the cart, he raised a questioning eyebrow.

Emmy shrugged. 'I know what you're thinking, they're hardly what you'd expect to see on the floor of a cottage, but Mother insisted.'

He grinned and lifting one of the larger ones he slung it across his shoulder and carried it outside.

The cart was almost fully loaded when Dorcas appeared in a smart claret-coloured two-piece velvet costume and a matching hat trimmed with peacock feathers that danced with each step she took. 'The rest of my bags are on the landing,' she told one of the men imperiously. 'And just mind you don't scratch the leather when you are loading them; they were very expensive.'

'We can give you a lift to the cottage, Aunt Dorcas, if you don't mind riding on the front of the cart,' Jake told her.

Dorcas visibly cringed. 'Do you mean to say your father hasn't sent the carriage for me?'

'I'm afraid not, but it's a lovely day, although it is a bit windy so you might have to hold on to your hat.'

When Emmy saw the mischievous twinkle in Jake's eyes it was all she could do to keep a straight face. Like herself he was probably thinking what an unlikely outfit her mother had chosen to wear but he was too much of a young gentleman to comment on it.

'In that case I suppose I have no choice.' Dorcas swept past them with her nose in the air and they both peeped round the door to watch as one of the workers manhandled her up on to the bench seat.

'Just mind where you are putting your hands, my man,' Dorcas scolded as the man put his hand on her rear and gave her a push up, and Emmy couldn't help but giggle, although she was painfully aware that she had precious little to be happy about. For the first time in her life her future was suddenly uncertain. Added to that, she was about to turn her back on the place she had always called home. But worst of all was the constant worrying about her father.

'How will you be getting to the cottage, Emmy?'

'What? Oh, sorry, Jake, I was miles away.' His voice had brought her back to the present. 'I shall walk over shortly, thanks, but I need to stay here for a while and make sure everything is ready for the bailiffs to come in.'

Abi appeared in a similarly inappropriate outfit to her mother's and asked, 'So how are we to get to the cottage? I'm ready to go.'

'I'm afraid you're going to have to walk with Hetty,' Jake apologised. 'The cart is fully loaded now.'

'*Walk!*' Abi looked horrified as she glanced down at the soft velvet skirt she was wearing, but then with a resigned sigh she stormed past them, closely followed by Hetty who winked at Emmy as she passed.

Suddenly the house was empty and as Emmy walked from room to room a lump formed in her throat. All her memories had been made here and it struck her just how different her life would be from this day on. Tomorrow the vultures would descend, valuing all the furniture and the treasures that her mother had collected over the years. Pulling herself together with an effort, she took a deep breath. It was no good crying over things that could not be changed. From now on they were all just going to have to make the best of things; it wasn't as if they were going to be homeless and sleeping on the streets, and after all the hard work that she, Jake and Hetty had done on the cottage it was very comfortable. There were so many people so much worse off than them, including the staff that her mother had had to let go; Emmy knew many of them well and she was going to miss them. She doubted her mother would see it that way, though.

Once again, she thought of her father and her heart ached. Was he somewhere sleeping rough with no place to call home? She could only imagine that he must have been in a desperate state to disappear as he had, but then her father had never been a strong man and had given in to her mother's every whim for as far back as she could remember, which she supposed was probably what had helped to bring them to this state. Why hadn't he put his foot down and curbed her mother's spending when the business wasn't doing so well? With a sigh she descended the stairs and after one last glance around the roomy hallway, she stepped outside, locking the front door behind her. It was time for their new life to begin.

When Emmy arrived at the cottage, she found Jake unpacking the few last-minute things her mother had insisted they brought with them, and after giving him a smile and a nod she entered the kitchen to find her mother sitting on the little gilt-legged sofa crying softly. Hetty was busy laying the Turkish rugs across the quarry tiles but there was no sign of Abi.

'She met Master Jasper and they went off together for a walk,' Hetty explained when Emmy asked where she was.

Emmy sighed. 'So, Mama, what do you think of it now after all our hard work?' Emmy asked cheerfully as she removed the pin from her hat.

Her mother gave her a fierce glare. 'What do I *think* of it? Why, I *think* it looks like a farm labourer's cottage,' she answered ungratefully and instantly the smile slid from Emmy's face. It seemed that all the hard work she and Hetty had put into making it homely counted for nothing, but knowing her mother as she did she supposed she shouldn't have expected any more.

'Well, I'm sure you'll get used to it eventually,' she said curtly as she went to throw another log on to the fire.

Jake had just entered the room and sensing the tense atmosphere he said hastily, 'Right, this is the last of the stuff. I'll get off and leave you to get settled in but if there's anything you need just pop across to the farm.'

He quickly placed the last of the things on the table but Dorcas didn't even acknowledge him as she sat staring moodily into the fire.

With a nod at Hetty he hurried outside, closely followed by Emmy who was mortified at her mother's behaviour.

'I'm *so* sorry, Jake.' She looked on the verge of tears as she gently laid her hand on his arm. 'I'm afraid this way of life is going to take Mama some getting used to but that doesn't excuse her awful behaviour. I really don't know what we would have done without you these last few days and I can't thank you enough.'

As he stared down at her small hand resting on his arm a flush rose in his cheeks and his heart gave a funny little flip. 'It was my pleasure,' he assured her. 'And don't forget if there's anything you need . . .'

'I won't.' She smiled and watched as he nimbly climbed up on to the driver's seat and lifted the reins. She had spent more time with Jake over the last few days than she had in years. Normally the Winters and the Chetwynds only got together for family occasions and it came to her that she was going to miss him when he went back to medical school.

He raised his hand as he set the horse in motion and she stood and waved until he was out of sight before turning slowly and making her way back into the cottage. Everything had happened so quickly since her father went missing that she hadn't really had much time to think about it, but now suddenly it hit her. This would be a completely new way of life for all of them and somehow, they were going to have to get used to it.

Once Emmy was back inside, Hetty closed the door firmly behind her then crossing to the corner of the room she opened a cupboard door and withdrew some towel-wrapped parcels.

'I managed to get these out, look,' she told them as she unwrapped them one at a time and laid them gently on the table. 'Me brother Micky will know who to take them to an' they should fetch a good price.'

'That's some of my Meissen,' Dorcas exclaimed. 'I remember them being very expensive when I bought them.'

'Aye, I can believe it, that's why I swiped 'em.' Hetty grinned.

Suddenly, to Hetty and Emmy's surprise, Dorcas leapt to her feet and reached for a large carpet bag at the side of her chair.

'You aren't the only one who's been naughty.' She grinned as she extracted a large jewellery box and when she lifted the lid the girls gasped. 'I was careful to leave some of my jewels,' she told them hastily. 'They would expect to find something, but I made sure I only left the cheaper trinkets. I left my pearls and silver pieces and some of the jewellery set with semi-precious stones, but I have all the expensive jewellery here and if needs be, we can sell some of these too. Although I hope it won't come to that,' she added as she fingered a ruby necklace. The stones sparkled in the sunshine that was pouring through the gleaming windows, and she sighed before placing it back in the box. 'Now we just have to find somewhere safe to hide them.'

'I know just the place.' Hetty stepped forward. 'There's a loose floorboard in the corner of your bedroom, ma'am. No one would think to look there. Would you like me to put them there now?'

Dorcas nodded and reluctantly handed the box over. While Hetty scampered off to hide the treasures, Emmy repacked the porcelain figures and followed Hetty out, placing them carefully under the floorboard. It was comforting to know that they had things of value they could sell should the need arise, although like her mother she prayed it wouldn't come to that.

She went to the sink then and began to prepare some vegetables for their lunch. Hetty was going to teach her to cook and bake bread and she was quite looking forward to it. They had brought all the supplies from the huge pantry back at the house and now it was all neatly stacked on the shelves or tidily put away in the much smaller pantry here.

Hetty returned and smiled appreciatively when she saw Emmy had made a start on preparing the meal.

'I thought I'd make us a nice steak an' kidney pie today,' she told her. 'You can watch how I do it an' next time you can 'ave a go at makin' one. The oven should be warm enough by now.' She began to get out all the ingredients as Emmy watched closely. Once the potatoes and vegetables were simmering on the top of the oven and the pie was cooking, Hetty went outside to fill the large dolly tub with buckets of water from the pump. 'Ever done the washin' or used a mangle before?'

When Emmy solemnly shook her head, Hetty laughed. 'Well, here starts another lesson then.' She dumped some

71

of the more delicate underwear she had sorted into the tub before lifting a small wooden device that looked like a three-legged stood with a handle. 'This is the posser,' she explained as she shaved some coarse soap into the water. She proceeded to prod the clothes down into the water with it and turn it so that the clothes were agitated. It looked like very hard work to Emmy and soon Hetty was sweating. 'I'll just do the lightly soiled things today,' Hetty told her. 'The dirtier clothes will need to be soaked overnight an' we'll need to get the copper on the go so's we 'ave 'ot water to wash 'em in tomorrow.'

Once the clothes were washed to Hetty's satisfaction they then had to be thoroughly rinsed in yet more buckets of cold water before being fed through the mangle and hung on the line in the yard that Jake had kindly fixed up for her.

'There, just look at that.' Hetty swiped the sweat from her brow and stood back to admire her hard work. 'There ain't nothin' more satisfyin' than seein' a line full o' clean washin' flappin' on the line.' Then she wiped her hands on her enormous apron and disappeared back into the cottage.

Emmy shook her head. Only now did she realise just how hard servants had to work and it came home to her once more what a privileged life she had led. But that was all about to change drastically and she didn't know how her mother and sister would be able to deal with it.

Chapter Nine

As they walked beneath the canopy of trees in the woods, Abi preened. Jasper was making no secret of the fact that he found her attractive and although he was her cousin, Abi enjoyed being the centre of any male attention. She knew she was pretty and before the shame of her father abandoning them, she was aware that her mother had had high hopes of her making a good marriage with some eligible rich young man. But what would her chances be now? she wondered. There would be no dowry and she had no doubt that once word got out of what had happened the whole family would be a laughing stock.

'Penny for them?' Jasper gave her a dazzling smile.

She toyed with a ringlet hanging over her plump shoulder and sighed dramatically. 'I was just wondering what was going to become of us,' she answered with a tremble in her voice. 'Until all this happened my future looked bright. I was going to attend a finishing school in France and once I came home, I dare say I would have married some rich young man and lived a life of luxury, but who will want me now?'

Jasper grinned. 'Oh, I shouldn't worry on that score. You must know that you're beautiful! Men will always queue for you.'

'Yes, but what *sort* of men?' Abi pouted. 'I'll probably be lucky to become the wife of a farm labourer with the circles we shall be moving in from now on, and I don't think I could bear that. Mama is already speaking of Emmy and me getting jobs! A *job* – me! Emmy says she likes the idea of becoming a nanny or a governess but that wouldn't appeal to me at all; so what could I do?'

'I can think of certain jobs where you would be highly in demand and sought after without having to work hard at all,' Jasper told her.

Abi stopped walking abruptly and stared up at him. 'Oh yes, and what jobs would they be then?'

He gave her a wry smile before leading her to a little clearing where they sat down on the grass to enjoy the sunshine. 'Well, there are certain clubs in London that I frequent where the ladies who work there are very much in demand.'

Abi frowned. 'You're not suggesting I should work in a whorehouse, are you?' She looked so horrified that Jasper laughed.

'No, of course not. I said clubs not brothels. They are two entirely different things.'

'Oh!' Abi's forehead puckered as she thought on his words. 'And exactly *how* are they different?'

'Women who work in whorehouses sell their bodies for sex. Women who work in the upper-class clubs are hostesses to the gentleman guests. Why, I've known a number of them marry rich men and live happily ever after,' he assured her.

Abi blushed at his frank words, but despite herself she was interested. 'And what exactly do these *hostesses* have to do?'

'They sit with the customers and encourage them to buy champagne and keep them company – that's it. The gentlemen that frequent these places are very rich as a rule and if one of the girls takes their eye, I've known them to be very generous. I've seen them give diamonds, even apartments if they really take a fancy to a particular girl. But the owners of the clubs often provide accommodation when the girls first arrive and they're very well paid for doing very little from what I can see.'

'Hm, I can't see Mama being very happy with that idea,' Abi told him, although she had to admit to herself that it sounded very appealing. 'And wouldn't I be too young? I'm not seventeen until next month.'

'I should imagine being so young would work in your favour,' Jasper assured her, watching her reaction closely. 'The men like the girls young and unspoilt, although I doubt many of them are.'

Abi stared ahead picturing herself being pampered and spoilt, and liking the thought very much. But then common sense took over and she sighed regretfully. 'It's the sort of life I would enjoy, I think,' she admitted. 'But Mama would never agree to me taking such a job so there's no point even thinking about it.'

'As you wish, it was just an idea. I was only trying to help,' Jasper said with a small smile. He had planted the seed and now all he had to do was sit back and let it grow.

Abi stood up and brushed her skirt down, saying glumly, 'I suppose I should show my face at the cottage; they'll be wondering where I am. I can't believe that awful little place is going to be my home from now on.'

Jasper offered his arm and once she had taken it, they began to stroll along in the warm sunshine. All around them the world was springing to life and lambs frolicked close to their mothers in the fields, but Abi didn't notice any of it. Her attention was focused entirely on the man by her side and her heart began to thump. Jasper was outrageously good-looking and even though he was her cousin she couldn't help but feel attracted to him. She could feel the warmth of him through the sleeve of his smart jacket and colour rose to her cheeks as she wondered what his skin would feel like.

He in turn was thinking of Emmy. Admittedly Abi was more of a classic beauty; she was petite and her figure was rounded, whereas Emmy was taller and her figure was almost boyish, but even so there was something about her that set his pulse racing.

And so they moved along, neither aware of the other's thoughts, until eventually the cottage came into view. After Jake's hard work on the outside, it looked like something out of a picture book with the smoke drifting lazily from the newly swept chimney into the pale-blue sky but Abi curled her lip at the sight of it.

'I don't know how I'm going to bear living here,' she groaned.

Jasper squeezed her hand. 'Well, think about the job I told you about,' he said persuasively as they walked towards the garden gate.

'Will you come in?' she offered.

Jasper shook his head. 'No, thanks all the same. Mother will be wondering where I am and I'm sure you need some time to settle in.'

'I shall *never* settle here,' Abi snorted derisively and flinging the gate open she marched up the path.

'Ah, Abigail, here you are. I was beginning to get concerned,' Dorcas greeted her the second she set foot in the room. Much as her mother had done, Abi glanced around and frowned. As far as she was concerned, no amount of fancy furniture or rugs could make it look any more than what it was: a lowly little cottage.

'I went for a walk with Jasper,' Abi informed her imperiously as she removed her bonnet and tossed it on to a chair. 'Where're Emmy and Hetty?'

'In the yard doing the laundry.'

Abi screwed her nose up in disgust but wisely said nothing, and it was just as well for at that moment Emmy came in wiping her hands on a large apron she had tied about her waist. Her face was flushed and some of her hair had escaped from its pins and curled around her face. Her sleeves were rolled up to the elbow and Abi was horrified at the sight of her.

'Why, you look just like a servant,' she spat in disgust but instead of being angry Emmy grinned.

'And so will you before much longer,' she said coolly. 'There's far too much to do with four of us here for Hetty to manage everything on her own so we're all going to have to muck in and help her, I'm afraid. And you can start by putting the kettle on and making a cup of tea. I'm sure we're all ready for one.'

'Call Hetty to do it,' Abi said coldly but Emmy stared her out.

'As I told you, Hetty is busy elsewhere, unless of course you'd rather go and finish the laundry?'

There was something in Emmy's voice that made Abi cross to the kettle and fill it from the pump handle on the sink, although she was mumbling under her breath the whole time and she was clearly not pleased.

'I'm glad none of my friends from school can see me now,' she grumbled as she slammed the kettle on to the range. 'I'd be a laughing stock and all because of our selfish father. How could he do this to us?'

Once again Emmy was instantly on the offensive. 'Father must have been in turmoil to go off as he did,' she scolded, heedless of the fact that her mother was listening avidly. 'And it might do you good to remember that we're still much better off than some.'

Abi and her mother glanced at each other, but sensing that Emmy was near to the end of her tether they both wisely remained silent.

It was mid-afternoon when they had their first visitor and when Hetty opened the door and Dorcas saw who it was she flushed to the roots of her hair with shame. Even so, her manners prevailed and she said graciously, 'Hello, Sybil, won't you come in? Would you like some tea?'

Sybil stepped inside and looked around as if there was a bad smell under her nose, then grimaced as she took in some of the fine carpets and pieces of furniture. 'I see you have made yourself comfortable, Dorcas,' she said patronisingly as she removed her white cotton gloves. 'And no, thank you, I won't take tea. I've actually come to deliver a message from Bernard. He asked me to tell you that from now on we shall supply you with milk, eggs and meat whenever any of the animals are slaughtered. I've no doubt that will be a great help to you?'

The words were threatening to choke her but nonetheless Dorcas managed a smile and said politely through gritted teeth, 'That is most kind of him. Do thank him for me. And thank Jake too. His help in moving all our belongings in has been invaluable.'

As Sybil took a seat in the wing chair to one side of the fire, she looked mildly surprised. 'Oh, I wasn't aware that he had been helping. He didn't mention it.'

'Well, he certainly has helped and we are most grateful to him,' Dorcas told her.

Sybil inclined her head and glanced around again before enquiring, 'I don't suppose there has been any word from Gerald?'

Dorcas flushed again as she shook her head, noting Sybil's expression. Just for a second Dorcas was tempted to forget her manners and swipe the smirk from her face, although she didn't of course. She was painfully aware that they were beholden to her brother and her sister-in-law while she and her daughters lived in their cottage and she couldn't afford to make things any worse than they already were – although as far as she was concerned, it was hard to imagine how they *could* be any worse.

'Do you think you will be comfortable here?'

Again, Dorcas plastered a false smile to her face. 'Oh, I'm quite sure we shall be, just as soon as we have settled in.'

'And is there any sign of jobs for the girls yet?' Sybil asked, driving the knife in even further.

Dorcas looked slightly taken aback. 'Not as yet; we haven't really had time to think about it.'

'Hm, and I've no doubt it won't be an easy task finding them posts when they have no experience at anything.'

'I dare say something suitable will turn up,' Dorcas said. 'But there's no rush as yet.'

Sybil, who clearly had no intention of staying, rose then and began to draw her gloves back on. It was uncomfortably hot in the small room but she realised that they had to have the fire on to cook.

'Just so long as you don't leave it until your money runs out,' she said as a parting shot and with a sickly sweet smile, she made for the door, saying, 'Good afternoon, dear.'

'Good afternoon.' Dorcas watched her leave and once she was out of earshot she growled, quite uncharacteristically, 'Stuck-up old *cow!*'

Hetty had just entered the kitchen and she quickly lowered her head to hide her grin. It was the first time she had ever heard her mistress curse.

Sybil, meanwhile, was making her way home to the roomy farmhouse with a smug expression on her face as she thought, *How the mighty have fallen!*

Chapter Ten

Four days after they had moved into the cottage, Jake came to say his goodbyes before he returned to London to finish his training.

As usual, Dorcas was seated regally in her chair beside the fire and from what Emmy had told him he gathered she had barely left it apart from to go to bed. Abi had also taken to staying in the room she had to share with her sister and he rightly guessed it was so that while she was up there she wouldn't be called upon to do any work. It was a damned shame, he thought, that everything should be left up to Hetty and Emmy, although he hadn't heard either of them complain. When he left after his brief visit, Emmy followed him to the gate and as they stood there with the warm sunshine beating down on them, he suddenly realised how much he was going to miss her.

'You really should put your foot down and make those two pull their weight,' he commented.

Emmy merely smiled ruefully. 'I think there's very little chance of that ever happening. But anyway, I hope not to be here much longer. I shall have to start to look for a job soon and so will Abi. But thanks again for all your help, Jake. As I've said before, I don't know how we would have managed without you. Your mother must be sad to see you go again.'

'I doubt that very much. As long as she has Jasper to pamper, she's happy. He's always been the favourite.'

'So, when will we see you again?' she asked.

'I dare say I shall be back in the summer sometime, but I can't say for sure when. I wanted to say, please be careful when you take a position . . . What I mean is, make sure that it's somewhere safe. Oh, and here's my address; I thought you could perhaps write and keep me up to date with how you all are and what you're up to.' He fumbled in his pocket and handed her a piece of paper and for no reason that she could explain, Emmy felt herself flush.

'I will. Goodbye for now and take care.' She stood back, a lump rising in her throat as she watched him walk away.

The next two weeks as they settled into their new home were not easy. Both Dorcas and Abi complained constantly about anything and everything, and now that they were living in such confined quarters, Emmy sometimes felt like screaming at them, although she managed to stop herself.

One day early in April as Hetty was preparing to catch the cart to Nuneaton Market Place, Abi suddenly decided to go with her.

'Anything is better than having to sit around this dump,' she said caustically and off she sailed to get ready.

When she appeared some minutes later in her best bonnet and all her finery, Hetty looked slightly worried. 'I ain't sure that's the right outfit fer walkin' round the market in, miss,' she said as tactfully as she could.

Abi waved her hand airily. 'And how would you have me dress then?' she snapped. 'One has to keep up appearances.'

Hetty shrugged and after she had collected her wicker basket, they set off to wait for the carrier cart at Astley crossroads.

When the cart pulled up, Abi was already complaining about the dust on the bottom of her fine gown but Hetty was unsympathetic and hopped into the back, leaving Abi to struggle up alone.

There were two farmers' wives already seated on the hard wooden bench seats and they watched with amusement as Abi flopped down beside them.

'*Surely* there is a more comfortable way of getting into the town?' Abi grumbled as the cart set off, bouncing along the uneven lanes. This was a very far cry from the fine carriage she was used to travelling in.

The farmers' wives exchanged a glance. The news of the Winters' downfall had spread through the town and the surrounding villages like wildfire and they had already guessed who Abi was.

By the time they reached Market Place, Abi's bottom was sore from bouncing up and down on the hard wooden plank seat and she was sure she would be bruised.

'I would have thought Uncle Bernard could at least arrange transport for us,' she complained churlishly as she brushed the dust from her skirt and straightened her bonnet.

Hetty grinned but made no comment as she set off for the stalls, and with no other choice Abi reluctantly followed her. The expedition proved to be nothing like the shopping trips she had been accustomed to when she could glance in a shop window and choose anything she liked, and soon she was bored and wishing that she had stayed at home. Soon Hetty's basket was almost full of fruit and vegetables and the other goods she had come for and they were just strolling past the dressmaker's shop when one of Dorcas's friends came out of the door with her daughter. Abi put her head down and hoped they wouldn't see her, but it was too late – she had already been spotted.

'Abigail, my dear girl!'

Abi had never been fond of Mrs Porter, or her daughter Miranda for that matter, but she forced a smile to her face and inclined her head politely.

'I was so sorry to hear what had happened to you girls and your poor dear mother,' the woman rushed on, looking anything but sorry. 'What a *dreadful* thing to happen, losing everything just like that!' She snapped her fingers. 'But I do hope you and your mother and sister are managing in the little cottage?'

'We're managing very well, thank you,' Abi forced herself to say, avoiding looking at Miranda who had a huge grin on her face.

'Oh good, good.' Then, adding insult to injury she patted the enormous bag she was carrying, saying smugly, 'We've just bought the gown you ordered. The dressmaker told us that you wouldn't be able to afford it any more and it's such a shame for it to go waste, don't you think? The colour suits Miranda admirably. But we must get on, dear. Do remember me to your mother, won't you?'

'Of course.' Abi watched the pair walk away and then to Hetty's amusement she stuck out her tongue in a most unladylike manner. 'Old *bitch*!' she muttered through gritted teeth. 'I bet she's loving what's happening to us. She always was jealous of Mama.'

Just for a moment Hetty felt quite sorry for her. 'Ah well, at least you'll 'ave the satisfaction o' knowin' that the gown won't look 'alf as good on Miranda as it would 'ave on you. She ain't the prettiest o' creatures, is she? An' I'll bet the dressmaker 'ad a right old game lettin' it out enough to make it fit 'er!'

Abi grinned and they walked on in companionable silence. But they hadn't gone far when she saw someone else she knew and she slowed her steps. 'Look, Hetty, there's James Prestatyn. His family are awfully well off and I think they've always hoped that James and I would make a match one day when we both came of age. I must go over and have a word.'

Before Hetty could stop her Abi lifted her skirts and was off. James had just come out of the tobacconist and when he glanced up and saw her advancing on him, he flushed a dull brick red. Abi had never been that fond of him but suddenly in her straitened circumstances, and knowing how wealthy his parents were, he looked much more attractive.

'Hello, James, how are you?' She batted her long eyelashes and gave him her most winning smile as she twirled the little lace parasol she was carrying.

'I, er . . . I'm very well, thank you, Miss Winter. And, er, yourself?'

He seemed a little tongue-tied, so Abi rushed on, 'I dare say you've heard what's happened with Papa leaving and everything, but we're getting settled into our new home now so you simply *must* come and see us.'

'I'll try.' He looked acutely embarrassed. 'But I can't promise anything ... what with going to university and everything, you understand? I'm only home for a few days.'

'I see!' Abi wasn't best pleased. James was usually all over her like a rash but today it seemed he was embarrassed to even be seen speaking to her. Even so her pride wouldn't let her show him how humiliated she was, so she nodded before saying cheerfully, 'Goodbye for now, then,' and without waiting for him to reply she turned away, tears springing to her eyes as she tried to lose herself in the crowds that were thronging the marketplace.

It was all Hetty could do to catch up with her and once she did, she caught her arm and drew her to a halt, saying softly, 'Don't let 'im an' 'is like upset yer, miss. Yer still as good as them all day long.'

'But I'm *not* any more, am I, Hetty?' Abi's voice was loaded with sorrow. 'Papa has ruined us and I don't think I'll ever be able to hold my head up again if I stay here. Perhaps I should start looking for a job! Somewhere far away where nobody knows me.'

'There'll be plenty o' time fer that. Come along now, I've just about got everythin' we came for so 'ow about we go an' wait fer the cart 'ome, eh?'

Abi nodded before remembering something. 'Oh, I just have to go to the post office first to post this letter for Mama.' She glanced at it curiously. It was addressed to someone in London. They had visited the capital with their parents many times but she had no idea who this person might be

86

and didn't much care, so keeping her head down she followed Hetty through the stalls.

The post office was quite full when she reached it, mainly with farmers' wives who had come into town to shop while their husbands bartered their livestock at the cattle market, but the second Abi set foot through the door the women, who were having a good old gossip, became silent immediately. Abi knew they had probably been discussing her family's situation and her humiliation was complete.

Later that evening as they sat around the fire, Dorcas asked, 'Did you remember to post my letter for me, Abigail?'

'What? . . . Oh yes, I did. I'm sure the people in the post office were gossiping about us. They all stopped talking the minute I went in; it was so embarrassing.' She scowled as she thought of it before asking curiously, 'Who were you writing to, Mama? I didn't recognise the name on the envelope.'

Dorcas sighed and laid down the sampler she had been embroidering. 'Actually . . . I was writing to my sister . . . to ask her for help, although it goes sorely against the grain. But then I suppose desperate times call for desperate measures.'

'Your *sister*!' Abigail exclaimed.

Emmy and Abi exchanged a shocked glance. They had never even known their mother had a sister.

'So why have we never known we had an aunt?' Abi asked in her usual blunt way. 'And why didn't she inherit the farm when Grandfather died?'

'There was never any reason for you to know, and my parents had washed their hands of her years before they

87

passed away,' Dorcas said primly. 'We were also estranged many years ago. She is some ten years older than me and was always our parents' favourite. Until she shamed them, that is, and then all their hopes were pinned on me.'

'So, what is her name? Tell us about her,' Abi pressed.

Dorcas took a deep breath. 'Very well, her name is Imogen and she was very beautiful and outgoing. I was always the quiet one and my parents never hid the fact that she was the favourite.' When Abi opened her mouth to say something, Dorcas held her hand up and she clamped it shut again, eager to hear what her mother had to say.

'When she was in her teens, she was keen to pursue a career in the music halls and of course our parents were horrified at the very idea. It's not the sort of thing well-brought-up young ladies do, and so eventually she ran away.' She sighed as her memory drifted back in time. 'For a while my father tried to find her to bring her home but after two years, he discovered that she had indeed made a name for herself in London. She was the darling songbird of the stage and the toast of the city by all accounts; she had no intention of returning home, so in the end my parents gave up on her and disowned her.

'Soon after, word reached them that she had married a very rich older Frenchman and that she was very happy. But her happiness was short-lived for they had only been married for a short while when he suffered a heart attack and passed away. Imogen was totally heartbroken, although he left her a very wealthy woman and from what I could get out of my parents she became something of a recluse after that. She did come to my wedding, and Bernard's when he married Sybil, and I also let her know when you and Emmy were born. I don't know if she is still at the same address in London or even if she is still alive but I thought I would chance writing to her to see if she is still there and ask if she might know of any suitable jobs going for Emerald.'

'Oh, *how* romantic,' Abi sighed dreamily. It was like something she read about in the novels she was so fond of. 'But why are you only asking her if she knows of work for Emmy? What about me?'

'You are a little younger,' her mother told her. 'And so it's only right that Emerald should find work first. Goodness knows there's little chance of either of you making a good marriage now, with no dowry to offer and our reputation in tatters!'

Abi's thoughts instantly returned to the way James Prestatyn had snubbed her in the town earlier in the day and she pouted as she recalled the incident to her mother.

Meanwhile Emmy was reeling with shock. To think that all this time they had had an aunt that they hadn't even known existed. She half hoped this unknown aunt would find work for her. It was certainly no fun living with her mother and Abi any more, all they ever did was complain rather than count their blessings, and neither of them seemed to be at all concerned about what might have happened to her father.

With a sigh, she rose and made her way to the room she shared with Abi where she sat on the bed staring thoughtfully into space. One thing was for sure, life was never going to be the same again for any of them and the sooner Abi and her mother got used to that idea the better it would be for all of them.

She washed quickly in the water that stood in a pretty jug and bowl on the small marble-topped washstand and after slipping into her nightgown she hopped into bed where she lay wondering where her father was and praying that he was all right, as she had every single night since he had disappeared. She had been racking her brains trying to think of a way that she might trace him but realised that with no idea where he might have gone, it would be like looking for a needle in a haystack. Would she ever know what had happened to him? she wondered. Because it was not knowing whether he was alive or dead that was eating her up inside.

Chapter Eleven

Over the next few days Emmy kept herself busy helping Hetty. They worked together on the small garden at the back of the cottage, clearing weeds and planting vegetables, and Hetty continued to teach Emmy to cook, although Abi stayed well out of the way. Dorcas meanwhile stayed firmly in her chair, almost as if she had been planted there, with a miserable expression on her face as she cursed the man she had married and felt sorry for herself.

Then one day, as Emmy was sweeping the path that led to the front door, she saw the postman on his bicycle riding towards her across the rough ground.

'Morning, Miss Emerald.' He doffed his cap. After delivering the Winters' mail to their former home for many years it still felt strange to find them living in this humble cottage.

He handed a letter to Emmy and she smiled and thanked him before turning to take it inside. It was addressed to her mother and she saw at a glance that the envelope was of the finest quality.

As usual, her mother was sitting staring into the fire, but when Emmy handed her the letter, she immediately opened it.

'Who is it from?' Abi asked curiously.

'It's from my sister, Imogen,' Dorcas replied.

Abi was all ears. 'Ooh, what does it say. Can you read it to us?'

'I suppose so.' Clearing her throat, Dorcas began.

Dear Dorcas,

I must admit to being very surprised to hear from you after all these years and was sorry to hear of your circumstances. I have heard nothing from you since you wrote to inform me of your daughters' births. I had always hoped to have children myself but sadly it wasn't meant to be. Unfortunately, I am no longer in the best of health so I may be able to offer your eldest a post as my companion-cum-maid if she should prove suitable. Perhaps she would like to present herself here within the next two weeks so I could explain what her role would be and see if we would be compatible. You are, of course, welcome to accompany her.

Yours sincerely,
Your sister,
Imogen.

'Oh, how exciting!' Abi clapped her hands. 'You will go, won't you, Emmy?'

Emmy was looking a little stunned but her mother answered for her. 'Of course she must go, and as soon as possible.' She stared thoughtfully towards the window for a time. 'We must decide what you are to wear, Emmy. We need you to make a good impression. You can catch a train to Euston and from there you can get a hackney cab to Islington. And if you do prove to be suitable, you must tell her that you are able to start as soon as she likes.'

Emmy smiled ruefully. 'It almost sounds like you can't wait to get rid of me, Mama,' she commented.

Dorcas waved her hand at her. 'Don't be so silly. This could prove to be a golden opportunity for you. No one there will know of your straitened circumstances and I've no doubt Imogen will know of many eligible young men in London. We might just find a rich husband for you yet, and in the meantime, you will be earning. For all her faults, Imogen was never mean so I have no doubt she will be generous to you.'

It seemed the decision had been taken out of her hands, so Emmy merely nodded in agreement.

Three days later, Emmy was up bright and early to catch the cart into Nuneaton with Hetty. As they waited at the crossroads, Emmy felt very overdressed. Her mother had declined to go with her but had insisted that she should wear her very best travelling costume, which was made of a fine sea-green cotton with a full skirt and a tiny jacket with a peplum at the waist. Beneath it she wore a white ruffled blouse and on her head was a matching bonnet trimmed with silk flowers.

'This is so excitin' fer you,' Hetty said enviously, although she knew she would miss Emmy dreadfully. 'Fancy goin' all the way to London on a train. I ain't never even been outside of Nuneaton!'

Emmy grinned. 'Well, I'm glad someone is excited about it,' she said quietly. 'I'm so nervous my stomach is in knots. What if my aunt doesn't like me?'

'O' course she will, 'ow could she not like yer?' Hetty answered as the cart rumbled towards them.

It drew to a stop beside them and soon they were rattling on their way. As they passed the castle and Astley Pool, Emmy realised how strange it was going to be if she did get the job and had to move away from everywhere that was so familiar. Over the years her parents had taken her and Abi on numerous holidays abroad. They had been to the South of France on many occasions and even as far away as Switzerland, so she considered herself to be fairly well travelled, but holidays were different. She had always come home when they were over, if she got the job she would be leaving for good. It was a daunting thought.

By the time she arrived at the train station she felt so nervous she was nauseous.

Hetty had insisted on coming to see her off and as they stood on the platform waiting for the train to arrive Hetty gave her a hug.

'You'll be fine,' she said reassuringly but Emmy wasn't so sure.

'What will I do if I don't get the post? Mama will be so disappointed.'

Hetty scowled and wagged her finger at her. 'Don't talk so daft. O' course you'll get the post. She's yer aunt, ain't she, so she can't say no. And yer a lovely person, nothin' like yer . . .' Her voice trailed away as she realised she had almost said too much.

Emmy grinned. 'If you were about to say Abi, don't worry. I know she can be a bit difficult. Just don't let her give you any grief while I'm gone,' she told her. 'I shall be back tonight, although I have no idea what time. But don't worry, Mama gave me enough money to get a cab to the cottage if it's too late when I get back to Nuneaton, so I shall be perfectly all right.'

At that moment they heard the train approaching and it was soon huffing into the station, belching steam and smoke that floated up to drift amongst the rafters. The guard hurried along the length of the platform opening doors so the passengers could alight.

Hetty pushed her towards the nearest door. 'Off yer go then. An' good luck.'

Emmy lifted her skirts and clambered aboard and once she was settled in a carriage, she waved at Hetty through the window. As the train chugged into life again, Emmy wondered what the day would bring. It would certainly be interesting if nothing else.

Back at the cottage, Abi was preparing to go for a walk regardless of the mountain of dirty breakfast pots piled high in the sink. As far as she was concerned, they were Hetty's job, no matter that the girl had gone shopping. So far since moving in she had managed to escape doing any of the menial jobs and she had no intention of changing that now.

'I shan't be long, Mama, I'm just going out to get some fresh air,' she told her mother as she fastened the ribbons of her bonnet beneath her chin, and the woman nodded absently.

Abi had almost reached the gate when she saw Jasper striding towards her looking very smart in a brand-new suit, a starched white shirt and a silk cravat.

'Ah, I thought I'd just pop in to see how you were all doing,' he told her cheerfully as he came abreast of her.

'I'm just off for a stroll and there's only Mama in,' she informed him.

His smile slipped. 'So where are Emerald and Hetty?'

'Emerald has gone to London to see an aunt we never even knew we had, and Hetty went into town to do some shopping and see her off,' Abi told him. As he fell into step with her, she told him about the job Emmy might get.

Jasper listened in astonishment, his lips set in a grim line. He hadn't known they had an aunt either, and he wasn't happy about the news that Emmy might be leaving. Although she was his cousin, he had suddenly developed an affection for her and the thought of her moving away was too painful to consider. Thankfully Abi didn't seem to notice the change in his mood and after a few moments he pulled himself together enough to ask, 'And what about a job for you? Have you thought any more about what I suggested?'

She fluttered her eyelashes and giggled. 'Of course I've thought about it, but what do you think Mama would make of the idea? Why, she'd have a fit if I so much as suggested it.'

'So, are you prepared to stay here with no prospects of making a good marriage?' he said somewhat unkindly. 'If you stay here the best you could hope for is for some farmer or labourer to ask for your hand and I can't see you being happy with that. Alternatively, you could become an old maid and grow old with your mother in the cottage.'

Abi's face fell at his words. He was quite right; she wouldn't be happy with that. She wanted someone who would spoil and pamper her and she certainly didn't want to stay in the cottage for a minute longer than was necessary.

'I . . . I will give it some serious thought,' she said slowly. 'But if I did decide to do it, Mama must never know where I'd gone. If I didn't like it then I could always come back and tell her I'd been staying with a school friend.'

'She certainly wouldn't find out from me,' he assured her as he turned to take another path. 'Just let me know what you decide.'

She stared after him thoughtfully. She had to admit that the life he had painted was appealing: being wooed by rich men and having expensive presents showered on her just for giving them her company sounded wonderful, and she was becoming more tempted by the idea every day.

Jasper's emotions, meanwhile, were in turmoil. He knew that the feelings he had formed for Emmy were unnatural but he couldn't seem to help it. Just the sight of her sweet face set his pulse racing, but how could he ever tell her how he felt? They were first cousins and it would be wrong for them to marry. He knew that nothing could come of his feelings. All the cousins knew the tragic story of the two children their grandparents – who had been first cousins – had had who had not survived infancy. Apparently, this had been due to an illness caused by the close familial connection. Jasper didn't understand much about that. Jake had tried to explain it to him, but really, it meant nothing. However, what he did understand was that under no circumstances would either his parents or Emmy's mother allow a union between the cousins. Personally, he didn't care if he never had children, but he knew his father would cut him off if he ever went against this unwritten rule. He had already had more than his share of young women but since Gerald had left, he had got to know Emmy better and seeing her spirit and courage in the face of adversity – so unlike Abi's whining – he felt sure he would never meet anyone who could measure up to her. If he had a woman like that by his side, he was sure the world would be his oyster. Somehow, he would have to let her know how he felt and come up with a plan on how he could persuade her to be his. Up to now he had kept his feelings well hidden, and if Emmy left for London, then he'd have no choice but to continue to do so. He sighed.

Hetty arrived home after lunch laden down with two bags of shopping and dropped them on the table with a sigh of relief. It had been a long walk from the cart and her arms felt as if they had almost been pulled out of their sockets

'Ah, Hetty, here you are at last,' Dorcas greeted her. 'Abigail and I are ready for our lunch now.'

Hetty's eyes stretched wide as she looked at the dirty pots still piled in the sink. 'So why didn't you make yourselves something?' she asked boldly.

Dorcas's head snapped up from the newspaper she was reading. 'Don't you talk to me like that, girl!' she scolded. 'Just remember you are the servant here and *I* pay your wages.'

'An' *you* just remember that I only 'ave one pair of 'ands an' I can't be in two places at once,' Hetty retaliated, at the end of her tether. 'In case it slipped yer mind I've been shoppin' all mornin' an' I come back to find neither o' you 'ave lifted a finger.'

'How *dare* you!' Dorcas blustered.

But Hetty was too angry to heed her warning as she faced her mistress squarely with her hands on her hips and her eyes blazing. 'Oh, I *dare*, missus!' Her voice was ominously quiet. 'An' I'll tell yer somethin' else, an' all! If yer don't alter the way yer treat me I'm gonna be gone. I'm sick of yer talkin' to me like I'm nowt but a skivvy! I've worked every single day from mornin' till late at night to meet yer demands since we got 'ere an' I didn't mind that – I even took a cut in wages – but I've 'ad enough now!'

Colour rose in Dorcas's cheeks as she snatched up her fan and furiously waved it in front of her. Half of her wanted to tell the young hussy to go if that was the way she felt, but then the more sensible side of her baulked at the thought of having to do all the menial tasks herself.

'Let's not be hasty,' she said, although the words almost stuck in her throat. 'Of course we appreciate what you do . . . don't we, Abigail, dear? It's just been such a difficult and upsetting time for all of us . . .'

Abi, who had been watching the argument avidly, her eyes round as saucers, didn't reply to her mother, merely waited to see what Hetty would say next.

Hetty's temper ebbed away as she began to unpack the bags. 'Right, in that case I'll make us all some sandwiches for now an' I'll cook us a meal this evenin, if that'll be suitable?'

'That will be very suitable . . . thank you, Hetty,' Dorcas forced herself to say.

Slightly mollified, Hetty pottered off to fetch the bread and some ham and cheese from the cold shelf in the pantry. A cup of tea to go with the sandwiches wouldn't go amiss either!

Chapter Twelve

The journey to London was uneventful and as soon as the train arrived at Euston Emmy got into a hackney cab to take her to her aunt's address. She had been to London so many times in the past that she had already seen many of the famous landmarks and the town held no excitement for her now. So as the cab rattled through the streets, she stared absently out of the window wondering what her Aunt Imogen would be like and trying to ignore the musty smell of the straw on the floor of the carriage. Barnsbury Road where her aunt lived was very close to Barnard Park and Emmy appreciated seeing a bit of green grass amongst all the hustle and bustle of the city. Soon they turned into a road that was lined with rows of three-storey townhouses and the cab stopped outside one of them.

The driver slipped down from his seat to open the door for her. 'This is it, miss. Do you want me to wait for you?'

'No, thank you; I don't know how long I shall be,' Emmy responded as she paid him and gave him a warm smile.

He touched his cap and hopped back up on to the driver's seat and as he steered the horse back into the traffic, Emmy turned to look at her aunt's house. It was surrounded by wrought-iron railings with stone stairs leading down to what she guessed would be the kitchen, and curved steps that led up to a brightly painted blue door with a shiny brass knocker. To either side of the door were long sash-cord windows hung with snow-white lace curtains and suddenly Emmy felt nervous again. Her mother had written back to inform her aunt that she would visit her today, but Emmy wondered if the letter had arrived yet and whether she would be welcome? There was only one way to find out, so after taking a deep breath and smoothing her skirt, she mounted the steps and rapped on the door.

After a few moments she heard footsteps pattering towards her and the door opened to reveal a young maid wearing a starched white apron and mop cap over a navy-blue dress.

'I'm Miss Winter and I'm here to see Mrs Dubois,' Emmy told her politely.

The girl nodded and stood aside to allow Emmy into the hall, which she saw at once was almost as large as the whole of their cottage put together.

'I'll just let madam know,' the young maid said in a broad cockney accent. She looked to be no more than sixteen or seventeen years old and had blue eyes, fair hair and a friendly smile. 'Will yer just wait 'ere, miss?'

As she hurried away Emmy stared around in awe. The place was so opulently furnished that she felt as if she had stepped on to a stage. Heavy gilt mirrors and portraits of a very attractive young woman adorned the walls and an enormous chandelier hung from the ceiling. Beneath it a huge vase of pure-white lilies stood on a highly polished table on the black-and-white tiled floor, their perfume filling the air.

Within minutes the maid was back with another friendly smile to tell her, 'Madam will see yer now, miss. Would yer like to foller me?'

She walked over to one of the many sets of double doors that led off from the hall and ushered her inside. For a moment Emmy was disorientated. The curtains at the window were firmly drawn and it was so gloomy that she had to stand and let her eyes adjust to the light. And the smell of heavy French perfume and yet more cut flowers almost took her breath away.

'So . . . you came then.'

The voice came from a wing-back chair to one side of an empty fireplace and Emmy's eyes flew towards it, although it was so dark that she could only just make out the shape of a small person sitting there.

Then suddenly whoever it was lit a match and seconds later an oil lamp on a small table at the side of them began to cast a shadowy glow about the room and Emmy found herself looking at a petite woman who seemed almost lost in the large chair. She was tiny and her hair, which was piled high on her head in intricate curls, was fair but peppered with grey. The low-cut pink silk gown she was wearing was so elaborate that it would have been more suited to a ballroom, and she was covered in jewels that caught and reflected the dim light. Her face was heavily rouged and her lips reddened, giving her the appearance of a china-faced doll Emmy had owned as a child.

'So, you are Emerald!' The voice was surprisingly firm for such a delicate frame and she stared at Emmy appraisingly as she bent forward, leaning heavily on an ornately carved ebony-topped silver walking cane. 'Well, I'll give our Dorcas credit where it's due, you're a good, strong-looking girl. Come over here into the light where I can see you properly. Aggie, who let you in, will be here with some tea for us soon. I dare say you'll be ready for a drink after your journey.'

Now that Emmy's eyes had adjusted to the light, they grew wider as she moved forward. The room was covered in ornaments, pictures, mirrors, ornate gilt-legged furniture and frills and furbelows everywhere she looked.

'Has the cat got your tongue?' Imogen quipped and Emmy blushed as she took a seat in front of her.

'Sorry, Aunt.'

'Now, tell me all about yourself and what's been happening to my sister,' Imogen ordered and so tentatively Emmy told her of all that had happened to them recently as Imogen listened intently.

'Hm, that must have brought our Dorcas down a peg or two,' Imogen said when Emmy had faltered to a halt. 'No doubt it was she who helped bring about your father's money problems. She always was a demanding little so and so. Can't pretend we ever got on all that well, to be honest, although she was still little more than a child when I left home.'

Emmy opened her mouth to defend her mother but thought better of it and clamped it shut again. She was in no position to upset the woman, after all, and she was only saying what Emmy herself had thought.

'And what of my brother Bernard?' Imogen asked next. 'And that terrible shrew of a wife he married? And their two boys? What are their names again?'

'Jake and Jasper. They are both a little older than Abi and me. Jake is in his final year at medical school and Uncle

Bernard is hoping to train Jasper to take over the running of the farm eventually.'

Thankfully the maid reappeared then and once she had laid the tray down and left the room, Imogen snapped, 'Make yourself useful, girl! Surely you know how to pour tea? You'll be no use to me if you're like your mother and expect to be waited on.'

Emmy felt a flash of annoyance as she rose to do as she was told. 'Actually, I'm not at all afraid of hard work,' she said shortly before she could stop herself. To her relief, Imogen threw back her head and laughed.

'Ah, so you've got spirit! I like that. I can't be doing with yes people. Now tell me about yourself.'

'There's not much to tell really,' Emmy admitted. 'Until . . . well, until we found ourselves in this position, I think Mama just expected that I would make a good marriage, but that's highly unlikely now.'

'And is that what you wanted?'

Emmy lowered her head. 'Not really,' she admitted.

'So what did you want to do then?'

'I'm not sure,' Emmy answered honestly as she passed her a dainty cup and saucer. 'I've always liked the thought of nursing or doing something useful, although of course I would never have been allowed to.'

'Fiddlesticks!' Imogen stated bluntly. 'You are in charge of your own destiny and should follow your heart.' She frowned before asking, 'Do you have a beau?'

Emmy shook her head and grinned. 'No, I don't. Although it isn't for want of Mama trying. She's been parading eligible young men in front of me ever since I left school but

I haven't met anyone yet that I would want to spend the rest of my life with, no matter how rich they were.'

Imogen smiled approvingly. 'Good, I'm glad to hear it. If or when you do marry it should be for love. My Marcel was the love of my life and although we didn't have too many years together, I would rather have had that short time with him than a lifetime with anyone else.' For a moment her eyes clouded as she stared towards a portrait of a dark-haired man with laughing eyes.

'Is that Marcel?' Emmy asked gently.

Imogen nodded. 'It is. He was almost twenty years older than me but I knew the moment I met him that he was my soulmate.' She looked back at Emmy and her voice was stern again as she said, 'I suppose you'd like to know what your duties would be if you came to live with me?'

Emmy nodded as she sipped at her tea.

'Unfortunately I haven't been too well for some time now,' Imogen went on. 'The doctors aren't too sure what is wrong with me. All they can tell me is that I am suffering from some sort of muscle-wasting disease that will only get progressively worse. The old ticker isn't too good either.'

Emmy had noticed how frail she looked and the slight tremor in her hands and she didn't know what to say.

'I have hardly been out of the door since Marcel died many years ago, apart from to visit my other home in Lytham St Anne's – I like to spend the summer there if I am well enough to travel. The air is so much purer there,' Imogen confided with no trace of self-pity. Seeing the sympathy that flashed in her niece's eyes she flapped her hand irritably. 'Don't look like that! Death comes to us all sooner or later; be we beggars or kings, there's nothing so sure! And what is death, after all? We merely pass from this life to another so I am never parted from my love, he speaks to me all the time.'

Emmy felt a shiver run up her spine but remained silent. What could she say?

'And anyway,' her aunt continued, 'my illness hasn't affected me as badly as it might have done if I was still gallivanting off all over the place as I did in my youth. I was the darling of the stage back in my day, you know. I had men falling at my feet. I could have been a baroness had I wished to be but there was never another for me once Marcel came into my life.' Once again, she fell silent as her mind went back to happier times. Then bringing her thoughts back to the present, she said, 'At the moment I only have two servants, although when Marcel was alive we had many more – even a housekeeper and a butler, can you believe? Anyway, that was a long time ago and now I only have Aggie, my little maid, and the cook who live in. I also have a woman who comes in once a week to do the laundry and a man who tends the greenhouse and the gardens. The trouble is my health is deteriorating and Aggie has more than enough to do keeping the house clean and so when your mother wrote to me I thought perhaps you could come as my companion? My eyesight is failing along with everything else, and it would be nice to have someone to read the newspapers and the romance novels that I love to me! I've tried spectacles but they are no help at all. Also there are days when I need assistance with dressing and getting up and down the stairs. Do you think these are things you could help me with?'

'I'm sure I could,' Emmy assured her. Despite her curt way of speaking and her stern demeanour, Emmy had already sensed that beneath her harsh exterior her aunt wasn't as hard as she made herself out to be and she felt herself warming to her.

'I would ensure that you received a fair wage and of course you would live here. I would also make sure that you had some time off. You're only a young woman and you need to get out and about with people your own age. All work and no play makes Jack a dull boy, or in your case, girl, don't you think? Now, will you be staying for lunch before you set off for home again?'

'I, er ... that would be very nice, thank you,' Emmy answered. 'As long as you're sure it won't inconvenience you.'

'I wouldn't have asked if it would,' Imogen replied shortly and Emmy hid a smile, sensing that her aunt's bark was worse than her bite.

'Right, I'll tell Aggie to set the dining room table in that case. I usually just have a tray in here but it's time the room was used again.' She leant over and pulled a rope at the side of the fireplace that would ring a bell in the kitchen.

Aggie was there in seconds and after bobbing her knee she asked, 'Yes, ma'am?'

'My niece will be staying for lunch. Inform Cook and lay two places in the dining room. What culinary delight does she have in store for us today, anyway?'

'I believe it's salmon, salad and new potatoes, ma'am. And there's rice pudding to follow.'

Imogen sighed and waved the girl away, telling Emmy, 'Cook isn't the most adventurous of souls when it comes to menus. She tends to be a very plain cook. It was different when Marcel was alive though. Oh, you wouldn't believe the things he introduced me to.' She chuckled. 'One day he persuaded me to eat snails. Ugh! But of course, they were a great delicacy where he came from. Anyway, take your bonnet off if you're staying for a while. You look like someone who has come calling.'

Once again Emmy managed to stifle a smile as she fiddled with the ribbons on her bonnet and laid it aside before patting her hair into place. Then they settled down to finish their tea while the cook put the finishing touches to their meal.

While they talked, her aunt watched Emmy closely. *She's not a bad-looking girl*, she thought. *Not quite beautiful, she's too tall and slim for that, but she'll do!*

Just as her aunt had predicted, lunch when it was served was plain but tasty, although Emmy noticed that her aunt only pecked at hers like a bird. It was no wonder she was so tiny, she thought.

'So if you take the job, when would you be able to start?'

Emmy quickly swallowed the food she was chewing and dabbed at her lips with her napkin. 'I could start whenever you like, Aunt.'

'Hm . . . very well, but it's only for a month's trial, mind! You might not suit.'

Emmy nodded.

'So shall we say next Monday?'

Another nod.

'Good, that's settled then. Now tell me all about your sister and then you'd best be off to catch your train. It's time for my lie-down.'

Knowing that she was being dismissed Emmy hurriedly told her a little about her younger sister then quickly rose and went to fetch her bonnet, asking Aggie to thank the cook for her meal.

Her aunt was making her way along the hallway, leaning heavily on her stick, when Emmy left the drawing room, and when she leant towards her to give her a goodbye kiss the woman scowled at her.

'There's no need for any o' that sloppy stuff,' she scolded. 'And don't think that just because you're my niece you'll get special treatment because you won't, girl. You'll be treated just the same as any other member of staff, do you understand?'

'Perfectly,' Emmy answered primly. A little shock coursed through her as she glanced again at one of the portraits of the woman hanging in the hall and realised that it was of her aunt when she was younger. She certainly hadn't been lying when she'd told her that she used to be beautiful.

'Goodbye.'

'Goodbye, Aunt.' Emmy watched the woman climb the stairs painfully slowly before slipping out into the street again and heading for Euston. It had certainly been an interesting day!

Chapter Thirteen

It was early evening when the train drew into Trent Valley Railway Station and Emmy was shocked to find Jasper waiting outside in his father's carriage for her.

'Ah, here you are.' He leapt down from the carriage and gave her a warm smile.

Emmy raised an eyebrow. 'What are you doing here?'

'Abi told me you'd gone to London to visit your aunt and as I was in Nuneaton anyway, I popped into the ticket office to find out what time the train was due in and thought I'd hang on to see if you were on it so I could give you a lift home.' He omitted to tell her that he had kept the poor horses and the driver standing outside the station for the last three hours.

'That was very kind of you,' Emmy told him as he took her hand and helped her into the carriage, although she found it strange that he was suddenly going out of his way to be helpful now when he hadn't lifted a finger to help them move into the cottage. *Still*, she thought, feeling slightly guilty for being so uncharitable, *better late than never.*

As she settled back against the luxurious leather squabs, she told him, 'I was just debating whether to walk home or get a cab.'

Jasper clambered up beside her and smiled. 'There you are then. You don't have to do either now. How did your visit go?'

She guessed Abi would have told him why she had gone to London and gave a wry smile. 'It went very well, as it happens. I'm going to do a month's trial to see if we suit each other.'

'And do you think you will?'

She shrugged. 'Time will tell, I suppose. Our aunt is a little eccentric to say the least, and I have the feeling she won't be the easiest person to please, but needs must. My mother's small inheritance won't keep us all going indefinitely.'

Jasper scowled as he took her hand, which made her feel rather uncomfortable. 'I just wish my father would do more to help you,' he said angrily. 'We are family after all.'

Emmy gently withdrew her hand from his. 'In fairness, it's very good of him to allow us to live in the cottage rent free, and once I've gone it will be one less person for Mama to worry about.'

Jasper had been livid when Abi had first told him of Emmy's possible move to London but now he was beginning to think that it wouldn't be such a bad thing after all. She was bound to have time off and once she was away from her mother's influence he could go and meet her and take her out.

'So when will you be going?'

'I shall start next Monday,' Emmy answered and his heart sank. He hadn't expected her to leave so soon, but he had many friends he could stay with in London so perhaps he could travel with her and spend some time there? He knew his father wouldn't be pleased at the idea; he had been on at him constantly to learn the business of managing the farming recently, but he could work on his mother. He was always able to win her round; she was like putty in his hands.

'That's a coincidence.' He flashed her his most charming smile. It usually worked like magic on the young ladies but it didn't seem to have much effect on Emmy. 'I'm going to London soon myself to spend a couple of weeks with a friend. Perhaps we could get together when you're not working and I could show you the sights?'

His spirits plummeted when Emmy shook her head. 'That's really kind of you but I think I've seen everything there is to see in London already. Papa used to take us there regularly for weekends in the summer and we would go sightseeing while Mama was shopping. She adores the big emporiums in London and we always seemed to come back with at least twice as much luggage as we went with. Anyway, I think until the trial period is over it would be wise not to go out too much, but thank you for the offer.'

Jasper struggled to keep his smile in place. Just being so close to her was setting his pulses racing and although he knew it wasn't right, he couldn't seem to help it. There was something about Emmy that drew him to her like a magnet.

'Perhaps we could meet up when you've settled in then?' he said quietly.

She nodded. 'Yes, perhaps.' For no reason that she could explain, Emmy felt uncomfortable so she was relieved when they fell silent.

'Thank you for the lift,' she said politely when the carriage had got as close to the cottage as was possible. She still had the best part of a field to get over but that was nothing compared to the walk she would have had.

'You're very welcome.' He helped her down, holding her hand a fraction longer than necessary, and gave a little bow as Emmy set off. It had been a long day and she would be glad to get home now.

'So how did it go?' Dorcas asked the second she set foot through the door.

Emmy smiled and stifled a yawn. 'Just let me get my bonnet and shoes off – my feet are killing me – then I'll tell you all about it.'

'I'll go an' make yer a nice cuppa,' Hetty said obligingly, heading to the sink. 'I dare say as you'll be ready fer one.'

Emmy smiled her thanks and once she was seated, she began to tell her mother about her day while Dorcas hung on her every word.

'And you say that she's ill?' Dorcas questioned.

Emmy nodded. 'Yes, it's some sort of muscle-wasting disease so she said. And I believe she has a weak heart too.'

'I see.' Dorcas chewed on her lip. It was hard to imagine Imogen as anything other than the beautiful young woman she had once been. 'And is the disease curable?'

'I don't think so,' Emmy told her.

'And is she still a little . . . strange?'

'What do you mean by strange exactly?' Emmy asked as Hetty pottered back to her with a welcome cup of tea.

'She used to be heavily into spiritualism and believed that she could communicate with the dead,' Dorcas told her. 'Our mother used to say that if she had been born a hundred years before she would have been branded a witch, but Imogen insisted that she had "a gift".'

Instantly Emmy remembered her aunt telling her that she often spoke to her dead husband and now she understood what she had meant, although the thought of it made her shiver. But then she supposed if it gave her aunt some comfort and she wasn't hurting anyone there was no harm in it.

The outer door opened at that moment and Abi appeared, as eager as her mother had been to hear how Emmy's visit to her aunt had gone.

'Well?' she said raising an eyebrow. 'Did you meet her? Have you got the job?'

Emmy smiled. 'Yes and yes. I'm to start a month's trial on Monday.'

Abi's face fell. It seemed so unfair. Living in London sounded so exciting compared to what she considered to be no more than a backwater hovel. And would she be expected to help with the housework once Emmy was gone? Up to now Hetty and Emmy had kept the place running smoothly between them, but was all that about to alter?

'Don't worry, I shall come and see you whenever I can,' Emmy told her gently, thinking that Abi's long face was due to the fact that she would miss her. 'And I shall send some of my wages home too, so that will be a help.'

Abi pouted but still managed to look beautiful. 'Oh, I'm *sure* you will,' she answered petulantly. 'Just so you can tell me what a wonderful time you are having in the capital while I am stuck here in the middle of nowhere with nothing to do and nowhere to go.'

Hetty chuckled before confirming Abi's worst fears. 'I shouldn't worry about being bored. There's more than enough to keep us busy 'ere an' you can always start to go into town to do the shoppin'. It would be one less job fer me to do at least.'

Abi sent Hetty a murderous glance and flounced away to her room.

When she was gone Hetty told Dorcas and Emmy, 'Me brother is callin' round this evenin' to take some o' the trinkets we brought from the house to sell 'em for yer.'

Dorcas didn't look too thrilled at the thought of being parted with any of her remaining treasures but understood that needs must. And so, Hetty retrieved them from under the floorboards and laid them out in front of her and they spent the next half-hour deciding which ones should go first.

'I reckon these would sell well,' Hetty said thoughtfully, holding up a fine pair of figurines. They were a Dresden shepherd and shepherdess and had cost a fortune when Dorcas had bought them as they were quite rare.

'They're actually worth a great deal of money. Can your brother be trusted not to break them and to get a fair price for them?' Dorcas fretted.

Hetty looked offended. 'Our Mickey ain't no mug,' she shot back. 'An' he don't sell things round 'ere. He'll probably take 'em to an antique dealer he knows in Warwick. He's allus on the lookout for interestin' stuff fer him an' he allus gets a fair price. But o' course if yer don't trust 'im . . .'

'Oh, I'm sure I can if you say so,' Dorcas said swiftly, seeing that Hetty was offended. 'And I shall be happy to pay him a percentage of whatever they fetch.'

115

'That goes wi'out sayin'. An' he'll expect 'is travellin' expenses an' all,' Hetty told her as she gently rewrapped the figures. 'An' what about this silver tray? We ain't goin' to 'ave much cause to use it 'ere, are we?'

The words stung when Dorcas thought back to how many visitors she used to have in Astley House. Every week without fail she would hold a coffee morning or an afternoon tea and everybody who was anybody had loved to come, yet since moving into the cottage not one of them had been to see her or even bothered to get in touch.

'I suppose not,' she said sadly. 'But I'd like to keep the silver tea set . . . for now at least.'

They also added another Meissen figurine of a little cherub to the pile and a pretty Wedgwood plate, but then Dorcas insisted that was quite enough for now and so the rest of the items were duly returned to their place beneath the floorboards and Hetty went off to rustle up some supper for Emmy, who was almost falling asleep now.

'Do you think you'll like working for Aunt Imogen?' Abi asked as they lay in their little beds that evening.

'Whether I do or not, I think I'm just going to have to make the best of it . . . for now at least. Mother needs the money.' Emmy yawned and turned over, and while Abi prattled on, she was fast asleep in minutes, although her dreams were full of ghosts and ghoulies floating out of the walls in Aunt Imogen's house.

Over the next few days, Emmy once again began to pack her things. It felt as if she had hardly settled into the cottage before she was off to live somewhere else again, but it couldn't be helped and Abi had been in such a bad mood that she sometimes thought she might actually be relieved to go. Neither her sister nor her mother were adapting at all well to their new lifestyle, but they were just going to have to get used to it.

'Don't you dare let them have you waiting on them hand and foot,' she warned Hetty.

'Ooh, don't you worry, I shan't,' Hetty replied with a grin. And then as something occurred to her she commented, 'Jasper's been around a lot over the last couple o' days, ain't he? What do yer think the attraction is all of a sudden?'

'Perhaps he just wants to make sure we're settling in.' Emmy didn't like to think badly of anyone, so why, she wondered, did Jasper's sudden concern for them all make her skin crawl? 'It might be that he's taken a shine to you, Hetty,' she teased with a twinkle in her eye. 'It certainly can't be me or Abi, can it, considering our parents would never allow a union between us.'

Hetty snorted. 'Huh! He might be rich but there's somethin' about that young bloke I just can't take to. Jake, on the other hand, is different, but Jasper . . .' She shuddered.

Emmy felt much the same, although she refrained from saying it as Hetty helped her to carry her luggage downstairs and place it by the front door. Jasper had offered to pick it up for her the following morning and drive her to the station and she was grateful to him for that at least, for Hetty had made her pack almost everything she owned.

'But why do I need to take two evening gowns? I'm going to be a paid companion to an older lady so I doubt very much if I'll ever get to wear them,' she had pointed out.

117

'Ah, but yer never know,' Hetty insisted as she had folded them carefully. 'An' it's better to take too much rather than not enough.'

And so Emmy had given in gracefully, although she had no idea how she was going to jiggle them all into a cab when she got to Euston.

On the morning of her departure, she got up early, and although Abi had chosen to stay in bed said a surly goodbye from beneath her blankets. But Dorcas was there to see her off, still in her dressing robe, and Hetty was there too.

While Jasper's driver carried the luggage over the field to the carriage, Emmy said her goodbyes. 'Write to us often, miss.' Hetty had tears in her eyes as Emmy gave her an affectionate peck on the cheek before turning to her mother.

'Take care.' Dorcas had never been one to show Emmy a lot of affection and was clearly finding it hard to know what to say.

'I will,' Emmy promised and, seeing no reason to prolong the goodbyes, she allowed Jasper to take her arm as they walked over the field towards the waiting carriage. As always, the touch of his hand made her stomach churn. He had shown them nothing but kindness for days now, so why, she wondered, couldn't she take to him?

'Goodbye, Mama, goodbye, Hetty,' she called, over her shoulder.

When she finally stepped up into the carriage, she leant out of the window to get a last view of the little cottage as it rocked across the bumpy grass. Then she sat back against the squabs; a new chapter of her life was about to begin and there could be no going back now.

Chapter Fourteen

'She's gone, then?' Abi said as she appeared in the kitchen, rubbing the sleep from her eyes at eleven o'clock that morning. Her hair hung down her back in a riot of shimmering brunette curls, and even sleepy-eyed and still in her night attire she was beautiful.

'She left hours ago,' her mother informed her shortly from her usual seat in front of the fire. Abi sometimes wondered if her backside was glued to it. Dorcas still hadn't stepped outside once apart from to visit the privy at the bottom of the garden since they had moved there.

Crossing to Hetty who was scouring a sink full of dirty dishes, Abi dropped two of her best gowns on to the floor at her side, saying curtly, 'These need washing.'

Hetty lifted her chin to stare at her calmly before replying, 'Well, yer know where the dolly tub is. I've to go into town shoppin' in a while so I'll not 'ave time to do 'em.'

'*What!*' Abi looked horrified. 'Are you daring to suggest that I should do them myself?'

Turning back to the pan she had just scrubbed, Hetty clattered it on to the wide wooden draining board and answered stoically, 'That's exactly what I'm suggestin', miss. I ain't quite got the knack o' bein' in two places at once as yet

119

so if yer want 'em doin' you'll 'ave to do 'em yourself. I've got to meet Mickey in the marketplace in a bit to see if he's managed to sell the missus's porcelain, an' if I don't get a move on I'll miss the cart. Oh, an' afore yer start on yer washin', yer might want to finish these pots an' all.' And with that she went off to get ready, leaving Abi with her mouth gaping.

'Are you *really* going to allow the servant to speak to me like that, Mama?' she queried, her voice trembling with rage.

Dorcas shrugged. 'I'm afraid it's out of my control,' she said in a self-pitying whine. 'Everything is out of my control thanks to your no-good father. How could he do this to us? I feel as if I am living in a no-man's land – shunned by the peasants and the gentry alike.'

With an annoyed click of her tongue, Abi approached the teapot only to find the tea was stewed and almost cold. 'She could have at least made sure my breakfast and a fresh cup of tea were ready for me when I rose,' she stormed. When she got no reaction from her mother, she stamped away to her bedroom and after throwing her nightgown across the room she dragged her clothes on and stormed outside. She had gone no more than a few yards when Jasper turned up.

One glance at her sullen face told him all he wanted to know and he smiled sympathetically and fell into step with her. 'Missing your sister already, are you?' he queried.

'Not in the least!' Abi tossed her pretty head. 'I'm just sorry that it wasn't me that got out of this godforsaken place! I think I shall go mad if I have to stay here for much longer.'

'Well, my offer of finding you a position in London is still open,' he said coaxingly. 'Just think how it would feel to be the belle of every gent you met. You would be cossetted and spoilt and I doubt very much if you would ever want to come back here.' He sighed. 'As it happens I had a hell of a row with Father last night over the very same thing. He's keen for me to start learning how to manage the farm so that he can retire, but I've told him I want to live a little first, instead of being buried in this backwater!'

Abi couldn't help but be curious. 'And what did he say?'

He grinned. 'He was dead against the idea but in the end, Mother coaxed him into a compromise so he's agreed I can have a few more months with a good allowance going where I please before starting to learn the business.' He shook his head and shrugged. 'To be honest, I would have liked a bit longer but I suppose it's better than nothing, so I shall be living in London too. I have lots of friends there I can stay with and I intend to make the most of every minute! You're only young once, after all.'

Abi stared at him thoughtfully. 'So you're saying that you would be close at hand if I went and I didn't like it?'

Sensing victory, he stifled a smile and his voice when he answered was sincere. 'Of course I'd be close by and if you were the least bit unhappy I would bring you back to your mother immediately. Although, as I said, I don't think there'd be much chance of that happening. I think you'd love it there!'

She stopped walking and gazed up into the cloudless blue sky as her mind raced. Suddenly she made her decision. 'I'll come!' she told him. 'When can we leave?'

'Whenever you like. But do you intend to tell your mother where you're going? And if you do, do you really think she'd allow it?'

Abi shook her head. 'No, she wouldn't. Never in a month of Sundays, so I won't tell her. If we were to go late one evening, we could catch the early train to London the next morning and be gone before she realises.' She frowned. 'But how would I get all my clothes out of the house without them realising?'

He laughed. 'Don't worry about that. If you sneak some out a few at a time and hide them somewhere dry at the back of the cottage I can collect them, and then on the night we leave I shall bring the carriage personally to collect you. I can leave it at the train station and pay someone to bring it back here for me the next morning.'

Excitement at the thought of the adventure ahead brought colour to her cheeks. 'When shall we go?'

He tapped his lip. 'Hm, today is Monday and you'll need a couple of days to sneak some of your clothes out, so how about we go Wednesday night? Is that too soon for you?'

'Not at all!' She clasped her hands. 'Mama and Hetty tend to go to bed quite early so I should be able to be ready by then.'

'Wednesday night it is then, but be sure not to breathe a word to anyone,' he warned. 'My head would be on the block if any of our parents were to find out that I was help-ing you to run away.'

'Not a word,' she promised solemnly but her heart was pounding and suddenly Wednesday evening seemed a very long way away. 'I shall leave some of my luggage in the little shed behind the washhouse this evening as soon as Hetty and Mama are asleep. It's nice and dry in there.'

'Until Wednesday evening then.' He gave a courteous lit-tle bow and as he turned and strutted away, he was smiling as he thought of the money he would earn for introducing a new girl to the Black Cat club in Soho. Lilly Flynn, the proprietor, would welcome a little beauty like Abi with open arms and he had no doubt that soon Abi would be well and truly under Lilly's spell.

Emmy arrived in Euston shortly after lunch and after locating a porter to fetch her luggage from the luggage van at the back of the train, she hailed a hackney cab and gave him her aunt's address. As usual the capital was teeming with people, but Emmy was so nervous she barely noticed as the cab wove its way through the traffic. At her aunt's, the maid was clearly expecting her, and was waiting at the door to help her to carry her luggage into the hall.

'The missus says I'm to show yer to yer room, miss,' Aggie told Emmy cheerfully. 'She's had me put yer next door to her in case she needs yer durin' the night.'

Emmy nodded and taking a valise in each hand she followed Aggie up the curving staircase to a magnificent galleried landing dotted with fancy little tables and bric-a-brac. They proceeded along it until Aggie stopped and threw a door open. 'This 'ere is your room, miss. An' that un next door is the missus's room. Oh, an' I'm Aggie by the way.'

Emmy stepped past her and once again blinked as she tried to take everything in. Just like the rest of the house the room was lavishly decorated and furnished. A huge four-poster bed surrounded by thick pink velvet drapes stood against one wall and matching curtains hung at the long sash-cord window. The bed was piled high with pink satin pillows trimmed with lace and a deep-pink eiderdown. A highly polished rosewood armoire with matching drawers stood against another wall and a pink deep-pile carpet covered almost all of the floor area. There was a dainty desk and chair in front of the window and an elegant chaise longue along the bottom of the bed. As in the drawing room, the walls were covered in gilt-framed mirrors and paintings of angelic cherubs.

Emmy couldn't help but chuckle. 'Crikey, I hardly know what to look at first,' she admitted in a whisper. 'There's so much to take in. It's all very . . .' She strove to find a way to describe the room before ending, 'Elaborate!'

Aggie giggled as she placed the bags on the bed. 'Oh, the missus likes it fancy,' she agreed. 'In fact, the fancier the better. But she ain't such a bad old stick. Her bark is far worse than 'er bite, if yer get what I mean?'

She opened the bags and began to lay Emmy's gowns across the bed, commenting, 'Some o' these will want a quick iron. I'll do 'em for yer, miss, just as soon as ever I get a spare minute.'

'Oh, please don't worry,' Emmy told her hurriedly. 'I'm sure you have more than enough to do cleaning this place. I'm quite capable of doing them myself. What's that door there?' Without waiting for an answer, she strode towards it and was pleasantly surprised to find her own bathroom, which was just as luxurious as the bedroom. The walls and the floor were marble and a tap was suspended above the deep claw-footed bath.

'We can pump hot water straight up here from the copper in the kitchen. Saves havin' to carry it up in buckets,' Aggie explained. 'An' when you've 'ad yer baff that hole there lets the dirty water drain straight out to a drain in the yard. It's good, ain't it?'

'It's very clever,' Emmy agreed as she fingered the soft towels that were laid ready on a chair.

'Anyway, miss, I'll leave yer to get yerself tidied up an' then the missus asked me to tell yer to join 'er in the drawin' room. I'll bring yer some tea then I'll come up an' put yer clothes away for yer.'

'Thank you, Aggie.'

The maid bobbed her knee and scuttled away, and after removing her bonnet and tidying her hair Emmy made her way downstairs, hoping she would remember which door led to the drawing room.

'You decided to come then?' her aunt greeted her when Emmy eventually opened the right door and entered the drawing room.

'Of course. I said I'd be here, didn't I?' Emmy retorted and a little smile hovered on the older woman's lips. She liked someone with a bit of gumption.

'And is your room to your liking?'

'It's very comfortable, thank you.' Emmy took a seat opposite her aunt and folded her hands primly in her lap.

'Good, then we'll start as we mean to go on. Once Aggie has served the tea you can read the newspaper to me. I can't be doing with these damn spectacles. I'm sure they make my eyesight worse and now I have a dog I'm not going to bark myself, am I? I shall expect you to earn your keep.'

It wasn't the friendliest greeting but Emmy hadn't really expected any more. Her aunt was clearly used to having her own way and Emmy sensed that they might well clash from time to time, but even so she was prepared to do her best to make her new position work. She really didn't have much choice because she didn't want to have to run home with her tail between her legs!

Chapter Fifteen

Much later that evening as Emmy began her first night in her new home, Abi lay on her bed listening carefully until Hetty's gentle snores echoed down from the attic room above hers. She rose quietly and began to cram some of her favourite gowns into a large travelling valise. When she was satisfied that she had packed everything she would be able to carry, she lugged it downstairs and out to the little shed. Unfortunately, the gowns she had taken down that day to be washed were still where she had dropped them after Hetty had refused to do them, but she consoled herself that if she proved to be half as popular in her new job as Jasper had promised she would be, she would soon be in a position to buy herself a whole new wardrobe if she wished to. Once the valise was in place, she crept back to bed where she tossed and turned until the first jewel colours of dawn streaked the sky, when she finally fell into an exhausted sleep.

The following two days seemed to pass interminably slowly but at last her mother and Hetty retired to bed and she went to her room where she waited on tenterhooks until she was quite sure they would be fast asleep. She then hurriedly changed into her favourite travelling costume and crept downstairs where she placed a letter she had written to her mother on the mantelpiece. She then tiptoed outside without once looking back to wait for Jasper. Within minutes she saw him striding across the field in the gloom and once they had collected her luggage from the shed, they carted it across the field to the waiting carriage.

She was surprised to see one of her uncle's labourers up on the driving seat and Jasper winked at her. 'I've paid Jim to run us into town and keep his mouth shut, that way the horse can go back to his stable this evening,' he told her as he bundled her up the steps.

Abi looked mildly concerned. 'But what if he goes back and tells them what we intend to do?' she whispered fearfully.

'By the time he gets back to the farm we'll be well on our way to London; I managed to get us tickets on the last train,' he promised her as he tapped the roof of the carriage to let Jim know they were ready. The carriage set off and Abi clung to the seat as it rocked across the uneven ground.

Soon after, as the train chugged out of the station in a smog of steam and smoke, Abi nervously bit down on her lip as she watched the lights of her home town falling behind her from the window. It was strange to think that she might never return and for the first time, nerves set in as she questioned whether she was doing the right thing. But as she thought of all the humiliation she had suffered since her father had run off leaving them all to clean up his mess, she raised her chin with a determined glint in her eye. *Of course I'm doing the right thing,* she tried to convince herself. *I might be young but I can look after myself!*

For a time, they sat staring from the window into the darkness beyond, but it had been a stressful day and soon

Abi was fast asleep and knew no more until Jasper nudged her awake.

'Come on, sleepyhead. We're at Euston.'

Bleary-eyed Abi stared up at him before knuckling the sleep from her eyes and following him on to the platform. A porter fetched their luggage and minutes later they emerged from the station into Euston Square. Despite it being close to midnight it was still teeming with people, but Abi just wanted her bed now.

'Where do we go now?' She didn't really care so long as she could lie down and rest.

In contrast, Jasper was still in fine spirits. 'I'm to take you to where you'll be living. Lilly is expecting you.' Stepping into the road he raised his hand and a hansom cab drew up next to them. They clambered inside and, thoroughly exhausted, Abi sagged against the stained leather squabs as the cab rattled across the cobblestones. It smelt of unwashed bodies and cheap gin, but Abi was past caring.

Eventually it drew up outside a soot-stained building with a large sign over the door that read 'The Black Cat' in bold gold letters. A burly-looking doorman with a large scar running all down one side of his face was standing outside it and he nodded at Jasper as he helped Abi down from the cab.

'We can't be staying here, surely?' she said nervously as she eyed the building and the street. There were some very dodgy-looking characters loitering about.

'Of course we won't. This is where you'll be working. Lilly's house, where you'll be living, is round at the back of it.'

'Oh!' Abi wasn't too thrilled at the position of her new home at all but as he lifted her luggage, she followed him down a long alley that ran along one side of the club. It was very dark and smelt strongly of urine, and Abi's spirits plummeted even further as she wondered what she had let herself in for. This wasn't the sort of place she'd imagined it would be at all. Once or twice she stumbled and had to steady herself on the wall, but at last they came to the end and after turning a corner she saw a large front door ahead of them.

'The house is built on to the back of the club, so you won't have far to go to work, will you?' he teased cheerfully as he rapped smartly on the door.

It was opened by a young girl in a drab grey dress. Her mousy hair was dragged into a ponytail and tied with a tatty ribbon at the nape of her neck and there was a scattering of pimples across her plain face. She was tiny and looked as if one good puff of wind would blow her away.

'I've brought Miss Winter. Mrs Flynn is expecting her,' Jasper informed the girl.

With a nod she stood aside to allow them to pass her.

It was the smell that Abi noticed first. A cloying smoky smell, although she had no idea what it might be.

'Miss Lilly is through in the club, sir,' the girl told him. 'If yer'd care to wait 'ere I'll run an' fetch 'er for yer.' And with that she was off like a miniature greyhound.

As Jasper toted her luggage inside Abi looked around curiously. They were in a long, narrow hallway with many doors leading off it and judging from the noise that was issuing from beyond some of the doors, a lot of the rooms were occupied. There was the sound of music, laughing and giggling and suddenly Abi had to stifle the urge to turn tail and run. The place was nothing at all like she had expected it to be. The noise of music grew louder as a door at the end of the corridor swung open and the young maid and a blousy-looking woman in a buttercup-yellow gown that left very little to the imagination appeared. The woman's hair was a bright red colour and piled into huge curls on top of her head and her face was heavily powdered and rouged. She was what Abi's mother would have scathingly called 'mutton dressed as lamb' but even though she was well into middle-age there were still traces of her being a beauty in her younger days.

'Jasper, me darlin'.' She strode down the hall in a rustle of silk and enveloped Jasper in a bear hug before releasing him and turning her attention to Abi.

'So this is the new girl you told me about, eh?'

Abi flushed as the woman stroked her chin thoughtfully, walking around her as if she were examining a beast she was thinking of buying at market.

'Well, just as yer said, she's a looker, I'll give yer that,' she told him. 'I'm sure she'll be in great demand wi' the punters.'

Abi began to feel as if she wasn't even there until the woman asked, 'Tired, are yer, queen?'

'Yes . . . I-I am rather.'

The woman giggled. 'Ooh, an' she talks all la-di-da too. That's another plus. Our richer clients'll be fightin' over 'er.' She clicked her fingers and the little maid who had been standing silently behind her hurried forward. 'Take this young lady to 'er room,' Lilly ordered. 'She can start work tomorrer but fer now she looks ready to drop.'

'Yes, Mrs Flynn.' The girl dipped her knee and snatched up one of Abi's heavy valises as if it weighed nothing before saying, 'Foller me, miss. I've got a room all ready fer yer.'

Abi hesitated as she looked at Jasper but he gave her an encouraging smile and a gentle nudge in the back. 'Go with Winnie and I'll see you in the morning after you've had a good rest. I'm going to go through to the club to try my hand at the gaming tables.'

He walked away with Lilly's plump arm tucked into his as if he didn't have a care in the world and sighing, Abi lifted her other valise and followed Winnie up the steep staircase.

At the top of the stairs was a long landing and if anything, the noise issuing from the rooms that led off it was even louder than it had been downstairs. They had gone a short way along when they passed one door that was standing ajar and when Abi glanced inside, she saw a young woman who was in a partial state of undress lying across a chaise longue with a gentleman kissing her passionately. Blushing furiously, Abi almost tripped and quickly averted her eyes.

''Ere we are then, miss. The missus said to put you in 'ere,' Winnie said as she pushed a door open.

Abi followed her into the room that was to be hers for the foreseeable future, should she decide to stay that was! The room was decorated entirely in rich scarlet and deep gold colours that made it look quite dark and Abi wasn't sure she liked it, although it was undeniably ornate. There was a silk chaise longue, much like the one she had just glimpsed in the room they had passed, and a large four-poster bed littered with lace-trimmed pillows, the blankets turned back to reveal what appeared to be silk sheets, dominated one wall. A highly polished armoire with a matching chest of drawers stood against another and fringed scarlet velvet curtains hung at the window. On another small table Abi noticed a selection of crystal goblets and bottles of champagne and wine and wondered why they were there. Surely the girls who lived there weren't encouraged to drink spirits in their rooms? But she had no time to dwell on it as Winnie asked, 'Would you like me to unpack your luggage for yer, miss?'

'What? . . . Oh no . . . thank you. I'll do it in the morning,' Abi assured her.

'It already is mornin',' Winnie giggled. 'But right y'are then, miss. Per'aps a cup o' tea or coffee then, or somefin' to eat?'

'A cup of tea would be nice,' Abi responded as she undid the ribbons on her bonnet. She was suddenly realising how exhausted she felt and was sure that the moment her head hit the pillow she would sleep for at least a month.

'I'll 'ave it up to you in two shakes of a lamb's tail,' Winnie promised as she headed for the door.

Once she was gone Abi was able to take a better look at the room. On the wall opposite the bed was a huge painting in a gilt frame of a plump woman, who was wearing next to nothing, reclining on a sofa, and once again she felt the colour rise in her cheeks as she wondered just what sort of establishment Jasper had brought her to. She had heard the girls at school whisper and giggle about places called brothels where women sold their bodies and now she was getting concerned. Surely Jasper would never bring her to such a place, and yet what else could account for the noises issuing from the bedrooms she had passed on the landing. Thoroughly worn out she shook her head. No, she was sure Jasper would never do that to her. She was here to be a hostess. If it turned out she was wrong, she promised herself, she would be on the first train home.

Winnie was back within minutes bearing a tray with a delicate china cup and saucer and a plateful of dainty sandwiches.

'Just in case yer get peckish, miss,' she said, placing it down on a small table.

'Winnie . . . do all the hostesses live here? And what time does the club close?' Abi enquired, choosing her words carefully. She was shocked that so many people were still there.

Winnie grinned. 'Oh no, miss. A lot o' the girls just turn in for work each night an' 'ave their own places. An' the place don't shut till the last clients leave, simple as that. Some of 'em don't go till breakfast.' As if to add credence to her words, she gave a big yawn and smiled apologetically. 'Sorry, miss. I'm ready fer me bed now.'

'Yes, of course. I'm sorry to keep you.' Abi smiled at her. 'You get off and get some rest.'

Once Winnie had gone she crossed to the door to lock it and was dismayed to see there was no key in the lock. So she drank her tea and after hastily unpacking her nightdress, she undressed and fell into bed. The rest of the unpacking could wait until later.

She soon discovered that silk sheets were nowhere near as nice to lie on as they looked and she found herself slipping and sliding about the mattress. Added to that the noise from the other rooms made it impossible to sleep so she lay thinking of home and wondering for the first time if she had done the right thing in coming here. Her arrival at her new home hadn't been nearly as exciting as she had hoped it would be but then, she consoled herself as she slipped into an uneasy doze, surely it could only get better?

Chapter Sixteen

Still in her dressing robe, Dorcas entered the kitchen the next morning to the sound of the kettle singing on the hob while Hetty was kneeling in front of a cheerful fire toasting bread on a long-handled toasting fork.

'Mornin', missus,' Hetty greeted her and Dorcas grunted. She had never been a morning person and Hetty's cheerful mood each day always made her cringe. 'I heard you movin' about so I thought I'd get your toast ready for you.'

Her words were met with yet another grunt from Dorcas as Hetty rose and began to liberally spread butter on the toast at the table.

'It's lookin' set to be another lovely day. I reckon I'll get out an' do a bit on the vegetable garden later; the carrots an' the cabbages are comin' on a treat.' She neither expected nor received an answer as she carried the plate of food to her mistress then bustled away to make the tea. Once she'd poured water into the pot, she covered it with a cosy and left it to mash while she prepared the cups and saucers. Only then did she notice the envelope propped up against the ornate ormolu clock on the mantelpiece.

She wiped her hands on her apron and went to fetch it before handing it to the mistress saying, 'This must be for you. Perhaps Miss Abigail 'as 'ad to go out early?'

Frowning, Dorcas put her plate aside and after running her thumb along the top of the envelope she withdrew a single sheet of paper and began to read.

Dear Mama,

By the time you read this I will hopefully be far away and beginning my new post. I shall be fine, I assure you, and once I am settled, I shall be sure to come and visit you. Forgive me for not telling you that I planned to leave, but I feared that you would not have allowed it so soon after Emmy left. I shall be working in London, not so very far away from Emerald, so hopefully once I am settled, I shall be able pay her and our Aunt Imogen a visit. I am so curious to meet her! I hope you under-stand that I couldn't stay there bearing the shame of what Father has reduced us to for a second longer. I only wish that you could make a new start elsewhere too, but I have every faith that Uncle Bernard will ensure that you manage comfortably.

Until we meet again, I remain,
Your loving daughter,
Abigail xxxx

The colour drained from Dorcas's cheeks like water down a plughole as she clutched her throat. Hetty grew quite concerned as she watched her read the letter. Her mistress was the colour of putty and her hands were shaking.

'Is everythin' all right, missus?' she asked anxiously.

Dorcas glared at her, her eyes bright with unshed tears. 'Does it *look* like everything is all right, you *stupid* girl,' she snapped as she waved the offending letter in the air. 'This is from Abigail! She's run away, but then I suppose you knew all about what she was planning!'

Hetty stretched to her full height and scowled at her indignantly, her hands fisted on her hips. 'As a matter o' fact I 'ad no bloody idea,' she snapped back. 'Though the way you speak to people and treat 'em, meself included, I can't say as I bloody blame 'er! An' I'll tell yer something' else an' all, unless yer buck yer ideas up an' start speakin' to me like I'm a human bein' an' not somethin' that's stuck to the bottom of yer bleedin' shoe I might well be followin' 'er before much longer!' And with that she turned and stamped out into the garden leaving Dorcas sitting there open-mouthed.

'Damn you to hell! This is *all* your fault, Gerald,' she muttered to the empty room. 'Look what you have brought me to!' And covering her face with her hands she began to sob with self-pity.

It was some time before the tears stopped and only then did she begin to feel fearful. As much as she loathed the girl, she was forced to admit that Hetty was a good worker. What would she do if she carried out her threat and left her? She could have managed without her had Emerald still been there – she had never been afraid to turn her hand to anything, unlike Abigail who was completely work-shy – but both girls had gone now and Hetty was the only one left to keep the cottage running. It never occurred to her that she could have done so herself; she had been waited on hand

and foot all her life and had no intention of changing things now, so she supposed she would just have to try to be a little kinder to the girl, although it went sorely against the grain because Hetty was only a lowly servant after all.

With a sigh she hauled herself out of the chair, dabbed her cheeks dry and went to the back door where she could see Hetty, looking none too pleased, digging in the vegetable patch.

'Hetty . . .'

At the sound of her name the girl glanced up and Dorcas swallowed deeply before forcing herself to say, 'I . . . I apologise for being so short with you earlier on . . . I-I think it was just the shock of discovering that Abigail had gone.'

Narrowing her eyes, Hetty stared at her mistress before swallowing the hasty retort that sprang to her lips. Dorcas did look upset and Hetty had always had a kind heart so after a moment she shrugged. 'Very well, we'll just 'ave to muddle along as best we can now, just the two of us. Apology accepted.'

Dorcas inclined her head and scurried back to her seat feeling very sorry for herself indeed as she thought of the long, lonely days stretching ahead of her.

That same morning in Soho, Abi was awakened by Winnie bearing a tray of tea and hot buttered toast.

'The missus said I should spoil you this mornin' seein' as it's your first day 'ere,' the girl told her cheerfully after placing the tray on a bedside table and crossing to pull the curtains aside. 'But after this you'll 'ave to 'ave your meals in the dinin' room wiv the other girls.'

'Thank you, Winnie.' Abi felt as if she had had hardly any sleep at all, but she sat up and after flicking her long hair over her shoulders, she yawned and took a sip of tea before asking, 'How many other girls actually live here?'

'Ooh!' Winnie paused and tapped her chin thoughtfully. 'There must be about a dozen or so,' she said eventually. 'Though I could be wrong. I ain't never been much good at countin'. But I must be off, if you don't need anythin' else. Mistress Lilly said to join her in the parlour when you're ready.' And with a last cheery smile she was off leaving Abi to eat her breakfast in peace.

Half an hour later, washed and dressed with her hair brushed neatly into a bun at the back of her head, Abi set off down the stairs. The house was quiet now and once in the hall she paused, wondering which door led to the parlour.

It was then that a pretty young woman came downstairs still dressed in a diaphanous robe that left nothing to the imagination. She was yawning and her loose fair hair was spilling across her shoulders.

'Ah, you must be the new girl. Lilly told us you'd be arriving,' she said in a surprisingly upper-class voice. 'Are you lost?'

'I am rather. Winnie said I was to go to the parlour to see Miss Flynn but I don't know which door it is.'

'It's that one there.' The girl pointed as Abi blushed and tried to keep her eyes averted from the flimsy robe. 'And I'm Bella. You are?'

'Abigail.'

'Well, I'm sure we'll be seeing more of each other,' Bella said. 'Goodbye for now.' She walked towards what Abi assumed must be the dining room, while she herself approached the parlour door. She paused and tapped on it and a voice from the other side said, 'Come in.'

When she opened the door, Lilly looked up from the pile of paperwork she was tackling and her face broke into a smile. She too was still in her night attire – a pale-blue silk negligee trimmed around the neck with ostrich feathers – and without the heavy make-up and with her hair loose about her plump shoulders, she looked younger.

'Ah, Abigail, I trust yer slept well?'

'Yes, Miss Flynn, I did, thank you.'

The woman laughed. 'It's Lilly, or Lil if yer prefer it. We don't stand on ceremony 'ere, queen.' She narrowed her eyes and peered at Abi closely and Abi felt herself blushing again. It felt as if that was all she had done since arriving.

'Hm, I reckon we'll need to get yer fitted out with some more suitable workin' clothes,' Lilly said, eyeing her gown critically. 'That gown yer wearin' is very nice but no good at all fer the job you'll be doin'. We'll need to sort yer hair out an' all. That style is far too severe fer in the club. My punters like me girls to show off their assets, if yer get me meanin'.' She threw back her head and laughed as Abi stood there looking completely confused. 'I reckon I might get young Bella to show yer the ropes,' Lilly went on. 'Met 'er yet, 'ave yer?'

'I have as it happens, just now,' Abi answered.

'That's good. She's one o' the favourites in the club is Bella. Come along now an' we'll see what we can find yer to wear.' Rising from the table she went out into the hallway and led Abi upstairs to a room that stood right at the end of the long landing where she took a key from the pocket of her robe and unlocked a door. They entered a room that had a number of clothes rails standing about the walls on which hung gowns of every colour of the rainbow.

'You can borrer some o' these till you've earned yerself enough to get some new ones,' Lilly told her as she began to lift them out one by one and study them. Eventually she smiled as she held up a soft-green satin gown heavily trimmed about the low neckline with guipure lace. It was quite exquisite and Abi gasped with pleasure as she fondled the heavy material.

'This should suit you down to the ground an' it'll go with your eyes an' all. Try it on,' Lilly urged and once again Abi looked uncomfortable.

'What now? . . . In front of you?' she said in a small voice.

'That's what I said, ain't it,' Lilly answered with a chuckle. 'An' don't worry, queen. You ain't got nothin' I ain't seen a million times afore.'

And so somewhat self-consciously Abi undid the row of buttons that ran up the front of her gown and slipped out of it as Lilly lifted the green dress and lowered it over her head. It fit as if it had been made for her, but while Abi thought it was beautiful, she was also acutely conscious of how low cut it was. She had certainly never worn anything like as daring before and could only begin to imagine what her mother would say if she could see her in it.

'Perfect,' Lilly declared when she had finished fastening the little pearly buttons on the back of it. She then took the clips from Abi's hair and let the chestnut curls spill across her shoulders. 'What do you think?' When she turned Abi to look at herself in a long cheval mirror, Abi anxiously chewed on her bottom lip.

'It's very beautiful,' she conceded slowly. 'But isn't it a little too . . .' She tugged at the neckline, trying to conceal some of her ample cleavage.

Lilly chuckled again. 'The punters will love it,' she assured her as she began to undo the buttons. 'So now I'll explain what will be expected of yer. Fer a start off it's your job to approach the men who frequent the club and get them to buy you a drink, preferably champagne.'

'But I've never drunk much before,' Abi told her worriedly.

'And you needn't now, queen. Just sip at yours and encourage them to drink it – the more the better. For every bottle of champagne your punter buys you'll get a bonus and all you 'ave to do is keep 'em happy an' chattin'. Flirt wi' 'em a bit too; I'm sure a pretty girl like you knows 'ow to do that.'

Abi smiled coyly and Lilly was pleased. The girl was a looker, there was no doubt about it, young and innocent too, and very well spoken, just as the gentlemen liked them.

'So, remind me, 'ow old did Jasper say you were?'

'Sixteen. Almost seventeen.'

'Ah, sweet sixteen an' never 'ad a sweetheart, eh?' Lilly said with a sad smile. 'What I wouldn't give to go back to bein' that age, knowin' what I know now.'

As she was dressing in her own gown again, Abi plucked up the courage to say, 'I couldn't help but notice when Winnie showed me to my room last night that some of the girls were, er . . . entertaining gentlemen in their rooms. Will I be expected to do that?'

'Not if you don't want to,' Lilly assured her as she placed the green gown back on its hanger. 'You make yer own rules, queen. You can go as far as you like as long as you get the chaps spendin' their money in the club. Anythin' you want to earn after that is entirely up to you.'

Abi sighed with relief as she took the dress from her new employer. 'And what are we expected to do during the day?'

'Not a thing, so long as you're in that club ready to start work come seven of an evenin', you can do what you like durin' the day. How does that sound?'

'Perfect!' Abi was feeling better by the second. What a job! She could dress up and flirt to her heart's content every night apart from Sundays and have every day off to do as she pleased. She would be able to visit Emmy and, better still, shop as much as she liked once she had started to earn. What could be better?

'Right, well I've got to get back to balancin' me books,' Lilly told her glumly. 'So, as you're up, why don't you go down to the dinin' room an' get to know some of the other girls? They should be startin' to get their arses out o' bed any time now. But hang that gown up in your room first an' remember it's only on loan. I ain't made o' money an' I can't afford to keep you an' dress you an' all.' And with that she went, leaving a waft of heavy perfume in her wake as Abi returned to her room to hang the gown in the armoire.

When she had managed to locate the dining room, she found two young women eating fat juicy sausages and crisp rashers of bacon. They greeted her cheerfully and pointed to the large brown teapot that stood in the centre of the table, so Abi poured herself a cup of tea and joined them.

'You must be the new girl Lilly mentioned would be joinin' us. What's your name, dearie?' a plump girl with thick fair hair and a broad cockney accent asked her in a friendly fashion. She had a peaches-and-cream complexion and Abi judged that she must be somewhat older than her, possibly in her early twenties.

'It's Abigail, but most people call me Abi.'

'Unless Lilly decides to give you a new name.' The girl chuckled.

Abi looked confused. 'But why would she do that?'

'Well, certain names suit the sort o' job we do better than our real ones,' the girl told her amiably. 'Take meself for an example, me real name is Agnes but while I'm workin' it's Maria.'

'And do you enjoy working here?' Abi asked tentatively.

'Hm, I'm not so sure I'd say as I enjoy it,' her companion answered. 'But a girl 'as to make a livin', don't she? An' this is money for old rope so long as you know how to handle the clients.'

When Abi frowned, she chuckled again as she helped herself to another sausage. 'What I mean is you 'ave to keep 'em in line.'

'In what way?'

Maria sighed at Abi's innocence. 'What I'm sayin' is you'll earn more takin' a chap upstairs to your room than you will just bein' a hostess in the club, if you get me meanin?' She winked cheekily and Abi blushed.

'Oh I-I don't think I'd like to do that,' she said falteringly.

Maria sighed sadly. 'We all say that when we first start 'ere,' she warned her. 'But it ain't long afore we get dragged into the money trap. That's why I've got a two-year-old daughter fostered out who I 'ave to pay for, bless 'er little cotton socks.'

144

'You have a child?' Abi looked shocked but Maria merely shrugged.

'It's me own fault. There's things you can do to stop a baby comin' along but I obviously didn't do it properly.'

'But why didn't the father of your baby marry you?' Abi asked innocently, and now both the girls laughed aloud.

'God bless yer! You've got a lot to learn,' Maria said, and a little ripple of unease made its way up Abi's spine. 'How did yer come to 'ear about this place anyway?' Maria enquired curiously, her head cocked to one side.

'Oh, my cousin Jasper told me about it,' Abi told her.

Maria chuckled. 'Hm, I thought as much.'

'What do you mean?'

Maria shook her head.

Abi was confused now. Jasper had told her about the job to help her escape from home, surely? Yet Maria seemed to be implying that he'd had something to gain from bringing her here. She wasn't too happy about the thought of having to entertain men in her room either, but then, she decided, Maria hadn't said that she would *have* to! No, she had come here simply to be a hostess and that was all she would be, and surely Jasper had helped her purely out of the kindness of his heart?

Chapter Seventeen

On the first Sunday since leaving home, Emmy was reading the newspaper in her room when Aggie tapped on the door to tell her, 'There's a young man waiting downstairs to see yer, miss.'

'To see *me*?' Emmy was surprised and had no idea who it could be. She laid the paper aside and smiled at Aggie. 'Thank you, I'll be right down.' It was her first day off and she was enjoying not having to run around after her aunt, although in fairness the first few days had gone far better than she had hoped they would. Imogen was demanding, admittedly, but already Emmy was discovering that she wasn't quite as hard as she liked to make out.

She checked her hair in the ornate mirror in her room and smoothing down the material of her full skirt she set off downstairs and gave a cry of delighted surprise when she saw Jake standing in the hall clutching his hat as he waited for her, realising with a little jolt how much she had missed him.

'Jake, how lovely to see you.' She hurried to him with her hands outstretched. She had written to him the evening after arriving there but as she had not heard back, she'd had no idea if he'd received her letter.

'I'm sorry to call unannounced,' he apologised as he returned the pressure on his fingers and a little thrill ran up her arm. 'But I didn't think a reply would get to you in time and seeing as I had a day off, I thought I'd come and see how you were settling in. I thought perhaps we could go for a walk? It's a lovely day.'

'I'd love to,' she told him. 'I was wondering what I was going to do with myself. I don't know my way about here yet.'

They were interrupted when Aggie hurried from the drawing room. 'The mistress wants to know who's 'ere.'

Emmy and Jake exchanged an amused smile as Emmy told her, 'You can tell her it's her nephew, Jake. Her brother Bernard's son. He works in London too and I told him where I was living.'

'Right y'are, miss.' Aggie zipped away, returning a moment later to tell them, 'The mistress says yer to take the young man into the drawin' room. She wants to meet 'im.'

Emmy glanced at Jake and gave a slight shrug before following the maid into the room where Imogen was sitting in her usual chair.

'So . . . it seems I see none of my family for years and then they all start turning up like bad pennies,' she said rather ungraciously.

'I apologise for not asking permission to call on my cousin, Aunt, but she only forwarded her address to me this week so I had no time,' he answered respectfully. He had been about to say that the reason she had never seen him was because, like Emmy, he had not been aware of her existence until recently, but he didn't want to hurt her feelings.

'Hm.' She narrowed her eyes and peered at him. 'And how is Bernard – your father?'

'He is very well, thank you, apart from a little trouble with gout.'

'Probably due to too much rich food and drink,' she said unsympathetically. 'Mind you, I would have turned to drink if I was forced to live with your mother.' As usual Imogen was quite happy to say what she thought and shame the devil. 'Anyway, don't just stand there making the room look untidy. Sit down, and I'll order us some coffee. I usually have a cup at this time as Emerald will tell you. Aggie, go and see to it!'

'Yes, ma'am.' Aggie raced away as if old Nick himself was snapping at her heels and Emmy felt quite sorry for her as she and Jake took a seat.

'Emerald told me you were training to be a doctor?'

Jake nodded. 'Yes, I am. I'm sitting my final exams in a few weeks so hopefully I shall be qualified soon.'

'Hm, and what will you do then? Will you return to the Midlands?' Imogen asked, looking at him closely. She could see nothing of her brother in him but then she supposed he must take after his mother.

Jake shook his head. 'No, I should like to stay in London and work in the poor hospitals.'

'But surely the money to be made is in private practice?' she queried.

'You're quite right but there are any number of doctors who are willing to tend the rich, not so many who are keen to help the poor,' he answered.

Despite herself Imogen was impressed with him. 'I dare say that's very commendable but it'll not make you wealthy,' she pointed out. 'What does our Bernard think of your idea?'

Jake smiled wryly. 'He's not too impressed, to be honest. He would rather I learnt how to manage the farm estate so that I could take over when he retires, but I prefer to do what I do. Father has pinned all his hopes on my younger brother taking over from him now, but Jasper isn't too keen on the idea just yet, so Mother has persuaded Father to allow him some time to enjoy himself before he has to buckle down to work.' He could have told her that Jasper had never been very keen on work of any kind and that he had even been expelled from school but he didn't feel it was his place.

'Huh! Sounds like she spoils him,' Imogen said in disgust.

Thankfully, Aggie reappeared then with a tray of coffee and biscuits fresh from the oven so the conversation steered to other things.

Once the coffee was drunk, Emmy and Jasper took their leave, Jake promising that he would visit her again soon.

'Crikey, she's a strict old bird, isn't she?' Jake remarked as he tucked Emmy's hand into the crook of his arm and they headed along the pavement.

Emmy giggled. 'She's not as hard as she likes to make out,' she assured him.

They came to the park shortly after and entered through the gates. It was a glorious day with the sun riding high in a cloudless blue sky and the park was full of people, with nannies pushing their charges about in perambulators and families sitting on the grass. Children raced about play-ing with hoops and balls and dewy-eyed young couples strolled along arm in arm staring at each other adoringly.

Eventually they came to a wooden bench beneath the shade of a large oak tree at the edge of a lake where they sat down to watch the swans gliding along the smooth surface of the water.

'Do you think you will like living with your aunt?' Jake asked after a time.

Emmy smiled. 'I think so. I miss my mother and Abi, of course, but I realised fairly quickly that I have to give as good as I get with Aunt Imogen, otherwise I think she'd be unbearable. Poor little Aggie, the maid you met, runs around after her like a headless chicken, although they seem fond enough of each other.'

Jake chuckled and Emmy went on to tell him of their aunt's interest in spiritualism. 'Some of her spiritualist friends are coming to the house this evening for a meeting,' she told him. 'But I have no idea what they do.'

'Ooh, I bet they'll hold seances and have tables floating in the air and ghosts coming out of the walls,' he laughed.

Emmy shuddered at the image he had conjured up. 'I certainly hope not, although I won't know about it anyway, seeing as it's my day off.'

After a while they rose and walked on until they came to a little café where they sat outside to enjoy a glass of lemonade.

'What will you do for the rest of the afternoon?' Emmy asked as she stared at his handsome face. She couldn't believe how thrilled she felt to see him.

'Oh, there's no peace for the wicked,' he said. 'I have so much revision to do for my exams that I'll probably have my head stuck in a book until bedtime. Speaking of which,

I shall have to make a move soon unfortunately because my landlady will have my lunch ready and she can be a right old harridan if any of us are late.'

'Well, we can't have that.' Emmy's eyes were twinkling. 'Come on, I'll walk back to the park gates with you.'

He offered his arm again and as she slipped her hand through it, she was suddenly very conscious of the warmth of his skin through his sleeve and she felt herself blushing.

At the gates, Jake promised to visit again the following Sunday provided he wasn't on call at the hospital before hurrying away. Emmy watched him go, feeling confused. *Pull yourself together, girl*, she silently scolded herself as she thought of the butterflies that had fluttered in her stomach when she first saw him that morning, *he is your cousin, there can never be anything between you.* She turned about in a flurry of silken skirts and headed back to her aunt's feeling very annoyed with herself.

That evening, Emmy sat at the top of the stairs peeping through the banisters to watch her aunt's visitors arrive. And what a strange crew they were. The first to enter was an elderly lady wearing the most enormous hat trimmed with peacock feathers that Emmy had ever seen. Aggie announced her to her aunt as Mrs Cuttingham. She was soon followed by a middle-aged gentleman who was so plump that his brightly coloured waistcoat strained across his stomach and he seemed to waddle rather then walk. Aggie greeted him as Mr Perry. Over the next few minutes yet more strange-looking people joined him. One lady in particular caught Emmy's eye. When she arrived, Emmy glimpsed a fine carriage and four with a liveried groom through the open front

151

door and so she wasn't surprised when she heard Aggie announce the regal-looking woman to her aunt as Lady Medville. It seemed that people from all walks of life were attending the meeting and, thoroughly curious now, Emmy almost wished that she could join them.

But her aunt hadn't invited her and she didn't wish to intrude, so when it seemed that everyone had arrived, she went to her room to write to her mother and Abi to tell them all about Jake's lovely surprise visit. She had already written to them once when she had first arrived but as yet she had received no reply. Although she was settling far better than she had expected, she was still deeply concerned about her father and thought about him all the time. She was also missing her old home and Abi's constant chatter and found that the evenings were the worst time. Her aunt tended to retire early and it was hard to fill the empty hours until bedtime and so because the nights were light, she had taken to strolling around the local area to get to know her way about.

In her new home behind the Black Cat, Abi was getting changed ready to go down to the club and start work. It had been a strange few days. At home her parents had ensured she led a very pampered, sheltered existence but the one she was living now could in no way be classed as that. She had quickly adapted to her new way of life, staying up until the early hours of the morning and sleeping in till lunchtime when she would rise to spend an idle afternoon with the rest of the girls. Now as she thought back to her first evening there, she smiled at her reflection in the mirror. She had been as nervous as a kitten when Lilly had first led her into the gloomy smoke-filled club but it was soon evident that she was going to be very popular with the clients, and within a few hours she had started to enjoy herself. Admittedly she had been very self-conscious in the low-cut gown that Lilly had allowed her to borrow but the admiring glances she'd received when Lilly had first introduced her to the gentlemen customers had soon dispelled her shyness. Unlike the other girls, who wore rouge and coloured their lips, Lilly had requested that Abi should remain natural with her glorious brown hair loose about her shoulders. She was the youngest girl working there and because of that it was soon clear that she would be in high demand. She too had written to her mother within days of arriving to assure her that she was safe and well and had found employment, but she had been careful not to include her address. The last thing she needed was an irate mother turning up on the doorstep to try and drag her home!

Once she was happy with her appearance, she stepped out on to the landing and almost collided with Maria, who was also making her way to work.

'You off downstairs an' all, are yer?' Maria said amiably as she patted her hair, which was piled into ridiculously high curls on the top of her head. Her face was heavily rouged and the perfume she was wearing was so overpowering that it almost took Abi's breath away. Before waiting for a reply, she went on, 'Gettin' the 'ang of it now, are you?'

Abi nodded. 'Oh yes, it's quite easy really. The customers who frequent this place don't seem to be short of money and once they've had a few drinks it's quite easy to persuade them to buy more.'

'Hm, so you ain't been tempted to invite anyone to your room yet?' Maria grinned. 'You could double the money you earn if you did.'

Abi blushed and shook her head as they lifted their skirts and made their way downstairs. Already they could hear the buzz of conversation and music coming from the club; it sounded like it was going to be a busy night.

'No, I, er . . .' Her voice tailed away and Maria giggled.

'Well, you're new to it as yet but I'll guarantee someone will catch your eye who'll tempt you.'

Abi didn't reply. She enjoyed the flirting and the attention that was being heaped upon her, but she had no intention of allowing any of the men she had met to go any further with her.

They went through the door to the club and immediately the smoky atmosphere made Abi's eyes water. They had gone no more than a few steps when a middle-aged, bald-headed man caught Abi's eye and beckoned to her.

'Would you care to join me for a drink, my dear?' He was well spoken and the cut of his clothes told Abi that here was a man who had money to spend.

'I'd love to,' she simpered as she sat down next to him. 'But I should warn you, I only drink champagne.'

Lilly, who was looking on, gave her a nod of approval as the man raised his hand to beckon one of the waitresses. 'A bottle of your very finest champagne for this charming young lady,' he told her.

Abi settled her skirts around her and batted her eyelashes becomingly.

To Abi's delight by midnight her companion had polished off four bottles of the club's very finest and most expensive champagne. She would receive a quarter of the price of every bottle she persuaded the customers to buy so she was more than happy, but he was now slurring his words and becoming more flirtatious and demanding by the minute. 'So how old are you, my likkle preshious!'

'I'm sixteen, sir,' she told him demurely.

'Ah, shweet sixteen an' never been kished. How much would it cost me to change all that? Perhaps we could go to your room for a little private party of our own, eh?' he said with a wink and a lewd smile.

'I'm sorry, sir.' Abi was desperately trying to catch Lilly's eye – she was an expert at keeping the men in their place. Thankfully Lilly noticed her silent pleas from where she was standing at the bar and strolled over.

'How are you, Mr Brewer?' she asked pleasantly. 'I see you've met our newest hostess. But you do look tired, if you don't mind me sayin' so. Why don't yer let me get George to 'elp you outside an' find a cab.' As she spoke, she raised her hand and instantly one of the men who she employed to keep order in the club appeared at her side. 'You can always come back an' see our little Abi another night.' She gave him a dazzling smile. It was her rule that unless it was absolutely necessary you never upset a paying customer. 'I'm sure you'd love to see 'im again, wouldn't yer, Abi?'

'Oh yes, I'd like that very much,' Abi lied as she tried to avoid his wandering hands. Then George, a great giant of a man with hands like hams, almost lifted Mr Brewer from his seat and all the man could do was raise his hand in farewell as he was led from the club.

'He was trying to touch my . . .' Abi gulped and pointed self-consciously at her chest.

Lilly threw her head back and laughed. 'You'll 'ave to get used to that, queen,' she told her. 'An' after all, when yer think what we charge 'em for their drinks who can blame 'em for wantin' a little feel o' yer titties, eh? Now come along; there are still customers requiring a little bit of attention. The night is young an' so are you, so go an' circulate.'

And so, stifling a yawn, Abi plastered a smile on her face and set off through the tables until she caught the eye of yet another gentleman. It looked set to be another very long night but she was getting used to it now.

Chapter Eighteen

It was the middle of Emmy's second week away from home when a letter arrived for her and she instantly recognised her mother's handwriting on the envelope.

'It's from Mama,' she told Imogen over breakfast, but she didn't attempt to open it. She would save it for later when Imogen went for her nap. She hadn't been too well for the last couple of days and Emmy was beginning to realise just how debilitating her aunt's condition was. Sometimes she could barely hold a cup without shaking and she was as pale as lint and clearly in pain, although to give her credit she wasn't one for complaining. On her bad days she would simply retreat to her room, leaving Emmy to do as she pleased. This morning was one of those days and Emmy could see the tremor in her aunt's hands as she picked at her food.

'Shall I read the newspaper to you after you've finished your meal?' Emmy offered, but Imogen shook her head as she pushed her plate away.

'Thank you but no, I think I might go and have a little lie-down. I didn't have too good a night so we'll read the paper after lunch.' With that she rose from the table and limped from the room leaning heavily on her stick. Emmy would have offered to help her up the stairs but she knew that if she did she would only get her head bitten off so she simply folded her hands in her lap and left her aunt to it.

As soon as she had gone, Emmy took the letter from her pocket and hastily opened it.

Dear Emerald,

I trust you are well and your aunt is satisfied with your services. I'm afraid I have yet more bad news for you. Abi has run away from home and is working somewhere in London. She wrote to me to assure me that she is safe and well but has left no forwarding address so I have no means of getting in touch with her. I can't believe she would be so selfish, worrying me like this when I already have so much to contend with! And then on top of that Hetty has informed me that the new owners have now moved into Astley House. I was tempted to go and introduce myself to them but felt too ashamed, given my present circumstances. How I hate to think of them living in what I shall always think of as 'our home'!

However, on a slightly happier note, when I rose one morning last week Hetty gave me an envelope that had been left on the doorstep and when I opened it, I found it contained ten one-pound notes. At first, I assumed it was from you but then I realised that it would have come in an addressed envelope with a London postmark rather than a plain one, so I have no idea who might have sent it. Needless to say, it will come in very handy. Hetty's brother has also managed to sell a few more of our trinkets for a very good price so thankfully we are comfortable for the time being, although of course any amount is always welcome.

Emmy smiled at the last sentence. What her mother was really saying was that she would expect a portion of her wages each month and Emmy would see that she got them.

> *There is still no sign of your errant father, damn and blast him to hell. Can you believe I had yet two more of my invitations to tea returned this week from women who I considered to be friends?*
>
> *Please, if you should happen to come across Abigail, do be sure to find out where she is living and tell Imogen that when I can afford it, I might journey to see her at some point.*
>
> *I remain,*
> *Your mother*

There was no kiss or 'with love from' at the bottom of the letter and Emmy didn't really expect it. But it was a shock to know that Abi had run away; how could she be so stupid? And to come to London of all places! Her first instinct was to put her bonnet on and go out searching for her, but then common sense took over and she realised how futile that would be. London was such a huge place that looking for one person there would be like looking for a needle in a haystack. And who could have left the money on her mother's doorstep? It was no doubt an acquaintance who sympathised with the position she was in. The only good thing was she had given Abi her aunt's address before she herself left for London so for now all she could do was pray that Abi would write to her.

With a sigh she rose from the table, wishing that she could speak to Jake and tell him about Abi running away; he was always so sensible. But there would be no chance of seeing him until Sunday, so somehow she would just have to be patient and hope that wherever her little sister was, she was safe. Meanwhile she would go and see if there was anything she could do to help in the kitchen. Anything was better than just sitting about worrying.

That evening Abi got ready to go into the club as usual. It was a week night so she wasn't expecting it to be too busy. She was getting better at staving off the men when they wanted to go to her room now. In truth, she hadn't yet met anyone who had made her even half want to, although she did enjoy the attention that was being showered on her. Just as Lilly had predicted she was already proving to be a great favourite with the customers, no doubt because of her pretty face, her comely figure and her age. One middle-aged gentleman in particular had taken a great shine to her and the night before had presented her with a beautiful gold chain bracelet.

Maria had chuckled when Abi had shown it to her the night before as they went to their rooms after the club closed.

'Just play yer cards right, kid, an' that could be the first o' many,' she told her. 'That old duffer is as rich as Croesus. I've known some o' the girls have diamonds given an' others have ended up in their own places, paid for by the men.'

'What? You mean like kept women?'

Maria nodded. 'Absolutely. Most of 'em are married, o' course, but that don't stop 'em havin' a mistress on the side.'

Abi thought of the rumours that had circulated back at home about her Uncle Bernard having a woman but she didn't mention it to Maria. It seemed that men were men wherever they lived. She wasn't at all averse to being flattered and spoilt but she had no intention of becoming a kept woman for any man.

The smell of expensive cigar smoke and perfume met her as she entered the club and Abi was surprised to see that there were quite a few customers there already. The majority of them were trying their luck at the card tables at the other end of the long room, but some eyed her appreciatively as she made her way amongst the tables before she decided who she would approach. Eventually Abi made for an elderly gentleman with a large handlebar moustache who was watching her hopefully. When she reached his table, she flashed him a dazzling smile. The gas lights mounted at intervals on the walls brought out the copper highlights in her gleaming brunette hair, and as he gazed into her lovely green eyes she knew that he would be like putty in her hands. He was easily old enough to be her grandfather but so long as she only had to drink with him, she didn't care about that. She had learnt quickly that a fool and his money were soon parted and she intended to play him for every penny she could.

She had been seated with her most recent admirer for about an hour or so when there was a slight commotion at the entrance and seconds later a crowd of rowdy young men appeared laughing and slapping each other on their backs. Abi glanced up curiously from the crystal goblet of champagne she was drinking and her face broke into a smile as she recognised Jasper at the bar.

'Do please excuse me, my cousin has just arrived,' she told her companion and before he could respond she rose and left him sitting there looking none too pleased.

'Jasper, I was wondering when you were going to come and see me,' she told him delightedly as she approached him and his friends who were now ordering drinks at the bar.

'How's it going?' he asked, thinking how pretty she looked. Tonight she was wearing a beautiful ivory satin gown trimmed with pearls about the neckline that showed off her creamy skin and the colour of her hair to perfection.

She opened her mouth to reply but his friend, who was standing beside him, turned and looked at her and she was temporarily struck dumb as their eyes met. Suddenly she felt as if they might have been the only two people in the room. He was easily the handsomest young man she had ever laid eyes on and her heart gave a lurch.

'So, this is your little cousin, is it?' The man took her hand and bowing over it he gallantly kissed it, sending shivers up her spine. He was at least a head taller than Jasper with thick fair hair that had a tendency to curl and his eyes were the most remarkable shade of blue she had ever seen, reminding her of the bluebells in the woods back home. His voice was well modulated and his clothes impeccable and she knew instantly that this was a young man of class.

'Yes, this is the one.'

Jasper's voice seemed to be coming from a long way away as Abi tore her eyes away from the stranger's and looked back at him with her heart racing.

'Abigail, this is my dear friend, Lord Hugo Medville.'

'I-I'm delighted to meet you, sir.' Abi curtsied in a billow of ivory satin as he held on to her hand.

'And the feeling is mutual, I assure you,' he answered, tucking her small hand into the crook of his arm. Then glancing towards Jasper, he told him, 'I shall entertain your cousin while you and the rest of the chaps go and have a game of cards.'

He was clearly a young man who was used to getting his own way and without even asking permission he led Abi to a table in the furthest corner and snapped his fingers for a waitress. One appeared at his elbow almost immediately and he told her, 'A bottle of your finest champagne.'

'Yes, sir. Right away, sir.' The little waitress bobbed her knee and scurried away as Abi sat staring at him as if she were in a trance. For one of the very rare occasions in her life she was utterly speechless.

'So Jasper tells me you've only recently started to work here?'

Wetting her lips Abi said throatily, 'Yes . . . yes I have.'

'And do you like it?'

She shrugged as he eyed her cleavage unashamedly. She was a very tasty little piece, there was no doubt about it. Jasper hadn't mentioned how pretty she was and she had come as a pleasant surprise. He wanted her more than any other young woman he had set eyes on for a very long time, and what Lord Hugo wanted he usually got.

'It's all right,' she forced herself to say. 'Although the unsociable hours can be very tiring and some of the men can be . . . shall we say – less than gentlemen?'

He knew then that he would have to take his time wooing this one into bed. She was a cut above the girls he usually took his fun with, but she was so pretty that he was prepared to wait – as long as it didn't take too long!

The waitress returned with the bottle of champagne in an ice bucket and shooing her away, Hugo popped the cork and poured their drinks into the crystal glasses provided.

'To us! I have a feeling we are going to see a lot more of each other in future. At least – I hope we are.'

Abi was so enamoured of him that she took a great gulp of her drink without even thinking about it. Normally she would make one glass last all night but Hugo made her feel reckless and suddenly she didn't care.

The noise Jasper and his friends were making at the card tables echoed down the club to them, but Abi hardly heard them; she was too busy staring into the eyes of this beautiful man. *Could this be love at first sight?* she wondered. She had read about it in novels but never having loved before she had no way of knowing. Whatever the feeling was she was ready to embrace it. She just wanted the night to go on forever with him gazing across the table at her with those incredible blue eyes. Occasionally their hands would brush together on the table and her heart would start its loud beating again, making her glad of the piano music, which masked the sound.

Eventually Hugo began to ask her about her life and she poured her heart out to him as he listened avidly. There was nothing she wouldn't have told him.

'And what about you?' she asked in a shy voice eventually. 'Are you really a lord?'

He chuckled as he swiped a lock of heavy blonde hair back from his forehead. 'I am indeed. I'm staying with my parents in their London home at present but they also have a large estate in Essex. But let's not talk about that. Could I possibly take you out for a meal one evening?'

Abi looked crestfallen as she shook her head. 'I'd love to but I'm afraid I work every night apart from Sunday and most of the restaurants are shut then.'

'Then how about I take you out for lunch?'

Her eyes glowed as if a light had been turned on within her. 'Thank you . . . that would be very nice indeed.'

At that moment Maria passed the table and as she glanced towards Abi and saw the way she was staring all starry-eyed at the handsome young man sitting beside her, she felt sorry for her. Abi may like to make out that she was worldly but Maria had soon discovered that she was, in fact, an innocent, as pure as the day she had been born.

But I bet she won't be for much longer, Maria thought sadly as she hurried by on her way to her next customer.

Chapter Nineteen

To her surprise, when Emmy told her aunt later that day about her mother's letter and that Abi had run away from home, her aunt merely smiled.

'And what are you so worried about?' she questioned her as she sipped at her customary glass of sherry following dinner. 'I did just the same when I was about her age and things turned out all right for me, didn't they? From what you've told me, Abigail is a very pretty girl so she won't go hungry.'

'But she isn't seventeen years old yet.' Emmy couldn't help but worry despite her aunt's assurances. 'And we don't even have an address to contact her.'

'Ah, but didn't you say she has this one?' Her aunt raised a finely plucked eyebrow as she stared at her over the mountain of ruffles of heavy lace that fell from her throat to her waist on the elaborate gown she was wearing. 'So that means that should she run into difficulties she can always contact you. I've no doubt she probably will anyway, so long as you promise not to pass on where she's living to her mother.'

Emmy looked doubtful. 'Do you really think she might?'

Imogen nodded. 'I'll guarantee it, so stop worrying.'

That proved to be a lot easier said than done and by the time Jake arrived on Sunday to take her for a boat trip along the River Thames, Emmy was a bundle of nerves. He had ordered a cab to pick her up and drive them through London and the second she climbed into it he saw that something was troubling her.

When she quickly told him what it was he stared at her with concern. 'I just wonder if Jasper hasn't had something to do with this,' he said with a frown. 'He was spending a lot of time with Abi before she left and he also spends a lot of time in London. It would be just like him to encourage her to come here if there was something in it for him.'

'But what could it be?' Emmy questioned.

Jake shrugged. 'I have no idea but I doubt he would do anything out of the goodness of his heart. Leave it with me. I know he's in London at the moment and I'll be seeing him for lunch one day in the week. I'll have a word with him and see if he can cast any light on the situation.' And with that, for now at least, Emmy had to be content and she tried to put it from her mind.

Despite her concerns the rest of the afternoon proved to be a resounding success and she found herself relaxing and enjoying herself. Today she was wearing a cream shantung silk day dress and a pretty matching bonnet trimmed with pale-pink silk roses that showed off her glorious brown hair to perfection. She was also carrying a small silk parasol heavily trimmed with matching lace, and as they sailed down the river he thought he had never seen her look so pretty. It was a beautiful day with a clear blue sky with just the occasional powder-puff cloud gently floating across it. The River Thames was as calm as a mill pond, although the smell that drifted up from the water made them wrinkle their noses.

Along the river banks they saw tiny homes, little more than hovels, surrounded by reeds and mud, and Emmy wondered how anyone could survive in them.

They passed several places of interest: the Tower of London, where in days gone by unfortunate queens had been incarcerated before being led to chopping blocks where they were parted from their heads; St Paul's Cathedral in all its splendour; and the Houses of Parliament and Big Ben. For a time Emmy managed to forget about Abi as she gave herself up to the pleasure of Jake's company. She had seen all the sights before but everything seemed so much more enjoyable when she was with him.

When they climbed out of the boat Jake bought her a tiny posy of violets from an old flower lady and took her to a pretty little café where they had hot chocolate and delicate pastries. Later they made their way to Westminster Cathedral where they bought small bags of seed from an old lady to feed the hundreds of pigeons that were busily pecking the ground outside.

Emmy was enjoying herself so much that the time seemed to pass in the blink of an eye. Finally, though, she told him, 'I really ought to be getting back now. My aunt will worry if I'm out for too long. It's only because we are cousins that she allowed me to come out with you at all.' She grinned. 'For someone who says she's so forward-thinking, she's very old-fashioned when it comes to allowing me out without a chaperone.'

'Well, you can rest assured you're safe with me,' he told her as he stepped to the edge of the pavement and raised his hand to summon a cab.

'I can't thank you enough for such a lovely afternoon,' she told him as they headed back to her aunt's house.

'It was my pleasure entirely.' Suddenly he was wishing wholeheartedly that they weren't related. He had always had a soft spot for Emmy but over the last few weeks as he had grown to know her better, his feelings had developed. He had no doubt whatsoever that had things been different he would have been asking her if she might walk out with him, but because of their blood ties that could never be and he wondered if he was being wise in continuing to see her. But then, he told himself, what harm were they doing by enjoying each other's company? They were merely friends.

When they arrived back at her aunt's house, Emmy invited him in for tea but he declined the offer politely, explaining that he must get back to his studying.

They parted after agreeing to meet the following Sunday, and as the cab rattled away across the cobblestones, Emmy let herself into the hall with the key her aunt had given her. Immediately she heard voices coming from the drawing room, and she wondered who it might be. As far as she was aware her aunt wasn't expecting her spiritual friends until later that evening.

Aggie came bustling towards her then with a cheeky smile on her face. 'You've yet anuvver young man called to see yer, miss. He's in there wiv the missus an' he's *ever* so 'andsome!' she whispered.

'Really?' Emmy approached the drawing room door and was shocked to see Jasper sitting opposite her aunt. She'd had no idea that he would be calling, even though Jake had informed her that he was in London.

'Jasper, what a surprise. I had no idea you knew where I was living,' she said, walking towards him with her hands outstretched.

'I didn't,' he confessed with a wide smile. 'But Abi passed your address on.'

'Abi . . . you've seen Abi?' She had gone quite pale and rising swiftly Jasper took her elbow and led her to the nearest chair.

'I had a letter from my mother in the week informing me that Abi had run away. She's most concerned and has no idea of her whereabouts.'

'Hm . . .' Jasper grinned. 'Abi didn't *quite* run away. She found a post in London but she didn't think her mother would approve of it so she decided not to tell her where she was going. But I assure you she is quite well and very safe. I saw her myself only last night as it happens.'

'Oh, that's wonderful.' Emmy felt as if a great weight had been lifted from her shoulders. 'Will I be able to see her? And where exactly is she working? Has she got the post of a nanny or perhaps a governess?'

'Whoa! One question at a time.' Jasper chuckled. 'All I can tell you is that she is working as a hostess in a club and from what I saw of her last night she's loving it. But I'm afraid I can't tell you any more without her permission.'

'A *hostess*!' Emmy looked shocked.

'Sounds like this little sister of yours is a girl after my own heart,' Imogen, who had been listening to the cousins' exchange with interest, said wryly. 'And why look so horrified? There's nothing wrong with being a hostess.'

'I quite agree,' Jasper butted in, directing a smile that would have charmed the birds off the trees at her aunt. 'All she has to do is entertain the gentlemen that frequent the club and get them to spend their money.'

'I see.' Emmy still wasn't that enamoured with the idea, and she grew even more concerned at Jasper's next words.

'Between you and me I think she's smitten with a certain young man that visits the club. She only met him a few evenings ago but they've been almost inseparable ever since.'

'I just hope she is being sensible; she's only sixteen – at least she is until next week,' Emmy commented.

Jasper chuckled again. 'Stop worrying, please. She's young and having fun. Now, how about you and I go for a stroll and you can tell me all about how you are settling in London.'

'But I've only just come in. Jake took me on a river trip along the Thames.' Just for a moment she saw Jasper's lips tighten and a look of irritation flash across his face, but then he was his usual charming self again.

'I'm sure our delightful aunt wouldn't mind if I whisked you out again,' he said confidently. 'She tells me it's your day off to do as you please.'

Her aunt stared at him and sniffed and Emmy got the impression that for some reason his charm hadn't worked its magic on her as it did on the majority of the women he met. Despite this, Imogen inclined her head. 'He's quite right. Today is yours to spend as you wish. I'm not your jailer!'

In actual fact, the last thing Emmy wanted to do was go out again but Jasper was her cousin so she supposed she couldn't snub him, particularly when she had just spent part of the day with his brother. 'Very well, I suppose we could take a short stroll about the park,' she said reluctantly.

With an exultant smile Jasper rose and kissed his aunt's hand. 'Goodbye for now, dear aunt. I'm sure we shall see each other again very soon.'

'I've no doubt we shall.' She was unsmiling as they left the room.

Outside, Emmy led Jasper to the little park. At some stage he tucked her hand into his arm and once again Emmy felt vaguely uncomfortable in his company. Why, she wondered, when she always felt perfectly at ease with Jake?

'So Abi is well?' she queried.

He nodded. 'Very well and having the time of her life from what I can see of it.'

'And you're quite sure that I can't persuade you to tell me where she is living?'

He sighed dramatically. 'I've already explained I can't do that until I've had her permission, but I'm sure she mentioned that she was thinking of coming to see you.'

He chattered on of other things but his words went in one ear and out of the other as Emmy thought about her sister. She didn't like the idea of what could happen to her in the sort of establishment she was working in, but there was nothing she could do about it for now, so she endured two laps of the park before politely but firmly informing Jasper that she wished to return to her aunt's as she was tired.

He sighed again as if he were mortally offended but led her back the way they had come and when they reached the house, she didn't invite him in.

'I shall come and see you again very soon, sweet cousin,' he told her, bending over her hand and planting a wet kiss on it.

It was all Emmy could do to stop herself shuddering, although she managed to keep her smile in place until he turned and strode away. Then, with a grimace, she wiped the back of her hand down her skirt before hurrying inside.

When she returned to the drawing room, her aunt was sitting where she had left her and gave Emmy a wry smile. 'I don't see any of my family for years then all of a sudden they're coming at me from all directions. That one is the double of his father when he was young.'

Emmy managed a smile as she removed her hat yet again. 'Yes, it does appear so.'

'Hm, and it seems that you have both of your cousins eating out of your hand.'

Emmy looked surprised. 'Whatever do you mean?'

'It's as plain as the nose on your face that they're both quite smitten with you,' her aunt said in her usual forthright way. 'But be careful – that last one, Jasper . . . I wouldn't trust that young man as far as I could throw him.'

'I'm sure you're quite wrong,' Emmy said primly. 'They're my *cousins*. After what happened with your brother and sister, you must know that even if what you say is true, nothing could ever come of it.'

'That might well be, but they're also young men an' you're a young woman,' her aunt told her tartly. 'The older one, Jake, now he seems a nice young chap and I can see him making something of himself, but Jasper . . .' She shook her head. 'He'll never be anything but a waster. Trust me, I'm a very good judge of character and I've come across plenty like him in my time so just be careful.'

Emmy couldn't help but smile. 'I must admit Jasper's not my favourite person either,' she admitted. 'And Jake and I are merely good friends.'

Imogen sniffed as she rang the bell for Aggie, and taking that as a sign of her dismissal, Emmy went to her room where she immediately threw open the window. Unfortunately, she found the fussy furniture and decor rather overpowering at times, although she would never tell her aunt so for fear of hurting her feelings. Plonking herself down on the window seat she stared into the garden and as she thought back to the time she had spent with Jake, she smiled. They'd had such a lovely day and were so easy in each other's company. She instantly felt guilty then when she remembered what her aunt had said and she was forced to wonder if it wasn't *her* who had feelings for him. The smile slid from her face and she frowned.

Over the last couple of years before the family had lost Astley House her mother had paraded a number of eligible young men in front of her but she had never felt for any of them what she felt for Jake. She found herself looking forward to spending time with him and listening to what he'd been up to since they'd last met. He was kind and thoughtful and undeniably handsome but she knew that nothing could ever come of any feelings she had for him and she wondered suddenly if it wouldn't be better to stop seeing him so often? She gave herself a little shake. *Stop being so fanciful*, she scolded herself. *It's nothing more than family affection you feel, so what's the harm in that? We are both working away from home so it's natural we should want to see someone we know.*

With her mind somewhat settled, she quickly made herself think of other things.

174

Chapter Twenty

June 1875

It was a beautiful evening early in June and as Abi was heading to the door that led to the club from the girls' living quarters, Lilly beckoned her into her office.

'Is anything wrong?' she asked anxiously as Lilly sat herself behind a pretty Queen Anne desk with dainty legs.

'Nor at all, queen.' Lilly smiled at her to put her at ease. 'It's just that some o' the customers are gerrin' a bit fed up cos you never keep them company.'

'Oh!' Abi flushed, not knowing quite what to say.

'Don't look guilty,' Lilly said quickly. 'It ain't your fault you're the youngest an' the most in demand of me girls at the minute . . . But the thing is, you've been spendin' a lot o' time wi' young Lord Medville an' it would be nice if you could spread yourself about more. Yer know, mingle a bit rather than spend the whole night sittin' wi' him.'

'I'm sorry . . . I hadn't realised I was doing that,' Abi said, although of course she knew full well that she had. He was all she thought and dreamt about and when she wasn't with him, she was miserable.

She was already aware that she wasn't popular with the other girls either because they were jealous of the attention she got, not that that was her fault. She couldn't help it if she was prettier and fresher than them, and at least Bella and Maria were kind to her, so all in all she was settling very well into her new lifestyle. She had learnt a lot in the few weeks she had spent there and was now fully aware that the girls could earn far more by entertaining the gentlemen in their rooms than they did by sitting drinking with them in the club, but she had no intention of going down that path. Her mother had drummed into her over the years that when she gave herself to a man, it should be her husband. That was why Lilly's next words made the colour burn into her cheeks.

'The other thing I wanted to talk to you about was takin' precautions.' Lilly smiled as she saw Abi squirm but she was used to it. Most of the girls arrived young and innocent but the majority of them didn't stay that way for long and she sensed that young Abigail would be no different, which was why she had been happy to pay Jasper a good sum for introducing her. 'I see yer know what I mean,' she went on.

'Oh . . . but I-I don't—'

Lilly held one hand up to stop her flow of words and rummaged in a desk drawer with the other. 'You've no need to be embarrassed, queen,' she assured her, then, with a triumphant smile she held aloft some small sponges and a tiny bottle of liquid.

'Oh . . . but I don't . . . I haven't . . .' Abi faltered. She had heard the other girls discussing them and had a good idea of what they were for.

'That's what they all say when they first come 'ere but Bella will tell yer how to use 'em should you decide to,' Lilly said, not wishing to prolong the girl's obvious embarrassment. 'So pop 'em up to your room an' then get to work. No doubt the young lord will be 'ere soon. But just a friendly word o' warnin': don't get too involved. He's a young man an' foot-loose an' fancy-free, though I've never known 'im visit so often till you arrived, but remember what I said, queen – he ain't the only customer we need to keep 'appy.'

Abi bobbed her head and stumbled from the room. She was just heading back up the stairs when she passed Bella.

'Everything all right?' she asked and when Abi opened her hand to reveal what Lilly had given her, Bella smiled. 'Better to be safe than sorry,' she chuckled. 'Go and put them away and I'll explain how to use them in the morning.'

Ten minutes later when she had composed herself, Abi entered the smoky clubroom and instantly her eyes swept the tables for a sign of the young lord, only to be bitterly disappointed. But then an elderly man in a smart pin-striped suit raised his hand to catch her attention and forcing a smile she went to join him at his table. *At least Lilly will be happy to see me with someone other than Hugo*, she thought as she spread her skirts on the seat beside him and flashed him a dazzling smile.

Despite the fact that she didn't have a moment to herself, the evening dragged intolerably and every time the door opened, Abi looked towards it hopefully, only to be disappointed.

'You've done well tonight, queen,' Lilly praised when the last customer finally left in the early hours of the morning. 'But get yerself off to bed now an' get a good night's sleep.' She turned back to counting the night's takings.

'What's wrong with you?' Maria queried as they made their way to their rooms, and when Abi shrugged, Maria looked concerned.

'Is it because the young lordship didn't put in an appearance tonight?' she asked gently.

Abi's glum face was her only answer and Maria placed a gentle hand on her arm. 'Try not to get too deeply involved with any of the customers,' she advised. 'I did exactly the same thing once and look what happened to me – I ended up with a child.'

Abi stared at her curiously. 'So you know who the father is then?'

Maria nodded. 'Oh yes. I was totally in love with him and he swore he loved me too and promised me that we had a future together. But as soon as I found out I was going to have a child he was gone like the wind, the lousy bastard! Eventually I found out where he lived and ventured round there and guess what? His *wife* answered the door with a number of small children hanging on her skirts an' a baby in her arms. He was married all the time and I felt so sorry for her I didn't even tell her why I were there. I just made some excuse and left. Not that I regret having my little girl; she's the apple of my eye and that's why I carry on working here so I can give her everything she needs.'

'Is she the one you go off to see every Sunday?'

Maria nodded. 'Yes, wild horses wouldn't keep me away from her and there's absolutely nothing I wouldn't do for her. The trouble is, if I were to leave here I'd never earn enough to keep her how I want her to be kept so . . .' She sighed resignedly and suddenly Abi felt sorry for her. Maria always put such a hard face on but she was as soft as butter underneath.

Even so, when they parted on the landing and Abi entered her room, she sat down heavily on the bed feeling thoroughly miserable. No one had ever made her feel the way Hugo did and although he hadn't said as much, she could see in his eyes every time he looked at her how much she meant to him. Not all men were like the one that had conned Maria, she reasoned, and he was sure to be back tomorrow. After all, he spent a lot of each evening at the card tables and she had frequently seen him lose a great deal of money so he had probably just decided to have a night away.

Feeling slightly more optimistic she hurriedly discarded the lovely gown she had bought with her first lot of earnings over the back of a chair and after scrambling into her nightgown she hopped into bed and was asleep in seconds, dreaming of Hugo's handsome face.

The following evening when Abi entered the club and found Hugo waiting at his favourite table for her, all was suddenly right with the world again. With her heart thudding erratically, she made her way towards him, completely ignoring everything Lilly had said, and consequently all the men who beckoned to her. A number of Hugo's friends were sitting with him but when they saw Abi, they quickly dispersed, nudging and laughing amongst themselves.

'I-I was worried about you when you didn't come last night,' she told him haltingly as he took her small hand

and raised it to his lips, causing the colour to rush into her cheeks.

'My dear girl, I can't be here *every* night.' He laughed as he beckoned to a waitress for a bottle of champagne. 'My father is on at me about the amount I spend, and all because I went a little over my allowance last month,' he said in an aggrieved tone. Then he fixed his remarkable blue eyes on her and Abi felt as if she were melting inside. 'But of course, I could never stay away for long . . . not now that I've met you,' he purred as he stroked her fingers, sending shivers up her spine. 'In fact, I have a little something here for you.' He withdrew a beautifully wrapped package from the pocket of his smart frock coat and gave it to her.

Abi pulled the paper back to reveal a small velvet box inside which was a tiny gold heart suspended on a fine golden chain.

'Oh . . . but it's *beautiful*,' she gasped as he fastened it about her neck.

'It's nothing,' he assured her loftily, then raising his hand to his head he said sadly, 'Though it would have been nicer if I could have given it to you somewhere a little quieter. I have a bit of a headache. I don't suppose there's any chance of us taking our drinks up to your room, is there?'

The colour drained from Abi's face as quickly as it had come as she stammered, 'Well, I, er . . . I've never entertained a gentleman in my room before.'

A flicker of annoyance passed over his face before he was all smiles again. 'Of course. I quite understand and I wouldn't want you to. You see . . . I very much consider you to be *my* girl. You *do* have feelings for me don't you, Abi?'

'I-I'm very fond of you.'

'Good!' As he leant towards her, she could smell the sharp clean scent of his cologne and when his lips pressed gently on hers her heart began to thump so loudly, she was sure that he would hear it, even over the sound of the piano.

Then he sat back in his seat and clipping the end off a costly cigar he struck a match and lit it, blowing a plume of blue smoke into the already smoky air as she stared at him adoringly.

It was then that Lilly approached them. She was smiling but the smile didn't quite reach her eyes as she said, 'Might I have a word, Lord Medville?'

He waved his hand at her as if he were batting an irritating fly away. 'Later, woman. Myself and this charming young lady are having a conversation.'

'You're also drinkin' me most expensive champagne, I see,' she answered and her eyes were as cold as marbles now. 'So perhaps if I bring yer the bill you an' your friends 'ave run up over the last few days you might like to settle it, eh?'

He had the grace to look uncomfortable as he told her, 'Oh, just put it on the tab . . . I'll pay you as soon as my allowance comes through.'

'An' when will that be?'

He shrugged. 'Within the next couple of days, I dare say. *Surely* you can wait?'

She inclined her head. 'Shall we say your bill will be paid in full by the end o' the week then?'

'Yes, yes.' He was more than a little angry by then as with a nod Lilly turned about in a swish of lilac satin skirts and drifted away.

'Bloody woman,' he cursed. 'Me and my friends must be amongst her best customers, the ungrateful old cow!' The night wasn't turning out half as well as he had hoped it would. For a start he had been convinced that tonight would be the night he would lure Abi into bed, especially after presenting her with the trinket that he had been ill able to afford until his allowance came through. No doubt that would mean another roasting from his father when the bill arrived with him. And then for Lilly to blatantly ask him to pay what was owed. Huh! She should just be grateful he and his friends chose to frequent such a hole.

Then suddenly remembering Abi was still sitting there, he pushed the thoughts aside and smiled as he turned on his charm again. He had thought she would be like putty in his hands but it appeared she was going to need a little more work, and because she was such a tasty little piece, he was prepared to take a bit more time in wooing her. But he wouldn't wait forever.

'I was wondering if you were free any time during the day tomorrow?' he said, leaning towards her and she almost swooned with pleasure.

'I-I could be,' she answered through suddenly dry lips. 'What did you have in mind?'

'I thought it might be nice if we had that little lunch together that I promised you to celebrate your birthday. Somewhere away from this place.'

She was nodding enthusiastically before he had even finished speaking. 'Good, then shall I pick you up at one o'clock?'

'Oh, yes please.' She was breathless with excitement and for the next hour until he rose to go for a game of cards, she hung on his every word, already going over in her mind what she would wear for their lunch date.

Chapter Twenty-One

'Are you not feeling well, Aunt?' Emmy queried when she entered Imogen's room to take her a tray of tea and toast early the next morning.

Without her heavy make-up and frills and flounces, Imogen looked very frail. Emmy surmised that she must only be in her early fifties but her illness had etched lines into her face and she looked pale and much older.

'I'm perfectly all right,' Imogen replied as she heaved herself up on to the pillows, wincing with pain.

Emmy placed the tray across her lap before bustling across the room to open the curtains and let the sunshine pour in. Like every other room in the house, this one was overly ornate. Pale-pink silk paper covered the walls and expensive pieces of Meissen, Spode and Royal Worcester were scattered along every surface. The elaborately carved four-poster bed was surrounded by fussy, heavily fringed velvet curtains, which matched the ones hanging at the window, and expensive multi-coloured Turkish carpets were laid across the floor. Emmy had now taken over the care of her aunt's wardrobe and she crossed to it to see what she might like to wear today.

'How about your lilac satin, or perhaps this pink muslin gown?' she suggested as Imogen lifted the dainty cup from its saucer and sipped at her tea.

'Actually, I thought I might have a bit of a lie-in,' Imogen told her and when Emmy looked concerned, she waved her hand impatiently at her. 'Now don't get reading anything in to it, my girl. I'm entitled to an extra hour or two in bed if I've a mind to, without you going into a flap, aren't I?'

'Of course you are,' Emmy told her hastily. 'But if you aren't feeling well I'd rather you say and I can get the doctor to call in to see you.'

'*Bah!*' Imogen sniffed impatiently. 'Just pass me that there bottle of pills from the mantelshelf and leave me in peace. I've decided to have an idle day so you might as well have it off. Go out and get some fresh air. It's not right that a young woman like you should be stuck in with an old biddy like me day after day. You need to make some friends of your own age. And I dare say you should be going home to see how your mother's getting on as well soon.'

'Very well, I'll just take this gown you wore yesterday down to the laundry room and then I will go out for a while if you're sure you don't mind? But if you do need anything be sure to ring for Aggie, won't you?'

'Oh, stop fussing, girl,' Imogen retorted irritably. 'You're like an old mother hen. Now get off with you and leave me in peace.'

Left with little choice, Emmy handed her aunt her pills and lifting the gown she left the room and almost collided with Aggie who was just passing the door.

'Ah, Aggie, you're just the one I wanted to see.' Emmy glanced at her aunt's bedroom door and lowering her voice to little more than a whisper she went on, 'I don't think Aunt Imogen is very well today, although she'd die rather than admit it, of course. I'm just going to wash this gown and get it hung out to dry and then she's given me the whole day off, but you will keep an eye on her, won't you?'

'Here give me that.' Aggie's plain little face broke into a smile as she took the gown from her. 'I'll launder that for yer. You go an' get yerself ready an' go an' enjoy yerself. It's a really lovely day.'

'Are you sure?' Emmy gave her a grateful smile. 'I think I might go into the city centre and do a bit of window-shopping then have a café lunch somewhere.'

'Don't blame yer,' Aggie answered good-naturedly. 'See yer later.' And with that she was off down the stairs as Emmy went to her room to fetch her bonnet.

An hour later she was strolling along Oxford Street enjoying the window displays and wishing that Jake could be there with her. Apart from her Sunday outings with him she hadn't ventured too far from her aunt's house and she felt quite strange being there all alone. Suddenly she heard someone call her name and turning she saw Jasper and another young man hurrying towards her.

'Jasper.' She smiled at him as he drew close. 'I didn't realise you were still in London. I thought you would have gone home by now.'

He shook his head, ignoring her hand and leaning in to kiss her cheek in a very familiar way, making her blush. 'No, I've told Mother and Father I shall be staying here for the summer. They're not too happy with the idea, mind. Toby here is kindly putting me up. Toby, this is my cousin Emerald. You've met her sister Abigail at the club. Emerald this is Tobias Bisset.'

His friend bowed courteously from the waist and Emmy inclined her head towards him.

'Where are you off to then?' Jasper enquired when the introductions were out of the way.

Emmy had to think quickly. The last thing she wanted was to have Jasper hanging on to her skirts so she chose to tell a white lie. 'I've come into town to get some things for our aunt,' she said, crossing her fingers behind her back.

He pouted like a spoilt child. 'Does that mean that you have to rush back?'

'I'm afraid it does.' She kept her fingers tightly crossed. 'And I'm in rather a hurry so I shall have to get on, but it was nice to see you.'

'I was hoping to take you to lunch. I'm sure you could find something to do to entertain yourself, couldn't you, Toby?' he said pointedly, turning his attention to the young man at his side.

His friend nodded. 'Of course I could, old chap.' He didn't blame Jasper at all for wanting to spend some time with this young woman. She was very attractive, although not quite as beautiful as her sister.

'That would have been very nice, but as I explained I really do have to get on.' She gave a little curtsey and hurried on, not daring to look back until she had gone some way.

Thankfully there was no sign of Jasper or Toby when she did and feeling like she'd had a lucky escape she turned into a side street and went where it led her. Soon she found herself in a labyrinth of narrow streets that led off into courtyards where grubby, undernourished children played in the gutters. Lifting her skirts, she quickened her steps, painfully aware of how closely they were watching her. She realised how out of place she must look to them in her fine gown and bonnet when most of them didn't even have shoes on their feet, and now she longed to come to a main road again. She could only begin to imagine how horrified her mother would be if she could see her now. At home, unless it was to go for a leisurely walk about the village or in the countryside, she hadn't even been allowed into the town without a chaperone. The thought brought a smile to her face, just as she emerged gratefully on to yet another busy road. This one she saw was dotted with clubs with lewd pictures of girls outside, some of them in a semi-undressed state. Blushing she hurried by as she realised that she must now be in the notorious Soho. The question was, how did she get back to the centre? It was lunchtime by now and as she paused to think what to do for the best, her heart suddenly skipped a beat as she saw a handsome-looking couple walking towards her. They were arm in arm and totally absorbed in one another but as they drew closer, she gasped with delight. She had thought the young woman looked familiar and now she saw that it was her sister. She let out a cry as she lifted her skirts in a most unladylike manner and began to race towards her.

'*Abi . . . Abigail!*'

The girl looked up and when she saw her sister bearing down on her a mixture of emotions crossed her pretty face.

Of course, she was happy to see her, but not if it meant losing precious time with Hugo.

'Oh, Abi, I'm *so* glad I've found you. I've been *so* worried about you,' Emmy cried as she drew close enough, and quite forgetting her manners, she flung her arms about the girl.

Nonplussed, the young man released his hold on her and stepped aside as Abi weakly returned the hug and forced a false smile to her face.

'I don't know why, I've been perfectly all right and I'm quite capable of taking care of myself,' she told Emmy churlishly. 'I'm not a child any more, you know?'

'No, of course you aren't,' Emmy agreed quickly. 'But it was just not knowing where you were that worried us all.' It was then that she remembered the young man at Abi's side and turning to him she apologised, 'I'm so sorry for interrupting.'

He bowed his head as Abi reluctantly told her, 'Emmy, this is . . . my friend, Hugo.'

'How do you do.' Abi gave a little curtsy and again he inclined his head.

'And, Hugo, this is my sister, Emerald.'

'A pleasure, I'm sure.' Raising her hand, he kissed the back of it lightly and Emmy felt a shiver run up her spine as he lifted his head to give her an arrogant smile. The young man was clearly upper class, immaculately dressed and quite handsome but Emmy took an instant dislike to him for no reason that she could explain.

Turning her attention back to her sister, Emmy said, 'I don't suppose you have time to come for a coffee with me? We have so much catching up to do, and I've missed you.'

Abi gripped Hugo's arm possessively and shook her head. 'Not now, I'm sorry but Hugo and I are just going out to lunch.'

As she stared adoringly up into his face, her cheeks flushed and her eyes sparkling, Emmy felt her heart sink. Her sister was clearly besotted with the chap, but did he feel the same way about her or would Abi be just one more in a long line of young women he would play with until he tired of her?

'Perhaps another day then, or one evening?'

'I work in the evenings,' Abi told her, clearly growing impatient to get away. But then seeing her sister's crestfallen expression, she added not unkindly, 'But I have Aunt Imogen's address. I'll come and see you as soon as I can.'

'That would be lovely. I'll look forward to it.'

Emmy watched them walk away, Abi chattering merrily to her companion, their meeting already forgotten. Suddenly the joy had gone from the day and Emmy walked a little further along the road until she saw a horse tram. Stepping aboard she paid her fare and headed back to her aunt's. *But still*, she consoled herself, *at least I've seen her, and she does look well.* All she could do for now was hope that Abi kept her promise.

She arrived back at the house to find her aunt in her favourite chair in the drawing room. She had changed her mind and decided to get up after all, although she was still in her night attire with a warm shawl draped about her shoulders.

When Emmy entered the room, she raised an eyebrow and asked shortly, 'What are you doing back? Didn't I say you could take the day off?'

'Yes, you did and it was very kind of you,' Emmy answered as she began to tidy the pile of magazines on the table at her aunt's side. 'I bumped into Abi, but unfortunately she was going out to lunch so we didn't get to spend much time together.'

'Out to lunch? Who with?'

'A young man, as it happens.'

Seeing the disapproving expression on her niece's face, Imogen chuckled. 'And what, may I ask, is wrong with that?'

'Erm . . .' Emmy hesitated. 'There isn't anything *wrong* with it exactly but she is only just seventeen. I was hoping to take her shopping and buy her a little gift for her birthday.'

'Good luck to her, that's what I say. I was exactly the same at her age. I had a list of suitors as long as my arm. It's a shame you don't take a leaf out of her book. You're too staid by half.'

'I am not staid!' Emmy denied, gritting her teeth. 'I'm just a different nature to Abi, that's all. I've never been a great one for balls and parties and such, like Abi is. I much prefer to read or go for long walks. It wouldn't do if we were all the same, would it?'

'I suppose not,' Imogen grudgingly agreed. 'But you're only young once, girl, and you should make the most of it. Don't forget that. But seeing as you're back, ring that bell and tell Aggie I'd like some tea.'

With a grin Emmy did as she was told.

Chapter Twenty-Two

'I suppose I should be thinking of getting us to the coast for the summer or it'll be winter again at this rate,' Imogen told Emmy one evening in late June. 'But first I should probably give you a few days off to go and visit your mother.'

Emmy eyed her aunt with concern, she was as prickly as a cactus but despite that Emmy had grown fond of her and was worried because she hadn't been at all well for the last couple of weeks. She had developed a summer cold and since then had rarely left her room, which wasn't like her at all. She had even called off her spiritualist meetings for the time being and knowing how much she enjoyed them, Emmy knew that she must feel very under the weather indeed. Because of her aunt's illness, Emmy preferred to be there to keep an eye on the woman, so apart from meeting Jake each Sunday, she hadn't ventured out of the house much either.

Today she had been particularly restless because she had received a note from Jake that morning informing her that he had spoken to Jasper who had given him the address of the club that Abi was working at. She hadn't managed to see Abi again since the day she had spotted her walking with the young man, and it troubled her. She'd hoped that Abi would visit her at her aunt's as she had promised, but as yet there'd been no sign of her, so after making sure that her aunt had everything she needed, she asked tentatively, 'Would you mind very much if I went out for a while this evening?'

Her aunt raised an eyebrow. 'Of course you can go out, but do you mind me asking where you're going? I know there's something on your mind. You've been like a cat on hot bricks all day.'

'Jake sent a message today telling me the address of the club where Abi's working and I thought I might pay her a visit and surprise her.'

Imogen snorted with derision. 'I don't think that's a very good idea,' she advised. 'Although I can't stop you going if you've set your mind on it. Most of the clubs in Soho aren't the sort of places young ladies go to unchaperoned, believe me.'

'Why not?' Emmy straightened her back and looked slightly offended. 'I'm only going to see my sister,' she pointed out. 'What's so wrong in that?'

Seeing that her niece was not going to be put off, Imogen shrugged. 'Have it your way then, but if you don't like what you see, don't blame me. And make sure you get a cab to bring you home. The streets of Soho are no place for a young woman to be wandering about on her own at night.'

'I'm sure I shall be quite all right; I'm more than capable of looking after myself,' Emmy answered primly, turning on her heel and hurrying to her bedroom. After changing her dress and putting on her bonnet, she asked Aggie to keep an ear open for her aunt, then snatching up her bag, she set off to find a cab to take her to the Black Cat club.

The cab dropped her right outside a short time later and Emmy felt the first little flutters of nerves in her stomach as she gazed at the outside. There were large posters of scantily dressed girls plastered on the wall and a burly man with hands like hams was standing outside the door.

'Er . . . excuse me,' Emmy said timidly. 'I'd like to come into the club.'

He threw back his head and laughed as if she had made a huge joke. 'Would you now, little lady? Well, I'm sorry but I can't allow you in, this is a gentleman's club.'

Emmy straightened her back and glared at him. 'But according to these posters there are women in there.'

'Yes, you're quite right, but they're the hostesses,' he told her with a grin.

'And my sister is one of them,' Emmy informed him imperiously. 'And it's her I've come to see.'

'Then why didn't you say so.' He pointed to an alley that led down one side of the club. 'The girls live in the back there, go and knock on the door and I've no doubt someone'll find her for you.'

Emmy inclined her head and with her shoulders back she marched away, wrinkling her nose in distaste as the sour smells in the alley wafted up to her. It smelt like the inside of a dirty toilet and she felt her heart sink as she wondered if the inside would be any better. It certainly wasn't what she had been expecting and she lifted her skirts to try to keep them away from the ground. Eventually she came to a door and rapped on it smartly. For a few moments there was no sign that anyone had heard her but then she heard footsteps and as the door inched open a mousy-haired, spotty-faced little maid stared out at her.

'I've come to see my sister. Her name is Abigail,' she informed her.

The girl's face broke into a smile that completely transformed her plain features. 'Come on in, miss.' The girl held the door open and as Emmy stepped inside, she was immediately aware of the sound of music and laughter coming from behind a closed door at the far end of a long corridor. The smell of cheap perfume was overpowering and she discreetly took her handkerchief from her bag and held it to her nose.

'I reckon Miss Abigail is already at work in the club, miss, an' Miss Lilly won't be none too pleased if yer disturb 'er,' the girl told her worriedly.

'And *who* is Miss Lilly?' Emmy questioned, but before the girl could answer a plump, gaudily dressed woman with flame-red hair emerged from one of the many doors in the hallway.

'I am, who wants ter know?' She looked her up and down and Emmy had the awful feeling that the woman could see right into her very soul.

'I-I've come to see my sister, Abigail Winter,' Emmy stuttered, suddenly feeling nervous.

'Ah! I can see the resemblance now you've said,' Lilly said with a broad smile. 'But she's workin' at the minute. Evenin's ain't a good time to catch 'er, queen. Couldn't you come durin' the day?' Seeing the girl hesitate she had a change of heart and told her, 'Look, I'll let yer go through an' see 'er, but just fer a few minutes – that's if she ain't entertainin' one o' the customers.' Abigail's sister, she noted, was taller and slimmer than Abi but a very attractive girl all the same. 'I don't suppose you fancy a job 'ere an' all, do yer?'

Emmy hastily shook her head. 'Thank you but no, I already have a job looking after my aunt.'

'Aw well, it were worth a try. You'd go down a treat wi' the punters, just like yer sister does, so if yer should ever change yer mind, yer know where I am. Foller me, queen.' She turned in a swish of heavy silk skirts and Emmy followed her to the door at the end of the hallway where all the noise was coming from.

Once they entered the club, Emmy found herself enveloped in a fog of cigar smoke and loud noise. The lights were dim but she could see gentlemen seated at many of the tables with girls who were almost indecently dressed fawning over them. A bar ran along one wall and she spotted Abi there, chatting to a young woman who was furiously polishing a glass behind it.

'Yer in luck,' Lilly told her. 'Seems she ain't entertainin' anyone just yet so go an' have yer word wi' 'er but make it quick, please.' Then she left Emmy to pick her way through the tables, her cheeks aflame.

She had nearly reached Abi when the girl spotted her. 'Emmy, what are you doing here?' she asked, looking very uncomfortable and not at all pleased to see her.

'You didn't come and visit me as you promised, so I thought I'd better come to you and make sure that you were all right. Jake gave me your address.'

'As you can see, I'm perfectly fine,' Abi quipped, on the defensive now.

Emmy studied her sister and her heart sank. Admittedly Abi's face wasn't heavily made-up as the other girls' were, but the gown she was wearing was cut indecently low and Emmy worried that if she were to lean forward her breasts might spill out of it. An awkward silence stretched between them for a while until Abi broke it when she said ungraciously, 'Seeing as you're here, you might as well have a drink. What would you like?'

'I don't drink, in case you'd forgotten,' Emmy replied primly, staring pointedly at the glass of wine in Abi's hand. 'And I don't think Mama would be very pleased to know that you were.'

'But Mama *doesn't* know, does she? And in case you'd forgotten, I don't have to answer to her any more. I'm making my own way in life now and loving it!'

Emmy silently cursed herself for putting her back up. This meeting wasn't going at all as she'd hoped it would. 'Sorry, I didn't mean to offend you,' she told her quickly. 'But I do miss you so. Couldn't you please come and visit Aunt Imogen so we can have a proper talk? She's planning on going to her second home at the coast for the rest of the summer and I won't be able to see you for months until we return.'

Abi's face softened for a moment as she stared back at her sister and she was about to say something when a commotion by the entrance doors distracted her and a rowdy group of young men entered. Jasper was amongst them but Emmy noted that it was another good-looking young man who immediately caught Abi's attention.

'Look, Emmy, my, er . . . friend has just arrived so I'm very sorry but I have to go.' Then seeing the way her sister's face fell, she added, 'But I will come and see you this week, I promise . . . Goodbye for now.' Then she was off like a March hare.

Emmy watched her go helplessly, suddenly recognising the man Abi was so interested in as the one she had seen her walking out with. It was more than obvious that she wasn't welcome and so with a sigh she headed for the exit.

Outside, the heat of the day had died down but it was still very humid and the smell of horse droppings and the sewers was overpowering as Emmy found her way back to the main road. More than once gentlemen tried to approach her but she hurried past with her head down until she was able to hail a cab. The smell inside it was even worse than the smell outside but Emmy was just glad to get away from Soho.

Once she arrived back at her aunt's, Emmy paid the driver and rushed inside to find Aggie coming down the stairs with a tray she had just fetched from Imogen's bedroom.

'You're back early,' she remarked. 'The missus ain't at all well tonight. I reckon she's in pain, though she won't admit it, the stubborn devil.'

'I'll go up and check on her,' Emmy promised as she removed her bonnet, then with a weary sigh, she began to climb the stairs.

Back at the club Abi was preening as Hugo gave her his full attention. Tonight, he had bought her a delicate silver bracelet and as he fastened it about her wrist he leant forward and kissed the skin on her smooth shoulder, making her breathless with delight.

She still hadn't let him go any further than kissing her, though, and he was growing ever more impatient.

'Why can't we go to your room where we could get some privacy?' He looked like a sad puppy as she gazed into his incredible blue eyes and Abi felt herself weakening. 'We could take a nice cold bottle of champagne up there with us and talk to our hearts' content,' he went on persuasively, staring at her through the pall of smoke.

Abi was very aware of what went on when the other girls took gentlemen up to their rooms. As they'd told her, it was a much easier way to earn money than sitting drinking all night and she was sure that Hugo was far too much of a gentleman to try to take advantage of her. Even so, something still held her back.

'Actually I was wondering how you'd feel about coming to meet my parents soon? As I've told you they have a rather nice town house in Mayfair and I'd love them to meet you.'

Abi knew that Hugo's father was a very well-known politician and her heart began to thump with joy. If Hugo was prepared to take her to meet his parents then surely his intentions towards her must be honourable? Suddenly any remaining doubts slipped away and her eyes were sparkling as she nodded. 'All right, we'll go up to my room, but you must promise to be a gentleman,' she said sweetly.

'When am I ever anything but?' Rising swiftly, he beckoned to the waitress to fetch them a bottle of champagne and once it was delivered, he grabbed it and two glasses and ushered her towards the girls' living quarters before she had chance to change her mind. With a bit of luck, tonight might just be the night!

Once in the privacy of her room he took a seat as Abi poured him a glass of champagne and sat down beside him. 'Aren't you having one?' he queried.

She giggled prettily. 'I'm afraid I already had a glass of wine just before you arrived.'

'Huh! Just one – that's nothing,' he said airily and pushing the glass she had just handed him to her, he hastily poured himself another one. 'Go on, relax and enjoy yourself,' he urged. 'What does it matter if you get a little bit tipsy? There's only me here to see you so let your hair down and enjoy yourself.' He began to take out the pins that fastened her hair so that it fell about her slim shoulders in all its silky splendour, then he ran his fingers through it and leant in for a kiss.

It was a kiss like nothing Abi had ever experienced before and as his tongue gently forced her lips open and began to probe the inside of her mouth she felt her desire rising. Soon his hands strayed to her breasts and when she offered no resistance, he gently lifted them from her low-cut gown and began to kiss her nipples. They instantly hardened and swelled as she gasped with pleasure.

Determined not to miss the moment, Hugo gently guided her to the bed, then kneeling in front of her, he began to caress her ankle, slowly stroking his way up her leg.

'Please let me look at you, you're so beautiful,' he gasped.

Panting, Abi had fallen back on the pillows while his hands awakened sensations inside her that she'd never felt before. She knew what she was doing went against everything her mother had ever taught her, but she didn't seem able to stop the feelings that were throbbing through her, so when he gently sat her up and began to fumble with the row of tiny buttons at the back of her gown, she offered no resistance.

Soon it lay in a silken pool on the floor to be joined by her petticoats and undergarments until finally, she lay before him as naked as the day she had been born. The bulge in his trousers showed her the effect she was having on him, but instead of feeling embarrassed and ashamed, she wanted him to own her. If he was aiming to introduce her to his parents, he was clearly planning on marrying her so why wait? she asked herself.

Soon his clothes had joined hers and as he stood before her she revelled in the sight of his young muscular body. He was so handsome that he took her breath away and as he gently nudged her back on to the bed she wrapped her arms about his neck, enjoying the feel of his strong chest against her breasts. Slowly, very slowly, he began to kiss every inch of her until she felt she was on fire, then finally he parted her legs.

As he entered her, she gasped with pain. But it was short-lived and soon their bodies found their rhythm and she moved with him as if it was the most natural thing in the world until her pleasure built to a climax.

When it was over, she lay with her head on his chest trying to ignore the blood on the sheet. It was a reminder of what she had just lost, but at that moment she had no regrets. He was hers for all time now, she was sure of it.

Chapter Twenty-Three

July

'Do you think I should ask the doctor to come?' Aggie asked worriedly one morning early in July.

'Yes, if you would please, Aggie.' Emmy had been up twice during the night to check on her aunt, who now seemed to be running a temperature. In fact, she had slept badly since discovering that her sister lived and worked in what she considered to be a seedy environment. She pushed her untouched breakfast away. She had no appetite today.

'I'll go straightaway,' Aggie volunteered. 'An' hopefully I'll catch Dr Logan afore he starts 'is rounds.' She went to fetch her bonnet while Emmy went back upstairs to check on her aunt again.

'How are you feeling now, Aunt?' she said cheerfully as she went to open the curtains. 'Do you feel like a bit of breakfast yet?'

'No, I *don't* and I wish you'd stop fussing, girl,' Imogen snapped, blinking in the sunshine that poured into the room as she struggled to sit up. Although it was only early, the heat was beginning to build already and it looked set to be another uncomfortably hot day.

'Do you feel like getting up for a while?' Emmy asked, apprehensive about telling her aunt that she had sent for the doctor because she knew that she would be cross with her. But there was no point in delaying, so without waiting for her to reply she rushed on, 'I sent Aggie to ask Dr Logan to look in on you.'

'What did you have to do that for?' Imogen was furious. 'Do you think I'm some invalid who can't tell you when I need a doctor?'

'No, I don't,' Emmy replied calmly as she helped her aunt get comfortable on her pillows. 'But why suffer when there's probably something he can prescribe to make you feel better? And don't say there's nothing wrong because I know that's a lie. You wince every time you so much as move.'

'I've told you before, this disease I have is only going to get worse and there's nothing we can do about it,' Imogen said irritably.

Still Emmy remained calm. 'I'm sure that isn't right. Anyway, we'll let the doctor be the judge of it when he calls. Aggie has already gone for him so I can't stop him now. And while we wait for him to come, I'm going to get you a tray of tea. You should have a drink inside you at least or you'll waste away.'

'Pah! Interfering little hussy,' Imogen muttered beneath her breath as Emmy headed purposefully for the door with a smile on her face. She was getting to know her aunt quite well now and was aware that she'd rather die than admit she was in pain.

The doctor arrived just over an hour later and after showing him into her aunt's bedroom, Emmy went to stand on the landing, leaving him to examine her. She was still there waiting for him when he came out.

He shook his head. 'I'm afraid there's nothing to do to halt the disease,' he told her. 'But what you can do is give her this if you feel she's in pain.' He withdrew a small phial of liquid from his bag and handed it to Emmy. 'This is laudanum and it will help with the pain but you must use it sparingly and only when absolutely necessary. A drop or two in half a glass of water to start with and as she gets worse you can slowly increase it.'

Emmy chewed on her lip and plucking up her courage she asked, 'Is this a terminal illness, doctor?'

He nodded gravely. 'I'm afraid it is, my dear. The time she has left is not going to be easy for her because she's such an independent woman.'

'And how long do you think that might be?'

He shrugged. 'Everyone is different; she could deteriorate quickly, but there again she could go on for a few years. But were you aware that on top of this disease she also has a heart condition so it could be that that finishes her before the muscle disease. There's no way of knowing.'

Blinking back tears Emmy nodded. 'Yes, I was aware of it, but what about travelling? She was hoping to go to her second home at the coast for the summer. Will she be well enough?'

'Ah, now that's a difficult one to answer,' he admitted. 'But what I would say is, if she wants to go and she feels up to it then let her.'

'Thank you, doctor. I'll see how she is in the next few days,' Emmy answered.

'What did he say?' Aggie asked anxiously when Emmy returned from showing the doctor out.

Emmy explained what he'd told her and Aggie sniffed sadly. She was fond of her mistress and hated to think of her being so ill. 'It's up to us to make sure that whatever time she 'as left is 'appy then, ain't it?'

Emmy nodded.

It was decided that Emmy should have the next weekend off just in case they decided to go to Lytham St Anne's and as she packed a small valise on the day she was leaving she was full of instructions for Aggie.

'Look, I'll take good care of 'er, don't you worry,' she promised Emmy. 'You just get off an' spend a bit o' time wi' yer ma. You've been runnin' up an' down the stairs like a blue-arsed fly after the missus all week so a break will do yer good.'

Emmy couldn't help but grin. Aggie had proved to be a rough diamond with a heart as big as a bucket and she knew her aunt was in good hands with her, so she went to say goodbye to her aunt and set off on her journey with an easier mind.

It was late afternoon before she turned on to the track leading to the cottage and the first thing she noticed was Hetty fetching in the dry laundry from the line that was strung across the yard between the outside shed and the kitchen wall.

Hetty let out a whoop of joy when she spotted her and dropping the clothes into a large wicker basket, she scooted to meet her. 'Eeh, it's lovely to see yer,' she greeted her with a warm smile. 'Yer mam will be well surprised, but why didn't yer let us know yer were comin'?'

'I didn't know myself until a couple of days ago,' Emmy admitted. 'So I would probably have got here before my letter did had I written.' She stopped and stared then as a lovely black and white puppy with his tail wagging furiously raced forward to meet her. 'And who is this?' She laughed as she bent down to him and he began to wash her face with his tongue.

'That's Bruno.' Hetty grinned. 'Your mam said she'd feel safer, what wi' us bein' here on us own, if we had a dog about the place, so me brother fetched him for us a couple o' weeks ago. O' course he's only a few months old so he ain't much of a guard dog yet but he will be when we've trained him. I think me brother said he were a Border collie.'

Emmy was shocked at her mother's change of heart but delighted. For as long as she could remember she had pleaded with her mother to let her and Abi have a dog but her mother had always insisted that they were dirty smelly things and far too much trouble.

'He's beautiful,' she told Hetty as he rolled over for a belly rub in the dust.

'Aye, he is that, and the missus is right taken wi' him,' Hetty chuckled. 'But come in now an' I'll make yer a cuppa. Yer must be parched after that long journey.' She took Emmy's arm and almost hauled her into the kitchen where she had yet another surprise when she saw her mother, clad in a volumin-ous apron, taking a golden-brown steak pie from the oven.

When Dorcas spotted Emmy she almost dropped it in her surprise, but then she slammed it on to the table and raced across to her to enfold her in her arms. 'Why, darling, how lovely it is to see you,' she said breathlessly. 'But is everything all right?'

'Everything is fine,' Emmy assured her, trying to get used to the sight of her mother in a plain gown with flour on her cheeks. 'I just thought it was time to pop home and see how you were. But what's this?' Emmy gestured towards the pie.

Dorcas blushed and grinned. 'Hetty has been teaching me to cook and she says I have a flair for it. I just got a bit fed up of sitting about and I quite enjoy cooking now,' she confided.

'She does an' all,' Hetty agreed with a nod of her head. 'And she's gettin' to be a dab hand at helpin' out in the vegetable patch an' all.'

Emmy was beginning to wonder if she'd come to the right place, although she was very happy with what she was seeing. Her mother had colour back in her cheeks and had gained a little weight, and with her long hair tied loosely in a ribbon at the nape of her neck instead of the neat chignon she usually favoured, she looked years younger. Softer, somehow, than Emmy remembered.

'How long can you stay?' Dorcas asked and when Emmy told her she looked vaguely disappointed. 'Aw well, we'll just have to make the best of the couple of days we have then. But first we'll have some dinner. These are all vegetables and potatoes that Hetty and I have grown in the garden.'

The meal that followed was delicious and throughout, Emmy was amused to see her mother passing titbits to Bruno under the table.

'I was amazed to see that you'd got yourself a dog,' Emmy commented innocently.

Dorcas had the good grace to blush. 'I know I always said you and Abigail couldn't have one because of the mess they'd make but in actual fact, apart from the odd little accident, he's as good as gold,' Dorcas said apologetically. 'And I feel so much safer knowing he's here now that your father's . . . Well, he keeps me company and I don't feel so lonely when he's around.' She quickly blinked back the tears that had welled in her eyes.

Emmy was even more shocked at that. It was the first time since her father had disappeared that she had seen her mother show any signs of missing him and she wondered what had brought about the change of heart.

The next surprise came after the meal when they were sitting enjoying a cup of tea. Emmy took some of the wages she had saved from her bag and pushed the money across the table to her mother, but instead of snatching it up as Emmy had expected her to, she smiled and slid it back to her.

'Thank you, that's very kind of you but we're managing very well now, aren't we, Hetty?'

Hetty nodded and Dorcas went on, 'Bernard supplies us with fresh meat, eggs and milk and we grow our own vegetables out the back. Hetty's brother has been wonderful too at selling some of the trinkets we fetched from Astley House, so we're actually very comfortable. And our anonymous benefactor is continuously leaving us money on the doorstep each month, although we still have no idea who it is. They tend to bring it on the same day monthly and I tried to stay up to catch whoever it was leaving it but I'm afraid I fell asleep. And now tell me, how is Imogen?'

The smile slid from Emmy's face as she sighed. 'Actually, she's very poorly. As well as the muscle-wasting disease she's suffering from, she also has a weak heart.'

'And is there nothing that can be done for her?' Her mother was finding it hard to imagine her once glamorous sister this way.

'I'm afraid not. All I can do is make her as comfortable as I can, which isn't easy because she's very independent.'

'At least that hasn't changed,' Dorcas commented. 'And what about Abi, have you seen her again?'

Emmy decided it was time for a few white lies. There was no point in telling her mother the truth about the place she had found her sister living and working in, it would only worry her. 'I have actually and she looks really well,' she said glibly, at least that was the truth because Abi had been absolutely glowing and was clearly enjoying her new life.

'And did she say if she might be coming home for a visit soon? I won't try and force her to stay if she does.'

'I think she's just settling in at the minute but I'm sure she will when she has time,' Emmy forced herself to say and she was rewarded when she saw her mother's face relax a little.

The following day seemed to pass in the blink of an eye and at one point Emmy took Bruno for a walk to take a peek at her former home. She could only view it from a distance because the new owners were in it now and she felt sad as she thought back to the happy times she had spent there. How their lives had changed since her father had left! Thoughts of the gentle man brought stinging tears to her eyes. She still constantly worried about him and wondered where he was. She knew that he must have been in a very dark place to abandon them as he had, for she had never doubted that he loved them.

Turning about she made her way back to the cottage and when she entered, she was surprised to see her Aunt Sybil seated at the table sipping tea from one of her mother's delicate cups and saucers. She was dressed in a dull-grey gown and with her hair pulled severely back into a tight little knot at the back of her head she looked just as formidable as Emmy remembered her being.

'Ah, Emerald. Your mother said you were here on a visit. Been to look at your old home, have you?'

Emmy detected a gloating look in her eyes and was instantly on the defensive. 'No, I just fancied a breath of fresh air,' she answered, not wanting to give her aunt the satisfaction of seeing that she was bothered.

'Oh, the new people who own it are *quite* delightful,' her aunt twittered on and Emmy saw her mother flinch. 'The Nelson-Hyams live there now and the lady of the house has been to take tea with me on a few occasions. They're extremely wealthy and distantly related to royalty, I believe.'

'How nice,' Emmy said through clenched teeth. Her aunt clearly hadn't changed a bit since she'd been away and was still as big a snob as ever. She certainly hadn't missed her, although she realised now that she missed the clean fresh air and the wide-open spaces, so different to the smoggy London streets. She took a seat and sat quietly as her aunt finished her tea.

Finally the woman stood up. 'I really must be off now, Dorcas. The maid will be preparing to serve afternoon tea soon and you know what a stickler Bernard is for routine.'

Dorcas inclined her head and after their goodbyes Sybil glided from the room like a ship in full sail.

'She's still as annoying as ever, I see,' Emmy commented once her aunt had gone, and to her surprise her mother grinned as she took the dirty cups to the sink.

'Ah well, she's on her own for most of the time. Bernard is always off somewhere or another and she has very little to do with all those maids to wait on her so I suppose she gossips to fill in the time. I sometimes get the impression that she isn't quite as happy with her lot as she makes out to be.'

Once again, Emmy was surprised at her mother's reaction. Not so long ago she would have been spitting feathers by now and calling Sybil all the names under the sun, but she was much mellower and Emmy approved of the change. 'Long may it last,' she muttered under her breath as her mother carried a cup of tea and a slice of Hetty's excellent fruit cake to the table to give her.

Before she knew it, it was Sunday evening and time to pack her bag to return to London.

'I shall miss you,' her mother told her with tears in her eyes as they said their goodbyes. Emmy would have to leave to begin the long walk into town very early the next morning to catch the first train to London, and so they had no idea when they might see each other again. It all depended on how well Imogen was or if her mother did decide to visit.

'I can't believe the change in her,' Emmy commented to Hetty as they sat enjoying a cup of cocoa together when her mother had retired to bed. 'It's as if someone's waved a magic wand and put someone else in her place.'

Hetty chuckled. 'Hm, I reckon I might 'ave had an 'and in that,' she admitted without a trace of remorse. 'She was sinkin' deeper an' deeper into depression so I had to put me foot up her arse an' give her a short sharp shock.'

'And how did you manage that?'

'It 'appened one day when I 'ad to ask 'er to lift 'er feet so as I could sweep underneath, 'em!' Hetty shook her head. 'Can yer believe it? It were as if her backside were bloody glued to that chair an' on this particular day I just 'it the roof an' told 'er if she didn't pull 'erself together an' make an effort I were off, I'd 'ad enough!'

Emmy blinked in surprise. 'And how did that go down?' At one time, she knew, had any of the servants dared to talk to her mother that way she would have dismissed them on the spot.

'Funnily enough it seemed to do the trick, cos after sittin' there cryin' for a while she actually got up to put the kettle on an' thankfully she ain't looked back since.'

'Well done you,' Emmy praised. At least she could return to London with her mind easier now.

Chapter Twenty-Four

'When are you going to take me to meet your parents?' Abi asked as she slipped a feather-trimmed peignoir over her curvy figure while Hugo lay in bed sucking on a cigar.

They'd been spending almost every night together for the past few weeks, but still he had made no move to introduce her to his family.

'What's the rush? We're happy, aren't we?' His lazy smile made her heart skip a beat. He was so handsome that just the sight of him turned her legs to jelly every time she saw him and he knew it.

'Er . . . yes, of course we are but . . .' She chewed on her lip as she chose her words carefully. 'But we've . . . we're, you know? Together in all ways now, aren't we, so shouldn't we be making it officially known that we are a couple?'

'Hold on, we're still both very young,' he pointed out. 'And I don't think my parents, or yours for that matter, would be too pleased if they thought we were becoming too serious about each other.'

'But we've . . . we're . . .' Abi was finding this very embarrassing but was determined to get her point across. 'I've given myself to you in all ways now so surely we should make some commitment to each other?'

'*What?* You mean get betrothed or something?'

She nodded eagerly. 'Yes, that's exactly what I mean. We wouldn't need to get married until we're both a little older, but it would be nice to show each other that this is forever.'

Crushing the cigar out in the ashtray at the side of the bed, Hugo clambered out and began to yank his clothes on and Abi couldn't help but notice that he didn't look at all excited about the idea.

'You *do* love me, don't you?' she whimpered uncertainly.

Instantly he came to take her in his arms. 'Why, of course I do, you silly little goose.' He kissed the end of her nose, trying to ignore the feel of her soft breasts pressing against his chest. Normally he would have dragged her back to bed and made love to her all over again but she'd quite put him off the idea now. He pushed her away a little. 'But because we're so young we don't want to have our parents objecting to the union. Let's just give it a little more time and then I'd love my parents to meet you. I'm sure they'll love you.'

Abi watched as he pulled on his boots and although he had said all the right things the first little niggling doubts about his intentions began to creep into her head. She'd noticed that over the last couple of weeks his visits to the club hadn't been quite so frequent and he'd been too busy to see her during the day too, although his reasons for not doing so had always seemed very valid.

'Surely you're not leaving yet?' she questioned him. 'It's barely ten o'clock.'

'I know and I apologise for having to dash off but I have to be up early in the morning to accompany my mother to France. Unfortunately, we've had word that my grandfather has taken ill; I might be away for a couple of weeks or so depending on how he is. I'm so sorry to drop it on you like this but I wanted to come and explain.'

'Oh, I see . . . I'm sorry about your grandfather.' Abi was feeling devastated. He was the first person she thought of every morning and the last before going to sleep each night so every day she didn't see him now felt like a year. How was she going to cope with him being away for weeks? she wondered.

He came over to kiss her and she clung to him like a limpet.

'I'll be back as soon as I can,' he promised as he eventually put her from him. 'You look after yourself. Goodbye.' He left without a backward glance, heading off down the stairs and back into the club again for a last game of poker with Jasper and his friends before he left.

Once he'd gone Abi got dressed and went back to the club too. If she didn't show her face early in the evening she would be in Lilly's bad books.

Lilly was at the bar when she entered the smoky room, and raising her eyebrow she nodded towards some of the customers who were sitting alone. And so with a sigh Abi approached one of them. He was a middle-aged gentleman with a red face and the most enormous moustache she'd ever seen. She batted her eyes at him and before long she had him eating out of the palm of her hand, although she constantly glanced towards Hugo who was seemingly unaware of her.

Eventually he rose from the card table. He had lost a lot of money again and knowing that he would have to go cap in hand to his mother for yet another handout he wasn't in the best of moods, so he didn't even acknowledge Abi as he walked out, leaving her feeling thoroughly miserable.

'Lover boy disappeared early, didn't he?' Bella commented when the last of the customers had finally left in the early hours of the morning. Then seeing the sad look on Abi's face, she patted her arm. 'You are taking precautions like I showed you, aren't you, queen?'

It was more than obvious that Abi had succumbed to the young lord's advances and Bella felt sorry for her, knowing Hugo as she did. He'd bedded almost every girl in the club since she'd been working there and had soon tired of them once he'd had what he wanted from them. It was no use telling Abi that, though. She knew love was blind and she had the terrible feeling that Abi was going to get her heart broken.

Abi blushed. 'Yes . . . of course I am, and he left early because he has to go away for a while. His grandfather is very ill,' she answered, although the first part wasn't absolutely true. She knew that if she should fall for a child Hugo would marry her earlier than they planned so what did it matter if she didn't take precautions?

'Good, but just, er . . . be careful, eh?' Bella liked the girl despite her hoity-toity ways. She'd clearly come from a good background and was nowhere near as streetwise as many of the girls that worked there, which meant she was as green as grass when it came to men and their needs. They parted at the top of the stairs and once in her room, Abi lifted the pillow that Hugo had lain on and breathed in the scent of him as tears slid down her cheeks. He loved her, she was sure of it, and although she dreaded the time they would be apart, she was confident he would come back to her as soon as his grandfather started to recover. *So why am I so worried?* she asked herself.

As Emmy yawned and stretched on the following Sunday morning, she smiled. Jake was coming to pick her up early today and they were going to take a picnic to the park. Hopping out of bed she smiled again when she saw the sun already shining and after slipping into her robe, she hurried along the landing to check on her aunt. She had been slightly better over the last few days but had decided that this year she wouldn't be going to her house at the coast.

'I can't be bothered to make the journey,' she had told Emmy, but deep down Emmy knew that it was because she didn't feel well enough – not that the stubborn devil would ever have admitted it. Emmy had noticed that her aunt's speech was beginning to be affected now and her hands sometimes shook uncontrollably to the point that she had dropped more than one cup of tea all down herself. It was a worry, but today Emmy was determined that everything would be perfect, so after looking in on her aunt who insisted she was 'as right as ninepence' she set off for the kitchen where Cook was preparing a hamper for her.

Emmy grinned as she peeked inside. 'There are only two of us going,' she told the cook. 'But there's enough to feed an army in here!' There was a freshly baked loaf sliced and buttered, fresh ham, cheese, pickles, pork pie and boiled eggs – and the dear woman hadn't even started to put the sweet things in as yet.

'Ah, but you're both young an' when you're out in the fresh air you'll soon build up your appetite,' Cook told her as she began to butter some freshly baked scones.

Emmy left her to it and hurrying back upstairs she took one of her favourite summer gowns out of the wardrobe. It was a pale-cream muslin sprigged with forget-me-nots and to go with it she chose a bonnet with ribbons in the same colour as the dress. Eventually she was washed and changed, but before going downstairs to wait for Jake she went in to say goodbye to her aunt.

'I reckon I might get Aggie to help me dress and go downstairs for a while today,' she told her niece.

Emmy instantly felt guilty. That was her job and here she was about to go out and leave her to it. She said as much but Imogen waved her comments aside.

'Rubbish, you know the old saying, don't you? All work and no play makes Jack a dull boy, that's why I always insist that Aggie should have each Saturday off, and you don't go out enough as it is, so get yourself off. Me and Aggie will be just fine.' She shooed her out of the room impatiently, so somewhat reluctantly Emmy went downstairs to wait for Jake.

He arrived exactly on time in the brougham that he had recently acquired. It was a small carriage with room for only two people with a hood that could be put up if it was raining, and as it only needed one horse to pull it, it was ideal for his house calls to the sick. There was usually some small boy about who would be happy to earn a penny and look after the horse while he visited those that were ill, and when he was wasn't working, the horse was stabled close to Jake's lodging house. He had finished sitting his exams now and while he waited anxiously for his results, he was working for a doctor to learn the practical side of medicine and diagnosing illnesses. But as Emmy lugged the heavy hamper outside to greet him, she noticed that his expression was grim.

'Is anything wrong?' she asked as he removed his hat.

'I'm afraid there is. I've been visiting a family down near the docks who are really ill. The father's been out of work for some time since an accident at work and they're almost starving. Now the children have come down with measles. The youngest, who was just a baby, died two days ago, and I fear the remaining three little ones could go the same way. They can't even afford to eat let alone pay for doctors' visits so I've been going to see them all week after my official hours are over. I know I promised we'd have a picnic today, Emmy, but would you mind very much if we put it off until next week? I've just bought some bread and cheese for them and my conscience won't let me rest if I don't go to check on them today.'

Emmy was horrified. 'Of course you must go to them,' she told him without hesitation. 'But I'm coming with you. There's far more food in this hamper than you and I could ever have eaten and from what you say they'll be glad of it.'

He shook his head looking concerned. 'That's really kind of you but I'm afraid it's not a place I'd care to take you. I never even realised such slums existed until I began to visit these places. The poor devils don't stand a chance, although the O'Flanagans do their best to keep their rooms clean.

The mother goes out doing whatever job she can get from morning till night to try to pay the rent and keep them, but she's so frail now. I dread to think what would happen to the family if anything should happen to her. No doubt they'll all end up in the workhouse.'

Emmy's chin rose as she stared at him defiantly with her hands on her hips. 'And what makes you think that I couldn't help?' she snapped. 'It sounds to me like the poor woman needs whatever help she can get. So just get this hamper into the carriage and let's be on our way.'

'But what if you should catch it?' His voice was fearful but she'd made her mind up and, as he was to discover, she could be as stubborn as their aunt when she wanted to be.

'I could say the same about you,' she pointed out as he took the hamper from her. 'So are you going to stand there arguing all day or are we going to get on our way?'

Somewhat reluctantly he stowed the hamper behind the seat then helped her up to sit beside him and minutes later they were on their way.

'So where exactly do they live?' she asked as they rattled along.

'In Whitechapel, but be warned it's, er . . .' Knowing how Emmy had been brought up he couldn't quite find the right words to describe just how bad the living conditions she was about to see were.

'Oh, stop worrying, I'm not a delicate china ornament,' she scolded and they drove on in silence.

As they entered the dark alleys that led to the O'Flanagans' home, Emmy was appalled when a rat bigger than some of the cats she had seen ran out in front of the horse. Hollow-eyed, barefoot children dressed in little more than rags played listlessly in the dusty gutters and the smell of open sewers was so overpowering that it was all Emmy could do to stop herself gagging. No sun shone here and moss and soot coated every wall. After passing through a labyrinth of alleys, they came out into a small square surrounded on all sides by tall terraced houses.

'Which one do the O'Flanagans live in?' she questioned.

He gave a wry smile. 'If only they were that lucky. All these houses are shared. Some families of ten share just two rooms.' He had drawn the horse to a stop and was putting a nosebag on him when a little boy approached. He was so thin that he was almost skeletal and his eyes were sunk deep into his grey face.

'Ah, Tommy, I was hoping you'd be here. Come to look after Daisy again for me, have you?' When the child nodded, Jake ruffled his hair sending a flurry of head lice scuttling across his parting. 'Good lad, you know the routine by now. Take good care of her and there'll be a shiny penny in it for you when I come out.'

'Right y'are, mister,' the child muttered as he took the reins and tenderly stroked Daisy's shining mane. Jake then lifted out the hamper and helped Emmy down.

She looked incongruously out of place in such poor surroundings but it didn't seem to bother her as she squared her shoulders and asked, 'So, where do they live?'

'In this house here.' Jake led her through a door that was barely hanging on its hinges and into a long hallway with a number of doors leading off. The smell of boiled cabbage, stale urine and something that she couldn't and didn't want

221

to identify, assailed her and suddenly the sound of babies crying, children squabbling and adults shouting seemed to be coming at them from every direction.

'They're on the third floor,' Jake told her solemnly. As they climbed the bare wooden stairs, Emmy had to blink back tears. On every landing sat dirty children so lethargic they barely had the strength to move.

At last he stopped at one door and rapped on it. It was answered some seconds later by a little girl who looked to be about six or seven. Her face was covered in a sore-looking rash and she blinked in the light struggling through the grimy window on the landing.

'Hello, Kathleen, I've come to see how you all are. Is your mammy in?'

'Sure she is, doctor,' the child answered in a soft Irish accent. 'Will you be comin' in now?'

He smiled as he entered a small room that seemed to be full of people and beds. The largest bed was set beneath the only window and on it lay a pale-faced man. He was dressed in a shirt and a pair of trousers but Emmy noticed that one of the trouser legs was pinned above the knee and she instantly felt sorry for him. He must have lost part of his leg in the accident that Jake had told her about, poor thing. In a chair by the empty grate a woman sat with a child on her lap and she gave the doctor a weak smile as he introduced Emmy.

'This is my dear cousin, Miss Emerald Winter. She wanted to come along today to see if there was anything she could do to help you.'

'You're very welcome, Miss Winter,' the man said politely as he inclined his head.

'Oh, and we've brought you this.' Jake laid the hamper on the scrubbed table that stood to the other side of the room and when he opened it the children's eyes grew round with longing, although the man of the house frowned.

'It's right good of you to think of us, doctor, but we ain't quite charity cases yet,' he muttered, feeling deeply ashamed of the plight they found themselves in.

'Oh, but it isn't charity, Mr O'Flanagan, sir,' Emmy quickly stepped in to assure him. 'Jake here and myself were going on a picnic today but we changed our mind and if you don't accept it, it will all be wasted.'

By now the remaining two children had sidled up to the table to peep inside and at the sight of the contents they gasped with delight. Like the little girl that had admitted them, they too were covered in a measles rash and their eyes were feverishly bright.

'Ah well . . . in that case, thank you kindly,' the man said, watching his children eye the food hungrily.

'Aye, thank you, doctor, miss,' chorused his wife. She was a small, dainty woman with a shock of red hair but she looked tired and worn from the hard life she'd led.

'Perhaps the children would like a little bread and cheese now?' Emmy suggested. 'If you could show me where the plates and the knives are, I can cut them some.'

Without waiting for an answer, the middle child, a boy who Emmy learnt was Finn, scampered away to get them and minutes later he, Kathleen and Niamh, the youngest child, were tucking into their feast as if they hadn't eaten properly for a month while Emmy served their parents with a generous slice of Cook's pork pie. They washed the food down with ginger beer and once they'd all eaten their fill, Emmy carefully wrapped the rest of the food and placed it in a cupboard for them for later while Jake examined his patients. At least she had the satisfaction of knowing that they would not go hungry that day.

'What a lovely family,' Emmy commented shortly after when she and Jake drove away after Jake had given little Tommy his precious penny. 'And how sad to see them having to live like that. After seeing the state of the rest of the house I didn't know what to expect but I was pleasantly surprised to see how clean the children and their rooms were.'

Jake nodded and sighed. 'I know. It breaks my heart to see anyone having to live in those conditions. They came from Ireland for a better life and I think they might have found it if Mr O'Flanagan hadn't had his accident. Goodness knows what will happen to them now. His job prospects are sorely limited with only one leg and his wife will work herself into the ground the way she's going on. It almost broke her when the baby died last week but her milk had dried up and he was so weak that he had nothing to fight the measles with, poor little chap. I heard they had to give the undertaker a penny to put him in with the next corpse they bury because they couldn't afford to give him a proper funeral. Poor souls will never even know where he is laid to rest, but at least they'll have the satisfaction of knowing he's buried in hallowed ground. But I was pleased to find the other three children all slightly better today. Thank you for giving them the food, Emmy.'

'Oh, you don't have to thank me,' she said distractedly, her mind still back with the family in their cramped little rooms. There had hardly been space to swing a cat and she had no idea how they managed. 'I left them half a crown with the rest of the food,' she admitted. 'I saw how proud they were so it was no use offering it to them but hopefully that will feed them for another few days when they find it. And I just wish there was more I could do for them.'

'Yes, they're a nice family,' Jake agreed. Then hoping to lighten the mood a little he glanced at her and asked, 'Now, how about we go for a stroll around the park and then I'll take you for tea and a bun seeing as you've given all our dinner away?'

'That sound like a very good idea,' she consented as they came out of the alleyways into the sunshine, but it was hard to banish the poverty she had just witnessed from her mind.

Chapter Twenty-Five

'Come on, queen, put a smile on yer face!' Lilly said as Abi came down the stairs a few evenings later. 'You've been mopin' about the place like a wet weekend, what's up wi' yer?'

'Nothing!' Abi said irritably as she strode past her into the club.

'What's wrong wi' 'er then?' Lilly asked Bella, who was close by.

Bella sighed. 'It's that bloody Hugo Medville,' she answered. 'He told her he had to go and visit his sick grandpa but between you and me I saw him and her cousin Jasper out and about with their little gang of mates yesterday. They were just coming out of a gambling den.'

'Oh dear, an' the girl's struck wi' him an' all,' Lilly said worriedly. 'But she'll 'ave to get over it. She's no good to me if she can't plaster a smile on 'er face fer the customers. Keep yer eye on 'er for me, would yer, queen?' She tutted as she moved off to speak to one of the other girls.

Bella bit her lip. *Poor little cow*, she thought as she slowly made her way into the club. *She's fallen for the two-timing bastard hook, line and sinker and I've a horrible feeling it's all going to end in tears.* She saw a gentleman smile at her and plastered a smile on her face as she hurried over to keep him company, forgetting all about Abi. As she had learnt, the show must go on.

It was a few days later before Jasper showed his face at the club again, and the second she saw him, Abi's face lit up, only to fall again when she realised that Hugo wasn't with him.

'Have you had any word from Hugo?' she asked eagerly as she drew her cousin to one side.

He shook his head sympathetically. 'Not as yet, no.' He could have told her that he hadn't seen him for days and that if the rumours that were circulating were true, his parents had finally put their foot down with him when faced with yet more of his gambling bills. He gave her a cheerful smile. 'He'll be back before you know it,' he told her instead. 'But how is Emerald? I thought I might call on her and our aunt tomorrow. Do you fancy coming with me?'

Abi's first reaction was to refuse but then as she thought of yet another day sitting in her room pining for Hugo, she had a change of heart.

'I suppose I could do,' she answered hesitantly, although she didn't sound too enthusiastic. 'Do you want to call for me?'

'Yes, I'll pick you up about one o'clock after lunch,' he promised and with a wink he went off to the card tables, hoping to win for a change, leaving Abi to go and entertain a red-faced elderly man who had hands like an octopus.

The next day Jasper arrived late as usual but Abi didn't say anything, she knew how unreliable he was. She actually didn't mind him being late today as she hadn't felt too well that morning, although she was fine now.

'So, what's Aunt Imogen like?' she asked Jasper as the horse pulling the cab trotted along weaving its way amongst the traffic.

Jasper chuckled as he straightened his immaculate cravat. 'Oh, I think you'll like her. I imagine she was a beauty in her day although from what I've gathered she's a bit of a recluse since her husband died, and she's quite poorly of course.'

'Hm, and why have you taken such an interest in her all of a sudden?' Knowing her cousin as she did, Abi was suspicious of his motives. From hearing the other girls talk, she had more than an inkling that Jasper would have been paid for introducing her to Lilly, which made her wonder why he was suddenly so keen to visit an aunt he had only recently discovered he had. Could it be that he was after her money?

Avoiding her eyes, Jasper shrugged. He could hardly admit that he only went because Emmy was there. 'I suppose I just find her amusing. You'll see what I mean when you meet her. She's very, er . . . shall we say, flamboyant? And that would be putting it mildly.'

Eventually they pulled up outside the house and after paying the driver Jasper knocked on the door.

Aggie admitted them, saying, 'The missus is up today so you're in luck. She's been abed poorly fer the last few days but I'll go through an' ask her an Miss Emmy if she's up to visitors.'

As she disappeared along the hallway, Abi stared around her in amazement at the silk wall coverings and the gilt-legged furniture and picture frames.

'I see what you mean about her being flamboyant,' she whispered to Jasper.

'Oh, if you think this is fancy wait till you actually meet *her*,' he warned with an amused chuckle. 'To say she's larger than life would be putting it mildly.'

Aggie soon returned and led them to the drawing room. When they entered, they instantly spotted Imogen sitting in a large velvet wing chair to the side of the fireplace.

She raised an eyebrow as she looked at Jasper. 'And to what do we owe the honour of this visit, young man?' She was dressed today in a yellow velvet gown that was covered from top to bottom in frills and furbelows and her pale face was heavily rouged, giving her the appearance of a fragile china doll.

'Why, Aunt, I could almost think you're not pleased to see me,' Jasper answered. 'But if you must know, your other niece wished to meet you.' He took Abi's elbow and led her forward.

'Hm, so you're Abigail!' Her aunt eyed her up and down, liking what she saw. In fact, Abi reminded her very much of herself when she was younger. She wasn't as tall as Emmy and was more curvaceous, but she was definitely the prettier of the two, Imogen decided.

'How do you do, Aunt Imogen.' Abi bobbed her knee and seeing the mischievous twinkle in the girl's eye, Imogen liked her even more. If she wasn't very much mistaken this young lady had spirit and she liked that.

'Come and sit down and let me get a better look at you. You're making the room look untidy,' Imogen barked, but rather than jumping to do as she was told, Abi casually strolled to the chair opposite and took a seat.

'And where is Emmy?' Jasper asked.

'I sent her to the kitchen to get me a cool drink. Why don't you go and hurry her up?'

Only too happy to oblige, Jasper shot off and once they were alone Imogen, said, 'Emerald tells me you're working at the Black Cat club in Soho? Are you enjoying it?'

'Oh yes, very much.' Abi's head bobbed setting the feathers on her hat dancing. 'I love being a hostess.'

Imogen glanced at the portrait of herself suspended above the mantelpiece and sighed. 'That's how I started out,' she admitted. 'But I went on to become a songbird, the darling of the music halls. That's where I met my beloved Marcel.' Even now, so many years after his death, just the thought of him could still make her eyes well with tears, but she blinked them away as she turned her attention back to her niece. 'And have you met anyone nice as yet?'

Abi blushed prettily. 'I have as it happens,' she confided.

'Hm, in that case I hope he's wealthy,' Imogen said shortly. 'It's all very well all these do-gooders saying money can't buy you happiness but there must be nothing worse than being poor and struggling, so choose wisely. You're still very young and have all your life ahead of you.'

'Oh, I have chosen wisely and he is wealthy. In fact, he's a lord.' Abi's eyes were shining.

'Is he now. And does he feel the same about you?'

Just for a second Abi's smile slipped. 'I'm sure he does . . . although he's had to go away for a while because his grandfather is very ill.'

Their conversation was interrupted when Jasper and Emmy entered the room. Emmy was carrying a tray full of glasses and a jug of home-made lemonade and Abi noticed the way Jasper's eyes followed her sister's every move. It was almost as if . . . Abi gave a little shake of her head. *No, of course he couldn't be looking at her that way*, she told herself. They were cousins! And Jasper would never risk getting cut out of his father's will for Emmy, surely? But Imogen was speaking to her again so she quickly turned her attention back to her as Emmy poured them all a long cool drink.

'What did you think of the old dear?' Jasper asked when they left over an hour later.

'I liked her.' Abi chuckled. 'As you said, she's quite a character, isn't she? I'd love to have met her before she was ill. I imagine she must have been really beautiful when she was younger. And Emmy looks well too, doesn't she?' she said innocently, watching for his reaction. 'I believe she sees rather a lot of Jake since working for Aunt Imogen. I know she sees him every Sunday at least.'

Jasper obviously wasn't too thrilled to hear this if his frown was anything to go by. 'Perhaps we all ought to meet up and see a bit more of each other on Sundays,' he suggested.

Abi shook her head. 'I shan't be able to, not once Hugo is back. I've no doubt he'll want me to spend my day off with him,' she said with a dreamy look on her face.

Jasper looked away, feeling guilty. He could hardly tell her that Hugo was tiring of her now that he had had what he wanted from her, could he? Or that he was in terrible trouble with his parents because of the huge gambling debts he had run up.

When Abi entered the house at the back of the club a short time later, she saw Maria coming down the stairs yawning. She was still in a flimsy negligee and her hair was in disarray as she had slept the day away after spending most of the night with an ardent customer.

'Been somewhere nice, 'ave you?' she asked Abi, stifling another yawn with her hand.

'I've been to see my aunt,' Abi informed her as she removed her bonnet.

'Oh, right . . . I thought p'raps lover boy 'ad come back an' taken you out.' Everyone who worked at the club was aware of Abi's infatuation with the young lord.

'No such luck,' Abi sighed and Maria felt sorry for her. The poor little cow had no idea what a cad Lord Hugo Medville was. It wasn't so very long ago that he had bedded her.

'Why don't yer come into the kitchen an' we'll 'ave us a nice cup o' tea,' Maria suggested and as she had nothing better to do until it was time to get ready to go into the club, Abi followed her.

'Look . . .' Maria said tentatively after a while seeing as they had the kitchen to themselves. 'I don't want to interfere but . . . Well, I wouldn't get too involved wi' young Hugo, if I were you.'

Abi was instantly on the defensive as she glared at her. 'And why not, may I ask? Hugo and I are in love. He's going to introduce me to his parents when he gets back from visiting his grandfather.'

Maria stared down into the steaming cup in front of her before trying again. 'I'm sure he told you that but yer know, yer both very young an' young men tend to flit from one girl to another. I've seen it 'appen time an' time again since I've worked 'ere. How do yer think I ended up wi' me belly full, eh? But soon as I got wi' child, I didn't see 'im for dust.'

'But my Hugo isn't like that!' Abi said defensively.

Maria realised that she was wasting her breath. 'Ah well, at least him bein' away made time fer you to go an' see yer aunt,' she said cheerily, happy to change the subject.

'Yes, although I thought for a time I wouldn't be able to earlier on. I felt really ill when I first got up. I hope I'm not coming down with something.'

'In what way ill?' Maria asked with an uneasy feeling in the pit of her stomach.

'Just sick,' Abi told her and it was all Maria could do not to voice her fears.

'Happen if yer feel the same tomorrer yer should have a word wi' Lilly an' she can get the doctor in to check you over?' she suggested.

Abi laughed as she rose from her chair and snatched her bag up. 'Oh, I'm sure it will be nothing. But now I think I'll go and have a bit of a rest till it's time to get ready for work.' And she tripped away leaving Maria with her thoughts.

Thankfully the club wasn't so busy that night and Abi was able to go to her room shortly after midnight, which was early compared to most nights. She slept like a log but woke the next morning feeling sick again, so sick that she only just managed to make it to her chamber pot before she was violently ill. Her breasts felt tender too and she wondered if she was due to have her course, before realising that she should have had it over two weeks ago.

It's probably late because I've been upset about Hugo being away, she thought. But an hour later, after resting on the bed for a while, she felt as bright as a button again and forgot all about it.

Chapter Twenty-Six

'It's a shame that we couldn't go to the 'ouse at the coast this year, ain't it?' Aggie said glumly the following week when Emmy went into the kitchen to fetch her aunt her mid-morning drink.

'I hardly think my aunt was up to the journey,' Emmy pointed out, but she had no time to say more because at that moment there was a rap on the front door and after quickly removing her apron Aggie hurried away to open it.

She came back smiling broadly to announce, 'There's a lady 'ere, Miss Emmy. She says she's your ma.'

Emmy was so shocked that she almost dropped the tray she'd prepared and slamming it on to the table she hurried into the hallway, much to Cook's and Aggie's amusement.

'Mama!' Emmy gaped at her mother. 'What a lovely surprise. You should have told us you were coming.'

'Why? I am family and allowed to visit, aren't I? Even if I haven't seen my sister for decades.'

'Yes, of course you are.' Taking her elbow, Emmy almost hauled her along the hallway. 'I'm so pleased to see you,' she gabbled. 'And I'm sure Aunt Imogen will be too.'

'Hm, well that remains to be seen,' Dorcas said stoutly as she removed her bonnet. 'But I have to say you are looking well. And have you seen anything of Abi?'

Emmy shook her head feeling guilty at the lie. She still hadn't given her mother Abi's address for fear she might turn up at the club. She could only imagine how horrified she would be if she was to see where she was living, but luckily Abi had written to her so at least Dorcas knew she was all right.

'You're just in time for morning coffee. Will you be staying?' Emmy asked eagerly. Her mother looked well.

'That all depends on whether I'm welcome or not.' Dorcas nodded towards the small carpet bag she had packed just in case. 'Let's see what sort of reception I get before I decide, shall we? But now, where is that sister of mine?'

'She's in there.' Emmy led her to the drawing room door. 'You go in and have a few moments alone with her while I go and get an extra cup. But I'd best warn you, she might not be the same as you remember her. She's very shaky today, so much so that I'm having to hold her cup for her while she drinks. I don't mind telling you she absolutely hates it! She's so independent, but I'm sure seeing you will perk her up.' And while Dorcas stood composing herself ready to go in to her long-lost sister, Emmy scooted back to the kitchen.

'Have I to get the spare guest room ready fer yer ma?' Aggie asked.

'I'm not sure yet,' Emmy told her as she bustled about adding extra biscuits and another cup and saucer to the tray. 'But we should know soon enough. I'm just giving them a bit of time alone as they haven't seen each other for years and I don't want to intrude.' She began to watch the clock but every minute seemed like an hour and eventually she made fresh coffee and lifted the tray. 'Well, they've had fifteen minutes to break the ice. If I know my aunt and my mother, they'll either be the best of friends or at each other's throats by now. I'm going in.' She took a deep breath and sailed along the hallway. Outside the drawing room door, she stopped to listen and not hearing raised voices she took it as a good sign and went in.

Her mother and aunt were sitting either side of the fireplace in the wing chairs and chatting animatedly.

'I was just telling your mother what a good help you've been to me but that I worry you don't get out and about enough, and even when you do it's always with Jake.'

'Jake and I have a lot in common and we get on well,' Emmy told her as she handed them both their coffee, but Imogen's hand shook so much that she had to take it off her almost immediately and place it back on the tray. She was clearly embarrassed about it and when Emmy lifted it towards her lips she waved it away.

'I'm not very thirsty. Just leave it on there for now,' she said irritably, then she turned her attention back to her sister and asked bluntly, 'So, you've fallen on hard times. All Gerald's fault, was it?'

For the first time in her life Emmy saw her mother look flustered as she replied quietly, 'I . . . I thought so at first and I don't mind admitting I hated him for bringing us all down but now . . . Well, I suppose I should have listened when he tried to tell me that the business was in trouble. Instead, I went on demanding.'

'Hm, even as a child you were demanding. Because you were the youngest you were spoilt,' Imogen commented unsympathetically, but it didn't seem to offend Dorcas.

'I suppose I was, but I had such high hopes for my girls.' There were tears in Dorcas's eyes as she glanced towards Emmy. 'I dreamt of them making good marriages to men who could keep them in comfort for the rest of their lives. But now . . .'

'But now they're making their own way in life and if and when they do marry it will be for love, be their choice a beggar or a king. I know I would have married my Marcel if he hadn't had a penny to his name.' Now it was Imogen who had to blink back tears but after pulling herself together she went on, 'As it happens I have more money than I know what to do with so if you need some I—'

'*No!* Thank you, but I'm managing very well,' Dorcas said proudly. 'In fact, I'm quite enjoying some aspects of my new life. For instance, when we lived in Astley House, I don't think I ever ventured into the garden apart from to show it off to visitors, but now I'm actually growing my own vegetables and my maid Hetty is teaching me to make jam from the fruit in the orchard and all manner of things. I'm getting quite good at making bread and pastry too, although I have to admit it isn't as good as Hetty's yet. I just wish . . .' Her voice trailed away for a moment until she said softly, 'I just wish I could have the chance to tell Gerald that I'm sorry.'

With a lump in her throat, Emmy slipped away to leave the two sisters to speak in private and once in the hallway she beckoned to Aggie. 'Would you mind preparing the guest room for my mother, please? I think she'll be staying for this evening at least, and I'll tell Cook that there'll be one extra for dinner.'

She could hardly believe the change in her mother and for the first time in her life she was proud of her.

Over dinner that evening Imogen surprised Emmy when she said, 'I've been thinking about that family you told me about, the O'Flanagans. I thought that perhaps on Sunday you might take them another hamper. I'll have a word with Cook. Of course, I realise that they're only one family out of hundreds who are in that dire position and I've had an idea I'd like to speak to Jake about, if you'd ask him to call in and see me.'

Emmy nodded; she was intrigued but didn't like to pursue it and so the rest of the meal was spent with the two sisters catching up on their lives. It had taken very little persuasion to get Dorcas to agree to stay for the night and seeing how much the two women were enjoying each other's company, Emmy retired early to leave them to chat.

Her mother was already downstairs when Emmy went to prepare a tray for her aunt the next morning and Dorcas greeted her warmly, something she had never done before. She had never made a secret of the fact that Abi was the favourite but now she said quietly, 'I realise that I haven't always behaved as I should towards you, my dear, and I'm sorry. But hopefully now I can put things right. I've finally realised that there are more important things in life than mere personal possessions.' She gave a hollow laugh. 'I've also realised that when the odds were stacked against us the people who I thought were my friends turned their backs on me. So please, come home and see me when you are able to, I have a lot of making up to do, and when you see Abi tell her the same. I don't suppose I can get you to change your mind and tell me where she is so that I can go and see her before I catch the train, can I?'

Emmy shook her head as she held her mother's hand. 'I can't do that because I promised I wouldn't. But I will get her to write to you again,' she promised. 'But you're not leaving already, are you? I'm sure Hetty is capable of looking after the cottage.'

Dorcas chuckled. 'Oh, she's more capable than me, to be honest, but I did say I wouldn't be gone for long. My life is there now and I intend to make the best of it.'

'And how are Uncle Bernard and Aunt Sybil?'

Her mother shrugged and gave a wry smile. 'Oh, the same as always. I don't see Bernard but Sybil still pops in to let me know how lucky I am that they helped us. In truth, she's right and do you know, I almost feel sorry for her now. I've only just realised that she's actually a very unhappy, lonely woman. Both of the boys are here in London and I don't think she and Bernard have ever been that happy together. But there we are. It's none of my business, so I just try to be polite. Shall we go into breakfast? And then I really must be on my way.'

'She's changed – and for the better from what I remember of her,' Imogen told Emmy when her mother had left. 'I reckon if your father would only go home now, they might make a go of things.'

'I agree,' Emmy told her as she passed her aunt the newspaper. 'The trouble is none of us have the faintest idea where he is.' She started to sort out what clothes her aunt would wear that day. Imogen had insisted the day before that she felt well enough to have her spiritualist friends round for a get-together that evening, and so Emmy would have plenty to do getting things ready for their arrival.

They began to arrive shortly after six that evening and Emmy showed them in while Aggie rushed about getting drinks for them. Lady Medville was the third to arrive and she looked down her nose at Emmy as she handed her her coat and commented, 'I wasn't aware that Imogen had employed a new maid.'

'She hasn't, ma'am. I am her niece.'

The woman sniffed and sailed past her as Emmy went to answer the door to yet another guest.

Soon they were all chattering like magpies and as Emmy passed the drawing room door, she heard Lady Medville say, 'Yes, it's been brought to my attention that Hugo has been associating with a little slut from a gentleman's club. It was the final straw, I don't mind telling you. I love my son dearly but he's been going off the rails badly lately and so his father and I have decided to send him to France to stay with his grandparents and work in one of our businesses for a few months. At least it will get him away from the terrible people he's fallen in with.'

As Emmy moved on to the kitchen she frowned. Hugo? She seemed to recall that was the name of the young man Abi had been seeing. And hadn't she said that he was the son of a lord? A cold finger ran down her spine. If this was

Abi's Hugo, she would be heartbroken when he was sent away. She decided that she would go and see her just as soon as it was possible.

The opportunity came sooner than she expected when her aunt told her irritably the following afternoon, 'Why don't you go out for a couple of hours and get some fresh air. You've been clucking around me like a mother hen all day and I want to get some rest!' She had clearly overtired herself the night before and was obviously not feeling at all well, although Emmy knew that she would have died rather than admit it.

'Are you quite sure you'll be all right?' She felt guilty leaving her and yet this would be the ideal opportunity to go and see Abi.

'Of course I will. Aggie will still be here if I need anything, won't she?' Imogen snapped.

Emmy was concerned to see the bluish tinge about her aunt's lips. She was sure it hadn't been there the day before and would have liked to send for the doctor, but knowing her aunt it would only get her into trouble.

'Very well, but I shan't be gone long. I might pop over to see Abi.'

At that her aunt smiled. She and Abi had got on like a house on fire but then that was no surprise to Emmy. Abi had always been able to charm the birds from the trees and Emmy was used to walking in her shadow. 'A girl after my own heart, she is,' Imogen said approvingly. 'She's not afraid to do and say what she wants and damn the consequences. I think she must take after me.'

Emmy smiled and after checking that her aunt had all she needed she set off for Soho.

The club looked just as depressing from the outside as Emmy remembered but she walked quickly past it and entered the stinking alley that led to the girls' living quarters. She found Winnie, the young maid, mopping the black and white tiles on the floor in the hallway and after asking if Abi was in, Winnie obligingly went to see.

'She is, miss,' she told Emmy breathlessly when she returned. 'An' she said I've to take yer up to 'er. She's in 'er room an' I don't think she's feelin' too grand.'

She obligingly led Emmy upstairs and after pointing to Abi's bedroom door she scooted away to get on with her jobs. Emmy was shocked when she entered the room. Abi was lying on the bed on black silk sheets and the room was very garishly decorated.

'Winnie told me it would be you,' Abi greeted her as she heaved herself up on to her elbows looking very fragile and pale. There was a terrible smell and glancing around Emmy was concerned to see that Abi had vomited into the chamber pot.

Striding across to the window, she threw it open but that only seemed to make things worse as the city smells and the sounds of the traffic rushed in. 'How long have you been ill?'

'I'm not ill,' Abi said defensively. 'I think it's just the champagne I drank last night, that's all. It will pass in a minute. But why are you here?'

Emmy chuckled. 'That's a nice greeting, I must say! Do I have to have a reason to come and see my little sister?'

Abi bowed her head and Emmy saw then that she had been crying. 'Why don't you tell me what's wrong?' she encouraged gently and when Abi went to tell her that nothing was, she quickly held her hand up. 'Don't bother to deny it. I can read you like a book and I can see you've been crying, so out with it.'

'It's just . . .' Abi's lip trembled. 'It's just that Hugo has had to go away for a time to see his grandfather in France who is very ill and I feel so lost without him.'

Emmy's heart sank as she realised that she must have been right. The Hugo Abi was in love with must be Lady Medville's son. But if he *truly* loved Abi, why would he lie to her about going to see his sick grandfather, when as far as she knew the man was in perfectly good health? Hugo was being sent away in disgrace for his gambling debts and mixing with a club girl, who could only be her sister. But if she told Abi that now she knew that it would break her heart!

Chapter Twenty-Seven

To her surprise when Emmy returned to her aunt's home it was to find Jake sitting at the side of Imogen's bed chatting away to her.

'I didn't expect to see you today,' she said with a smile and he grinned.

'I've been given a half-day off, so I thought I'd come and see you both. In the next week or so, about mid-September, I should get my exam results hopefully.'

'Then let's hope you've passed them all. Anyway, it's a good job he did call, Emmy, because I've got a proposition to put to you both.' Imogen looked slightly better as Emmy pulled a chair up to sit beside Jake. 'The thing is . . . I've been thinking about that poor family you told me about, the O'Flanagans. Sadly, they're only one of dozens of families from the slums who can't afford medical care and it got me to thinking. How about if we hired a room somewhere and Jake could treat anyone who couldn't afford to pay on his day off for free? I know you're not a trained nurse, Emerald, but you could help out with the organising of it and I'd pay for the hire of the room and any medication you needed to use. What do you both think?'

Emmy's face was radiant. 'I think it's an absolutely brilliant idea and I'd be happy to help out in any way I can. But it's down to Jake, really. He's the doctor, or at least he will be if he's passed his exams.'

Jake's smile stretched from ear to ear as he stared at Imogen. 'Are you quite sure about this? It's a wonderful offer and I know it would make a huge difference to so many families.'

'I wouldn't have offered if I wasn't sure, would I?' Imogen barked. 'But you two would have to do all the hard work – finding a suitable room, etc.'

'Of course.' As he looked at Emmy, she saw the excitement in his eyes and it was as infectious as a smile.

'We could set up two surgeries: one in the morning and one in the afternoon,' she suggested.

'Yes, but first we'd have to find somewhere that would give us a waiting room and a surgery where I could carry out consultations and treatment. Oh, and we'd need some chairs and an examination couch, and that's just the beginning.'

Imogen shrugged. She'd said what she wanted to say and was tired again now. 'Why don't you two go down and put your heads together. Then tell me how much you'll need and I'll make sure that you get it.'

Emmy and Jake rose from their chairs and Jake looked at Imogen with admiration. 'This is a very kind thing that you're doing,' he said softly, but she waved the compliment aside.

'It's not, not really. It's something my Marcel always said he'd like to do, to help the poor, so I'll be doing it for him really.'

Jake inclined his head and taking Emmy's elbow, they hurried down into the drawing room where they began to talk excitedly.

'I think we should look for suitable premises somewhere in or near Whitechapel,' he said thoughtfully. 'If we go to somewhere too upmarket the poor won't want to come, they'll feel too uncomfortable. I could start to have a look around this afternoon . . . But listen to me chattering away – I'm sorry, Emmy, your aunt said you'd gone to see Abi, how is she?'

'Oh, she's, er . . . fine,' Emmy answered, although she had a terrible feeling that Abi wasn't. There had been something not right about her but as yet Emmy couldn't put her finger on what it was. She went on to tell him about her mother's visit and the change in her and then they went back to speaking of finding new premises for the venture they were to embark on. Barely able to wait to start, Jake left soon after to begin the search.

The next few days passed slowly and Emmy wondered how Abi was, and how Jake was doing in his search. At last, at the end of the week, he arrived one evening with a smile that lit up the room. 'I've passed my final exam! I heard today; I am now a fully qualified doctor.'

'Oh Jake, that's *wonderful*, well done and congratulations!' Emmy was genuinely thrilled for him. She knew how hard he had worked to achieve this, although Imogen wasn't quite so enthusiastic. She could see nothing glamorous in the career he had chosen but she supposed someone had to do it!

'It takes all sorts, although I have to say well done. It's a shame, though, with looks like yours you could have gone on the stage.'

Both Emmy and Jake laughed but he had yet more good news for them. 'I think I've found some suitable premises.'

'Really?' Emmy's eyes were shining.

'It's two downstairs rooms in a house in Whitechapel. They've just become available and although they're in a bit of a state at the moment I'm sure it's nothing that a bit of elbow grease and paint couldn't put right.' When he told Imogen how much they would cost she raised an eyebrow.

'That sounds very cheap. Couldn't you find somewhere a little more salubrious?'

'The people we are going to be treating are all from around that area and if we go somewhere too posh, they wouldn't come,' he pointed out.

'Hm, I suppose you have a point,' Imogen admitted. 'I'll have the money for the first month's rent ready for you tomorrow and I'll give you a little extra to buy the things you'll need to do the rooms up. How does that sound?'

'Excellent, thank you. This will mean so much to so many.' And to Imogen's huge embarrassment he leant over and planted a big kiss on her cheek making her blush furiously as she self-consciously pushed him away.

'Go on, you daft ha'p'orth!' She flapped her hand at him. 'Take Emerald to have a look at these rooms. She's got her head screwed on and if they're too bad she'll tell me.'

Emmy was only too happy to do as she was told, and soon after they hurried outside and flagged down a passing cab to take them to Whitechapel, as Jake hadn't come in his carriage that evening.

Her first sight of the gloomy rooms at the bottom of a tall tenement filled her with despair. The smell in them was appalling and Emmy pinched her nostrils together to stop herself gagging as they entered.

'You weren't joking when you said they needed a little cleaning, were you?' she said wryly as Jake lit a stub of candle he found on the windowsill. Then seeing the way his face fell she went on hurriedly, 'But of course it can be done. Perhaps we could persuade Jasper and Abi to come and help.'

Jake laughed aloud. 'I wouldn't hold my breath on that,' he answered. 'I can't really see either of them wanting to get their hands dirty, can you? One nice thing though, I called in to check on the O'Flanagans yesterday and Mrs O'Flanagan said she'd be happy to come along and help get the rooms ready. She said she'll bring some of her neighbours to muck in and then put the word about when we're ready to open.'

Emmy nodded with satisfaction, suddenly eager to get started, although as she looked around she realised they had an awful lot to do. The windows were so grimy both inside and out that they allowed hardly any light in and the floor was strewn with rubbish. Fingers of thick black mould snaked up the walls and out of the corner of her eye she saw a fat tail disappear into a hole in the skirting board and she shuddered. 'Right, I suggest tomorrow you start to get the limewash and all the cleaning things we'll need. I'll make you a list when we get back to the house and then we'll come early on Sunday and get stuck in, although we'll have to get rid of all this rubbish and give it a good clean out before we can do anything.'

'Yes, boss.' He grinned and gave her a mock salute.

She slapped his arm playfully. It was surprising how easy she felt in his company, she thought, and she couldn't wait to work with him, although she realised that he would be doing the lion's share. All she was going to be able to do was assist where she could.

The next few weeks passed in a blur as Jake and Emmy worked on the two rooms every spare minute they had, and at last at the end of September they were ready to do business.

The walls had been limewashed and fresh oilskin had been fitted on the floors.

One of Jake's professors had kindly given him an old examination table, and they had bought some mismatched chairs from second-hand shops and markets, which had been thoroughly scrubbed and were now neatly lined up in what was to be the waiting room. Jake had also managed to get hold of a couple of trolleys for holding bandages and suchlike and had also purchased a small stove for heating water – luckily there was already a sink in the corner of one room where Jake could wash his hands. Now, finally, they felt ready to open.

'I could put a sign in the window to let people know we're open for business and when,' Emmy suggested and he nodded in agreement. And so when they finally left that evening it was decided that they would officially open the doors the following Sunday.

'Just don't expect people to flock to you straightaway,' Imogen warned when Emmy told her about it. 'Even poor folk have pride and some of them would rather suffer than take charity.'

'Hm, I hadn't thought of that,' Emmy admitted. 'But surely they won't let their children suffer unnecessarily? I could buy some candy canes and liquorice sticks to encourage the children in, perhaps?'

'Not a bad idea,' Imogen agreed. 'But why don't you just hold on and see how it goes?'

Emmy nodded and stifled a yawn. She seemed to have had hardly a minute to herself for weeks and felt as if she could have slept for a month. Not that she minded; she'd enjoyed working side by side with Jake and seeing the filthy little rooms transformed, although they couldn't take all the credit because Mrs O'Flanagan had been true to her word and had turned up with some of her neighbours to help. The only thing Emmy was concerned about now was that she hadn't seen Abi for weeks, but she promised herself that just as soon as things settled down a bit, she would make a point of visiting. Feeling happier she went off to bed and was asleep almost as soon as her head hit the pillow.

Jake picked her up bright and early on Sunday morning and Emmy tripped out to climb into his carriage. She had chosen to dress in a very plain dove-grey gown with a large apron tied about her waist, and instead of one of her smart coats she had worn a warm woollen shawl.

'This is it then,' she said cheerfully as he helped her up on to the seat. 'I'm ready if you are, Dr Chetwynd.'

'I am indeed.' He climbed back into the driver's seat and they were on their way.

When they arrived at the rooms in Whitechapel, Jake went off to settle the horse in the stable of a nearby inn for the day. The weather was turning cold now and he didn't want to leave her tethered outside. If he were honest, he also realised that in this neighbourhood there was every chance old Daisy might not be there when they closed and he didn't want to risk losing her.

While he was gone, Emmy hurried inside to fill the kettle and place it on the small stove to boil, then she pottered about making sure everything was just right. Cook had made up a hamper of food for them to eat throughout the day, promising that she would have a hot meal ready for them that evening. She'd also added a small jug of milk, some twists of tea and some sugar so that they could have a hot drink. By the time Jake got back, Emmy had made them both a strong brew and had turned the 'Closed' sign on the window to 'Open'.

'All we can do now is wait for the first patient.' Jake looked slightly nervous as they sat on the chairs in the waiting room and Emmy gave his hand a squeeze.

'They'll come,' she said confidently, feeling proud of him. There weren't many young newly qualified doctors who would offer their services for free, she was sure. But as the minutes ticked away and the little surgery remained empty, she began to feel nervous. What if they had gone to all this work and effort for nothing?

At last, at almost eleven o'clock, there was a timid tap at the door, and smoothing her apron, Emmy hurried to open it.

''Scuse me, miss – is this where the doctor'll see you fer nowt?' A young woman clutching the hand of a grimy boy who looked to be about six or seven years of age was standing in the hallway. In her other arm was a tiny baby and she looked nervous.

'Yes ... yes, it is,' Emmy told her encouragingly. 'Do come in and I'll get the doctor to see you. What seems to be the problem?'

'It ain't me, it's young Perce 'ere.' The woman nodded towards the little boy who was hanging his head. ''E's gorra boil, see? Just 'ere, poor little bleeder. It ain't 'alf givin' 'im some gyp.' She pointed to the child's backside.

Nodding, Emmy took the child's hand and led him in to Jake, then returned to the waiting room to sit with his mother.

Half an hour later Jake appeared with an arm about the boy's thin shoulders. 'All done,' he told the woman. 'It was a nasty one and I'm afraid I had to lance it but he was very brave. So brave, in fact, that I think he deserves a little treat, don't you, Emmy?'

'I most certainly do.' Hurrying to the hamper Emmy took out a liquorice stick and handed it to the child, thrilled to see his face light up. The poor little chap clearly didn't get treats very often.

'I've dressed the wound,' Jake told his mother. 'But I would like to see him again next Sunday if you could pop him in, just to make sure it's healing. Meantime, try to keep it clean to avoid infection.'

'Fanks, doc.' The woman flushed as she opened her palm to reveal a penny. 'I'm afraid that's all I've got. Is this enuff?'

Jake shook his head and gave her a kindly smile. 'There's no charge, I assure you.'

'An' you really won't take this penny?' When he shook his head once more she quickly stuffed the coin back into her pocket as if she was afraid he might change his mind.

'Then fanks again, doc. Come on, Perce.' And with that they left, all with smiles on their faces as Jake washed his hands at the deep stone sink, which Emmy had scrubbed until she could almost see her face in it.

'Congratulations, Doctor Chetwynd,' she told him warmly. 'That was your very first patient and a lovely job you did, I have to say. The poor things; the woman clearly didn't have two pennies to rub together. I felt so sorry for her I made her a cup of tea while you were treating the little boy. It got me to thinking, perhaps if we could offer a hot drink as well as treatment, it might attract a few more in?'

'You really do come up with some wonderful ideas,' he praised.

Emmy placed her arms about him to give him a celebratory hug. And then time seemed to stand still as their eyes met. Slowly he lowered his head until their lips were only inches apart and Emmy held her breath in anticipation. But then Jake released her abruptly and quickly turned away. He so wanted to put his arms about her again and kiss her and thank her for all her help and hard work, but the harsh reality was she was his cousin and given their family situation, it wouldn't have been right. With a sigh he sat down to wait for his next patient, truly wishing she wasn't, while Emmy stood there feeling exactly the same and more shaken than she cared to admit.

Chapter Twenty-Eight

'Are you all right, queen?'

Abi glanced up from the chamber pot she was hanging over and stared crossly at Maria who had entered her room uninvited.

'Sorry, I know I shouldn't 'ave just barged in but I was passin' an' could 'ear yer bein' ill an' I were worried for yer,' Maria explained as she came further into the room, closing the door softly behind her.

Abi swiped the back of her hand across her mouth and leant up looking absolutely ghastly and Maria frowned with concern. 'Look . . . I know it ain't any o' my concern, but this 'as been goin' on fer a while now, ain't it?' she said tentatively and when Abi nodded miserably, she went on, 'Per'aps it's time yer went to see a doctor, although I reckon I've got a good idea what he's gonna tell yer. I reckon you 'ave an' all, ain't yer, queen?'

When Abi began to cry the girl crossed to her and put her arm about her shoulders.

'So 'ow many of yer courses 'ave yer missed now?'

'Two . . . at least. Possibly three.'

'Hm, don't yer think it's time you 'ad a word to 'is lordship?'

'I can't,' Abi told her, dabbing at her eyes. 'He still hasn't come back from France yet and I don't know when he will. He told me he wouldn't be gone long.'

'Then I reckon it's time you 'ad a word wi' that cousin o' yours an' got 'is London address,' Maria advised. 'You could go round there then. Just to check if 'e's home.'

Abi nodded. She knew that what Maria was saying made sense and prayed that Jasper would visit the club very soon.

Her prayers were answered that very night when at about nine o'clock Jasper and some of his pals strolled in. Forgetting all about the elderly gentleman who she had just encouraged to buy champagne, Abi shot off across the club like a greyhound, catching Jasper at the bar.

'Have you heard anything from Hugo yet?' she asked.

He grinned. 'That's a nice greeting I must say, and no I haven't as it happens,' he lied as the rest of his group wandered off to the card tables.

'Then I'm afraid I must ask you for his London address; I need to see him, or at least get in touch with him,' Abi told him forcefully.

Jasper ran his finger around the inside of his shirt collar as he asked, 'What for?'

'That's for me to know and you to find out. So unless you want me to cause a stink, I suggest you give me the address *right* now.'

As he looked into her flashing eyes Jasper's heart sank. Hugo would be none too pleased if he were to do as she asked, but then, as his parents had sent him to France, what did it matter? When Abi arrived at the house, the maid would probably simply tell her that he was not in the country and she'd have to go away with no harm done. That is unless she was . . . Jasper couldn't even let himself consider the possibility. It was he who had encouraged Abi to run away from home and he who had introduced her to the club, and all for nothing as things had turned out. As well as the money he'd got for introducing her to Lilly, he had hoped that with Abi out of the way he would have more time to get Emmy to himself by sending the sisters down different paths but it hadn't worked out that way, because Emmy had surprised him by moving here first, and despite following after her, he'd not managed to make any progress with her, thanks to his saintly brother. Today he'd received a letter from his father telling him he wanted him home and quickly, so it looked as if his little holiday was about to end without him managing to win Emmy over. And the thought of having to leave her in London cut like a knife. His liking for her had grown into an obsession, and the fact that she seemed indifferent to him made him all the more determined to press his case with her. And if it should ever come out that it was he who had encouraged Abi to run away, he would be in water up to his neck!

'Very well. He lives at Medville Towers, Park Street, Mayfair,' he told her grudgingly. 'And now if you'll excuse me, I'd like to go to my friends.' With an icy smile he left her.

Abi watched him go with a thoughtful expression on her face. She had seen another side of Jasper since coming to live at the Black Cat. The attention he had once bestowed on her had disappeared and she correctly guessed that it was because she held no more interest for him now that he had introduced her to Lilly. She knew that he had run up a large debt at the club and that Lilly was very unhappy with him, which was hardly surprising. It was obvious now that Jasper's drinking and gambling habits were out of control and she shuddered to think how his parents would react if they ever found out. But then, it wasn't her problem, so she turned away and put him from her mind.

Abi was up bright and early the following morning but she had to wait for the sickness to subside before she was able to travel to Hugo's parents' London home.

It was one of the most imposing houses in the street and she stood uncertainly on the marble steps that led up to the magnificent oak front door, trying to pluck up the courage to knock on it. She had chosen to wear one of her prettiest day gowns, although it felt quite tight across the chest now. It was in a lovely shade of pale green the same colour as her eyes and with the matching bonnet she had worn with it she knew she looked her best, which gave her a little confidence. Finally she pulled the rope to the side of the door, which rang a bell inside, and swallowed hard when she heard footsteps coming towards it.

'May I help you, miss?'

Abi found herself looking into the eyes of a stern-faced gentleman and realised that this must be Davies, the butler Hugo had mentioned.

Straightening her back, Abi refused to feel intimidated as she answered, 'Yes, please. I wish to see Hugo.'

'I'm very sorry, miss. I'm afraid Master Hugo is out of the country at the minute.'

'Oh . . . I see.' Abi was temporarily nonplussed. She had prayed that he would have returned by now, but then lifting her chin she made a decision. 'Then I would like to see Lady Medville.'

The butler looked as if was about to burst a blood vessel. 'And may I ask if you have an appointment?'

'Er . . . no, but I'm sure she'll see me if she's in . . . it's about her son,' Abi gabbled as nerves got the better of her.

The butler tutted in annoyance but realising that Abi wasn't going to go away quietly until she got whatever it was she wanted, he opened the door a fraction more to admit her and nodded towards a small gilt sofa. 'If you would care to take a seat, miss, I shall go and see if Lady Medville is receiving visitors. Who may I say is calling?'

'Miss Winter . . . Miss Abigail Winter.'

He inclined his head and strode away, his back as straight as a line prop as Abi began to sweat and wonder what she had got herself in to.

'Her ladyship will allow you ten minutes,' he told her pompously when he returned. 'If you would come this way, miss.'

Abi felt as if she was walking through the foyer of a stately home as she followed the man across the glossy tiles until he stopped before double doors and threw them open to introduce her, 'Miss Winter, ma'am.' He ushered her ahead of him and she found herself in the largest drawing room she had ever seen. The butler then quietly closed the door and as her eyes ranged the room, she saw Lady Medville sitting beside a tea trolley in a large bay window.

'It is customary for visitors to make an appointment when they wish to see me,' the woman informed Abi icily. 'But now you are here, what is it you want?'

It wasn't much of a greeting and Abi felt herself shrinking as the woman looked her up and down, her expression scathing.

'*Well*, girl? Speak up, I haven't got all day.'

'It . . . it was actually Hugo, your son, I wanted to see,' Abi said in a voice husky with unshed tears. 'I need to see him . . . *desperately.*'

She saw a flash of something that might have been fear in the woman's eyes but it was gone so quickly that she couldn't be sure.

'And what *exactly* is so desperate?'

Abi stared at her helplessly for a moment before saying, 'It . . . it's rather a personal matter.'

'I see.' The woman continued to stare at her for a while before asking, 'Would you by any chance be the young . . .' She seemed to struggle to give her a description. 'The young *woman* my son has recently been seen out with?'

Abi's eyes shone as she nodded vigorously. 'Yes, we have been walking out together.'

'And where are you from?'

'I'm actually from Astley, a small village near Nuneaton in the Midlands, but I moved here to work earlier in the year and that's when I met Hugo.'

'Work *where*?'

Abi felt as if she was being interrogated. 'Er . . . I work in a club, actually,' she answered in a small voice.

Now Lady Medville's worst fears were realised and with a snap in her voice, she asked, 'And are you in some sort of trouble? Is that why you wish to see Hugo?'

Abi sniffed as a tear slid unchecked down her cheek. 'I-I just need to see him. If you could perhaps give me his address . . .'

'I'm afraid that is quite out of the question. Hugo will be gone for some long time.' The woman studied her for a moment. The girl was very pretty, admittedly, and much better turned out than she would have expected a common little club hostess to be. She was well spoken too, but Hugo had been earmarked to marry the daughter of a wealthy family they knew when he came of age and this girl would have to be got rid of.

'So when is the child due?' she asked bluntly and Abi's head shot up as she stared at her in shock. The woman had crossed to an ornate French escritoire and removing a little book from it she tore a page out and began to write on it. 'Don't think you are the first girl that has come to me in this condition,' she said harshly. 'And I do sympathise. But of course, you must realise that you are not in Hugo's class so nothing could ever come of your short relationship. Here, take this and present it at the bank, then do as you will. Get rid of the child or, if you don't wish to do that, this should see you right for some time to come.'

Abi stared down in shock at the amount written on the paper. Fifty pounds.

'But if, as I fear, I am having a child, it will be your grandchild,' she told the woman with a look of disbelief on her face.

The woman waved her hand dismissively. 'I consider the matter closed,' she said, looking Abi directly in the eye. 'And now I wish you to leave and I must tell you that should you ever return I shall have the police called to remove you. Good day.' And with that she turned her back.

Abi stood staring at her for a moment, then very deliberately tore up the paper in her hand and dropped it on to the carpet, and with what dignity she could muster she sailed from the room and out of the door the butler was holding open for her.

It wasn't until she had turned a corner in the road that her shoulders sagged and the tears came. The woman was heartless and it seemed that Hugo, the man she loved with all her heart, was too. *But what are you going to do now?* a little voice in her head asked her and Abi sighed as she forced herself to move on. She had no idea whatsoever.

'So 'ow did yer get on at Hugo's pad?' Maria asked when she got back to her living quarters. As Abi haltingly relayed what had happened, Maria shook her head.

'I did *try* to warn yer about 'im, didn't I?' she said glumly. 'But now you've got to make yer mind up what yer goin' to do. I've got the address of a woman who'll sort yer out, if yer know what I mean, so give it some thought, eh?' Then she quietly walked away, leaving Abi to run to her room and sob broken-heartedly all over her silk sheets.

After a time, she managed to pull herself together and she sat up on her bed. Crying would get her nowhere, but what was she to do now? Hugo's mother was clearly going to do all she could to keep them apart and if what she had said was true – that she was just another in a long line of girls he'd associated with – then perhaps he wouldn't want to know about the baby anyway. *Perhaps it's just a false alarm*, she told herself, but she didn't really believe it. *I could go to Emmy and Aunt Imogen for help*, she thought, but dismissed that idea almost immediately. She still had her pride, for what good it would do her, so she couldn't go home either, and soon it would be harder to keep her secret and then what would happen when Lilly found out? She would probably dismiss her instantly, and where could she go with no job and only the small amount of money she had saved?

That left only one alternative and although the thought of it broke her heart, she wearily crossed the landing to Maria's room and once inside she asked her, 'C-could I have the address of the woman you told me about. The one who . . .'

'O' course. Her name is Mrs Duffy, she lives in a small cottage on the Thames embankment an' she used to be a midwife apparently. I'll draw you a map, if yer like. But are yer sure about this? I mean, havin' sumfin' like this done ain't wi'out risk.' Only the year before one of the girls who had worked at the club had visited the same woman and had died of an infection days later.

'I shall have to take my chance,' Abi told her dully.

Maria sighed as she drew a rough map for Abi to follow. 'When are yer thinkin' o' goin to see 'er? An' would yer like me to come with yer?'

'I haven't decided yet.' Abi took the piece of paper from Maria and pushed it into the pocket of her skirt. 'And thanks, but I think I'd sooner go alone.'

'Well, it's your decision, queen, but my advice to you would be don't leave it too long.'

Abi thanked her and went back to her own room where she sat nervously chewing on her nails for the rest of the afternoon until it was time to get ready for work.

'Ah, Abi, here you are.' Lilly pounced on her the moment she got to the bottom of the stairs that evening. 'I've been meanin' to 'ave a word with you. Come through.'

Left with no choice, Abi followed Lilly into her room and once the door had closed behind them Lilly immediately asked, 'Is there anythin' wrong? You ain't seemed yerself for some time an' yer heart certainly ain't in the job at the minute. I've 'ad a few complaints from customers, queen.'

'N-no, there's nothing wrong and I'm sorry,' Abi stammered, wishing the ground would open up and swallow her.

'Hm, well yer'd best pull yer socks up then! I can't keep girls on who ain't popular wi' the customers. You've lost yer sparkle an' I've a good idea it's somethin' to do wi' that young lord you've been seein'. Let you down, 'as he?'

'Something like that,' Abi mumbled, feeling thoroughly miserable.

'I ain't surprised,' Lilly stated. 'He's got a reputation fer likin' the girls. But now plaster a smile on that pretty face o' yours an' get out there an' entertain the customers. That's what I pay yer for an' forget all about Hugo, the young sod. There's plenty more fish in the sea and wi' your looks you can take yer pick.'

'Thanks, Lilly.' Abi was in such a rush to escape that she almost tripped over her skirts in her haste to leave the room but once in the hallway she took a deep breath and pulled herself together. If Jasper came to the club that evening she would try to get Hugo's address in France off him, but if he didn't she would go and see Mrs Duffy first thing on Monday morning, and once the baby was gone she would try to put this whole sorry mess behind her.

Chapter Twenty-Nine

'How did the first day go?' Imogen asked when Emmy carried her tea tray up to her the next morning.

'Not all that well, to be honest,' Emmy admitted. 'We sat twiddling our thumbs for most of the day. I think we had four patients and that was it. The first little boy had a boil that needed lancing, the second was a little girl who needed stitches in her leg after gashing it on a fence and the last two had terrible coughs. Hardly worth staying there for really.'

'Rome wasn't built in a day.' Imogen took the cup and saucer Emmy held out to her and stared thoughtfully ahead as she sipped at her tea. 'I think you need something to attract them in. Most of the people you'll be seeing live on the breadline and are always hungry, so what if I got Cook to bake a load of loaves on Saturday night and you could give each patient one to take away? That way they'll be getting free medical treatment and something to eat.'

'But won't that be rather a lot of work for Cook?'

Imogen shook her head. 'I shouldn't think she'll mind at all. In fact, I think she'd feel she was doing her bit. She's thoroughly behind what you and Jake are trying to do.'

'I suppose it's worth giving it a go. I'll put the idea to Jake, and thank you.'

'Huh! It's nothing, but now get me some clothes laid out. I've got Lady Medville calling today for morning coffee. I think I'll wear the mauve bombazine.' And so Emmy rushed about doing as she was told.

Early on Monday morning Abi stood on a bridge staring down at the small cluster of cottages on the embankment that Maria's map had led her to. They looked almost derelict and outside one of them a cluster of grubby, underfed children were paddling in the dirty water of the Thames. She walked further along until she came to a small opening where a set of rickety wooden steps led down to the cottages and once at the bottom she stepped through the mud and approached the children to ask, 'Which cottage does Mrs Duffy live in, please?'

''Ow much will yer give us to tell yer?' a small boy of indeterminate age asked cheekily.

Abi fished in her bag and held out a shiny penny and the boy's eyes, which were sunk into his thin face, lit up as he snatched it from her and pointed to the one closest to the shoreline. 'Ma Duffy lives in that one there, but she won't be up yet, miss, not if she 'ad a bellyful o' gin last night.'

His words did nothing to inspire confidence in Abi who was shaking with fear already, but having come this far there was no point in going back so picking her way through the mud she approached the cottage and tapped at the door.

There was no answer so she tapped again, a little harder this time, and suddenly a voice barked, 'Clear orf, yer little bleeders, afore I come an' clout yer one!'

'Er . . . Mrs Duffy, I wondered if I might have a word with you,' Abi said quickly before she followed her instincts and fled.

For a moment there was no sound but then she heard a shuffling noise and the door inched open to reveal an old woman in a shabby shawl with so many lines on her face that it was impossible to determine her age. Her sparse grey hair stood out in disarray about her head and her bloodshot eyes blinked in the light. The shabby dress and blouse she was wearing were so worn that it was difficult to say what colour they might once have been and she looked as if she had slept in them. She didn't look or smell any too clean either and Abi began to feel even more apprehensive.

'Who give yer me address?' she demanded suspiciously as she eyed Abi up and down.

'O-one of the girls I work with at the Black Cat club in Soho,' Abi answered haltingly.

'Ah . . . I see now . . . yer in a spot o' bother, are yer, dearie?'

When Abi hung her head and nodded miserably, the old woman stood aside and reaching out almost hauled her into the room. 'Come on in then, ain't no point lerrin' the whole world know yer business, is there?'

Abi's nose wrinkled at the stale smell of the place as she glanced around. It was little more than a hovel with a sink and a table to one side of the room, an unmade bed to the other and an old wing chair to the side of a small fireplace. She noticed an empty gin bottle lying on the floor beside the chair, which did nothing for her confidence at all.

She had no more time to take in anything else, however, as the old woman asked, 'So, were yer lookin' for me to 'elp yer out?'

Blinking back tears Abi nodded mutely.

'Hm, yer do realise it'll cost, don't yer?'

Another nod from Abi.

'A guinea up front, that's what I charge. Have yer got it?'

'Y-yes.' Abi fumbled in her bag and when she withdrew the guinea, the old woman's eyes latched on to it greedily before she reached out and snatched it and pushed it down the front of her blouse.

'Good, that's that bit out o' the way. So now we'll get on, shall we? No sense in waitin'. 'Ow far along are yer?'

'About two to three months, I think.' Abi was cringing with shame and embarrassment as the old woman went to a cupboard and withdrew a bowl containing a long, lethal-looking knitting needle and some pieces of rag.

'Right.' She nodded towards the table. 'I want yer to take yer drawers off an' gerr up on there fer me. You'll feel a sharp stabbin' feelin' fer a few moments then you've to go straight 'ome an' the rest should follow naturally. It'll all be over by this evenin' but afore I do it you need to swear that should anythin' go wrong you'll not bring my name into it.'

'I won't . . . I promise.'

Tears were coursing down Abi's cheeks now as the implications of what she was about to do hit home. This was her baby she was about to kill. Hers and Hugo's, the man she loved. Until that moment she had never really thought of the baby as a real living little person but now she wondered what it might have looked like. Would it have been a little girl who looked just like her or a baby boy who looked just like Hugo? Very slowly and shaking with humiliation she removed her skirt and drawers as the old woman slopped a grimy cloth across the table. Abi felt as if she was caught in the grip of a nightmare and her legs suddenly turned to jelly and she found that she was frozen to the spot.

'Well, come on then,' the old woman snapped with not a trace of sympathy. 'Yer weren't so worried when yer took yer drawers off fer the father, were you? An' I ain't got all day, yer know! Me time is precious.'

As she lifted the knitting needle and wiped it with the same grimy cloth, Abi's courage fled and she knew in that moment that she couldn't go through with it. She would rather go through the shame of giving birth to an illegitimate child than die trying to get rid of it.

'I-I'm sorry, but I've changed my mind!' Snatching up her drawers she shoved her legs into them and hoisted them up then did the same with her skirt.

The woman's eyes narrowed. 'What do yer mean – yer've changed yer mind? You'll not get yer money back. I can't do wi' people wastin' me time. Another five minutes an' it'll all be over.'

'No, no really. I can't do it . . . and it doesn't matter about the money.' Abi was shaking so much that she couldn't fasten the buttons on her waistband. Eventually she gave up and grabbing her bag, she raced from the cottage leaving the door to flap open after her in the breeze washing off the river.

She stumbled more than once as she tackled the stairs back up to the bridge and by the time she'd managed it her skirt and hands were muddied and her eyes were wild, and she looked nothing like the sedate young woman who had arrived there shortly before. As she pelted along, lifting her skirts in a most unladylike manner, people stared at her curiously. But she paid them no heed, her only wish was to get as far away from the hellhole she had just visited as possible.

Once back at her living quarters she nearly fell through the door and Maria, who had only just risen after spending most of the night entertaining a customer in her room, caught her arms to steady her.

'Whoa! Hold up there, queen! What's wrong?'

'I-I went to see Mrs Duffy.'

Maria frowned. 'Ah! So it's all over bar the shoutin', is it?'

Abi's head drooped and she began to cry. 'N-no, it was so *awful* th-there, Maria, I couldn't go through with it. I'd paid her and everything but then—' She hiccuped to a halt as Maria led her into one of the downstairs rooms where the girls entertained their gentlemen friends and closed the door firmly behind them.

'But what are you goin' to do now?' Maria looked worried. 'It won't be long afore yer can't hide yer condition, an' nothin' much gets past Lilly.'

'I-I really don't know.' Abi dropped on to a chair and sobbed afresh as Maria bit on her lip.

'Why don't yer just get yerself back 'ome to yer ma an' come clean wi' her?' Maria suggested. 'Per'aps she'll forgive yer an' let yer keep the baby there.'

Abi shook her head. The mother she knew would never get over the shame. 'No, I could never do that. I shall have to think of something else.'

'Right well, while yer do I'm goin' through to the kitchen to get yer a nice strong, sweet cup o' tea. They reckon it's good fer shock an' yer look like yer could do wi' a cup.' Maria headed for the door, her floaty peignoir swirling about her legs.

That evening Abi got Maria to tell Lilly it was the wrong time of the month and she was feeling unwell, and while all the other girls went to work, Abi lay curled up in a ball softly sobbing as the wonderful future she had planned for herself crumbled to ashes. Before her father had left them, she had dreamt of a rich young man coming along and sweeping her off her feet but that dream had died when she and her mother and Emmy were left homeless. Then Jasper had dangled a new and exciting life in London in front of her and after snatching at it she had met Hugo and given him her heart. Even now she couldn't believe that he had willingly left her. Surely he would come back from France if only she could get word to him about the baby?

Suddenly it hit her like a blow between the eyes. What a fool she'd been to believe all that his mother had said. Hugo *did* love her, she was sure of it, and if he couldn't come to her then she must go to him. She realised that she would never get his address in France from his mother but she wouldn't mind betting that Jasper would know where he was and if she were to fully explain the situation to him, surely he would give it to her?

Without stopping to ponder, she leapt out of bed and pulled on one of her beautiful gowns, then after brushing her hair till it shone, she made her way down to the club room.

'I thought you were feelin' poorly,' Lilly greeted her.

'I was but I'm feeling much better now.' Abi's eyes swept past Lilly to scour the smoky room, but as yet there was no sign of Jasper. Still, she wasn't overly concerned. The night was young and he still had time to appear.

It was actually four nights before Jasper put in an appearance and by then Abi's nerves were as taut as violin strings.

'Jasper, you *must* give me Hugo's address in France,' she told him without preamble before he had even had time to reach the bar. 'It's *imperative* that I see him.'

Jasper frowned. 'I don't think his grandparents will be too pleased if you just turn up there uninvited,' he pointed out, hoping to put her off, but she wouldn't be swayed.

'I'm not expecting to be asked to stay,' she told him shortly. 'I just need to see him and once I have I'll come back again.' *Hopefully with Hugo*, she thought but she didn't say it aloud. 'You do have his address, don't you?' she hedged.

'Well, yes, yes I do.' Jasper had stayed with Hugo at his grandparents' home in France many times during the summer holidays when they had attended school together, but he was reluctant to part with it. He had a pretty good idea why his cousin wished to see him and knew that Hugo wouldn't thank him for it. But what choice did he have? Abi clearly wasn't going to take no for an answer. She was like a dog with a bone.

'Get me a piece of paper and I'll write it down for you,' he eventually told her reluctantly. 'But take my advice and write to him rather than visit. It's a long way to go only to have to come all the way back again.'

Abi stood impatiently tapping her foot as he quickly jotted down the address, then snatching it up, she nodded at him. 'Thank you, and when are you planning on going home?'

Now it was he who looked glum. 'This weekend. I've had the royal summons from my father saying the holiday is well and truly over and I've got to go back and buckle down to work. If I don't, he's going to stop my allowance. That was one reason I called in this evening – to say goodbye. For now at least.'

'I'm sure it won't be as bad as you're expecting,' Abi told him with a sigh. She couldn't imagine Jasper settling down to anything.

'Hm! It means I won't see nearly as much of Emmy . . . or you, of course,' he hurried on when he saw Abi raise an enquiring eyebrow. Abi was aware that he had been visiting Emmy and their aunt regularly and just for a moment she could have sworn he was talking of leaving a lover when he mentioned her sister, but surely she was imagining it, she told herself. But then Lilly was at her elbow looking none too pleased, so after quickly saying her goodbyes Abi hurried away to entertain one of the elderly gentlemen that had just arrived, safe in the knowledge that she now at least knew where Hugo was.

Chapter Thirty

'Your cousin Jasper is 'ere to see you, miss,' Aggie told Emmy one morning and Emmy scowled. It was very early; she hadn't even had time to help her aunt get dressed yet.

'What does he want, Aggie?' She couldn't keep the note of annoyance from her voice as she carried her aunt's breakfast tray out on to the landing and handed it to the maid. 'He was only here the day before yesterday.' Smoothing her skirt and patting her hair she sighed as she descended the stairs to find Jasper in the hallway clutching his hat in his hands.

'Ah, Emmy, there you are.'

Emmy frowned, wondering where else he had thought she might be at that time of day. 'Of course I am. As it happens, I was just about to help Aunt Imogen get dressed, so whatever it is you want you shall have to make it sharpish,' she answered shortly, then felt guilty when she saw his face fall.

She led him into the drawing room where he told her, 'I've come to say goodbye . . . for now at least. Father wants me home before the weekend, I'm afraid.'

'Oh, is that all?' She smiled. 'I thought there might be something wrong.'

'It *is* wrong,' he snapped sulkily. 'I'm to start work learning how to manage the farm apparently, even though he knows that's not what I want to do with my life.'

'I see.' He reminded Emmy of a large, petulant child and suddenly her patience was done with him. 'So perhaps it would help if you told him what you *do* want to do?' she suggested caustically. 'You've been in London for months and life can't be one long holiday.'

The conversation wasn't going at all as he had hoped it would and he frowned. 'I'd like to find some sort of a job here in London . . . so that I could be close to you,' he said, his heart sinking as he saw the look of shock on her face.

'B-but why would you want to be close to me?' She was confused now and a little afraid as she remembered back to what Imogen had said. Hadn't she hinted that she thought Jasper had romantic intentions towards her? Well, if that was the case, he'd better get over them fairly quickly. They were cousins; surely he knew that even if she returned his affection, which she most certainly did not, nothing could come of it?

Before she could stop him, he stepped forward and took her hand in his and her heart missed a beat as he stared earnestly into her eyes. 'Why do you think? You must have guessed how I feel about you? Why do you think I've stayed in London all this time? It was just so that I could be close to you.'

Emmy snatched her hand away as if had been burnt and hot colour rose in her cheeks. 'Don't be so silly,' she told him firmly. 'You must realise there could never be anything between us because we are so closely related.'

'I don't *care* about that,' he said doggedly. 'I only know that I love you and it doesn't matter that we're related. It's not wrong to feel like I do, you know. We could go somewhere away from our family. I can't help how I feel, after all.'

Emmy's mouth gaped open in shocked surprise as she saw that he was in earnest. 'If we did, Uncle Bernard would cut you off, so what do you suppose we'd live on? And that's assuming that I have feelings for you, which I don't!'

'We could get jobs,' he said desperately. 'And we'd manage somehow.' He stepped forward again but she backed away from him as if he had the plague.

'Go home, Jasper,' she told him firmly. 'I think you've developed a rather silly crush on me but once you're back at home I think you'll see how ridiculous it is. You're a good-looking young man and I'm sure you'll be able to have your pick of girls back in Nuneaton.'

'Haven't you listened to a word I've said?' His voice was rising now. 'I don't want any other girl – I want *you*!'

Emmy turned so suddenly that her skirts swirled about her. 'I think you should leave now and for both our sakes we should forget this conversation ever took place. If Aunt Imogen asks why you came, I'll tell her it was to say goodbye to her. Now please leave, Jasper, and if you come to London again, I'd prefer it if you only came to visit our aunt.'

His face was an ugly mottled red but he wasn't finished yet and leaning towards her he ground out, 'This isn't the end, Emmy! When I want something, I usually get it and I want *you* so get used to the idea because as God is my witness, I'm telling you that if I can't have you no one else will!'

And with that he rammed his hat on, barged past her and left the house, slamming the door so loudly behind him that it danced on its hinges.

'Lordy, what were that tantrum all about?' Aggie asked as she appeared from the kitchen.

Flustered, Emmy shook her head. 'Oh . . . it's, er . . . nothing to worry about. Jasper's just upset because my uncle has told him it's time to go home and get to work.' Then lifting her skirts she fled up to her room to compose herself. After all, wasn't she as bad as Jasper for having feelings for someone she shouldn't have them for? As a picture of Jake's face swam in front of her eyes, a tear slid down her cheek and she couldn't deny how she felt about him any longer. The slightest touch of his hand could send shivers up her spine. A smile from him could make the day brighter and the more time she spent with him the more her feelings grew. And yet she knew that it was hopeless, they could never come together and she felt as if her heart was breaking. She stood for a while, trying to pull herself together before going in to see her aunt.

'What was all the commotion downstairs about?' Imogen asked when Emmy entered her room some minutes later. 'I could hear the door slam from up here. I'm surprised it didn't come off its hinges!'

'Oh, it was just Jasper. He came to say goodbye. His father has told him he's got to return home and buckle down to some work and he's none too pleased about it.'

'I see.' Imogen raised her eyebrow. 'And . . .?'

'And what?' Emmy said innocently as she lifted the gown her aunt would wear that day from the armoire. It was yet another frilled concoction, but then all of her clothes were.

'Oh come on, girl. I wasn't born yesterday, you know. If that was all that was upsetting him why would he take it out on you? Or even come to say goodbye for that matter? He was only here a few days ago.'

When Emmy remained mutinously silent her aunt nodded. 'Hm, declared how he felt about you, did he? And when you told him you didn't feel the same it upset him, did it?'

'What? I don't know what you—'

Her aunt held her hand up and scowled as she wiggled painfully to the edge of the mattress. 'Don't try to hoodwink me. I've been around a lot longer than you and I know when a man is smitten. But he's not the only one, is he? I think Jake has feelings for you as well.'

'Oh, Aunt, really!' Emmy was squirming with embarrassment now. 'I think you've been reading too many of those romantic novels you're so fond of. Now come along or we'll never get you dressed at this rate.' And with a shake of her head Imogen did as she was told.

The following Sunday, Jake picked her up bright and early as usual and once they had packed the freshly baked loaves Cook had made for them into his carriage they set off for Whitechapel.

'Let's hope this will encourage a few more patients in,' he said hopefully as he guided the horse through the busy streets. Even on Sunday London always seemed to be busy, Emmy had noticed. 'And I've had some good news this week. I applied for a job with a doctor in Harley Street and I received a letter yesterday telling me that I got the post. The other doctor he worked with is retiring so it left the way open for me. I shall have to find new lodgings, but that shouldn't be a problem, and it means I shall finally be earning and able to pay my father back some of the money it's cost to get me qualified. I start in two weeks' time so I thought I'd pop home to see my parents for a few days before I start.'

'That's wonderful, well done.' Emmy was genuinely pleased for him. 'You worked really hard for this. It still seems strange, though, to address you as Dr Chetwynd.'

'I suppose it does.' He chuckled.

'I imagine the patients you see in Harley Street will be very different to the ones you treat on Sundays,' she said.

'Oh yes, they're all very wealthy and I couldn't believe it when the doctor who owns the practice told me what they pay for a single consultation. Still, they must be able to afford it. It doesn't seem fair, does it, when you think of how differently the classes live?'

His words made her think of her mother's position and she nodded in agreement. 'No, it doesn't. I didn't think my mother would cope when my father first left and she was forced to go and live in the cottage but she seems to be coping admirably now. In fact, in some ways, she seems more content than I've ever known her.'

When Jake guided the horse down the narrow alley leading to the rooms they'd rented, they saw little Tommy waiting for them, his face expectant.

'Take Daisy round to the stables for me and there'll be an extra penny in it for you,' Jake told him with a wink and the boy's grubby face was transformed when it broke into a cheeky grin. 'But first you can help me and Emmy get all this bread inside.'

The job was done in minutes and Emmy felt sorry for the little chap as he stared at the food hungrily.

'When you've got the horse settled come back and you can take one of these loaves back for your mother,' she told him.

He was off like a shot and she smiled as she saw him leading the old horse back up the alley. Soon the kettle was bubbling on the little hob and they were ready for business, but again by ten o'clock they had not had one single patient and Jake was walking up and down the small rooms like a caged tiger.

'I'm not so sure this is going to work,' he said worriedly, but the words had barely left his mouth when Tommy appeared again with a small woman clutching a baby in a grubby shawl.

'This is me ma, doc,' he said proudly for all the world as if he was introducing royalty. 'An' this is me baby sister, Nance. She's gorra wicked rash on 'er an' I told me ma you'd 'ave a look at 'er.'

'Of course I will, Tommy.' Jake held his hands out for the baby and Tommy's mother reluctantly handed her over. He carried her through to the other room where he gently unwrapped the faded shawl from the little girl, praying that she wasn't going to be yet another victim of the measles.

'Fanks fer doin' this, doc,' Tommy's mother said. 'An' fanks fer the loaf an' all. The kids really enjoyed it.'

'You're very welcome. And I'm pleased to say this isn't the measles.'

The woman breathed a sigh of relief. 'Are you feeding her yourself?' he asked as he gently ran his hands over the child, and she shook her head.

'I were till a couple o' weeks ago but then me milk dried up so I'm weanin' 'er on to solids.'

'Hm, it looks like some sort of allergy to me,' Jake said. 'Where do you get your water from?'

'Out o' the tap in the road,' the woman answered.

'In future I want you to boil it before giving her drinks,' he advised and she nodded. 'Meanwhile I'm going to give you some ointment to put on the rash and I'd like to see her again next Sunday if she's no better.'

'Fanks, doc.'

Once the woman had wrapped the child tightly back in her old shawl and shuffled away with Tommy in tow, Jake shook his head.

'That damn water tap causes half of the problems in this place,' he said. 'The water is not at all clean and most of the folks round here don't bother to boil it before they drink it or cook food in it.'

She nodded in agreement but they had no chance to discuss it further for another patient peered in at that moment and Jake ushered them into the treatment room. Over the day they got gradually busier and between patients Emmy told Jake about Jasper's visit earlier in the week and that he was going home, although she didn't tell him about Jasper's feelings for her.

'About time too,' Jake said. 'The little devil has been running up gambling debts left, right and centre from what I can see of it. It'll do him good to buckle down to a bit of work for a change.'

As Emmy watched him, she couldn't help but compare the two brothers. Jake was conscientious and caring while

Jasper was selfish and greedy. They were as different as two people could be, but then she supposed that she and Abi were too – in their natures at least.

The light was beginning to fade from the day, and after sweeping the floors and tidying the two rooms, Emmy finally blew the candles out late that afternoon while Jake went to fetch the horse and carriage from the stable. She was feeling happy; they'd had quite a few people through the door that day – not enough to say they were actually busy, but far more than they'd had previously, and she was beginning to think this venture of Jake's might just be a success after all and she was proud of him.

Chapter Thirty-One

'Lilly . . . I was wondering if I might have a few days off this week?' Abi asked tentatively. It was now the beginning of October and she knew that she couldn't wait much longer before she went to track Hugo down in France. 'I, er . . . I haven't been home to see my mother since I arrived here and I feel like I should.'

'I suppose so,' Lilly muttered, looking up from the paperwork she was doing. 'To be honest I shan't much miss yer, the way you've been carryin' on, queen. You've been walkin' about wi' a face on yer like you've lost a bob an' found a penny, so I suggest yer try an' get yer sparkle back while you've gone, eh? Cos you ain't no use to me if yer can't keep the customers 'appy!'

'Sorry, Lilly,' Abi muttered as she turned and fled up the stairs. Her bag was packed and ready to go whether Lilly had given her permission or not and now all she had to do was get through the night and she'd be on her way. She had booked a berth on a cross-Channel ship bound for Le Havre the following morning, and her excitement was growing. Surely Hugo would be pleased when she told him that she was going to have his child? She could picture him sweeping her into his arms and dancing her around the room, and then they'd have a fairy-tale wedding. She would look like a princess, all in satin and lace, and they'd live in a beautiful house with servants to wait on them and a nanny to look after the child. Oh, they were going to be *so* happy! But first she must get through one more night entertaining the gentlemen in the club.

Even the maid wasn't up when Abi crept down the stairs early the next morning. She felt sick and ill and had been sorely tempted to roll over and go back to sleep, but her need to see Hugo was greater, so she swallowed her nausea and tiptoed to the dining room where she left a note addressed to Maria on the shelf. She had hoped to see her the evening before to tell her where she was going, but Maria had still been entertaining a gentleman in her room when Abi went to bed, so she'd resorted to writing her a quick message in which she told her she was going to visit Hugo at his grand-parents' chateau in France and that she would hopefully be back within a week.

She inched the back door open and set off down the side alley and soon she was heading for the docks, which were already surprisingly busy with burly seamen loading cargo and livestock on to the ships, and she had to step over thick coils of rope and wind her way amongst barrels to get to the ship she had booked a passage on.

The Mermaid was actually a cargo ship and judging from how low it sat in the sludgy water it was already fully loaded, but the captain wasn't averse to earning a few extra shillings by taking the odd passenger across the Channel, providing they didn't expect luxury, which Abi didn't. The gangplank stretched from the dock up to the ship and, gripping her bag, she climbed it as quickly as she could, clinging on to the rope handrail for all she was worth. Far below she could see the flotsam swirling on the dark water as it slapped against the quay and she shuddered.

'Ah, Miss Winter.' The captain, a swarthy-faced man, hurried to meet her, his calloused hand outstretched. 'I'll put you in the dining room, if you could call it that,' he chuckled. 'As I explained when you booked, it ain't very salubrious but it's probably where you'll be most comfortable for the journey an' I'm sure our cook will make sure as you have plenty o' cups o' tea. I'm sorry I ain't got nothing better to offer you.'

'I'm sure I shall be perfectly fine,' Abi assured him as she followed him across the deck and down a short ladder, which proved to be quite difficult to negotiate in her wide skirts. He led her into a gloomy room where trestle tables and benches were spaced along the walls. It smelt strongly of overcooked cabbage, tobacco smoke and stale sweat but Abi didn't complain. She would have swum the Channel if it was her only means of getting to Hugo.

'Right, I'll leave you to make yourself comfortable,' the captain told her. 'There's only two more passengers to come an' then hopefully we'll be off wi' the mornin' tide an' in Le Havre by late evenin', weather permittin'. Do you have somewhere to go when we get there?' There was something about this young lady that made him concerned about her. She was about the same age as his own daughter and didn't look well at all, and he wondered what it was that made her want to cross the Channel unchaperoned. But still, it was none of his business and it didn't do to ask too many questions.

'I'm sure I shall be able to find a hotel, thank you,' Abi answered politely. She had no idea as yet how far she would have to travel from Le Havre to reach Hugo's grandparents' home. 'But could you tell me where the, er . . . bathroom is please.'

He laughed. 'It's hardly what I'd term a bathroom but if you go out o' here an turn right you'll find what passes as a toilet at the end o' the corridor. Oh, an' would you mind stayin' below till we've sailed, please, then once we're out o' the dock you're more than welcome to go up on deck.' He touched his cap and left her.

Soon after a middle-aged couple joined her and nodded a greeting. By that time the gentle swaying of the boat was making Abi feel queasier than ever and suddenly she rose and made a rush for the door and fled down the corridor. The toilet the captain had referred to was simply a plank of wood with a hole in it stretched across a bucket half full of cold ashes. The smell in there was horrendous but as Abi leant over it and vomited up almost everything she had eaten the day before she hardly noticed. At last, when there was nothing left to bring up, she straightened and dabbed at her mouth with her handkerchief. She had sailed on many ships over the years with her parents when they'd holidayed abroad and she had never been ill like this, but then, she realised, the ships they had travelled on had been far more luxurious than this one and she hadn't been expecting a baby!

Feeling weak and exhausted she staggered back to the dining room and tucked herself away in a corner as she wondered how she was going to manage the journey. But worse was to come, for shortly after, as the ship moved out into deeper waters, it began to rock alarmingly and in no time at all Abi was back up and racing towards the toilet again.

Eventually she managed to clamber back up the ladder on to the deck where she swayed towards the rail and stared down into the choppy water. The weather had taken a turn for the worse and the wind that whipped around her was biting as the ship rose and fell alarmingly. A tear trickled down her cheek as she clung weakly to the ship's rail and prayed as she had never prayed before.

Back in Nuneaton, Hetty was just about to set off on her morning journey to the Chetwynds' farm to fetch a jug of milk, but as she opened the door her eyes were instantly drawn to an envelope lying on the doorstep.

'Looks like our anonymous friend 'as called again, missus,' she told Dorcas who was sitting in front of the fire in her dressing robe. 'An' I sat down 'ere nearly all night an' all hopin' to catch 'em an' never 'eard a blummin' thing!'

'Really? This is getting to be a habit.' Dorcas took the envelope from Hetty and when she opened it and saw the folded notes inside she sighed. 'I wonder who it could be from?' she mused as Hetty shook her head. 'It's not from any of my so-called former friends, I'm sure. They soon disappeared off the scene when the chips were down.'

Looking slightly uncomfortable, Hetty suggested tentatively, 'Yer don't think it could be the master as is leavin' it do yer, missus?'

'Gerald!' Dorcas looked shocked. It had never occurred to her that it might be him but the money had turned up monthly ever since they had moved in to the cottage. 'Bu-but surely not? I don't even know where he is. He could be miles away; he might even have gone abroad for all I know.'

Hetty shook her head. 'Ner, not the master. He thought too much o' you an' his girls to go too far away an' 'appen this is just 'is way o' makin' sure you 'ave enough to get by.'

'What? You think he may be working somewhere around here?' Dorcas said. 'But if that was the case, surely we would have heard about it on the grapevine.'

'Not necessarily,' Hetty answered stoutly. 'But I got to thinkin'. It's always at the beginnin' o' the month that the money turns up. Next time why don' we both stay up to try to catch him?'

'That's an excellent idea,' Dorcas declared, wondering why her heart was pounding with excitement. Since Gerald had been gone, she'd gradually began to realise how much she still cared for him. But even if she ever managed to see him again, would his feelings for her still be the same? She could see all too clearly now how demanding she had been and how much she had taken him for granted, to the point that the poor man had felt he had no choice but to run away. Guilt, sharp as a knife, pierced her. *If only I could have the chance to speak to him one more time, I would tell him how sorry I am*, she silently promised herself.

Once Hetty had set off to fetch the milk, Dorcas stared down at the money in her lap, lowered her head and cried, feeling lonelier than she had ever felt in her life before.

Later in the morning as Dorcas was rolling pastry for a steak and kidney pie, Sybil arrived dressed in her usual drab gown with a warm cloak around it.

'Come in and sit down. I'll make you a cup of tea,' Dorcas invited and Sybil raised her eyebrow as she settled in the wing chair to the side of the fireplace. 'I hear Jasper is home; how nice for you.'

'Hm.' Sybil stared moodily into the flames as Dorcas filled the sooty-bottomed kettle and stood it on the hob.

'Yes, he's home but he doesn't seem very happy about it,' Sybil admitted. 'He and his father have had words already. I don't know what gets into the boy, I really don't. He's had the best of everything all his life: the best clothes, the best holidays, the best education, but he still doesn't seem to want to buckle down and learn how to manage the farm.'

'I suppose I could say the same about Abigail,' Dorcas admitted. 'She couldn't settle down to this way of life at all and soon flew the nest for the bright lights of London. Emerald is there too, admittedly, but at least she went to help out.'

There had been a subtle change in her and Sybil's relationship over the last few weeks, for the more she saw of her the more Dorcas realised that she was actually a very lonely woman. Of course, Sybil was far too proud to admit it, but now that they lived so close together Dorcas couldn't help but notice how much time Bernard spent away from home. She had an idea that he probably spent that time with the fancy woman it was rumoured he had, and suddenly she found herself feeling almost sorry for her sister-in-law.

'I'm sure he'll settle down eventually.' Dorcas spooned some tea leaves into the best china teapot she always used when Sybil came to call, although she and Hetty tended to use the sensible old brown pot for themselves now. As Dorcas had discovered, it didn't have to be fine bone china for the tea to taste nice – that was just one of the lessons she had learnt. She only wished she could have learnt them sooner.

'Emerald tells me that the new venture Jake has set up for treating the poor is going well now. You must be very proud of him,' Dorcas said, hoping to change the sombre mood.

'Yes, I suppose I am,' Sybil said thoughtfully. 'But Jake was always the more thoughtful of the two boys – probably because, being the oldest, he didn't get as much attention as Jasper did.'

'I must admit the same applies to Emerald and Abigail. If only we could turn the clock back, eh? And try to put everything right.'

She took a seat next to Sybil and poured the tea as each of them sat silent and thought back over their lives.

It was very dark, rainy and windy when *The Mermaid* pulled into the port at Le Havre late that night. Bad weather had slowed the journey and Abi felt as weak as a kitten and couldn't wait to feel solid ground beneath her feet again.

'I'll fetch your bag up for you, Miss Winter,' the captain offered sympathetically as Abi hung over the rail like a limp rag while the sailors began to haul the gangplank into place.

While he was gone Abi noticed that the docks were teeming with people, despite it being so late at night. Ships of all shapes and sizes were lying at anchor while sailors loaded them with cargo so they would be ready to sail with the morning tide.

'There y'are, me dear.' The captain took her elbow with one hand and gripped her bag with the other. 'Let me 'elp you down the gangplank, eh?'

Abi felt so weak that she was glad of his help and once they were on the quay, she gave him a grateful smile.

'Now, if you're lookin' for somewhere to stay the night, I suggest you walk straight up that street there. At the top of it you'll see a little guest house wi' blue shutters at the winders. Madame Bisset runs it; it's cheap an' cheerful but it's clean enough an' if you tell 'er Captain Marks sent you she'll see you right. She talks quite good English an' all so you shouldn't have any problems wi' her. Goodbye, me dear.' And with that he turned and was off back up the gangplank to shout orders at his crew.

Abi turned in the direction he had pointed and as she picked her way across the quay she was shocked to see some women with heavily made-up faces and wearing indecently low-cut dresses hanging around the sailors who were just coming in to port. No doubt they were after the sailors' hard-earned wages and as she passed them, they glared at her, fearing she was a threat. She smiled. Little could they know that there was only one man in the world for her and hopefully she would be seeing him very soon.

She had no trouble in locating the small guest house, and Madame Bisset, a small, motherly looking woman with soft grey hair and a plump figure, ushered her inside out of the cold.

'I 'ave one room that might suit you, mademoiselle,' she told Abi in broken English. 'It is at the top of the 'ouse but it eez warm and comfortable. Please to follow me.'

As they mounted the stairs she asked, 'Do you know 'ow long your stay might be? And 'ave you eaten?'

'I'm afraid I don't know how long I shall be here,' Abi answered. 'And no, I haven't eaten. I'm afraid I was rather ill on the ship.'

'Ah, then you must 'ave some soup,' the woman told her with a kindly smile. 'Eet will settle your stomach.'

The room she showed Abi had sloping ceilings and it was sparsely furnished but there were crisp white sheets on the small iron bed and it was clean. 'This will be satisfactory, yes?'

Abi was so exhausted that she would have said yes to anything and she nodded as she dropped her bag on to the floor. 'It's very satisfactory. Thank you.'

'Good, that ees good. Now you must take off your coat and come down for some food. You weel feel so much better with food in your belly, *mon cherie*.'

Abi gave her a weak smile. She doubted she would be able to eat a thing but, not wishing to appear rude, she did as she was told, then followed the woman back down the stairs where she was led into a small homely dining room. She was the only person there and within minutes Madame Bisset bustled back in with a tray containing a steaming bowl of chicken soup and some thick slices of freshly baked bread spread with rich creamy butter.

Abi thanked her and picked up her spoon tentatively, but seeing that Madame Bisset was waiting for her to start, she took a sip from her spoon and suddenly realised how hungry she was. The kindly landlady left the room with a smile and it wasn't long before Abi had eaten every morsel and felt remarkably better for it.

'Would you be able to tell me how far away this is?' Abi asked, handing Madame Bisset the address of Hugo's grandparents when the woman returned to clear the dishes. She was keener than ever to see Hugo now and was even contemplating going there and then, despite the lateness of the hour.

'Ah yes. It ees a good way but not so far that you cannot walk it,' the woman told her. 'First theeng in the morning I will draw you a leetle map, oui?'

Abi swallowed her disappointment and nodded before climbing the stairs to her room. It didn't take long to undress and get into bed where she instantly fell into a deep sleep and didn't stir until the morning.

Following a hearty breakfast, which Abi was unable to eat much of, she set off bright and early. She felt sick and poorly but there was a swing in her step at the thought of seeing Hugo again. From the map that her landlady had drawn for her she could see that the chateau was beyond the town and set on a hill. She passed the church and the town hall, peeping into the shop windows set in between them, and after a time the houses began to be more spaced apart and she began to climb through a wooded area. Eventually the noises of the town faded away and all she could hear was birdsong. She had felt much better for the first part of her journey, but now her steps slowed as the dreaded feeling of nausea came over her again and she stopped to sit on the grass at the side of the track until it had subsided a little. When she set off again the hill became steeper and glancing at the map again, she realised that she must be very close now.

Soon she rounded a bend in the lane and there were the gates to the chateau that Madame Bisset had described to her. They were very tall and grand and made of intricately shaped wrought iron but they opened easily enough. Once through, she shut them securely behind her and began to follow the gravelled drive that she assumed must lead to the chateau. When it came into view it quite took her breath away and she could understand why Jasper had enjoyed holidaying there so much. With its turreted roof and nestled into the hillside against a backdrop of trees, it reminded her of one of the small fairy-tale castles she had seen in the story books she had loved as a child.

Her heart began to beat faster as she realised that she might be only minutes away from seeing Hugo again and the thought made her quicken her steps.

Chapter Thirty-Two

'What do you mean she's gone to France? Whatever for?' Imogen said when Emmy returned all of a fluster from the club.

'Just what I say!' Clearly agitated, Emmy began to pace the floor. She'd gone to see her sister on a whim as she was coming home from collecting a gown for her aunt from the dressmakers, only to be told by Lilly that Abi had gone home to visit her mother for a few days. She would have been quite happy with that but as she had left, she had met Maria in the alley leading to the house and she had informed her of where Abi had really gone. And now Emmy was seriously concerned. Admittedly she and Abi had travelled to France many times over the years when they'd holidayed with their parents, but neither of them had ever undertaken such a journey alone.

'She's gone to find Hugo. He's there staying with his grandparents apparently and Abi clearly couldn't stand being apart from him any longer.'

'How romantic.' Despite her harsh ways, Imogen was a great romantic at heart, especially when she thought back to how her Marcel had swept her off her feet.

Emmy glared at her. 'But she's only seventeen,' she pointed out distractedly. 'Don't you think that's rather young to be travelling all that way on her own? Why – anything could happen to her and how would we know?'

Imogen glared right back and flapped her hand. 'Of course nothing will happen to her. The girl's got her head screwed on, much as I had at her age,' she added with a nod of her head.

'Hm, well I'm not so sure,' Emmy fretted. 'And Maria seemed concerned too.'

Imogen snorted impatiently as she waved her hand towards the clothes Emmy had laid out for her. 'Oh, for goodness' sake, you must want something to worry about. Now help me get dressed and do what I pay you for.'

Thoroughly chastened Emmy did as she was told.

When Abi climbed the marble steps up to the broad oak door that was the entrance to the chateau, her heart was in her mouth. Lifting the heavy black knocker, she rapped on the door and soon it was opened by a pretty fair-haired maid in a starched mop cap trimmed with broderie anglaise and a matching pinafore over a plain navy dress.

'*Puis-je vous aider?*' the girl asked and Abi gulped. She had never been much good at French at school but she remembered just about enough to know that the maid was asking how she might help her.

'Yes, I—*Puis-je vous aider* . . . Hugo?' she stuttered, hoping the girl would understand it was him she wanted to see.

'Ah.' The girl smiled. '*Maître* Hugo.' She turned and disappeared inside and seconds later an older woman appeared dressed in a severe grey gown with a chatelaine about her waist who looked at her enquiringly. This, Abi thought, must be the housekeeper.

'I wish to see Mr Hugo,' Abi said again and was relieved when the woman nodded.

'Unfortunately, you are too late,' she said with a heavy French accent. 'He already leave with hees *grand-père* for work.' She inclined her head and made to shut the door but Abi stuck her hand out desperately.

'Then *please* could you tell me when he will be back?'

The woman tutted with annoyance. 'Theese evening. You wish to leave a message?'

'No . . . no, thank you. I'll come back later,' Abi told her as disappointment ripped through her, and she turned and made her way back along the drive. There was no point in causing a scene. However, by the time the town came into sight again, Abi's spirits had lifted considerably. The nausea had worn off and it wasn't so very much longer to wait after all. It wasn't as if Hugo could have known she was coming. And so she browsed the shops for a while to pass the time before strolling down to the harbour to look at the boats. It really was very busy and she was fascinated as she watched the sailors loading the cargoes.

Shortly before lunchtime she returned to Madame Bisset's and asked if she might stay for another night and the woman was only too happy to oblige her.

'But 'ave you eaten?' she asked and Abi shook her head. 'Then you should . . . for the sake of the child.'

Stunned, Abi stared at her as her hand instinctively dropped to her stomach. 'But how did you—'

The woman sighed at her shocked expression as she tapped the side of her nose. 'I can spot woman with child twenty yards away,' she answered solemnly, staring pointedly at Abi's bare fingers. 'In the mornings they are oh-so pale and seeckly but by midday they 'ave a glow about them. But come, I have roasted chicken and vegetables.'

And so Abi shared a meal with the woman and as they were eating Madame Bissett asked, 'You ask me the way to the Medvilles' chateau. Do you know them?'

'I, er . . . don't actually know *them* but I know their grandson, Hugo,' Abi told her as she ate another piece of chicken. It was very juicy and tender. 'It was him I went to see but he won't be in until this evening.'

The woman nodded and just for a second she looked worried before fixing a smile back in place and saying knowingly, 'Ah . . . I see. And would thees young man 'ave anytheeng to do with the child you are carrying?'

Abi's blush told her all she wanted to know and she shook her head. 'You 'ave come to tell him about the child, yes?'

Abi nodded miserably. It was clear she wasn't going to be able to pull the wool over this lady's eyes.

'Then let us 'ope he does the right thing by you,' the woman said soberly as she gathered the dirty pots on to the tray and quietly left the room, leaving Abi to her thoughts.

Abi spent the rest of the afternoon in her bedroom. The nights were drawing in now but she waited until it was really dark before venturing back downstairs where she found Madame Bissett's other boarders about to sit down to their evening meal.

'Do you wish to dine?' Madame Bissett appeared from the kitchen with a loaded tray as Abi headed for the door.

Unable to meet her eye, Abi shook her head. 'Thank you, but no. I'm going to see if Hugo is in yet.' She let herself out on to the still busy street and turned in the direction of the Medvilles' chateau.

The journey seemed to take twice as long now that it was dark and every so often an animal noise from the woods made Abi glance about nervously, but at last she reached the drive leading to Hugo's grandparents' home and once again her heart began to hammer.

The same little maid she had seen earlier in the day answered the door. 'Could you tell me if Master Hugo is home yet, please?' Abi asked.

The girl turned to say something in French to someone behind her and a second later the housekeeper appeared again.

'Yes, he is home,' she informed Abi. 'Please wait there, mademoiselle, and I will see if he is available.' She closed the door firmly in Abi's face, making her flush with humiliation.

There was nothing to be heard but the sound of the night creatures and the wind in the trees and as she stood there Abi's teeth began to chatter with a mixture of nerves and cold. But at last the door opened again and Hugo almost erupted on to the steps. Closing the door firmly behind him and taking her elbow, he began to haul her on to the drive.

'What the hell are *you* doing here?' he demanded, sounding none too pleased to see her.

Abi's eyes gleamed with tears as she was dragged unceremoniously around the side of the house until they were out of sight of the windows at the front.

'*Well?*' He drew her to a halt and let her go so quickly that she swayed.

'That's hardly the greeting I was hoping for,' she told him in a wobbly voice. 'You didn't write to me so I had no idea when you were coming home.'

'*So?*'

'Well, I-I had to come as it happens!' Abi was beginning to lose her nerve completely now. This reunion wasn't going at all as she had hoped. She had imagined that he would be so thrilled to see her that he would drag her into the chateau to introduce her to his grandparents as his future bride, but instead it appeared that he was trying to hide her from them as if she was someone to be ashamed of.

'And why would that be? Surely whatever it is could have waited until I got back to London?'

Abi stood straight and glared at him now. 'I'm afraid it can't. You see . . .' She gulped deep in her throat and before she could lose her nerve completely, told him, 'I'm going to have a child!'

He looked momentarily shocked but then quickly pulling himself together he shrugged. 'Oh! And why would you come all this way to tell me that?'

Abi gasped, the colour draining from her face like water from a dam. 'I came because it is *your* baby I'm carrying!'

His lip curled as he stared at her with contempt. 'What you mean is you wish it *were* my baby,' he spat at her. 'But how can I believe that? You're nothing but a dirty little hostess whore from a backstreet club that entertains gentlemen. I've no doubt your bastard could belong to any number of the men you've entertained.'

'*Hugo!* How could you even *say* such a thing? You're the only man I've ever lain with!' she told him in a strangled voice. 'You *must* know that . . . you were my first and my only lover.' Arms outstretched she took a step towards him.

He knocked them away with a growl and stepped back. 'Just *go*,' he snarled. 'And try and palm your brat off on some other mug!'

With tears streaming down her face Abi drew herself up to her full height and glared at him. 'You won't get away with it that easily,' she warned. 'This is *your* baby and one way or another you're going to take responsibility for it even if I have to come and tell your grandparents about it!'

Now she could see the rage flashing in his eyes and for the first time she felt afraid as he caught her arm in a vicious grip and swung her about so abruptly that she almost fell. 'You do that and you'll wish you'd *never* been born!'

She could see he meant every word he said as he pushed her again.

'Now *get* out of my sight. I never want to see you again.'

'B-but you said you loved me,' she whimpered desperately as she fought to take him in her arms.

'I say that to all the girls. What makes you think you were any different?' And with that he gave her a final push that sent her sprawling on the ground then turned and strode away without so much as a backwards glance.

Surrounded by darkness Abi sat there too numb with shock to believe what had just happened as all her dreams of a happy ever after with the man she loved turned to ashes.

What shall I do now? she asked herself. She didn't even have enough money for her passage home. Most of the money she had earned since working at the club had been frivolously spent on glamorous gowns and she had truly believed that once she was here, Hugo would take care of her. The money she had left would stretch to a few more nights in Madame Bisset's guesthouse but what would she do then? Broken-hearted and shaking uncontrollably, she finally rose and staggered back towards the town.

Chapter Thirty-Three

'Good morning, Aunt, I've brought you your break-fast,' Emmy said cheerfully as she laid the tray down and hurried across her aunt's room to draw the curtains. Through the glass she could see the leaves beginning to flut-ter from the trees. The October morning was cold and she shuddered before moving to the small fireplace and throw-ing some coal on to the fire.

She had spent a sleepless night worrying about Abi and had finally decided in the early hours of the morning that she had no choice but to go to France and bring her home. But first she would have to sweet-talk her aunt into letting her have some time off.

She turned towards the bed and her heart leapt in her chest as she saw her aunt's blue lips. Her head was hanging limply to the side on her pillow and she was staring blankly. Racing out on to the landing, Emmy screamed, 'Aggie go for the doctor at once, my aunt is very ill!'

Within seconds Aggie appeared at the bottom of the stairs, her face ashen as she asked, 'What's 'appened, Miss Emmy?'

Emmy had no time to answer, for at that moment there was a rap on the door and when Aggie went to open it she found Jake standing there.

He was like the answer to a prayer and grabbing the sleeve of his coat she dragged him unceremoniously over the doorstep.

'Whatever is the matter?' he asked with concern. 'I was only nipping in to drop these bread baskets off to Cook on my way to work.'

'It's the missus,' Aggie told him with a catch in her voice. 'She's took bad apparently. Miss Emerald is up there with her now. She told me to run fer the doctor but seein' as 'ow yer 'ere, 'appen you could see what's wrong?'

Jake dropped the baskets, scattering them all over the floor, and took the stairs two at a time, calling over his shoulder, 'Go out to the carriage and bring me my doctor's bag please, Aggie.'

Aggie hurried off to do as she was told as Jake burst into the bedroom where he found Emmy hanging over her aunt with tears on her cheeks.

She looked up when he came in, and she was sure she had never been so pleased to see anyone in her life. 'I just . . . just brought her breakfast and found her like this,' she sobbed. 'What's happened to her, Jake?'

Jake didn't answer as he started to unbutton Imogen's high-necked nightgown, and when Aggie returned with his bag, he quickly withdrew his stethoscope and listened to her heart. But he had no need to examine her really, the way her face had dropped on one side told him all he needed to know.

'Wh-what's wrong with her?' Emmy whimpered as he rose and began to adjust Imogen's pillows.

'She's suffered an apoplectic seizure – or a stroke as it's now being named,' he answered gravely. 'Now, help me to raise these pillows and then pass me the little white tablets you'll find in the front of my bag.'

Emmy was all fingers and thumbs, but she managed to do as he asked and when her aunt was propped up and he had placed a tablet beneath her tongue, she asked fearfully, 'She is going to be all right and get better, isn't she?'

Jake felt as if his heart was breaking seeing Emmy so fearful and upset but he was well aware that their aunt may be able to still hear them so after making sure he had made her as comfortable as he could, he drew her out on to the landing, leaving Aggie to sit beside her.

'I'm afraid I can't answer that question, Emmy.' He really wished that he could. 'A lot will depend on what happens in the next forty-eight hours. If she can get past that she has every chance of making a recovery, although I doubt she'll ever be quite as she was before and she'll have to be very careful. She's going to need constant nursing for some time.'

As he spoke, Emmy's hopes of going in search of Abi flew out of the window and she felt as if she were being torn in two. She was in a no-win situation. If she stayed to care for her aunt she would continue to worry about Abi and if she went looking for Abi she would worry about her aunt.

'What can I do for her?' she asked, wiping away her tears with the back of her hand and lifting her chin, determined to rise to the challenge.

'Keep her very quiet and get as much liquid into her as you can,' he advised. 'And of course, she'll need to see her own doctor to see if he agrees with my diagnosis. It's lucky that I stopped by when I did. Will you manage, Emmy?'

His voice was so kind and gentle and so full of concern for her that she was afraid she'd start crying again, but somehow she held herself together as she nodded.

'Yes, I will.' She gave him a tremulous smile. 'It's my aunt we should be worrying about not me. Poor soul, what a dreadful thing to happen to her.' She paused before saying, 'I was going to ask her today if I could have some time off to go and try to find Abi and bring her home but that's out of the question now.'

'Wouldn't Aggie be willing to care for her?'

She nodded. 'Oh yes, I'm sure she would, but I'd feel so guilty leaving her. We'll just have to see how she is in a few days' time. Perhaps if I know she's on the road to recovery I might risk leaving her but certainly not until then.'

'What about if you were to ask your mother to come and take over for a short while? I'm sure she wouldn't mind if you explained the situation to her.'

That idea hadn't occurred to Emmy. 'Hm, you could be right. I shall have to write to her today and tell her what's happened anyway and we'll take it from there. It could take her months to arrive, however, she wrote this very week to say that poor dear Hetty has broken her ankle. For now, I just need to see that she's going to recover.' She brushed a stray tear from her cheek with the back of her hand. 'I don't think I'd realised just how much I'd come to care for her until now. But anyway, you get to work. I'm sure we've made you late already. I'm just so relieved you happened by when you did.' And with a sad smile she turned to go back to her aunt as Jake took a deep breath and left.

Imogen's doctor confirmed Jake's diagnosis when he arrived shortly after. Her aunt was still semi-conscious and seemed unaware of anything or anyone so Emmy sat holding her hand and quietly talking to her for the rest of the day as Aggie nipped in and out checking to see if there was anything she needed.

That night Emmy sat in the chair at the side of her aunt's bed, refusing to go to her own room, but in the early hours of the morning exhaustion finally claimed her and she dozed on and off with her head laid on the side of the bed. She woke with a start as the light started to seep into the room early the next morning and as she glanced up her face broke into a smile as she found her aunt awake and staring at her.

'Thank goodness,' she cried, planting a kiss on her cheek. 'You had us worried for a while back there.'

'Ugh . . . ugh . . .' Her aunt tried to answer her but the only sounds she could manage were grunts. Still, Emmy knew it was very early days and she was just relieved that she was properly conscious again.

'You've had a nasty turn,' she explained as she gently lifted the woman higher on her pillows. 'But don't worry. We'll get you well again. But first would you like something to drink?'

Her aunt shook her head as a single tear slid down her cheek and knowing how independent she was Emmy realised how much she would hate being like this. 'Very well. The doctor is coming back in to see you first thing so let's get you washed and into a clean nightgown, eh?' She bustled away to fetch a bowl of warm water from the kitchen.

She and Aggie managed her aunt's wash between them and once she was propped against her pillows with her long hair neatly brushed and plaited, Emmy gave her an affectionate smile, although her heart was breaking. One side of her aunt's face was pulled down and she dribbled continuously but Emmy kept up a cheerful chatter. 'Right, now you're all clean, it's time we got something inside you.'

'Uh! Uh!' Her aunt's head wagged from side to side but Emmy was insistent as she gently held the cup of lukewarm tea to her lips.

'Sorry, but it's important you have your fluids,' she told her bossily and somehow after a lot of spilling down her aunt's chin she managed to get about half a cup inside her.

'And now I reckon *you* should have a lie-down, miss. You've only catnapped an' yer must be tired,' Aggie told her. 'Go on, go an' have a rest. I'm more than capable o' copin' wi' the missus an' I'll call yer when the doctor comes.'

And so somewhat reluctantly after taking the letter she had written to her mother the night before downstairs to be posted, Emmy wearily made her way to her room and lay on the bed. She was sure she wouldn't sleep as she sank back against the pillows, but what with worrying about her sister and now her aunt, she was utterly exhausted and was fast asleep in seconds.

Jake called in that evening to see how Imogen was and was pleased to see that she was awake, although very frustrated. It appeared that the stroke had affected the whole of her left side and her hand lay limply on the bed at the side of her.

'Will she ever get back to being how she was?' Emmy asked him when she took him downstairs for a cup of tea. He had come straight from work and looked tired.

He sighed. 'To be honest there's no way of knowing,' he told her truthfully. 'Some people get all their mobility back, others don't. But I have to tell you it's extremely unlikely she'll ever be completely back to normal.'

'I see, then it looks like I'm going to have to take on the role of nurse as well as companion,' Emmy commented.

The next week passed in a blur for Emmy as she saw to Imogen's needs and tried her best to keep the woman's spirits up. She was not proving to be a good patient but Emmy wouldn't have expected her to be and she was endlessly patient with her even when Imogen got frustrated because she was having to be spoon-fed and knocked the spoon out of Emmy's hand. And all the while the niggling worry about Abi was in the back of Emmy's mind until finally one morning, she asked Aggie, 'Do you think you could sit with my aunt for a while so that I can go and find out if Abi is back from her trip to France?' Imogen still had no control over her left side and was still unable to speak apart from making unintelligible sounds, but the doctor was pleased with her progress and so Emmy felt she was well enough to leave for a short time now.

'O' course I can,' Aggie answered obligingly.

Soon after Emmy set off, shivering in the cold October morning air. It was still early and hoar frost was sparkling on the grass in the park as she passed it but she was so intent on getting news of her sister that she didn't even notice it. Once on the main road she flagged down a cab and as soon as it dropped her outside the club she hurried through the alley and rapped on the back door of the girl's living quarters.

'I've come to see if my sister has returned yet,' Emmy said urgently when Winnie answered the door.

The girl bit her lip as she solemnly shook her head. 'No, we ain't had sight nor sound of 'er, miss, an' Lilly ain't none too pleased about it, I don't mind tellin' yer.'

Emmy stepped past her into the long narrow hallway just as Lilly appeared in a flounced dress and reeking of expensive perfume. Spotting Emmy she narrowed her eyes.

'Come to collect yer sister's things, 'ave yer?' she asked bluntly.

Emmy blinked. 'Well . . . er, no, I hadn't.'

'Hm, seein' as yer 'ere yer might as well go up to 'er room an' collect 'em then,' Lilly said brusquely, clearly disgruntled. 'Girls who just swan off an' come an' go as they please for weeks at a time ain't no good to me,' Lilly said vehemently. 'I've already got another girl to take 'er place so the sooner 'er stuff is shifted the better. Winnie, show 'er up to Abi's room.'

Winnie bobbed her knee and shot off up the stairs and, too shocked to do any other, Emmy quietly followed her.

Much as her room at home had always been, Abi's room was in disarray with discarded clothes strewn about the floor and thrown across the bed and the chair.

'Thank you, Winnie. I'll see to it,' Emmy said as she retrieved some bags from the bottom of the wardrobe and began to pack Abi's things. There would be far too many for her to carry, she realised, so once the packing was done, she'd have to flag down a cab to take her back to her aunt's.

As well as the extravagant gowns that Abi had purchased, there was a number of gifts that Emmy assumed different men had bestowed on her, including expensive perfumes and items of jewellery, and she packed it all safely away. She had almost finished when there was a tap at the door and Maria's head peeped round it.

'You ain't 'eard nothing from her then?' she queried, looking concerned.

Emmy shook her head and was about to tell her what had happened to her aunt, but she was just too weary to so she clamped her mouth shut as tears threatened.

'Never mind, she's probably 'aving the time of her life wi' Hugo,' Maria said kindly.

'I certainly hope she is and that nothing's happened to her.' Emmy snapped the last bag shut and glanced around the room to make sure she hadn't missed anything. 'I'm taking her stuff back to my aunt's so if she should come back will you ask her to come there?' she asked.

'Course I will, queen.' Maria's eyes were sad as she hoisted one of the bags up. 'Let me 'elp yer get all this stuff downstairs.' And without another word she left the room.

When Emmy arrived back at the house, Aggie took Abi's things up to one of the spare rooms as Emmy went to check on her aunt whose eyes found her the minute she entered the room.

'I've been to the club to see if Abi has returned from France,' Emmy told her as she removed her bonnet and held her cold hands out to the small fire. 'But she hasn't, and now she's lost her job.'

When she approached the bed, Imogen clutched her arm with her good hand and gave her a lopsided smile. 'Shee . . . bee . . . all right . . .' she managed and Emmy smiled despite her fears for Abi. It was the most her aunt had managed to say since she had suffered her stroke and although the words were slurred, Emmy took it as a good sign.

Chapter Thirty-Four

It was the beginning of December and as Emmy was carrying her aunt's dirty washing down the stairs, someone knocked on the door. When Aggie hurried from the drawing room, where she was polishing, to answer it, Dorcas appeared.

'*Mama!*' Emmy was so shocked and delighted to see her that she almost dropped the clothes she was holding and after slamming them down on to the hall table she hurried over to embrace her mother. 'What are you doing here? Is Hetty better?' she gabbled joyously. Emmy had been horribly disappointed that Dorcas had been unable to come when she'd first written to tell her what had happened with Imogen and Abi. But Hetty had fallen and broken her ankle, so her mother couldn't leave her.

Dorcas smiled. 'Hold on and let me get in. And shut that door, for goodness' sake, you're letting the cold in.'

Aggie hurriedly closed the door and helped Dorcas off with her coat.

'Brr, it's enough to freeze you out there,' Dorcas commented as she undid the ribbons on her bonnet and handed it to Aggie. 'And yes, Hetty is much better. The minute she was able to get out and about again, she insisted I come. I'm so sorry I couldn't get here sooner. I've been so worried!

But at last, I've come to help look after my sister. Now, is there any tea going? I'm frozen through and I swear we're in for some snow before long.'

As Aggie bustled away to make the tea, Emmy led her mother into the drawing room where she quickly brought her up to date with everything that had happened.

'So, Imogen is making a good recovery then?' she said when Emmy had finished.

'Yes, she is, but because of her heart condition the doctor told me that she's still in danger and if she should have another stroke, it's unlikely she would survive it.'

'I see,' Dorcas said sombrely, regretting all the years she and her sister had spent apart. But there were so many regrets now. 'And is there any news from Abigail?'

When Emmy shook her head, Dorcas sighed and gazed towards the window.

'Until Aunt Imogen took ill, I was thinking of asking her for some time off so that I could go to France to try to find her,' Emmy continued. 'But of course, with her being so poorly I didn't like to leave her. But tell me, is Hetty really all right now?'

Dorcas raised her eyebrows. 'Poor love. Yes, she's getting stronger. And at least she can walk and look after the cottage and Bruno for me. You'll hardly recognise him the next time you see him, he's really grown and he's bright as a button. But things aren't so good over at the farm, I'm afraid. Jasper has cleared off again and Bernard is furious and threatening to disinherit him if he doesn't come back soon. That boy has no sense of responsibility whatsoever, I can understand them being so annoyed with him.'

Aggie arrived at that moment with a laden tea trolley and as Emmy poured the tea into fine bone china cups she wondered where Jasper might have gone. After the last conversation they'd had when he'd professed to have feelings for her, she sincerely hoped that he wasn't back in London but she didn't say as much to her mother. She'd had enough to deal with over the last few months, although now she seemed to be coping with everything admirably well. In fact, she seemed almost content.

'Ah, that hit the spot, but I'd like to go and see Imogen now, if you don't mind,' Dorcas said after her second cup of tea and Emmy obligingly led her upstairs.

When the bedroom door opened Imogen's eyes turned towards it and as she saw Dorcas standing there they filled with tears, showing Emmy that she wasn't quite as hard-hearted as she tried to make out.

'D-Dori . . .' At the use of the affectionate nickname she had always used for her younger sister when she was a child, Dorcas began to cry too and not wanting to intrude on their reunion, Emmy left the room, closing the door quietly behind her.

As always Jake called in on his way home from work that evening, just as he had every night since Imogen's stroke, and when Emmy told him of her mother's arrival he was thrilled.

'Good, that might take a little of the strain off you.'

'It isn't a strain,' Emmy assured him as he helped himself to one of Cook's delicious scones fresh out of the oven. He'd been staying for dinner some evenings too and Emmy had been glad of his company now that she couldn't get out and about. Sadly, she was no longer able to help him at what they had christened the 'poor surgery' on Sundays any more but thankfully a friend of Jake's who had been at medical school with him and was also newly qualified was helping him out for now.

'While your mother is here it might be a good idea if you took advantage of the fact and got out for a bit of fresh air,' he suggested, noticing how pale Emmy was.

She gave him a guilty grin. 'Actually, I was wondering if Mother might be prepared to stay on for a while to take care of Aunt Imogen so that I could go to France to look for Abi.'

Jake frowned. 'I hope you're not thinking of going on your own?'

'Why ever not? Abi did.' Emmy grinned.

'Quite, and now we don't know where she is,' he pointed out.

'But we *do*.' Emmy told him. 'Maria gave me the address of Hugo's grandparents. I thought of writing to them but didn't like to.' Something occurred to her then, and she went on, 'My mother told me Jasper is in trouble for clearing off from home again. You don't think he's gone to Hugo in France too, do you?'

'I'd say that was a possibility.' Jake looked thoughtful. 'He's certainly spent enough summers out there in the past but I've never known him to go in the winter.'

'There's a first time for everything and I wouldn't put it past him if it saved him from having to work,' Emmy snorted.

The door opened and Dorcas appeared. 'Imogen is having a nap so I thought I'd pop down for a cup of tea. How are you, Jake?' She smiled at him.

317

'I'm very well, thank you, Aunt.' Jake gave a polite little bow, then he turned and looked at Emmy pointedly and she gulped. She supposed he was thinking now was as good a time as any to ask her mother to stay for a while. And so, she tentatively put the idea to her and was surprised when Dorcas readily agreed without any argument.

'But I don't want you travelling all that way on your own,' she said, wagging a finger at her.

'That's exactly what I told her,' Jake said. 'But leave that with me. I'll have a word with my boss tomorrow and see if I can get a few days off so that I can go too.'

The next evening Jake informed them that he'd booked a week off work starting on Saturday and had organised for his friend Richard to hold the fort at the poor surgery while he was gone. Suddenly everything was hustle and bustle as Dorcas helped Emmy pack for the journey.

'You must take plenty of warm clothes, it's going to be cold on the ship,' she warned. 'And when you do find Abi, please persuade her to come back if you can.'

'Of course I will,' Emmy promised. The trip was only two days away and she was alternately looking forward to it and dreading it. What if Abi wasn't there? Or worse still, what if something had happened to her? But then she would have Jake with her no matter what happened and the thought was comforting, although she wasn't sure how she was going to be able to be in his company for so long without betraying how she felt about him.

Before she knew it, it was Saturday morning and time to be off. After hurriedly kissing her mother and aunt, Emmy clambered into the cab Jake had waiting for her outside and they headed for the docks to board *The Neptune*.

Unlike the day that Abi had sailed, the sea was as calm as a millpond and the boat was covered in frost that made climbing the slippery gangplank a treacherous affair. Emmy would have slipped more than once had it not been for Jake's strong arm about her and once they were safely on deck she breathed a sigh of relief.

'I-it's so cold!' she said through chattering teeth as Jake led her towards the passengers' cabins.

'Hopefully they'll have left us plenty of blankets to wrap ourselves in,' he said as they negotiated the treacherously slippery stairs that led down into the ship. 'Ah, here we are,' he said eventually, 'Number 5. I could only get one cabin, I'm afraid, but, all being well, we won't be sleeping aboard so we'll just have to make the best of it. Once the ship has set sail we'll go and find the dining room. Hopefully it will be a bit warmer in there and we'll be able to get a hot drink and something to eat.'

Almost an hour later the ship began to rock and they were on their way and by the time they had climbed back up on deck they were just in time to see a foggy London fading into the distance.

Within no time the ship's cook had made them a very tasty breakfast and with that and two cups of hot sweet tea inside them they began to feel warmer. Emmy would have liked to wander on the deck but now that they were out at sea the wind was cutting so they stayed where they were in the warm and chatted about the patients who were now attending the surgery.

'Word's getting around and I think the free bread is an added attraction,' he told her with a grin that made him look so handsome her heart turned over.

The day passed in a flash and soon it was dark and Emmy glanced nervously towards the window.

'I hope they know which direction they're heading in,' she said.

Jake chuckled. 'Don't worry, we should be there soon and the captain knows exactly where he's going,' he assured her. 'If it wasn't so cold we could go and stand on deck and watch the lights of Le Havre come into view.' He smiled and pointed towards the window where the first snow of winter was fluttering down.

Emmy nodded. It looked so pretty but not pretty enough to tempt her out on to the deck. 'I hope we can find some-where to stay tonight,' she said.

'Don't worry. I happen to know there's a rather nice hotel not too far from the docks,' he told her. 'We can stay there tonight and then we'll go and find Hugo, and hopefully Abi too, first thing in the morning.'

She nodded in agreement and they spent the rest of the journey sitting in a companionable silence.

When they disembarked, Jake lifted their bags and after taking directions from a sailor, they found their way to the hotel where they hurried to the reception desk.

'It ees a double room you are needing for yourself and your wife?' the man behind the desk asked and colour flooded into Emmy's cheeks.

'Oh no . . . we're not . . . I mean, thank you but we'd like a room each please,' Jake told him hastily, looking rather amused.

The hotelier was a small man, almost as far round as he was high with a waxed handlebar moustache and oiled black hair.

'Ah, forgeeve me, monsieur. I assumed the mademoiselle was your wife.' He turned and took two keys from a board behind him and snapped his fingers to summon the porter who was slouching on a sofa in the far corner of the foyer.

'Pierre, take the guests' luggage up to their rooms, if you pleeze.' He turned back to Emmy and Jake. 'I am afraid the dining room eez now closed but perhaps you would like some coffee or hot chocolate and croissants brought to your room?'

Jake thanked him and they followed the young porter up a sweeping staircase to the first floor where they were shown to two very comfortable rooms. They ate their supper together in Emmy's room looking out of the window at the boats in the harbour and then Jake retired to his own room while Emmy took the pins from her hair and got ready for bed.

Once again the doubts set in. What if Abi wasn't there? What if they had come all that way for nothing? What would she tell her mother if she had to go home without her? But then taking a firm grip on herself, she pulled on her night-gown and slid into bed, very aware that Jake was just a few doors away from her. She tossed and turned for some time but eventually she slept. She would know soon now and the morning couldn't come quickly enough.

Chapter Thirty-Five

'You look tired,' Jake commented the next morning as they sat together having breakfast in the hotel dining room.

'I didn't get that much sleep,' Emmy admitted as she poured them both a cup of tea. 'What if she isn't here?'

'Where else would she be?' He patted her hand. 'Stop worrying, we'll find her and hopefully persuade her to come home with us. She's probably been staying with Hugo's grandparents. I hope you've brought some strong footwear. The Medvilles' chateau is a good step past the town from what the man on the reception desk told me and it hasn't stopped snowing all night.'

Emmy glanced towards the window. He was right, the snow was still coming down in thick white flakes but thankfully she had thought to pack a pair of stout walking boots, although she wondered if even they would be any use in this weather. Still, her need to see Abi was so great that she would have walked barefoot if need be so she wasn't overly concerned.

The breakfast in front of them was very different to the ones they were accustomed to back at home. There was a basket of small rolls and pastries fresh from the oven and a selection of jams and thick creamy butter to spread on them. Jake was tucking in with a will but Emmy could hardly swallow a thing and was glad when he finally sat back and rubbed his stomach appreciatively.

'That was delicious,' he declared. 'But you're like a cat on hot bricks so shall we go back to our rooms and get ready to go?'

'Yes please.' Emmy rose hastily and they hurried back to their rooms.

They met up again in the foyer shortly after, wrapped in layers of clothes.

'Right, we'll get off then,' Jake said and taking her elbow they stepped out on to the street.

The bitterly cold wind took their breath away and as the snow was blown into their faces, they had to bow their heads as they set off for the outskirts of the town.

'I c-can't believe how big and how busy this place is,' Emmy panted as they slipped and slid their way up the main street. Thankfully the traffic had flattened the snow, but it was now treacherously slippery and Emmy clung on to Jake's arm for dear life.

'Le Havre is a very busy seaport,' Jake agreed and as they moved slowly along, they passed sailors of all nationalities, colours, shapes and sizes.

When they eventually reached the outskirts of the town, though, the snow deepened as the road rose through trees up a steep hill, and they passed fewer people. By now the bottom of Emmy's skirts were sodden and they were both so covered in snow that it was impossible to see what colour clothes they were wearing. Her boots had proved to be rather ineffective and already her feet were so cold and wet that she was losing all feeling in them.

'I h-hope it isn't too much further,' Emmy said breathlessly as they steadily climbed. The snow was much deeper here and they had left the sounds of the town far behind. All they could hear now was the wind gusting through the leafless trees. Then suddenly Jake squeezed her hand and glancing up through narrowed eyes Emmy saw someone heading towards them from the opposite direction. As the person drew closer, he lifted his head and Jake gasped with amazement as he dragged Emmy to a halt.

'Jasper! What are you doing here?'

'I could ask you the same thing,' Jasper replied as he stared pointedly at Emmy's arm, which was tucked through Jake's.

'We . . . we've come to find Abi.' Emmy's teeth were chattering and she was sure she would never be warm again.

'Abi?' Jasper frowned. 'What would Abi be doing here?'

'She left the club some weeks ago to come and find Hugo,' Emmy told him, her heart thudding painfully. 'She told Maria at the club that he was staying here with his grandparents.'

'He is,' Jasper agreed. 'But we've seen nothing of Abi, I assure you.'

'But you must have!' Emmy was clearly distressed now.

Jasper shook his head. 'I've been here a while and I'm sure Hugo would have told me if she'd visited him,' he insisted, then with a guilty expression he looked back at Jake. 'I got fed up with Father barking orders at me. I wonder what it will take for him to realise that I don't want to be a bloody farmer!'

'Well, you've got to do something with your life,' Jake said unsympathetically. 'How are you going to live if Father stops your allowance?'

Jasper sniffed as he swiped the snow from out of his eyes. It was almost blizzard-like now. 'He already has,' he sneered. 'But thankfully, Mother is sending money out to me. But come on, I think we need to get Emmy out of the cold, she looks frozen through. Where are you staying?'

Emmy hesitated but realising there was nothing to be gained from going any further if Abi wasn't there, she sighed with disappointment and they started the downward climb. It seemed much harder going down than it had going up and more than once she would have fallen had it not been for Jake and Jasper supporting her. At last, they reached the hotel and staggered into the foyer, wet through and gasping for breath.

'Go upstairs and get out of those wet clothes before you catch your death of cold,' Jake ordered, taking control. 'Then come back down and I'll have some hot coffee waiting for you.'

Too afraid and miserable to argue, Emmy climbed the stairs and went to her room, her mind whirling. If Abi wasn't here, then where was she? Maria had been so specific; surely, she couldn't have got it wrong?

She hung her wet cloak and bonnet on a hook on the back of her door and peeled off her clothes, throwing them into a sodden heap on the floor. Her best travelling gown looked as if it could well be ruined, but that was the least of Emmy's worries right now. All she could think about was where her sister might be.

She found Jasper and Jake sitting in front of a roaring fire in the foyer when she went back downstairs. They had steaming cups of coffee in their hands and Jasper leapt up to draw her towards the fire. 'Come and get warm. You're as white as a ghost.' The touch of his hand on her arm made her shudder and she was glad that Jake was there. She didn't feel comfortable with Jasper any more.

'Are you quite sure that Hugo hasn't seen Abi?' she questioned when the feeling started to return to her hands and feet.

'Quite sure. So, what are you going to do now?'

Emmy shrugged, feeling defeated. 'I suppose I shall have to go home without her.'

'Hm.' Jasper thought for a moment. 'But what if she *is* here in Le Havre and she just hasn't been to see Hugo yet? Wouldn't it pay to hang around for a while so we can ask about and see if anyone has seen her?'

'I'm afraid I can't stay here indefinitely,' Jake told him. 'Some of us have work to go back to.'

'So you go back and Emmy can stay here with me. We can search for her together,' Jasper suggested.

As much as Emmy hated the thought of having to spend any amount of time with Jasper, she supposed it did make sense.

'And how does she get home?' Jake said irritably. 'The whole point of me coming along was so that she wouldn't have to travel by herself.'

'That isn't a problem.' Jasper stretched his long legs out towards the fire. 'If we find Abi they can travel home together and if we don't, I shall accompany her.'

Jake wasn't at all happy with the idea but couldn't come up with a better one so he shrugged. 'Very well, but only if Emmy feels comfortable with that?'

She nodded, feeling like she didn't have much choice. 'But you don't have to go immediately, do you?'

'I can stay for three days but then I really should be getting home. So later today let's start to ask about and see if anyone has seen her.'

Jasper and Emmy nodded in agreement as Emmy tried her best to be optimistic.

Later that afternoon they went out and each of them started to stop people in the streets and enter shops to give them Abi's description and ask them if they had seen her but by the time it was dark, they'd had no luck at all.

'It's as if she's vanished off the face of the earth,' Emmy fretted when they made their way wearily back to the hotel again.

'We'll find her,' Jake promised comfortingly.

Jasper glared at him, although he said nothing. Seeing Emmy and Jake together was like a knife in his heart and he couldn't wait for Jake to sail home so he could have her all to himself.

For three days they scoured the streets with no success and reluctantly Jake went to book himself a passage home.

'I hate to leave you,' he told Emmy on the morning of his departure. 'Why don't you come back with me today?'

'I shall be fine and I'd only fret if I left,' she answered truthfully. 'But I will come back just as soon as I'm convinced that she didn't come here.' And with that Jake had to be content.

Emmy walked with him to the harbour and saw him aboard a cargo ship that was heading for London on the morning tide and as the ship was swallowed up by the falling snow her spirits sank. Despite her reason for being here she had enjoyed their time together and she knew that she was going to miss him. She was all alone with Jasper now but having to put up with him would be a small price to pay if they managed to find Abi, she decided.

For the next two days the search continued but it was fruitless and eventually Emmy admitted, 'I think perhaps Abi didn't come here after all. Surely if she had we'd have found her by now? I can't stay much longer so I think I'll start to make enquiries about getting a passage home.'

Jasper had been like her shadow ever since Jake had left, only leaving her late each night and now he was horrified at the thought of her going.

'But we *can't* give up yet.' He caught her hand and a shiver ran through her. She'd been grateful for his help but she still didn't feel at ease with him, even though he had behaved like a perfect gentleman.

Gently withdrawing her hand from his she primly laid it in her lap. They were in the foyer of the hotel and after a long day walking the streets she was tired and despondent and just wanted her bed.

'This is a big place,' he rushed on. 'And we haven't covered a fraction of it yet.'

Narrowing her eyes, she peered at him. 'And you say that Hugo was quite adamant that he hadn't seen her when you asked him if Abi had tried to get in touch with him?'

'Quite,' he lied, looking her straight in the eye.

'Then I'm sorry but tomorrow I shall make enquiries about returning home. Aunt Imogen was very ill when I left and I can't leave my mother to cope with her alone any longer.'

Seeing that she meant what she said, Jasper's shoulders sagged. He had hoped that having her to himself after Jake's departure would draw them closer together but although Emmy had been polite and civil to him, she'd made it more than clear by her actions that she still only looked on him as her cousin.

'In that case I shall come with you,' he stated. 'I suppose I've got to go back and face the music sometime. The money my mother sent me is running out anyway so leave it with me and I'll book us a passage out of here on the next available ship.'

Emmy nodded, stifling a yawn. 'Thank you. Goodnight, Jasper.' And with that she rose and went to her room without another word, leaving him to stare after her with a frown on his face.

As he made the long walk back to Hugo's grandparents' house, up to his ankles in snow, an idea occurred to him.

He knew all too well that at the moment Emmy regarded him as a young waster but if anything were to happen to his father – an accident, for example – that made him unable to manage the farm any more, then his father would have no choice but to let him have free rein with how the farm was run, and as there was a perfectly reliable manager, Jasper could leave the main running of it in his hands and do as he pleased while still having access to his father's wealth. Admittedly, as the oldest son, Jake would probably inherit the farm when his father passed away, but he wouldn't want to live back there. He was too wrapped up in his work in London, which would leave him in charge and he could wrap his mother around his little finger. Surely Emmy would look on him more favourably if he was a man of means? What woman didn't like having money spent on her and being showered with extravagant gifts?

A smile hovered about his lips and he was so taken with planning how his father might meet with his 'little accident' that he didn't even notice the cold.

Chapter Thirty-Six

The next morning, Emmy came down to breakfast to find Jasper already waiting for her.

'You're an early bird,' she remarked.

'Oh, I've been up for hours. I've already been down to the docks and managed to get us a passage home tomorrow.'

'Well done.' Part of her was thankful to be going home but the other part was devastated that the trip had been in vain. 'In that case perhaps you'd care to join me for breakfast and after that we can spend this last day having a final look around?'

He nodded obligingly as he followed her into the hotel dining room and an hour later, they set off through the snowy streets to continue their search.

Once again, their efforts came to nothing and when it was dark Jasper escorted her back to the hotel. 'I thought perhaps we might have a meal together seeing as it's our last night here?' he suggested.

Emmy shook her head as the snow from her boots melted into pools on the floor of the foyer. 'Thank you for the offer but I've my packing to do if we have an early start tomorrow.'

Swallowing his disappointment, he nodded and they parted until the next day when he returned to escort her to the boat.

The return crossing was nowhere near as calm as the outward journey and at times Emmy clutched her seat in fear of her life as the boat pitched in the stormy seas. But at last, late that evening, they sailed into the docks in London and after disembarking Jasper hailed them a cab to take them back to Imogen's.

'I thought Aunt Imogen might let me stay the night,' he said on the journey through the quiet streets. 'I doubt I'd get a train home this late.'

'I'm quite sure she wouldn't mind,' Emmy assured him and they went the rest of the way in silence.

'Oh, Miss Emerald, I'm so glad to see yer back,' Aggie told her when she opened the door to them shortly after. 'Yer ma an' yer aunt 'ave been worried sick about yer. Did yer 'ave a good journey back?'

'No, I'm afraid we didn't, Aggie,' Emmy answered wearily as Aggie helped her out of her cloak. 'But how is my aunt?' Her legs felt as if they were made of rubber and she was longing for a cup of tea.

'Well, she's certainly got 'er voice back, albeit slurred,' Aggie answered with a wry grin. 'An' she's certainly no worse, which is sumfin' I suppose. Now go an' sit by the fire while I get yer both a hot drink.'

Emmy gave her a grateful smile. 'Thank you, and do you think you could prepare the spare bedroom for my cousin? It's too late for him to get a train home this evening.'

'O' course I can,' Aggie answered obligingly. 'But first I'll get yer both a drink an' tell yer ma yer back.'

Aggie disappeared up the stairs while Emmy led Jasper into the drawing room where a low fire was still burning.

Minutes later Dorcas burst into the room. 'Oh, thank goodness you're safe,' she said. 'Is there any news?'

'I'm afraid not.' Emmy shook her head and seeing that she didn't look at all well her mother didn't press the point.

'Try not to worry,' her mother soothed. 'I'm sure you did your best. We'll talk tomorrow when you've had a rest; you look all in.'

'I am, and I imagine Jasper is too,' Emmy answered. 'He's going home tomorrow.'

'In that case we may as well travel home together,' Dorcas told him. 'There's no point me staying on here now that you're home. Imogen is no worse, which the doctor says is a good sign. She's out of danger for now, thank goodness.'

Just for a second Emmy thought she saw Jasper frown at the suggestion but it was gone as quickly as it came and she wondered if she'd imagined it.

After they'd had a cup of tea, Emmy went straight to bed and was asleep as soon as her head hit the pillow.

Aggie woke her the next morning with yet more tea and Emmy realised that she hadn't eaten since the morning before. The sea journey had been so bad that she hadn't been able to face eating, afraid that she might bring any food straight back up. Now, though, she was suddenly starving. But before breakfast she wanted to see her aunt, so after swallowing the hot drink as quickly as she could she dragged her dressing robe on and hurried to her aunt's room.

'Ah . . . you're back.' Her aunt's voice was weak and slightly slurred but that was a huge improvement to what it had been before Emmy left and she sighed with relief.

'Yes, I am and I'm thrilled to find you on the mend.' As she bent and quickly pecked the woman's cheek Imogen waved her aside with her good hand.

'Th-at's quite enough of that sloppy stuff,' she admonished her but Emmy noticed the little smile that hovered around her mouth.

'Y-your m . . . other is packing,' Imogen went on. 'She's going h . . . ome today now that you're back.'

'So I believe, but I'm afraid I didn't manage to find Abi,' Emmy answered, finding it strange that her aunt hadn't asked after her.

Imogen raised her hand and flapped it. 'Don't g-get worrying about her. She's a strong girl and we-well able to take care of herself.'

'I hope you're right. But now I'm going to go and get dressed and see my mother before she leaves, then after breakfast I'll come and read the newspaper to you.' She tucked the covers snugly around her aunt, noting that she was on the verge of sleeping again, before quietly leaving the room.

On the landing she almost bumped into Jasper who was washed and dressed and on his way downstairs. He drank in the sight of her. With her hair loose and tumbled about her shoulders and in her nightclothes, he thought she looked beautiful, although he didn't comment on it.

'I was just going down to breakfast,' he said instead. 'Your mother and I are hoping to make an early start, will you be joining us?'

Emmy nodded as she swept past him, feeling vaguely embarrassed to be seen in her night attire.

'Yes, just give me time to get dressed and I'll be right down.' And she disappeared into her bedroom closing the door firmly behind her.

Her mother and Jasper were already seated at the table when she went into the dining room a short time later and her mother smiled at her, asking, 'Did you sleep well, dear?'

Emmy helped herself to some toast. 'Like a log. I think I must have dropped off the second my head hit the pillow and I think I'd probably be there still if Aggie hadn't wakened me.'

Her mother sighed. 'And what can we do to find Abi now?' She was obviously very worried about her.

Emmy shrugged. 'I don't know, but first I'm going to pay a visit to the club to make sure she hasn't gone back there.' Deep down she felt that she'd probably be wasting her time. All Abi's things were stored in one of her aunt's spare bedrooms and if Abi had come back, she would surely have come to fetch them, but she couldn't think what else to do.

Her mother nodded. 'Jake has called in every day since you've been gone. I'm sure he'll be happy to know you're back safe and sound.'

'Why wouldn't she be? I was there taking good care of her,' Jasper commented sullenly and Emmy was shocked to see the dull colour rise in his cheeks. 'But anyway, we'd best get our coats on. I got Aggie to go and order us a cab to take us to the station and it will be here in fifteen minutes.' He scraped his chair back and strode from the room.

Now that they were alone her mother asked, 'Are you quite sure you'll cope with your aunt, Emerald? I'm afraid she's very frustrated at being bedridden and it makes her quite grumpy.'

Emmy grinned as she spread marmalade on her toast. 'Don't worry, Mama, I'm used to her moods now and I'm just relieved that she seems a little better. I've no doubt Hetty and Bruno will be pleased to have you home.'

Dorcas nodded. 'And believe it or not I shall be glad to be home. I'm afraid London with its crowded streets has no lure for me now. I'm used to peace and quiet living in the cottage, although I doubt it will be very peaceful at the farm when Jasper arrives back,' she confided. 'Your Uncle Bernard was absolutely furious with him when he just took off again and who can blame him? I'm afraid Sybil has spoilt him shamelessly.'

Emmy was tempted to say, 'Just like *you* spoilt Abi,' but she managed to refrain and clamped her lips shut. There was no point in causing ill feeling when her mother was on the verge of leaving.

Soon after, the hackney cab arrived and while the driver piled the luggage on to the top of it, Jasper and Dorcas said their goodbyes.

'Be sure to keep me informed about the search for Abi,' her mother called when Jasper had helped her into the cab.

'I will,' Emmy promised as she stood on the step waving and soon the cab pulled away and was swallowed up by the snow.

As the day wore on Emmy found herself getting excited at the prospect of seeing Jake again. She had missed him far more than she had thought she would after he had left her in Le Havre, so when he finally arrived it was all she could do to stop herself throwing her arms about him.

'Emmy, it's good to see you home.' As he took a step towards her, dripping snow all over the hall floor, and gently took her hand, a shiver ran up her arm.

'It's good to be back, although I'm afraid I had no luck finding Abi.' She sighed as she helped him off with his coat. 'I can only think that perhaps she didn't go to Le Havre after all. She must still be in London somewhere. But wherever she is why didn't she take all of her clothes?'

Jake shook his head, as confused and worried as she was. And then Emmy hauled him off to the drawing room to sit by the fire and get warm.

On the train back to Nuneaton, Dorcas noticed that Jasper was unusually quiet, although she wasn't really surprised. No doubt he would be worrying about what sort of reception he was going to get from his father when he arrived home, and she couldn't really blame him. Bernard had been absolutely furious about Jasper being so unreliable the last time she had spoken to him and she was glad that she wouldn't have to be there to witness the reunion. She settled back into her seat and watched the fields passing by in a blur as she wondered about her husband and Abi. She thought about both of them every single day and wished that she could turn the clock back. But it was much too late for that now so all she could do was hope that eventually they might both decide to come home.

It was dark by the time the train pulled into Trent Valley Station and Jasper grasped their bags and hurried her outside where the hackney cabs sat hopefully waiting for fares, their horses covered in thick blankets and with their noses stuck in nosebags.

'Crossroads Farm, Astley,' Jasper told the driver as he helped his aunt into the cab and the driver frowned at him through the snow.

'I'll get yer as close as I can, me man, but I can't promise as I'll be able to get yer all the way,' he admitted. 'A lot o' the lanes around that way are impassable an' under drifts but as I said, I'll do me best.'

They set off with the snow still falling so thickly that it was impossible to see more than a few feet beyond the windows. It was after they had passed Astley Pool and were nearing Astley House, Dorcas's former home, that the real problems began and the poor horse slowed until finally the driver drew him to a halt.

'Sorry, mister, but I'm afraid I can't risk goin' any further,' he shouted down to Jasper and Dorcas. 'The mare is gettin' skittish an' I can't risk 'er goin' off the road an' into a ditch. It'll be 'ard enough to get back the way we've come wi' how it's comin' down now.'

Dorcas and Jasper clambered out of the cab to find themselves almost knee-deep in snow and after Jasper had paid the driver and retrieved their luggage, they set off with their heads bent low against the wind.

'Phew, have we much further to go?' Dorcas gasped as she struggled along. All the familiar landmarks were buried and already she had lost all sense of direction.

'No . . . the castle and the church should be just ahead,' Jasper answered as he struggled with their bags, and sure enough shortly after the buildings loomed into view.

Now that she knew where she was, Dorcas took heart and, staying close to Jasper, tried to quicken her pace, until finally the lighted windows of the cottage came into view. There had never been a more welcome sight and as she got closer, she heard Bruno begin to bark and she smiled. Seconds later the cottage door opened and Hetty peered out into the silent white world holding a lantern aloft as Bruno sniffed at the air. Then picking up the scent of his mistress his tail began to wag furiously and he leapt into the snow and ploughed towards her, knocking her clean off her feet.

'Hello, boy, miss me, did you?' Dorcas laughed as his wet tongue licked the snow from her frozen cheeks. 'Let me get up and out of the cold and then I'll give you a fuss.'

Minutes later she sprawled unceremoniously over the step and into the cosy sitting room as Hetty looked on with a smile on her face.

'That's some entrance, missus.' Hetty giggled as Dorcas tried to rise past Bruno's searching tongue with Jasper close behind her.

'Will you stay for a hot drink?' Hetty asked Jasper.

He shook his head as he set Dorcas's bag down. 'Thank you but no. I'd best get back and face the music.' With his face set in grim lines, he turned and went back out into the swirling snow.

Hetty led her mistress to her favourite chair by the fire.

'Oh, it's good to be back,' Dorcas said, and in that moment she realised that she meant it. However humble this little cottage was, it was now the place she called home and it came as a shock to realise that she was now more content here than she ever had been in Astley House, or at least she would have been if her husband had been there with her.

Chapter Thirty-Seven

Emmy had been home for three days when her aunt patted the bed at the side of her one morning indicating that she wished to speak to her. Emmy went and perched on the edge of the mattress and stared at her expectantly as her aunt licked her lips.

'I . . . I have something I should tell you,' Imogen began slowly. 'And I'm only doing it to stop you worrying. I'm sick of seeing you walk about as if you have the weight of the world on your shoulders.'

'Oh?' Curious, Emmy raised her eyebrow.

'I know where Abi is,' her aunt went on after taking a moment to get her breath back and now Emmy's face registered her shock.

'So where is she? Is she safe?' Emmy's heart was pounding but Imogen ignored her stricken face. It wasn't easy for her to speak and so any sort of conversation they had could take a long time.

Eventually Imogen nodded. 'Yes, she's very safe . . . she came to see me a couple of days after you left for France to find her . . . A friend had helped her and found someone to take her in, but her money had run out and well . . . Luckily she came very late at night when your mother was in bed so

Dorcas never knew she'd even been here. Aggie answered the door to her and I . . . I made Aggie promise that she wouldn't say anything to either of you. I wasn't going to tell you but I can see you're fretting. The thing is, though . . . Abigail has had her heart broken and she needs time to heal so before I tell you where she is, I want you to promise that you'll make no attempt to go to her. Abigail will come back in her own good time. Can you do that?'

Reluctantly Emmy nodded and after a while her aunt went on, 'She is at my home in Lytham St Anne's. I couldn't think of anywhere else to send her.'

'And is she there alone?'

Imogen shook her head. 'No, I have a live-in housekeeper and her son that live there and keep the place up to scratch for me. Of course, at such short notice I had no chance to let them know that Abi would be coming so I got Abi to write a letter from me to take with her for Mrs Merryweather, my housekeeper there, and then I signed it. Abigail will be quite safe with them and I made sure she had enough money for her fare to get there before she left.'

'Oh, thank goodness!' Tears of relief pricked at Emmy's eyes but after a moment she asked, 'How long do you think she'll stay there?'

Imogen shrugged her frail shoulders; she seemed to be shrinking by the day. 'How long is a piece of string? As long as she needs to. For months at least I should say. It takes time to heal.' She deliberately omitted to tell Emmy about the baby Abi was carrying. If things worked out as she had planned there would be no need for Emmy or anyone else to even know there had been a baby. In her letter she had asked Mrs Merryweather to find the child a decent home when it was born or put it into an orphanage if that was what Abi wanted, and then she could come home with her reputation unblemished if she chose to.

'Thank you for telling me,' Emmy said sincerely. 'Although I can't think why Abi didn't come to me for help if she just wanted to hide away. She could have gone home to lick her wounds at Mama's.'

'Like I said, she's had her heart broken and she needs to be away from everyone.'

Emmy seemed to accept that explanation. 'Then thank you again for helping her. But may I at least write to my mother just to let her know that she's safe?'

'Of course you may.' Imogen inclined her head and dropped back on to her pillows, exhausted. She clearly needed to rest, so after making sure that she had everything she needed, Emmy left the room in a much happier frame of mind.

At that moment in Lytham St Anne's, Abi was sitting in the large bay window of her aunt's house watching the ships far out at sea. She sometimes wished she was on one of them heading for a far-off land where no one would know of her shame. She also wondered what would have become of her if Madame Bissett hadn't taken pity on her the night that Hugo had rejected her and broken her heart. She wondered if the woman Maria had persuaded to take her in for two months had any kindly feeling towards her, even if she was just in it for the lodging money. The good-hearted French woman

343

had loaned her the money for her fare back to England and once there the only person she could think of who might keep her secret and help her was her Aunt Imogen. The suggestion that she might like to hide out at her aunt's holiday home had been like the answer to a prayer for Abi and although the combined train and coach journey to get there had been tedious, she could think of nowhere better to be in her condition. Mrs Merryweather, a plump motherly widow with a heart as big as a bucket, had welcomed her with open arms and had never once made her feel wicked for being an unmarried mother-to-be.

'You are not the first and I'm sure you won't be the last, lass,' she had said stoically when she had read Imogen's letter.

'And you'll help me find a home for the baby when it's born?' Abi had asked hopefully.

Mrs M, as she preferred to be called, had shaken her head. 'There's no need to be worrying about things like that yet,' she had advised. 'Let's just get the little one here and then see how you feel, eh?'

Angry colour had risen in Abi's cheeks. 'But I *already* know how I shall feel!' she had argued. 'This child will be a bastard and my reputation will be gone forever if I consider keeping it.'

'Even so I think we should take one step at a time.' It was very clear that Mrs M would not be swayed on this matter and so now Abi was just trying to take one day at a time as her waistline expanded. She spent much of each day letting out the seams of the few gowns she had brought with her but she was aware that soon even they wouldn't fit her and she felt fat and awkward. She was also very prone to tears. The least little thing could set her off, but again Mrs M took it all in her stride.

'It's quite normal in your condition,' she told her. 'You'll settle down again once the baby arrives.'

Abi wasn't so sure. Some days she felt so depressed about the way Hugo had treated her that she wanted to die. The only bright spot in her day was the time she spent with Mrs M's son. Bertie was twenty-two years old and worked as a carpenter in the nearby town of Blackpool, which was also a very popular holiday resort during the summer months. When he wasn't at his day job, he was busy seeing to anything that needed to be done about the house and garden. He was tall and slim with a thatch of fair curly hair that no amount of Macassar oil seemed able to tame. He could never be termed as handsome: his nose was a little crooked after he had broken it as a child and he could be quite shy, but his eyes were his saving grace. They were the colour of bluebells and seemed to twinkle when he spoke to her and she soon discovered that his nature was as kindly as his mother's. Not once did he condemn her for the position she found herself in, but instead he tried to speak positively to her of her future.

More than once he had tried to persuade her to go for an evening stroll along the pier with him to get a blast of fresh air but Abi always refused.

'*Why* would I want anyone to see me like this?' she had snapped on the last occasion and had felt instantly contrite when he looked upset. 'I'm sorry,' she had mumbled, close to tears. 'I just feel so ashamed. If my mother ever found out . . .'

'If your mother ever did, I'm sure she would come to love the baby once she was over the shock, it will be her first grandchild after all,' he had pointed out gently, but she had shaken her head.

'No . . . you don't understand. My mother had high hopes of me making a good marriage. But now who will want me? I am soiled goods.'

'No, Abigail, just look in the mirror; you are beautiful.' Then he had turned and slowly left the room leaving her with tears of self-pity streaming down her pale cheeks.

Dragging her eyes from the window Abi stared about the room. It was furnished very much in the style of Imogen's house in London with elaborate furniture scattered about and gilt-framed pictures and mirrors on the walls. This room and many more in the house had been shut up when she had first arrived, the furniture hidden beneath huge dust sheets as Mrs M and Bertie tended to live in the large kitchen that overlooked the well-kept garden at the rear but Mrs M had soon whipped the covers away insisting, 'You need somewhere where you can be private and sit and watch the world go by. Mrs Dubois would want you to be comfortable and it's no trouble at all to light an extra fire.' And so now Abi spent a great deal of each day in there and found it surprisingly relaxing being able to gaze out to sea from the window.

She was still sitting there that evening. The lamplighter had just passed by and the glow from the lamps made the fast-falling snow sparkle like shattered diamonds. She was admiring the scene when she noticed a familiar figure heading her way dragging something behind him. Realising it was Bertie she quickly rose and hurried to the door to let him in.

Mrs M was busy in the kitchen preparing the evening meal for them all and Abi didn't want to disturb her.

'Hello, Bertie, what have you got there?' She gave him a welcoming smile and gasped with delight when he hauled a Christmas tree into the hall, leaving trails of snow across Mrs M's polished tiles.

'I thought a tree might cheer you up,' he told her with a cheeky grin. 'It is almost Christmas after all. I'll set it in a bucket of earth after dinner and then you could perhaps decorate it for me ma tomorrow. It will give you something to do.'

Despite how miserable she had been feeling, Abi clapped her hands with delight. She had always loved Christmas and though this tree was nowhere near as big as the tall stately ones of about ten foot that used to grace the hall of Astley House – it was perhaps only half the height at the most – she loved it all the same.

'And I thought when you'd done that you could perhaps come for a walk with me to the park where we could cut some holly.'

Abi opened her mouth to refuse but he held his hand up. 'I know – you don't want to be seen out because you think people will know you're not married, so I got you this.' Fumbling in his pocket, he produced a small box and handed it to her and when she snapped the lid, she saw a thin gold wedding band nestling on a bed of silk.

'People won't see your hand if you're wearing gloves but I thought you might feel better with it on anyway.'

It was such a thoughtful gift that tears sprang to her eyes and she lowered her head as he lifted it from the box and gently placed it on the third finger of her left hand.

'There, now if anyone asks you can say you're married . . . to me if you like.' He flushed to the roots of his hair as Abi rose on tiptoe and gently pecked his cheek, then grabbing the tree again he began to haul it towards the kitchen, saying in a choky voice, 'I'd best get this into the kitchen before me mam skelps me for mucking up her hall floor. I'll see you at dinner.'

Abi stared down at the thin gold band thinking how wonderful it would have been if it had been Hugo who had placed it on her finger. And then with a sigh she returned to her seat to resume her lonely vigil at the drawing room window staring out at the snowy vista beyond.

As Bertie had suggested, she spent the next day decorating the tree with the dainty glass baubles that Mrs M fetched from the loft. She had just finished it when suddenly she felt the baby kick inside her. A look of shock crossed her face as her hand flew to her stomach.

Mrs M smiled. 'Gave you a kick, did it?'

Abi nodded numbly. 'Y-yes. I've felt a funny sort of fluttery feeling before but never anything as strong as this.'

'Well, you'd best get used to it, lass.' She chuckled. 'When I was having my Bertie there were times I felt as if he were playing football inside me. Now, I think it's time we got the doctor to check you over.' When a look of panic crossed Abi's face, she held her hand up. 'It's nothing to worry about. It's just to make sure that everything is as it should be. And I can tell him you're my niece that's been widowed if that will make you feel better?'

'Very well.' Abi was reluctant but knew that it made sense. Feeling the baby move had made her realise that this was a real little live person she was carrying and it was a strange sensation.

Soon after they heard the front door open and Bertie appeared carrying a huge box that he struggled to get through the door.

'Goodness me, whatever have you got there, lad?' his mother asked.

Dragging his cap off he blushed. 'Open it and see.'

Both Mrs M and Abi stepped forward to do as he asked and when the lid of the box was opened Abi gasped. Inside was a baby's cradle.

'I've been carving it at work in my spare time and during my lunch break.'

He and Mrs M manoeuvred it out on to the floor where the wood gleamed softly in the light from the oil lamp. It was on little rockers and he had painstakingly carved tiny animals all around the outside edge. The wood was so smooth that it was easy to see a lot of time and patience must have gone into the making of it but instead of the reaction he had hoped for Abi's eyes filled with tears.

'And what would we need *that* for?' she snapped. 'Haven't I told you that I don't intend to keep the baby?'

'Aye, you have.' Bertie nodded solemnly as he twisted his cap in his hands. 'But it will still need something to lie in when it's first born, won't it? And every baby is a gift as far I'm concerned and deserves somewhere comfortable to sleep at least.'

Abi instantly felt guilty. He had obviously gone to a lot of trouble for her and she knew how ungrateful she must sound but this and feeling the baby move was suddenly making everything seem all too real.

'I'm sorry,' she said in a wobbly voice, and lifting her skirts she waddled from the room, leaving Bertie to stare after her with a sad expression on his face.

Upstairs in the privacy of her room, Abi stood at her window staring out across the snowy street to the wild sea beyond where the waves were crashing on to the shore. The wind was howling like demented souls in torment and rattling the window panes and she sighed. She wished Bertie wouldn't be so kind to her all the time. It made her feel . . . How did it make her feel? she wondered. Finally she settled for confused as she tried to picture Hugo's handsome face.

Chapter Thirty-Eight

'Where's Father?' Jasper asked his mother at breakfast a week before Christmas. His homecoming had not been a happy one to say the least and the atmosphere between himself and his father had been fraught with tension.

'He's out shooting rabbits with the gamekeeper,' his mother told him as she helped herself to a thick rasher of bacon from the sideboard.

'Oh, so, er . . . I don't suppose I could persuade you to lend me a few pounds to tide me over, could I?' he asked cajolingly. His father had refused to reinstate his allowance until Jasper agreed to start work and so they were at stalemate, and because he had no money Jasper had barely set foot out of the house and was becoming increasingly frustrated.

'You know I can't give you any more without your father knowing.' Even Sybil was becoming impatient with him now and was forced to see that he really should be learning the business.

'*Fine!*' he stormed, flinging his chair back so abruptly that it crashed to the floor and, turning about, he stamped from the room.

Over in the cottage Hetty was carrying the envelope she had found on the doorstep to Dorcas who was frying eggs.

'Our phantom helper has called again,' Hetty said.

Taking it from her, Dorcas chewed her lip as she stared at the money it contained.

'Blast!' she said suddenly. 'I stayed up all night again to try and catch whoever is calling and I never heard a thing.'

'Well, you wouldn't, would you?' Hetty glanced towards the window. 'The snow would have muffled their footsteps.'

'Yes, you're right, but you're forgetting that Bruno's hearing is much more finely tuned than ours. I wouldn't mind betting that he at least woke up when he heard whoever it was. I'm just surprised that he didn't bark.'

'Then perhaps it's someone friendly?'

Dorcas nodded and turned back to preparing the breakfast. 'It could well be but one way or another I'm going to get to the bottom of it.'

A thought occurred to Hetty and crossing the room she opened the door and peered out. 'I just realised there was no snow on the envelope,' she said thoughtfully. 'And look, these footsteps are fresh. Whoever left it must have only just come.'

Dorcas flew to the door and sure enough she saw that Hetty was right. Without a second thought she rammed her feet into her boots and dragged her coat on. 'In that case whoever it is can't have gone far. I'm going to try and find them. Come on, Bruno.' And before Hetty could say another word her mistress set off into the thickly falling snow with Bruno prancing delightedly at her heels.

The footsteps led into a small copse and once beneath the barren trees it was harder to follow them but Dorcas plunged on regardless, Bruno romping at her side. As they emerged from the copse, he began to bark and race ahead, and holding her hand above her eyes Dorcas peered into the snow. She could just make out a hunched figure striding some way in front of her.

'Hey . . . *wait!*'

The figure paused and turned towards her and as Dorcas moved forward her mouth gaped open in shock and her heart began to thump.

'*Gerald!*'

Shamefaced he lowered his head. He was dressed in workmen's clothes with a cap covering his thatch of thick hair. His hands were plunged deep into his coat pockets and his shoulders sagged.

'Gerald . . .' Dorcas's voice was softer now and clogged with tears. '*Where* have you been?'

'Working.' His voice was so low that she could barely hear it and she drew closer, shocked at the change in him. His face looked at least ten years older than she remembered and his hands when he removed them from his pockets were calloused and rough.

'But why did you run away like that?'

He shrugged. 'What else could I do? I'd let you all down and I was ashamed. I thought you'd all be better off without me.'

It was she who held out her hand to him. 'No . . . no, you didn't let us down! I was as much to blame as you for what happened. Please come back to the cottage with me. I think we need to talk.'

His head wagged from side to side. 'I don't think that's a good idea, Dorcas. It's too late for talking now.'

Her chin rose in the determined way he remembered so well. 'I don't agree. Please come back with me. Just to talk . . . *please.*'

He hesitated like a bird about to take flight but then with a laboured sigh he fell into step beside her as they turned back towards the cottage.

When they entered the kitchen sometime later, Hetty was just throwing some logs on to the fire and she dropped the one she was holding so heavily that the fire crackled and spat.

'*Mr Winter!*'

'Hello, my dear.' He stood nervously by the door but not for long because Dorcas dragged his coat from his shoulders and ushered him towards the warmth of the fire.

'You sit there while I get us a hot drink,' she ordered bossily and with a wry smile playing about his lips he did as he was told. It seemed that some things never changed.

'I, er . . . I think I'll go an' give me bedroom a good tidy,' Hetty said tactfully, then bustled away upstairs.

Neither spoke as Dorcas busied herself making tea, but finally, when they were both seated either side of the fire facing each other with steaming mugs in their hands, she asked, 'Why didn't you tell me the business was in such dire trouble?' But before he could answer she rushed on. 'I think I know the answer to that . . . it was because I wouldn't have listened to you. I was too demanding. Nothing was ever good enough, I always wanted more . . . and I want to say . . . I'm sorry. So *very* sorry!'

He raised his head to stare at her in surprise. He had expected her to be shouting and screaming at him but instead she was being more than reasonable. In fact, as he looked at the simple gown she was wearing, with her glorious hair tied loosely in a ribbon at the nape of her neck, he was suddenly reminded of the girl he had fallen in love with.

An awkward silence settled between them for a few moments then and he stroked Bruno's silky ears.

Finally, Dorcas asked, 'Where have you been living? Have you found someone else?'

'What?' He looked startled at her suggestion. 'Of *course* I haven't. For all my faults I've never been a womaniser – you should know that. I've been working at Bates Farm near Bedworth and living in a room above his barn. But where are the girls?'

Slowly Dorcas began to tell him of all that had happened since he had left and he hung on her every word.

'So Abigail is at Imogen's house in Lytham St Anne's and Emerald is looking after Imogen?'

'Yes.' She nodded. 'I didn't even know where Abigail was until I received a letter from Emerald yesterday. I'm afraid she took the move here very badly which is why she ran away to London. But at least I know she's safe now and I also know that both girls will be so relieved that I've found you. We've all been so worried not knowing what had happened to you.'

He looked at her incredulously. '*You* were worried?' He could hardly believe what he was hearing. Was this really the same woman he had run away from?

'Yes, my love – I was.' She reached across the distance between them to gently take his hand. 'I admit I was angry – furious, in fact – when you first went. And then when we discovered that we were to lose the house and I would have to throw us all on Bernard's mercy I hated you for a while. Coming here' – she spread her hands to encompass the cosy kitchen – 'seemed like a fate worse than death. Yet after a while I found that it wasn't so bad. Of course, I was also heartbroken because my so-called friends had all turned their backs on me, until I realised that they had never been true friends after all. Hetty has stood by me through thick and thin and I think I now have more feelings for her than I ever did for any of them.' She sighed. 'Sometimes it takes something life-changing to make you realise what is important and I've come to love this little place. I also slowly came to realise that I still love you too.'

He looked infinitely sad. 'I was terrified I had destroyed all your lives. And don't worry, I shall continue to support you as much as I can. I don't need much to get by on out of my wages, which is why I've been leaving them outside here for you. But now I really should be going. Thank you for the warm and the hot drink.'

'Oh!' As he rose from his chair, tears flooded into Dorcas's eyes, and making a snap decision she asked in a small voice, 'Is there no way I could persuade you to stay?'

'I think I've put you and the girls through enough heartache, don't you?'

'I only got what I deserved . . . But the thing is . . .' She took a deep breath. She had a feeling she must speak now or forever hold her peace. 'I meant it when I said that I still love you, Gerald, it just took me a time to realise what's important. But of course, I'll understand if you don't have any feelings left for me any more . . .'

'I've always loved you,' he said softly. 'And you just reminded me of why I fell in love with you in the first place.'

She too rose and they stood facing each other until suddenly without quite being aware of who made the first move, they were in each other's arms both sobbing.

'Does this mean you'll stay?' she asked gingerly.

He raised her chin and gently kissed her mouth. 'Only if you're sure?'

'I've never been more sure of anything in my life,' she told him in a choky voice.

Hetty, who was crouched at the top of the stairs, punched the air in delight. It seemed that the master and mistress might just get their happy-ever-after ending and she couldn't have been more pleased for them. With a broad smile she crept back to her room, leaving the lovebirds to themselves.

Chapter Thirty-Nine

'I think you should have your Sunday off this week and go and help Jake,' Imogen said one morning as Emmy was getting her dressed. 'I bet he'll be busy with all the winter illnesses that are going around. Aggie can see to anything I need while you're out.' Imogen was now well enough to get up and sit in a chair for a while each day and Emmy thanked God for it. There had been a time following Imogen's stroke that Emmy had feared they would lose her and it had made her realise just how much her aunt had come to mean to her.

'Well, if you're sure, I'll just make sure it's all right with her.'

Aggie was all for the idea when she put it to her. 'Course it's all right. As long as I don't 'ave to give up me Saturday,' she said with a becoming blush. 'I've met a young man, see, an' he 'as Saturday afternoons off from the fish market where he works, so we could walk out together.'

'Then I'm really pleased for you, Aggie,' Emmy said warmly.

Jake was delighted when he called in that night after work and she told him. 'I'll be glad of the help, to be honest, even with Richard helping we're run off our feet,' he admitted. Then with a sigh he confided, 'To be honest, I'm thinking of working at the practice in Harley Street part-time. If I cut my hours, I'd have more time to work with those who can't afford to pay, which is where my heart is, and the wealthy clients pay ridiculous sums for their treatment so I'd still earn more than enough to survive comfortably.'

Emmy's heart swelled with pride. He really was the kindest young man she had ever met, very different to his brother, and yet again she found herself wishing that they weren't so closely related. But it couldn't be helped and she knew that she must stop thinking of him as anything more than her cousin.

And so bright and early on Sunday morning, Jake called to pick her up and once they had loaded all the bread Cook had baked for the less fortunate they set off for the little rooms that had become Jake's surgery. Richard wandered in within minutes of them arriving and soon they were all busy preparing for the day ahead, which turned out to be just as busy as Jake had predicted. The bitterly cold weather had caused a glut of colds and influenza and when Emmy saw how inadequately dressed the majority of the patients were, it gave her an idea.

'I noticed that most of the people who came in for medicine today didn't even have decent shoes,' she commented to Jake and Richard. 'And it got me to thinking. Aunt Imogen's spiritualist friends have started to call to see her again now that she's a little better and most of them are quite wealthy. I'm sure if she asked them to put the word out that decent quality second-hand clothes and shoes are needed for the poor we'd get a good response.'

Richard and Jake nodded in unison as they sipped at the tea she had made them during a lull in patients.

'That's an excellent idea,' Jake said approvingly. 'We could hand them out to the most needy.'

So that evening when she got home Emmy put the idea to her aunt who was only too happy to oblige. 'Lady Medville is calling to see me tomorrow as it happens,' she told Emmy. 'And I'll get her to pass the word around.'

Just three days later Aggie answered the door to Lady Medville's butler who unceremoniously dumped two laden boxes of assorted garments on the hall floor. 'Her ladyship asked me to deliver these to you,' he said pompously and without another word he turned and left, his back as stiff as a ramrod.

'Ooh, would yer look at some o' these, miss,' Aggie cooed as she and Emmy went through the bags a short time later. She pounced on a very pretty blue gown with a full skirt and held it up against her. 'Why, these clothes must 'ave come from toffs. I ain't never owned nothin' as posh as this in me whole life!'

'Then I think you should keep that one,' Emmy told her kindly. 'It would be just right for walking out with your young man. Oh, and look, here are some shoes that might fit you as well. What size are you?'

'I ain't got a clue,' Aggie admitted. 'Me ma allus bought us kids shoes an' boots from the rag stall at the market. If the shoes were too big we just stuffed the toes wi' newspaper. These what the missus bought me when I started workin' 'ere are the first new pair o' boots I've ever owned in me life.'

Emmy glanced at the boots. They were very practical and serviceable but not very pretty so she was delighted when Aggie slid her feet into the dainty shoes she'd found and they fit her.

'I shan't wear 'em yet though, nor the gown,' Aggie confided with a pretty blush. 'If my Archie ever pops the question, I'm goin' to save 'em to be married in.'

Emmy was touched and patted Aggie's hand as they resumed sorting through the clothes.

'I'm afraid some of these would be very impractical for the people they're intended for,' Emmy said when they'd finished sorting the various garments into piles. 'But just think how many smaller garments could be made out of this gown alone.'

Aggie nodded in agreement as Emmy showed her a fine warm woollen gown with a huge skirt. 'This would make at least three smaller dresses for children.'

'It would that,' Aggie agreed. 'An' I 'appen to know that most o' the women these are intended for can turn their 'ands to a bit o' sewin' – they 'ave to be able to. Things get passed down an' reworked, see, as their families grow.'

By the end of the week quite a few more donations had arrived and Emmy was delighted.

'Look at this,' she said to Aggie as she held up a wide cotton underskirt trimmed with broderie anglaise. 'Just think how many babies' nightgowns could be made out of this one item of clothing alone. At the rate it's all arriving Jake will have to make two trips to the surgery on Sunday to get everything there.'

Her good mood improved further the following day when a letter from her mother arrived and she sat at the side of her aunt's bed to read it to her.

'Oh, Aunt Imogen.' Her face was radiant as she waved the letter at her. 'Father is home! He's at the cottage with Mama and they're back together! Oh, it's such a relief to know that he's safe.'

'About time too!' Imogen sniffed. 'I always did like your father; he's a good man. Let's hope your mother has learnt a lesson now and won't be so demanding.'

Emmy grinned. 'I think she's changed quite a lot over the last few months. And now they can have Christmas together. Talking of which I must go and check that Cook has everything she needs for the Christmas dinner. It's just days away and knowing that Father and Abi are safe I shall be able to enjoy it now, although I do have a favour to ask of you. Would you mind very much if Jake joined us? He isn't going home and I'd hate to think of him spending Christmas Day alone.'

'The more the merrier,' Imogen answered, her eyes becoming dreamy as she thought back to Christmases past. 'When my Marcel was alive this house would ring with laughter and be full from morning till night. He was such a generous man and he hated to think of anyone he knew being alone.'

'Thank you, I'll tell him.' Emmy rose and made for the door, smiling happily. 'Meantime, you just stay there and rest. I want you to build your strength up so that you can enjoy Christmas Day.' She bustled off leaving Imogen with a thoughtful expression on her face.

In Imogen's other house in Lytham St Anne's, the Christmas preparations were also well under way and Mrs M was rolling pastry for yet another batch of mince pies while Abi sat at the table watching her.

'I reckon I'll hide this batch,' she chuckled. 'Our Bertie has been scoffing them as fast as I can bake them. I can't even say it's because he's a growing boy now because if he grows any taller his head will be in the clouds. Still, I shouldn't complain. I like a man with a good appetite; his dad was just the same. I used to tell him he'd got hollow legs because I could never seem to fill him up.'

'Is there anything I can do to help?' Abi offered.

Mrs M wagged a floury finger at her. 'You'll sit right where you are, young lady,' she told her sternly.

Abi sighed. 'I feel so fat and useless,' she complained. 'I've forgotten what my feet look like now.' As she spoke the baby began to kick again and her hand self-consciously rested on her bump.

'Well, according to the doctor it shouldn't be too much longer now. He reckons somewhere early in March and it will be all over. You could get on with that little nightgown I'm sewing for it if you're bored.'

Abi scowled. Mrs M had spent every night for weeks sewing tiny clothes in readiness for the baby's arrival. Abi had argued saying that there wasn't any point seeing as she had no intention of keeping the child but Mrs M had carried on regardless. 'It will need clothes even if you don't keep it!' she'd insisted and so Abi had given up objecting and left her to it.

At that moment the door banged open and Bertie appeared bearing the largest goose Abi had ever seen.

'Here you are, Ma. Is that big enough for you?' He laughed as he swung the poor bird on to the table. 'The boss let me finish early seeing as it's the last day before the holidays and I thought I'd pick it up on me way home. I can start to pluck it for you if you like. Do you fancy helping, Abi?'

Horrified, she shook her head as she pushed her chair back. She was sure the poor thing was watching her from its glassy dead eyes.

'No, I certainly do not. The only way I like to see geese is running about the farmyard or ready cooked on a plate,' she said in disgust and with that she sailed from the room with Bertie and Mrs M's laughter following her.

Later that afternoon, she and Bertie took a gentle stroll to the nearby park where Abi cut some bunches of holly with bright-red berries to decorate the mantelpiece in the dining room. It had temporarily stopped snowing and in the fading light everywhere looked clean and bright. The sea was as still as a mill pond as they made their way home, with Bertie insisting that she hook her arm through his.

'We don't want you falling and hurting you or the baby,' he told her and she couldn't help but be touched. He was such a caring young chap. She couldn't understand why some girl hadn't snapped him up ages ago and she told him so.

He grinned. 'I've had me chances,' he admitted. 'But there's no one ever really caught me attention until . . .' He stopped speaking abruptly and even in the dim light she saw that his cheeks were glowing. 'Anyway, let's concentrate on getting you in out of the cold. We don't want your ankles swelling again, do we?'

Abi shook her head as she stared thoughtfully ahead. It had been a very strange year one way or another but now, despite everything, she found that she was actually looking forward to Christmas Day.

The church bells woke her on Christmas morning and after washing quickly and struggling into her clothes she waddled down the stairs to join Mrs M and Bertie in the warm kitchen.

The smell of bacon sizzling in the pan met her when she entered the room and they both turned towards her with broad smiles on their faces, 'Merry Christmas,' they said in unison and she smiled back.

'And the very same to you.'

Bertie hurried over to the table and returned carrying a small parcel wrapped in pretty paper. 'It's nothing much,' he muttered, looking embarrassed. 'But I hope you like it.'

Abi flushed as she stared at it in horror. 'But . . . but I haven't bought you anything,' she garbled. 'I-I don't like to go out as you know and—'

'Shush!' He held a hand up to silence her. 'I didn't want or expect anything. Now just open it, will you?'

With fingers that were suddenly shaking, Abi fumbled with the wrappings to reveal a small box. She snapped open the lid and a lump formed in her throat as she stared down at a small gold heart-shaped brooch. Upstairs she had a selection of expensive jewellery given to her by the gentlemen admirers back at the Black Cat club. She had been meaning to pawn them when she could get into town, but she knew that she would treasure this trinket forever.

Seeing the tears that had sprung to her eyes, Bertie looked dismayed. 'Er . . . if you don't like it, I could always take it back and change it,' he volunteered but she shook her head as she fastened it to the bodice of her gown.

'Oh no, I love it.' Without thinking she stood on tiptoe and kissed his cheek and much to his mother's amusement, his face turned as red as a beetroot.

'And you'll find another present from me on the table.' Mrs M nodded towards another package. 'But you'll have to get it yourself. My hands are greasy.'

Inside this one was a beautiful silk shawl in soft autumn colours and again Abi was so touched that she could barely speak. These dear people had been instructed to take care of her by her aunt, their employer, but in the months that she had been there they had done so much more. They had taken her into their hearts and made her feel a part of the family and she didn't know how she could ever repay them.

'A-as soon as this is out of the way I'll make it up to both of you,' she mumbled in a choky voice as she patted her stomach but they both shook their heads and Mrs M frowned at her.

'There'll be no need for that, lass. And please don't refer to the baby as "this"! It's a real little person and doesn't deserve to be spoken of like that. Come along now, the dinner's all prepared so we'll go to the Christmas morning service at the church then we'll come back and have a lovely day.'

Abi looked hesitant but Bertie patted the ring on her finger. 'No one will turn a hair,' he promised her and so Abi went to fetch her cloak and they set off with her arm tucked in Bertie's. The day before Christmas Eve she had received a letter from her aunt telling her that her parents were reconciled and while it had surprised her, she was pleased. All in all, it wasn't turning out to be such a bad Christmas after all.

The atmosphere was also light at Imogen's house in London, for the evening before Emmy had answered the door to find her parents standing there laden down with presents.

'Let me in,' her father said, his eyes twinkling. 'I've carted these all the way from Nuneaton and I feel like a packhorse.'

'B-but I had no idea you were coming,' Emmy breathed as her father discarded the packages and wrapped her tightly in his arms while her mother looked on beaming.

'Imogen wrote and invited us but we wanted to surprise you,' her mother laughed.

Emmy's heart swelled. Her mother looked at least ten years younger and her face was radiant as she looked at her husband.

'Oh, this is going to be one of the *best* Christmases ever! And Jake is joining us for dinner too,' Emmy said ecstatically as she led them into the drawing room where a cheery fire was roaring up the chimney. 'I just wish . . .' Her voice became sombre as she thought of her sister. 'Abi could be here with us too.'

'Imogen assures me that she's doing just fine,' Dorcas told her as she undid the ribbons on her bonnet. 'She keeps in close touch with Mrs Merryweather by letter, and apparently Abi is coping much better now. I wouldn't be at all surprised if she didn't come home soon.'

Emmy instructed Aggie to fetch them a hot drink and they settled down to catch up on all that they'd been doing.

Chapter Forty

At Crossroads Farm, the atmosphere was strained. Bernard had left early that morning to join the traditional Christmas morning shoot at a neighbouring hall and Sybil was barking orders at the servants as they prepared the dining room for the Christmas dinner.

Jasper, meanwhile, was pacing up and down his room with his hands clasped behind his back, scowling with frustration. He had hoped to be back in London with Emmy by Christmas but both his mother and father had refused to give him so much as a penny piece, so now he was simmering with resentment. Then an idea occurred to him. If he could get into the safe in his father's study, he could take whatever was in there and disappear. He knew there would be plenty of cash as his father's agent had recently collected all the rents from the tenant farmers on his estate, so all he had to do was work out the combination on the padlock – unless his father had been lax and forgotten to lock it, which he had been known to do in the past.

Deciding there was no time like the present, Jasper quietly made his way downstairs, keeping a cautious ear open for his mother. He could hear her shouting at the servants from the direction of the dining room and slipping silently along the hallway he let himself into his father's study. He knew that time was not on his side; his father could return at any minute – even he didn't dare to be late for his Christmas dinner – so crossing to the safe he tried the door and sighed with vexation when he found that it was securely locked. Ever since returning home he had racked his brains to think of a way to cause his father to have an accident that would confine him to bed, but so far he had come up with nothing and even if he had, he wondered if he would have had the guts to see it through, so this was the only option left.

Cursing softly, he fiddled with a combination of numbers but the padlock remained obstinately shut and he thumped the door in his frustration. In the hallway he could hear the servants bustling past like busy little ants as they went to and from the dining room to the kitchen, but he tried to remain focused on what he was doing. Suddenly, he had an idea, and he tried the numbers of his father's birth date and the lock snapped open. Turning the handle on the safe, he pulled it wide, to reveal piles of pound notes.

He had to stifle his cry of glee as he reached hungrily inside. There was a fortune there if he wasn't very much mistaken. Certainly enough to get him and Emmy somewhere far enough away where they could begin a new life, if he could only persuade her to go with him. And how could she refuse him, he wondered, when he showed her his fortune?

He began to cram the money into his pockets, not even bothering to count it. There had to be at least two to three hundred pounds in there he reckoned and that would keep them happy for some time. Admittedly, he had realised that he wouldn't be able to go to her today as there would be no trains running but with this amount of money at his disposal he was sure that he would have no trouble finding somewhere to hole up until they started to run again and then the world would be his oyster.

His smile stretched from ear to ear as he rammed the last of the notes into the pocket of his waistcoat and he turned to leave, only to stop dead in his tracks when he saw his father standing in the open doorway with his gun in his hand glaring at him. Bernard had just dropped two hares, a rabbit, three partridges, a pheasant and two woodcocks off to the kitchen following a very successful morning's shooting but now his happy mood dispersed as he saw his son in the process of trying to rob him.

Striding into the room he slammed his gun down on the large mahogany desk that stood in pride of place in the centre of the room and glared at Jasper. 'Just *what* the bloody hell do you think you are doing? Surely to God you haven't sunk so low that you would steal from your own family?'

'Why *shouldn't* I?' Jasper's face was red with humiliation at being caught red-handed and rage that he hadn't managed to get away with it. 'You treat me like a child, doling out bits of pocket money here and there so I thought I'd help myself to what I'm entitled to! I'm a grown man now and deserve more than you give me!'

'Then perhaps it's time you *behaved* like a grown man and stopped acting like a spoilt child!' Bernard's voice had risen now and his hands were clenched into fists of rage. 'Now put that money on the table and get out. Until you learn to buckle down and behave, I don't want to set eyes on you again – do you hear me?'

Jasper stared back at him in horror. '*What!* You mean you would throw your own son out into the cold on Christmas Day? What sort of a father are you?'

'A very tired, fed up one,' Bernard grated, his eyes flashing fire. 'Now put the money down or I swear I shall strike you.' He took a menacing step towards him but stopped in his tracks when Jasper shot forward and snatched up the gun.

He pointed it at his father's chest as he warned menacingly, 'Step away, Father. Or as God is my witness . . . I'll shoot you.'

It was at that moment that Sybil appeared in the doorway to find out what all the shouting was about and as she saw what was going on her hand flew to her mouth.

'Jasper . . . put that gun down this *instant*,' she commanded.

He turned briefly to glare at her and while he was distracted, his father leapt forward to grab the barrel of the gun as Sybil screamed, bringing the servants running.

Suddenly there was a resounding bang that reverberated around the room and as Jasper looked up, he saw blood explode from his father's chest as he dropped heavily to his knees staring up at him in shock. Scarlet blood began to trickle from his mouth and he fell back as if in slow motion as the women began to scream.

Sybil raced forward and dropped to her knees, cradling her husband's head in her lap as she cried, 'Someone get a doctor . . . *now!*'

Dropping the smoking gun as if it had burnt him, Jasper panicked and pushing his way through the group of servants in the doorway, he fled as if the devil himself was snapping at his heels. He had no idea where he was going, he just knew he had to get as far away from there as he could. If his father died the police would be looking for him for murder and he might well end up dangling from a rope. Tears of self-pity sprang to his eyes as he raced blindly through the woods adjoining the farmhouse. There would be no chance of wooing Emmy now. From this day on he would have to be invisible, a wanted man. The prospect was terrifying. Not once did he have any sympathy for the man who had fathered him; his thoughts, as always, were all for himself.

Back at the farm chaos reigned as the servants ran about like headless chickens, the dinner forgotten. One of the grooms had ridden for the doctor who arrived almost three-quarters of an hour later after attending a difficult birth in the town, but Sybil knew by then that he needn't have rushed. Bernard had been dead within minutes of Jasper shooting him.

'I'm so sorry, my dear,' he said gravely as he helped her to her feet and covered Bernard's face with a clean white handkerchief. Her skirt was soaked with blood and she was as white as the snow outside and clearly in shock. Turning to the groom who was hovering in the doorway, he instructed, 'Ride back into town again and get the constable, would you, my good man?'

'Yes, sir.' The groom touched his cap and left to do as he was told as silence descended on the farmhouse. This had certainly turned out to be a Christmas that no one present would ever forget.

Chapter Forty-One

Both Emmy and her parents read about Bernard's murder in the daily newspapers two days after his death. There had been no time for anyone to write to them to inform them what had happened and they were all deeply shocked.

'We must get home immediately,' Dorcas told Gerald. 'Sybil will no doubt be in a terrible state.'

'Of course, my dear.' He quickly rose from his seat, hardly able to take in what they had just read. It appeared that there was a big manhunt going on for Jasper and he shuddered to think what would happen to him when they caught him, as they surely would eventually. 'I'll go and ask Aggie if she'll do our packing for us,' he told his wife gently. 'And if we hurry, we should be able to catch the twelve o'clock train back to Trent Valley.'

They were soon ready, and once a hackney cab had been found, they stood on the steps and said a tearful goodbye to Emmy. She had wanted to go to the station with them but they had told her they preferred her to stay with Imogen, who wasn't too well that day and had chosen to stay in bed. A short time later the cab dropped them at the station and they caught the train home.

It was dark by the time they entered the cottage that night and Hetty welcomed them with a faltering smile.

'Have you heard what's happened?'

Dorcas nodded as she dropped wearily into a chair. 'Yes, we read about it in the newspapers. I still can't take it in, though. I always knew that Jasper was spoilt but why would he want to kill his father?'

'He was robbing the safe when his father walked in on him, apparently.' Hetty shook her head as she filled the kettle at the sink.

'And has there still been no sight of Jasper?'

'No, missus. They've had police scouring the surrounding neighbourhood but he seems to 'ave vanished into thin air. But 'ere, let me 'elp you off wi' your cloak while we wait for the kettle to boil.'

'It's all right, Hetty.' Dorcas gently shooed her away. 'I'm going to go and see how Sybil is first.'

Hetty sighed. 'From what I've 'eard she's in shock,' she confided. 'She ain't said so much as one word since they took the master away to the chapel o' rest, apparently. She just sits there starin' off into space.'

'Then I'll go immediately.' Dorcas stood up and Gerald joined her at the door, telling Hetty, 'We'll be back shortly and look forward to that cup of tea. A sandwich wouldn't go amiss either.'

'O' course, sir.'

As they tramped through the deep snow to the farm-house, Dorcas gripped Gerald's arm. Thankfully the snow had stopped falling for the first time in days but the journey was still heavy going and by the time they arrived they were both out of breath.

A red-eyed young maid met them at the door and informed them, 'The mistress is in the drawin' room, ma'am. Shall I tell 'er you're 'ere?'

'No, it's all right, Polly, thank you.' Dorcas and Gerald handed the girl their coats and hats. 'We'll just go in to her.'

They found Sybil sitting by a roaring fire staring into the flames, but she glanced up when they entered.

'I'm so sorry, Sybil.' Dorcas crossed the room and, kneeling down in front of her, took Sybil's hand. 'We came back from Imogen's just as soon as we heard what had happened. I can hardly believe it. Is there anything we can do?'

Sybil shook her head. 'No, but thank you. Everything is in hand. Bernard will be buried next Monday.'

'And Jasper?'

'I haven't heard a peep from him.' She shook her head. 'To be honest, I blame myself for what has happened. I always spoilt him shamelessly. Bernard and I had more rows about it than I care to remember but never in my wildest dreams did I think he would ever be capable of doing something like this.' She rose from her chair and went to a side table where a small book lay open. 'The police found this.' She tossed it to Dorcas. 'It's Jasper's diary and it seems that he has formed an obsession for your Emerald.'

'*Emerald!*' Dorcas glanced at Gerald in alarm. 'Then if that's the case, do you think there's any chance he might turn up at Imogen's?'

Sybil shrugged. 'I doubt it and don't worry, even if he did, he would be caught. They have policemen watching the house.'

Dorcas could hardly take it in. Jasper knew very well that given their family history, there could never be any sort of a relationship between them. They had all been well schooled in that fact. What was he thinking of?

Seeing the worried frown on her face, Gerald squeezed her shoulder. 'Emerald will be fine,' he told her.

Sybil noted the affectionate gesture and it seemed to be her undoing as the tears finally began to fall.

'At least you two are happy again,' she said sadly. 'In truth I don't think Bernard and I were ever happy together from day one. I was never under any illusions; he married me for my dowry and I was just grateful not to be left on the shelf. Who else would have married such a plain Jane? Within months of our marriage, I was aware that he was seeing other women, but what could I do?'

'You are far too hard on yourself,' Dorcas soothed, although she was well aware of her brother's shortcomings. 'But now we'll leave you to rest. I just wanted to let you know that we are back should you need anything.'

Their relationship had been undergoing a subtle change ever since she had moved into the cottage. At first, Sybil had visited her simply to gloat and yet despite that Dorcas had soon seen through her sister-in-law's hard front to the lonely woman beneath it and now she felt nothing but pity for her, for she had lost not only a husband but a son.

'Try not to worry, I'm sure they'll find Jasper very soon,' she said reassuringly.

Sybil snorted. 'I half hope that they don't.' Her face was bleak. 'Because then all I can look forward to is seeing him dancing at the end of a rope. No, what's done is done and nothing can bring Bernard back so I hope he manages to get away, preferably somewhere abroad where nobody knows him. I have to face the fact that he's gone forever now as well as Bernard.'

Dorcas had no reply to that so she and Gerald quietly left the room.

Bernard was buried quietly in the little churchyard adjoining Astley Church the following week after a simple service. There were only a handful of people present in the church. Sybil and her staff and Jake, who had come from London to attend, and a few of the farm workers, plus Dorcas and Gerald and a heavily veiled woman who took a seat right at the back of the church when the service had just begun.

'Of course, I'm sure you can guess who the mystery mourner was,' Sybil said bitterly as they rattled their way back to the farmhouse following the interment.

Dorcas raised an eyebrow. She hadn't really given the matter much thought.

'It was Bernard's fancy woman,' Sybil informed her quietly. 'I knew that he'd set her up in a little love nest years ago but he didn't know I was aware of it. I just hope he made her happier than he made me. But there, it's done now and when we get back to the farm, I have something I'd like to discuss with you, Gerald.'

'With me?' Gerald frowned, wondering what it could be but he kept his silence until they were back in the warm with glasses of whisky in their hands.

'So, what was it you wanted to talk to me about?' Gerald asked when he could no longer contain his curiosity.

'I've been thinking' – Sybil glanced at Jake – 'I don't suppose you will wish to give up your career to come home and take over the running of the farm, will you?'

Jake regretfully shook his head, so Sybil went on, 'Our farm manager will be retiring soon so I shall need someone reliable to take his place, especially now that Bernard is gone. What do you say, Gerald? Would you be prepared to take it on? I can't think of anyone I'd rather have to do it if Jake doesn't wish to, and of course I can afford to be generous.'

'W-well,' Gerald spluttered. 'I'm honoured that you've asked me, but do you think I'd be up to it?'

'Of course you would. You can come over and go through the books with the undermanager to see what's what whenever you like and then when you feel ready, we'll introduce you to the tenants and you can have free rein to manage everything as you see fit. I have neither the time nor the inclination to do it myself and you would be doing me a service if you agreed to it.'

Gerald smiled. Since coming to live in the cottage with his wife he had spent hours each day tramping to and from his poorly paid job on the outskirts of Bedworth, whereas if he worked here he would be close at hand to attend to any problems that might arise.

'Oh, do say you'll give it a try, dear,' Dorcas urged. 'You deserve another chance.'

Gerald nodded. 'Very well, we'll give it a try.'

Jake returned to London the next morning and soon after he had gone Gerald arrived at the farmhouse for a meeting with Bernard's undermanager. These meetings continued for some days, after which Gerald was introduced to Bernard's tenants and then he was ready to begin his new role.

Once again he was his own boss but this time Dorcas was determined not to put any pressure on him. Surprisingly enough she found she had all she needed in the little cottage and she was content for the first time in many, many years.

On the same day in January that Gerald began his job as the farm manager, Jasper's new life looked set to begin too when he boarded a ship at Dover bound for Calais. He had lain low for weeks in dirty bed-and-breakfast places until he felt certain that the police would no longer be searching for him so he could attempt to leave the country. Even now he was still nervous to be seen out and about, although he had changed his appearance drastically – his hair had grown and he now had a beard and wore workmen's clothes. No one seeing him would ever have believed that the rucksack he kept in sight at all times contained a small fortune. Now, as he climbed the gangplank, he paused briefly to take one last look over his shoulder at his homeland. He knew that once the ship set sail, he would never see it again.

But his biggest regret was leaving Emerald behind. As he thought of her now his stomach churned . . . if only he could have plucked up the courage to go and see her. He might have been able to persuade her to come with him and they could have started a new life together far away and everything would have been perfect . . .

Chapter Forty-Two

On a bright morning at the beginning of March, Mrs M frowned as Abi entered the kitchen looking pale and tired.

'Not slept very well, lass?' she enquired as she dried her hands on a tea towel and reached for the teapot.

Abi was still in her nightgown and robe and she shook her head as she held her back and manoeuvred herself awkwardly on to a chair at the table.

'No.' She rubbed her back. 'I've had backache all night and I couldn't get to sleep for it.'

'Have you now? Well get this down you and some breakfast inside you and happen you'll feel a bit better.' Mrs M was well aware of what was happening but not wishing to frighten the girl she kept up a cheerful chatter as she poured the tea and passed a cup to Abi.

'I don't think I want anything to eat, Mrs M, thank you,' Abi answered as she sipped at her drink. 'I'll just have this for now and then I'll go and get dressed.'

'Why bother if you're more comfortable as you are? We're not going out so it's not as if anybody is going to see you.'

'Hm, I suppose you're right. Bertie gone to work, has he?'

Again, Mrs M nodded. 'Yes, he was up with the lark and off early as usual. Why don't you go and sit out in the garden for a while? It's so lovely to see the daffodils and the crocuses coming through and a bit of fresh air would do you the power of good; you're looking a bit peaky.'

'Actually, I might just do that.' Abi rose and turned to the door then gasped with horror as she felt something warm between her legs and looked down to see a puddle of water on Mrs M's clean floor. 'Oh, I-I'm so sorry!' She was clearly mortified. 'I seem to have had an accident all over your kitchen floor.'

Mrs M chuckled as she hurried over to pat her arm and help her to sit down again. 'You haven't had an accident,' she assured her. 'If I'm any judge your waters have broken, lass.'

'*What?* . . . Y-you mean the baby is coming?' Abi looked so horrified that Mrs M couldn't help but smile.

'That's exactly what I mean, so let's get you dried off then I'll go and tell the midwife that you've started.'

'But what if she can't get here on time? What if I have it while you're gone?' Abi gabbled in a panic.

Mrs M shook her head. 'I don't think there's much chance of that happening so stop worrying. First babies have a habit of taking their time. You could be hours yet.'

She helped Abi back up to her room but they had only just reached the top of the stairs when Abi suddenly gripped her stomach and bent over. '*O-oh!* I just had a pain.'

'That'll be the contractions starting but like I say, there's no need to panic, this is only the beginning. Now come along so we can make sure we have everything ready for you and the baby before I shoot off to find the midwife.'

Once in the bedroom, Mrs M deftly stripped the sheet from the bed and padded the mattress with wads of old newspapers she had been saving and a layer of towels before putting the sheet back on. She helped Abi into a clean nightgown then dragged the crib that Bertie had so lovingly carved in from the spare room and placed it beside the bed along with some of the tiny baby clothes she had painstakingly stitched over the last few months.

'There, that should do it.' She stood back to eye her handiwork with satisfaction before helping Abi on to the bed. 'I'm just going to slip off now but the midwife doesn't live far away so I won't be long.'

'But what if she's out delivering another baby?' Abi's eyes were round with terror as she stared at this kindly woman who had taken her to her heart.

'We'll wait until the other baby is born and then she'll come here to you. Now will you stop panicking and try to relax, please. You need to save your strength.'

It proved to be easier said than done and once she heard the front door close Abi wriggled off the bed and hurried to the window to check Mrs M's progress down the street.

'Oh, Hugo, this is your baby about to be born and you'll never see it,' she wailed to the empty room, yet somehow when she tried to picture his handsome face it was just a blur. Then another pain gripped her and she forgot all about Hugo. She felt as if someone had put a tight band around her stomach and was squeezing it and she began to cry. She had never realised that giving birth would be anything like this. Thankfully she didn't know that there was much worse to come.

She had no idea how long Mrs M had been gone but by the time she returned it felt like hours and she was pacing up and down like a caged animal.

'Where is the midwife?' she cried, seeing that the woman was alone.

'It's all right, she'll be here shortly,' Mrs M assured her. 'She's just popped to see another mother-to-be who is close to her time and then she'll come.'

'Oooooh!' Abi grit her teeth and leant heavily on the foot-board of the bed as another much sharper pain gripped her. 'Ow, that one *really* hurt!'

'Why do you think they call it labour?' Mrs M gave her a hug. 'But just remember, every single one of us entered this world the same way and it's a pain that is soon forgotten once you see your baby.'

Abi glared at her. 'Haven't I told you a million times that I don't even want to see it?'

Mrs M nodded. 'You have that, but let's just wait and see if you're still singing from the same hymn sheet when it arrives, eh? Now stop getting yourself all worked up and concentrate on the job in hand.'

The midwife arrived almost an hour later and after washing her hands in the bowl that Mrs M had ready for her, she examined Abi and cheerfully told her that everything was fine and coming along nicely.

'It doesn't *feel* very fine!' Abi growled through gritted teeth as another pain ripped up her. 'How much longer is this going to . . . to take?'

'Babies have a habit of not coming until they're good and ready.' The elderly midwife had delivered many babies in her time and didn't seem overly concerned, which Abi supposed she should take as a good sign. 'So now I suggest Mrs Merryweather should go and make us all a nice cup of tea, then I'm going to go home for an hour or two and come back later. I'm afraid you're nowhere near ready yet.'

'*Wh-what?* You're going to leave me?' There was an edge of raw terror in her voice but the woman had seen it all before, especially with the first-time mothers. And so a short time later they drank the tea Mrs M fetched upstairs for them and the little midwife, who was almost as round as a little barrel, left Abi to it with a promise to be back later.

She reappeared at three in the afternoon by which time the contractions had become much stronger and Abi was sobbing with fear.

'I'm going to die!' Abi whimpered but Nurse Blye merely smiled and shook her head.

'No, you are not,' she told her stoically. 'Now let's have a look what's happening, eh?'

After examining Abi again, she smiled with satisfaction. 'A few more hours and your baby should be born.'

'A few more *hours*!' Abi was horrified. Never in her wildest dreams had she ever imagined that giving birth could be this traumatic. 'But I'm exhausted already.'

'Just breathe your way through the pains,' the midwife told her as Mrs M, who was sitting at the side of the bed, let Abi grip her hand.

'Grip as tight as you like, lass. You won't hurt me.' Mrs M gave her an encouraging smile and Abi did her best to be brave although she was rolling in agony with each contraction that came.

Bertie arrived home from work that evening to the sound of Abi's screams echoing down the stairs and the colour drained from his cheeks as he threw his work bag down and took the stairs two at a time. Once on the landing he pounded on the bedroom door and his mother's face peeped out at him.

'Is Abi having the baby?'

His mother nodded. 'She certainly is and I'm afraid I haven't had time to cook dinner.'

'It doesn't matter about that. What can I do to help?' He knew he couldn't have eaten a thing even if a feast had been waiting for him. 'Can I come in to see Abi?'

'No, you most certainly cannot,' his mother scolded. 'The birth room is no place for a man so go downstairs and get some bread and cheese. Oh, and put plenty of water on to boil. I think we may be needing it soon.'

Bertie did as he was told but after another hour of hearing Abi's agonised screams, he was beside himself with fear. Surely it shouldn't take this long for a baby to come? What if something was wrong? He tortured himself with possibilities as upstairs Nurse Blye checked on the baby's progress again and rolled her sleeves up.

'Well done,' she praised. 'You're ready to start pushing now so on the next pain give it all you've got. Your baby should be born soon.'

Abi did as she was told to the best of her ability but despite her best efforts the baby still refused to come and after another hour even the midwife became concerned.

'I think the baby is breech,' she quietly confided to Mrs M above Abi's screams. 'Do you think your son could run to tell the doctor he's needed?'

'Of course.' Mrs M was gone almost before the words had left the midwife's mouth and seconds later they heard the front door slam as Bertie raced to do as he was asked.

By the time the doctor arrived they were no further forward despite the midwife's best efforts and Abi was slipping in and out of consciousness.

'She's in a bad way, doctor,' Nurse Blye told him. 'And the baby's heartbeat is becoming erratic now.'

'Then we must deliver this child with all speed.' The doctor quickly removed his jacket, rolled up his sleeves and washed his hands, then he leant over Abi and told her gently, 'I am going to have to examine you internally and turn the baby if I can, my dear. I'm afraid it's going to hurt dreadfully but if we are to save your baby there is not a minute to lose.' Then without even waiting for Abi's consent, he bent to do what had to be done as her screams echoed around the room.

'You were right, the baby is breech,' he told the midwife as sweat stood out on his brow. 'And it's too far down the birth canal to turn it now. Hand me the scalpel please or we're going to lose both of them.'

As the midwife obliged him Abi's screams suddenly stopped abruptly and when Mrs M looked at her she saw that the girl was unconscious and began to pray. 'Please dear Lord, let them both survive,' she said quietly as the doctor and midwife worked on. Suddenly the doctor gave an exultant cry as a tiny leg appeared and with the doctor's help the rest of the baby followed soon after.

The child lay motionless between Abi's bloodied legs and as the doctor battled to stem the flow of blood gushing from

387

the mother, the midwife held the child aloft and sharply smacked its bottom. There was no reaction so next she lay the child back on the bed and began to gently blow into its mouth. Mrs M anxiously wrung her hands as she looked on helplessly until suddenly a thin mewling little cry made her heart beat with joy.

'Phew, you gave us a rare turn there for a moment, madam,' the midwife said as she wrapped the child in a towel and handed her to Mrs M. 'Would you take her and give her a bath while I help the doctor with Abigail?'

'Gladly.' As Mrs M took the tiny scrap in her arms her eyes filled with tears. The baby looked just like her mother with a thick thatch of soft tawny-coloured hair and she was quite beautiful, although very tiny, which was no surprise really when she thought of how little Abi had eaten throughout her pregnancy.

'Come on, little one, let's take you down to meet my Bertie,' she crooned as she left the room, throwing one last anxious glance towards Abi.

Bertie bounced out of the kitchen chair the second she appeared and within seconds the baby had him eating out of her tiny hand as he cradled her while his mother prepared the water for her bath.

'But how is Abi?' he asked eventually when he managed to tear his attention from the baby.

'Not good at the minute,' his mother admitted, carrying the bowl to the table. 'But she's in good hands so we have to stay optimistic.'

Bertie glanced towards the ceiling as he reluctantly handed the baby back to his mother. An hour ago he would have done anything to stop the agonised screaming yet now the dreadful silence seemed infinitely worse.

Finally, the doctor appeared in the doorway looking haggard and tired. 'I've managed to stop the flow of blood and Nurse Blye is washing her now,' he told them.

'Will she be all right?' Bertie's eyes were tortured.

'She's young and healthy so provided she doesn't start bleeding again I see no reason why she shouldn't make a full recovery. But now let's have a look at this little lady before I go.'

The baby, now swaddled in a shawl that Mrs M had knitted and dressed in one of the tiny nightgowns that she had stitched, was fast asleep in the drawer of the kitchen dresser.

'Is she all right, doctor?' Bertie asked.

Once again the doctor looked grave as he removed his stethoscope from his ears and straightened. 'I'm afraid one of her legs is broken. I had to be quite brutal to deliver her so that will have to be set but also . . .' He paused, seeing the look of concern on their faces. 'I'm afraid she may have a heart condition. Of course, the erratic heartbeat could just be down to the traumatic birth, in which case it will right itself.'

'And what can you do for that if it doesn't?'

The doctor sighed as he looked at Bertie. 'There is nothing that can be done,' he admitted. 'We can only hope that she grows a little stronger over the next few weeks. I'm not even going to set her leg just yet. I think she's been through quite enough trauma coming into the world, but I'll call back to see how she and the mother are tomorrow. Good evening, Bertie, Mrs Merryweather.'

They both inclined their heads as he left the room and Bertie lifted the baby protectively against his chest. 'I wonder what Abi will call her?' he mused. He was clearly besotted with the infant already and held her as if she was made of pure gold.

'That's the least of our worries for the minute,' his mother responded. 'I'm going to prepare a pap bag for her and you can see if you can get any milk into her while I go up and see if there's anything I can do to help Nurse Blye.'

Abi had been washed and changed and lay limply back against the pillows when Mrs M got upstairs.

'She did come round for a few minutes,' Nurse Blye told her. 'But what she needs now is rest and good nourishing food.'

'And I shall see that she gets both,' Mrs M assured her as she smoothed the blankets across Abi's stomach. 'I don't mind telling you I thought we were going to lose her for a while back there.'

'So did I, but between you and me it's the baby I'm the most concerned for,' the nurse told her in a low voice as she rolled her sleeves back down and prepared to leave. 'Still, it's all in God's hands now. Goodnight, Mrs M.'

'Goodnight, nurse.' Mrs M took a seat at the side of the bed and gently took Abi's hand as she waited for her to wake up.

'Come on, lass, don't let me down now. You've got a little daughter downstairs waiting to meet you, and me and Bertie need you to wake up so that you can tell us what you're going to call her,' she said softly, but Abi slept on.

Chapter Forty-Three

'I had a letter from Abi today,' Emmy told Jake when he picked her up the following Sunday. 'It's the second I've had from her since she ran off to Aunt Imogen's house at the coast and she said she might be coming home soon. But she still won't give me the address for me to write back to her and neither will my aunt. I really can't see why,' Emmy ended peevishly.

'I've no doubt she has her reasons,' Jake said sensibly as he urged the old horse forward. 'And I really can't see what the problem is if you know that she's all right.'

'I suppose you're right,' Emmy admitted in a small voice. 'But I still can't stop worrying about her.' As she glanced at Jake she noticed that he looked tired. He was now working four days a week at the practice in Harley Street and the other three at the poor surgery. 'Don't you think it's time you started to have a day off each week? You're working far too hard!' she suggested tentatively.

He shook his head. 'I'm fine. I just feel guilty that I haven't gone home to help Mother run the farm now that Father is gone.'

'Well, don't. Mama told me in her last letter that my father is doing a sterling job of managing it. I'm actually very grateful to Aunt Sybil for giving him the opportunity. It's given him his pride back and he and Mother are like a pair of lovebirds.' She giggled. 'I never thought I'd say this but they seem happier now than when they were living in Astley House.'

'Life is a funny thing,' Jake commented. 'And as for me looking tired, you look a little peaky yourself.'

'Oh, I'm fine.' Emmy was a little tired but she would never admit it. Her aunt hadn't been at all well for the last few days and Emmy had spent a few sleepless nights getting in and out of bed to check on her, much to her aunt's disgust.

'There's no need to keep checking on me like a mother hen,' she had scolded. 'I'm quite capable of calling you if I want anything.' At which Emmy had smiled and slunk away. She knew that her aunt was grateful under her tough exterior.

Whatever few minutes or hours she did have spare was spent collecting clothes for the poor. She would then take them back to her aunt's where Cook and Aggie would sort them into piles and launder any that needed washing. Every Saturday night she spent in the kitchen helping Cook to prepare and bake the bread she would take to the poor surgery the following day, along with the huge pan of soup she now took each week. She had also started to collect donations for the poor from her aunt's wealthy friends and this, along with what Imogen gave him, went a long way towards helping Jake to buy the pills and potions he prescribed for the patients. Somehow, she never seemed to have a minute to herself. Not that she begrudged a moment of the time she spent helping Jake; she would have walked through fire for him if need be and had been forced to admit to herself that her feelings for him had deepened further. She suspected he felt the same for her but knew that it was useless to even imagine that they had a future together. Somewhere along the way she had resigned herself to becoming a spinster for she knew now that no other man would ever match up to him in her eyes.

As they rounded the corner to the poor surgery, her thoughts were pulled back to the present when they noticed a straggling line of people already waiting for them and Jake chuckled. 'Look at that. How things change, eh? We couldn't persuade them to come in at the beginning and now we struggle to see them all each day.'

Richard had also just arrived and was unlocking the door and soon they were all busy carrying the food and clothes they had brought with them in before Richard and Jake saw the first patients. Since she had been helping at the surgery, Emmy had become adept at dressing wounds and administering medicine and she found that she enjoyed it. She certainly seemed to have a calming influence on the patients and sometimes wondered if she shouldn't go into nursing as a career if anything happened to her aunt. Just the thought of that made her feel sad but she had been forced to face up to the fact that her aunt's health was deteriorating rapidly despite the constant care that she and Aggie gave her, and she realised that it was just a matter of time before she lost her.

It was late that evening by the time Jake drove her home and they were both feeling tired but satisfied with what they'd achieved that day. They both realised that many of the people who attended only came with mild ailments so that they could go away with a loaf of bread or a much-needed pair of shoes or item of clothing, but others came with more serious complaints and they felt that this was a good thing.

'Will you come in for a drink?' Emmy asked when he drew the horse to a halt outside her aunt's.

He nodded. 'That would be lovely. You go in and put the kettle on and I'll be in when I've put his nosebag on,' he answered as he hopped down from the driver's seat and tethered the horse to the lamp post.

Minutes later they were seated at the kitchen table with steaming mugs in front of them and as Jake sipped at his and stretched his long legs out, he sighed with contentment. 'Oh, I have to say you make a lovely cup of cocoa.' He gave her the smile that could turn her legs to jelly if only he'd known it. 'This is just what the doctor ordered.'

'Hm, I was thinking, we're going to need bigger premises if this goes on for much longer. We had more patients than ever today. Soon we'll be turning them away.'

He nodded. 'I understand what you mean but I don't think we can expect Aunt Imogen to do more than she does. She's already paying the rent on where we are now, bless her.'

They talked of the various patients they had seen for a while until Jake said tentatively, 'I noticed that you and Richard are getting on well.' He watched her closely for her reaction.

'Yes, we are.' Emmy smiled. 'He's so nice, how could anyone not get on with him?'

A little ripple of jealousy coursed through Jake like iced water. Richard had confided that he admired Emmy enormously. Sometimes Jake would catch his friend's eyes following her around the room and he knew that Richard was developing feelings for her. He also knew that he shouldn't mind, but he did and sometimes he tortured himself with images of them getting together – not that there was anything he could do about it. Suddenly the precious few quiet moments they had been sharing were spoilt and scraping his chair back he rose abruptly, leaving his cup half empty.

'I'll be off then,' he said shortly as Emmy blinked with surprise. 'Got another busy day ahead tomorrow.'

'B-but aren't you going to finish your cocoa?'

'No, I ought to be going. Goodnight, Emmy.'

She watched the door close behind him and listened to the echo of his footsteps in the hallway, then lowering her head she sighed sadly.

In Lytham St Anne's, Abi was slowly recovering from the birth, much to Mrs M's and Bertie's relief. The baby was a day old and although Abi was weak, she was now fully conscious. Mrs M was plying her with tasty titbits and nourishing chicken soup, which the dear soul thought was the cure for all ills, and downstairs Bertie was once again trying to persuade the baby to take some milk, although as yet he'd had no success at all.

The doctor had been in twice that day to check the mother and baby but while he was pleased with Abi's progress he was now gravely concerned about the child. Its tiny heartbeat was as erratic as it had been following the birth and although the doctor hadn't told them to prepare for the worst, he fully expected it.

'I was thinking it's time you met your daughter now you're properly awake again,' Mrs M told Abi as she prepared to carry a tray downstairs.

Abi looked uncertain but the kindly woman wasn't going to take no for an answer and pottered from the room before Abi could refuse.

Minutes later she was back with the baby wrapped in a snow-white shawl and as she approached the bed, she saw Abi flinch as if someone had struck her.

'I-I'm not sure I'm strong enough for this yet,' she said in a choky voice as Bertie hovered in the doorway, his face concerned.

'Rubbish, of course you are.' Mrs M gave her no more chances to refuse and marching to the bed she laid the child on her mother's chest.

And then the strangest thing happened, for as Abi reluctantly looked down at her daughter a look of awe appeared on her face and her arms instinctively closed about her, much to the onlooker's relief.

'Oh . . . but she's *beautiful*!' she breathed as she tenderly stroked the baby's soft cheek. A wave of love swept through her and suddenly she was crying as she realised that this child was a part of her and that she would never be able to give her up.

'Didn't I tell you so?' Mrs M said smugly. 'And now it's time you thought of a name for her.'

Bertie had come to sit by the bed and as Abi glanced at him, she noted the way he was staring at the baby. She had obviously stolen his heart too, just as she had hers.

'Right, I'll leave you pair to look after her for a while. I'm going to have a cuppa and put me feet up for a bit.' Mrs M smiled with satisfaction and marched from the room, closing the door behind her.

'Had you got any names in mind for her?' Bertie asked, delighted to see the way Abi was cuddling the child.

Shamefaced, Abi shook her head. 'I'm afraid because I wasn't planning on keeping her, I didn't bother to think of any,' she admitted and she began to cry. 'But how *can* I keep her, Bertie? I'd never be able to go home again and people would always class me as a scarlet woman. What sort of a life would that be for her?'

Bertie nervously cleared his throat and said gently, 'I've got a solution to that. If you married me, she'd take my name and I'd bring her up as my own and I'd make sure that she never wanted for anything.'

Abi looked so shocked that he gave her a smile. 'Don't look so surprised. I'm not just saying this out of the goodness of my heart! You must have realised how I feel about you, Abi. I love you and have since the moment I first set eyes on you.'

'B-but how can you say that? I've just given birth to another man's child! I'm soiled goods.'

He shook her head. 'You just made a mistake and you could never be soiled to me. I don't expect you to give me an answer straightaway but if you say yes, you'll make me the happiest man on earth. We'll go off somewhere and get married quietly and no one need ever know that she isn't my baby. Will you at least consider it?'

Abi was speechless for a moment and merely nodded at this gentle young giant who had never shown her anything but kindness. Unlike Hugo, he had never expected anything from her and she suddenly realised with a little jolt that she had grown to be more than fond of him. But was that enough?

She turned her attention back to the baby, who hadn't so much as whimpered and as she cradled her against her breast, she knew what true love was. 'How about the name Grace?' she suggested and Bertie nodded enthusiastically. 'And what is your mother's name?'

'It's Rebecca.'

'Then Grace Rebecca it is.'

When she came back upstairs some half an hour later, Mrs M was thrilled with the choice and proud as punch that Abi had chosen to give the newborn her name. She gently took Grace out of her mother's arms. 'You might be on the mend but you've still a long way to go before you get your strength back,' she scolded when Abi objected and Bertie chuckled as he leant over to peck her cheek. 'But I'll tell you what I'll do, I'll get Bertie to carry her crib back up here and she can sleep beside you once I've fed her.'

Once Mrs M had left the room, Bertie grinned. 'Just think, she could be your mother-in-law!'

Abi smiled back feeling tired but more contented than she had for a very long time, then she turned her head on the pillow and within seconds was fast asleep.

Chapter Forty-Four

'I can't believe we're into March already,' Emmy said as she tied the ribbons on her bonnet beneath her chin. Aggie had agreed to watch Imogen for her while she popped to the apothecary to pick up her aunt's heart tablets and she was looking forward to a gentle stroll in the sunshine. It wasn't often she managed to get out during the day.

'I shouldn't be long,' she promised as she lifted her bag and set off. Soon she was strolling past the railings of the park enjoying the fresh air.

'Psst . . . Emmy . . . over here!'

Emmy paused and peered through the hedge on the other side of the railings only to gasp when she saw a rather dishevelled looking Jasper crouching there. Her first instincts were to pick up her skirts and run for dear life, but then common sense prevailed. It was broad daylight so he wasn't likely to try and harm her, surely.

'What are you doing here?' she hissed. 'Don't you know that the police are looking for you?' She could hardly believe the change in his appearance. His clothes were shoddy and with his beard and his workman's cap he looked nothing like the smart young whip she remembered.

'I didn't mean to shoot my father,' he hissed back, looking over his shoulder to make sure he couldn't be overheard. 'It was an accident . . . he was trying to take the gun off me. But I'm not here about that.'

When Emmy hovered uncertainly, he hurried on, 'It's about Jake . . . he's been hurt, *badly* hurt, and I need you to come with me. I can hardly fetch anyone to help him, can I? You were the only one I could think of.'

Her eyes were wide with fear now. 'What do you mean – he's hurt?'

'He went to help some tramp in a warehouse down by the docks and they turned on him. I saw Jake go in then the tramp ran out and when I went in to check on him, I found him lying on the floor. He was unconscious and there was a lot of blood. I didn't know what to do.'

'Oh no!' Emmy's heart was thumping painfully now and she didn't even think to ask how Jasper had just happened to be there. All she could think about was Jake lying injured. Without waiting for his reply she went on in a shaky voice, 'Take me to him at once.'

Jasper disappeared, joining her on the pavement a moment later, looking left and right to make sure they were not being observed.

'Hurry!' she urged as they moved on, half running and half walking.

Sometime later, he pointed ahead. 'The warehouse is down there.'

Above the roof of the near-derelict building, she could see the ships at anchor in the dock and the first feeling of something being not quite right began to niggle away at her insides. 'B-but I didn't think these warehouses were in use any more,' she said uncertainly as her steps slowed.

'They're not. The vagrants tend to sleep here, that's why Jake was going to help one. You know what he's like when it comes to helping the needy. But hurry or we might be too late to help him.'

It was all she needed to spur her on and seconds later they entered the building and she came to a halt as her eyes adjusted to the gloom. Just as Jasper had said there was evidence that people had recently slept there. Cardboard boxes were strewn about with layers of newspapers inside them and empty bottles and food wrappers were discarded across the floor. The smell of sewage and stale bodies was appalling and she almost gagged.

The only daylight that filtered in was from the holes in the roof but she had no time to take in any more for Jasper was hurrying towards a door that led down into what appeared to be a cellar.

'He's down here.' He was out of breath now and so was she but she found a new strength suddenly and ran after him, picking her way down the steep wooden stairs. It was even darker down there and when something warm and furry suddenly ran across her foot she screamed.

'S-so where is he?'

He pointed towards a pile of sacks by the far wall. 'Over there.'

Emmy instantly flew towards them, narrowing her eyes to try to see in the dark. It was then that Jasper suddenly caught her from behind and because she hadn't been expecting it, she toppled over in a heap with him on top of her.

'What are you *doing* . . . and where is Jake?' She began to beat at him with her fists as panic coursed through her.

'I've no idea,' he admitted as he held her in a vice-like grip. 'But this was the only way I could think of to make you see sense.'

As she stared up at him, appalled, she saw the glimmer of tears on his cheeks and a desperate look in his eyes.

'You must *know* how much I love you,' he choked. 'But because of what happened with Father I can't stay here now. I have to get out of the country and I want you to come with me. I was actually boarding a ship that would get me away but at the last minute I couldn't leave you. We are meant to be together!'

'Don't talk such *rubbish*!' she snapped.

His expression changed and he glared down at her. 'I know you don't love *me*,' he snarled. 'You only have eyes for Jake. I've seen how you look at him and how your eyes light up whenever his name is mentioned. But if I can't have you, no one will, especially not my goody-goody brother, damn him to hell! If you'd just agree to come away with me, I could make you love me in time, I know I could!'

Emmy was furious as she lashed out at him as best she could. 'Stop talking such nonsense! You know very well we can never be together; we're cousins!'

His lip curled. 'You're a *hypocrite*,' he snarled. 'That doesn't seem to bother you when it comes to Jake and he's as much your cousin as I am! And anyway, there's no reason we can't be together now. The only thing holding me back before was the threat of being cut off.' He gave a short bark of laughter. 'But that's not a problem any more. And I don't want any children. All I want is you!'

'Just go and give yourself up to the police,' she implored him. 'If your father's death was an accident as you say it was, they'll listen to you.'

'Huh!' he sneered. 'Fat chance of that happening.' Then suddenly without warning he flipped her over on to her stomach as if she weighed nothing and after fumbling in his pocket, he took out a length of fine rope, and began to bind her hands behind her back.

The first real feelings of panic began to rush through Emmy as she tried to reason with him. 'Look . . . just let me go and I'll forget I ever even saw you,' she begged but her words fell on deaf ears and once her hands were securely tied, he flipped her over again and proceeded to tie her feet together until she was trussed up like a turkey.

'This is silly,' she told him, trying to keep her voice calm. 'You can't keep me here indefinitely. Aunt Imogen will have the police out looking for me if I don't go back.'

He was breathless again now as he sat back to survey her. The rope was cutting into her wrists and ankles and she had to blink back tears when she realised what a fool she had been to follow him.

'I have no intention of keeping you here forever,' he told her, his eyes cold. 'Just until you decide to see sense and come away with me.'

She opened her mouth to tell him that this would never happen but immediately thought better of it and clamped it shut again as he struggled to his feet and lifted his rucksack.

'I've got a small fortune in here,' he bragged and she detected a strange glint in his eye. 'Enough to set us up for some time to come. Think of it . . . a life in the sun, no more having to pander to dear old Aunt Imogen. We could be so happy if you'd only give us a chance. I'm going to go and get us some food and drink now. We can stay here while you think about it. Oh, and don't bother screaming. No one ever comes here apart from the down-and-outs when darkness falls and they're usually in such an opium-induced state they wouldn't take any notice of you.' Without another word he turned and climbed the stairs, closing the door at the top behind him, plunging the cellar into total darkness. Next came the sound of the outside door slamming shut.

Emmy's tears came then, so fast that she could hardly see, but after a while she forced herself to calm down so she could think what to do. All around her, creatures were foraging in the darkness and the hairs on the back of her neck stood to attention as a pair of tiny red eyes passed within a hair's breadth of her face.

'*Ugh!*' She began to wriggle and roll across the floor until she came to the wall where, somehow, she managed to manoeuvre herself into a sitting position. The wall was damp and within minutes she could feel it seeping into the back of her gown as she wrestled with the rope on her wrists. But it was useless; the more she struggled the tighter the rope became and so eventually she sat very still listening for the sound of anyone who might be within earshot.

On the far wall was a tiny window covered in a metal grill but it was so high up she knew there could be no chance of escape there, even if she managed to get free. It finally sunk in that she was Jasper's prisoner and there wasn't a single thing she could do about it. But he was saying that he loved her so surely he wouldn't hurt her? Remembering the hint of madness she had seen in his eyes, she suddenly wasn't so sure and as she sagged back against the damp bricks she let her tears fall once more.

'Good evening, Aggie. And how are you all this wonderful evening?' Jake said cheerily when Aggie opened the door to Imogen's house that evening.

Aggie frowned as she looked past him, ignoring his cheery greeting. 'But ain't Miss Emerald wi' you, sir?'

The smile slid from his face as he handed her his hat. 'Of course not. Why would she be on a weekday? I've been at the Harley Street practice today.'

'But she popped out on an errand fer the missus this mornin' an' she ain't come back,' Aggie told him fearfully. 'The missus is in a right two an' eight about it an' she's convinced somefin' 'as happened to 'er.'

'Have you reported it to the police?'

Aggie shook her head. 'No, Mr Jake. The missus were convinced she'd be wi' you if she were anywhere but if you ain't seen 'er, where could she be? She don't know the place like I do. Yer don't fink she's got lost do yer?'

'It's highly unlikely.' Jake was frowning now as worry descended. 'If she did get lost, all she'd have to do is hail a hackney cab and it would bring her home. Was she in good spirits when she left?'

'Oh yes, sir. Bright as a button she were.'

'Right, I need to see Aunt Imogen. Is she upstairs?'

When Aggie nodded he took the stairs two at a time. Minutes later he came pounding down again and snatched his hat from the hatstand. 'I'm going to inform the police of her disappearance,' he told Aggie. 'Although I doubt they'll do anything about it at this early stage. She hasn't been gone for long enough. Still, it won't stop me having a scout around for her. Perhaps she's gone to the poor surgery.' Deep down he knew this was highly unlikely but he was prepared to try anything.

It was late that evening before he returned, footsore and downhearted. 'No one has seen her,' he told Imogen who had insisted on coming downstairs to wait for him. 'I think you'd best write to her parents and tell them how worried we are in case she's turned up there.'

'I'll do it immediately,' Imogen answered as she lifted her stick and hobbled over to her dainty escritoire in a waft of expensive French perfume. 'Then Aggie can run and put it in the post box and it will go first thing in the morning.'

Jake nodded. Now there was nothing else they could do but wait, although every minute that Emmy was missing seemed like an hour and he wondered how he would bear it.

Chapter Forty-Five

'It's no good, Mrs M, she just won't feed,' Abi said with frustration as she fastened her nightdress yet again.

'Try not to worry, she will when she's hungry,' the kindly woman told her, although she herself was now gravely concerned about the child. They'd tried everything to get her to drink her milk but whatever they did she just let it dribble out of the side of her mouth and with every day that passed, her mother grew a little stronger and Grace grew a little weaker.

The doctor had called in a couple of days ago and had set her leg as gently as he could, which had made the poor little soul whimper with distress, but there was nothing he could do to make her take her milk and her heart was still beating erratically – not a good sign at all, although he hadn't dared to tell the young mother that.

'I think you should run and ask the doctor to call again, Bertie,' Mrs M told him when she carried the baby into the kitchen minutes later. 'She seems to be wasting away despite our best efforts and I feel so useless.'

Bertie was off like a hare. There was nothing he wouldn't have done for Grace. He already loved the child as much as if she had been his own and he loved her mother even more, if that were possible. He just prayed she would agree to be his wife.

Thankfully the doctor attended within the hour and after weighing the child on Mrs M's kitchen scales, he shook his head. 'It's usual for newborn babies to lose a little weight immediately after the birth,' he told her with a grim expression. 'But I'm afraid this little one isn't thriving at all. I think you should all prepare yourselves for the worst.'

Mrs M wrung her hands as her eyes filled with tears. 'But surely there's *something* you can do for her, doctor? She's only a few days old, God love her!'

He sighed. 'If only there were, Mrs Merryweather, but to be honest, I didn't expect her to survive this long. Her heartbeat is sadly erratic, that accounts for the tinge of blue you can see about her lips, and unfortunately there is nothing anyone can do about that in a child so young.'

Bertie tenderly took Grace from his mother's arms and began to gently rock her to and fro as his heart broke. He'd had such plans for her but now it seemed they might never happen. He'd pictured them building sandcastles on the beach when he got home from work each evening and giving her donkey rides. He'd imagined them paddling in the sea with the sun warm on their backs – that was if Abi agreed to marry him. But now it looked as if his dreams weren't going to come true and worse still, how would Abi take it if anything happened to Grace? She had gone from not wanting the baby to adoring her within minutes of seeing her and he knew that she would be broken-hearted.

'What should we tell Abi?' he asked in a shaky voice.

The doctor sighed. 'Perhaps we should wait a while and just see how things go?' he suggested. 'While she's on the mend there's no point in upsetting her until we have to. And after all, I could be wrong; it wouldn't be the first time.'

'Let's just pray that you are.' Mrs M saw him to the door before once again warming some milk for the little one. If she didn't survive, she was determined it wouldn't be through lack of her doing her very best for her.

That night when all was quiet Mrs M tucked the baby into the crib at the side of her mother's bed and bent to kiss Abi's cheek. 'Now you just call if she wakes and you need any help during the night,' she told her, although Abi hadn't had to do that as yet. The baby seemed to spend most of her time sleeping.

'I will,' Abi promised as she lay on her side gently stroking the baby's cheek. She looked like a little angel lying there with her eyelashes curled on her baby cheeks and Abi's heart overflowed with love for her.

'I love you so very much, little Miss Grace,' she whispered and she watched her for a long time until eventually she fell into a deep contented sleep.

The next morning after seeing to Bertie's breakfast, Mrs M made Abi a cup of tea and carried it upstairs to her. Once in Abi's room she placed it on the small table at the side of the bed and crossed to flick the curtains open, letting the early morning sunshine spill into the room.

'Morning, lass,' she said cheerfully as she approached the bed where Abi was stretching and yawning. 'This little one gave you another undisturbed night, did—?' She stopped talking abruptly as she glanced into the crib and the smile slid from her face.

'What's wrong?' Abi levered herself up on to her pillows and as her eyes followed those of Mrs M she saw that Grace was lying unnaturally still.

Bending, Mrs M lifted the child and as her tiny arms dangled to either side of her small body her worst fear was confirmed. The child was cold to the touch and her skin, normally like peaches and cream, had taken on a grey tone.

'Oh, my poor little lass!' Mrs M began to cry as Abi looked on in horror. 'I'm so sorry but I'm afraid she's gone.'

Without thinking, Abi swung her legs out of the bed, wobbling dangerously as the floor rose up to greet her. Then she rushed over and snatched the baby from Mrs M's arms.

'Grace, it's Mummy. Wake up, sweetheart . . . Oh, *please* wake up!' But even as she said it, she knew that Mrs M was right. Her sweet little baby was quite dead.

Mrs M meantime had run to the door and bellowed downstairs to Bertie, 'Run for the doctor, son. Tell him to come *immediately*!'

Bertie appeared at the bottom of the stairs, his face ashen. 'Is something wrong with Abi?'

'No, lad . . . It's the baby . . . sh-she's gone,' his mother informed him as tears ran in rivers down her cheeks.

Bertie looked stricken, but pulling himself together he snatched up his coat and within seconds the front door banged behind him as he raced off to fetch the doctor, praying that his mother was wrong with every step he took.

Thankfully the doctor was at breakfast when Bertie appeared breathless on his doorstep and he went back with him immediately to the house overlooking the sea.

'I'm so very sorry,' he said eventually when he'd examined the child. 'To be honest with you, her heart being so bad, I did fear this.'

Abi was sitting as if she had been turned to stone. She hadn't shed so much as a single tear and he wrote out a prescription for Bertie to take to the apothecary. 'It's something to help her,' he explained. 'She's clearly in shock. And perhaps while you're out you might ask the undertaker to call?'

'Of course.' Bertie himself was shaking uncontrollably as he tried to take it in and the happy future he had planned for them all disappeared like mist in the morning.

The rest of the morning passed in a blur. Soon after the doctor had left, the undertaker arrived to take Grace's tiny body to the chapel of rest and to organise her funeral. It was decided that she would be buried in the pretty little graveyard of the church that Mrs M and Bertie attended and the service would take place in three days' time. Then he too was gone and still Abi sat staring from the window, seemingly in a place where no one could reach her, dry-eyed and silent.

Throughout the day either Bertie or Mrs M were with her constantly but she didn't even seem to know they were there.

'She needs to cry,' Mrs M whispered to her son worriedly. 'It doesn't do any good at all to bottle everything up like that.' She had plied her with endless cups of tea and coffee and tasty titbits to try to get her to eat and drink but everything went back to the kitchen untouched, and as darkness fell the kindly woman was at a loss as to know what to do.

'Perhaps we should give her some space?' Bertie suggested, his eyes tight on the girl he loved as he gripped her hand.

His mother nodded and after planting a gentle kiss on Abi's cheek and telling her that they would be there if she needed them, they quietly left the room and dejectedly made their way down to the kitchen. They both knew there would be no point in going to bed, neither of them would sleep, so Mrs M made yet another large pot of tea, and they sat miserably at the kitchen table.

It was well after midnight when Mrs M suddenly looked up and frowned. 'Did you hear something?' She cocked her ear. 'I thought I heard the front door shut just then.'

Bertie shrugged, his eyes gritty from lack of sleep and red from weeping. 'No, I didn't, but I think I'll just go up and check on Abi again.' He had been up and down the stairs a dozen times at least, but each time he had found her in the same position, staring from the window.

Wearily he mounted the steps once more and quietly opened Abi's door, and then his heart skipped a beat. She wasn't there.

He flew back to the kitchen. 'She isn't in her room. It must have been her you heard going through the front door, but where would she go at this time in the morning?' Without even waiting for an answer, he rushed along the hall and through the front door, pausing on the step to look up and down the street but there was no sign of her. And then as he looked ahead to the beach, he glimpsed someone dressed in white heading towards the sea. Without stopping to think he started to run and sure enough he saw a figure knee-deep in the waves that were crashing on the shore.

'Abi! *STOP!*' His heart was pounding now but his steps didn't slow and he ran as if his life depended on it, but by the time he reached the sea, the water was past Abi's waist and her nightgown was floating about her.

He plunged in, oblivious to the cold water that took his breath away and somehow a few seconds later he managed to grab her.

'Get *off* me! I want to be with my baby!' She began to pound at him with her fists and they fell beneath the waves, but he dragged her back up to the surface, coughing and spluttering as she continued to fight him.

Slowly and painfully, he hauled her back to the damp sand where she collapsed in a heap.

'You should have let me die,' she shouted. 'It's all my fault Grace is dead. I don't deserve to live!'

Appalled, Bertie stared at her. 'What do you mean – it's your fault?'

As she looked up at him he saw the raw pain in her eyes and his heart broke afresh for her. 'Don't you understand? She was conceived in sin, a bastard! And I didn't want her. I used to wish I could have a miscarriage. I even considered getting rid of her at one stage but I was too much of a coward to go through with it. That's why God has taken her, because I'm wicked. I didn't deserve to have her!'

'Ah, but all that changed when you saw her, didn't it?' She was shivering uncontrollably now and he drew her into his arms and gentled the wet hair from her face. 'No mother could have loved her child more than you loved her. God isn't punishing you; she had a bad heart, Abi. We knew from the start but we were praying for a miracle.'

She blinked up at him as if she could hardly take in what he was saying and suddenly she began to cry, great gulping sobs that shook her slight frame.

'That's it, cry it all out,' he soothed as she sobbed against his chest. 'And then we'll get you home and into some dry clothes before you catch cold.'

Three days later Grace was laid to rest. Only Mrs M, Bertie and Abi attended the short but sweet service and when they turned to leave the tiny grave Abi left a piece of her heart there with her little daughter. She had had her for such a very brief time but she knew that she would never forget her. They went back to the house where Abi stood once again silently staring from the window.

'You know . . . what I asked you a while ago still stands,' Bertie told her as he stood close behind her. 'I love you, Abi, and I would be honoured if you would agree to become my wife.'

She turned to face him and her hand rose to stroke his cheek gently. 'You're a good man, Bertie,' she said softly. 'And I just might take you up on that offer one day. But first there are things I have to do.'

When he raised a questioning eyebrow she went on. 'I realise now that I've been a very selfish person. I ran away to London when my father left us with no thought of what would become of my mother and then I fell in love with Hugo. All I cared about was wearing pretty gowns and getting what I wanted, doing what I wanted. When I got into trouble my aunt saved the day when she sent me here to you and your mother. But my poor mother doesn't even know that for a very brief time she had a little granddaughter.'

'But surely she doesn't need to know?'

Abi shook her head. 'No, I don't want there to be secrets and lies between us any more otherwise I will never be able to mention Grace. It will be as if she had never been here and I don't want to forget her. One day, if I ever have other children, I want to be able to tell them about the big sister they never met . . . Can you understand that?'

With tears glistening on his lashes, he nodded. 'Yes, I think I can. So, what are you going to do now?'

'I'm going to see my aunt then I'm going home to make my peace with everyone and apologise.'

He gulped as he gently took her hand. 'Do what you must. But just remember – if ever you want to take me up on my offer . . . I'll be here waiting . . . for always.'

She stood on tiptoe and gently kissed his lips. 'I'll remember.'

Chapter Forty-Six

The sparse light that had struggled through the window in the cellar was now gone again and once more Emmy found herself in total darkness. All around her she could hear creatures scuttling across the floor and, taking deep breaths, she tried not to panic. She knew that this must be at least the second night she had been imprisoned there but the hours were running into one another and she had lost all sense of time. Her wrists were so sore now that she had stopped struggling; the blood where the rope had chafed her skin had dried and she felt weak from lack of food. She desperately wanted to use a toilet too and tears of humiliation began to course down her cheeks as she squirmed in her damp underclothes. And then she heard a sound upstairs. Someone was up there and she began to shout.

'Help! . . . Help me *please*! . . . I'm down here in the cellar.'

There was no response and her shoulders sagged. It sounded as if there was more than one person up there but if they had heard her, they were turning a deaf ear.

At last, when she had almost given up hope of Jasper ever returning, there was the sound of the door at the top of the steps opening and a shaft of dim light spilled into the dank room. She saw the flare of a match as someone paused to light a candle they had placed ready. As it wavered towards her, she saw that it was Jasper. He was holding a newspaper-wrapped parcel that smelt delicious and from his rucksack he produced a bottle of ginger beer.

'I got us a pie,' he informed her cheerily as if they were on a picnic.

'I need to go to the toilet . . . *now*,' she spat furiously and he instantly looked remorseful.

'Oh yes, yes of course you must do by now.' Without argument he came to stand behind her and undid the ties on her wrists, then he did the same with her ankles and she sighed with relief, although the pain in her arms when she straightened them was horrendous after being tied in one position for so long.

'Where is it? The toilet?' she demanded.

He waved towards a far corner of the cellar. 'You can go over there.' Seeing the look of horror on Emmy's face, he grinned. 'It's all right. I won't be able to see you from here.'

Knowing that she had no option, she tentatively picked her way across the filthy floor until she came to the far wall. As quickly as she could she lifted her skirts and relieved herself, keeping her back to him the whole time. When she returned, he had undone the food and placed the pie on the chair for her, but hungry as she was, she swiped it off with a single stroke.

'I won't eat *anything* you bring me,' she snarled and turning she headed towards the cellar steps.

She had only taken a few paces when Jasper had her in a firm grip again and she began to struggle and kick out as he manoeuvred her back to the chair and slammed her into it.

417

'I was hoping you'd have calmed down a bit by now,' he grunted as he struggled to tie her again. It took every ounce of strength he had as she put up a fight but eventually, she was trussed again and she began to scream.

'Carry on,' he told her nonchalantly as he lifted the pie from the filthy floor where it had fallen and bit into it. 'None of them up there will take any notice. They're all off their heads with drink or opium.'

Emmy's chin drooped to her chest and she began to cry, great heaving sobs that shook her body.

Clearly upset to see her so distressed, Jasper rose and began to pace up and down the room, his eyes wild. 'It's your own fault. You don't think I like having to do this to you, do you?' he said peevishly. 'If you'd only calm down and see sense, you'd see what a wonderful life we could have together . . . look!' Upending his rucksack, he let the money he had stolen from his father's safe flutter to the ground like confetti at a wedding. 'We're rich; this could keep us for ages and we could go anywhere you like. Just name the place!'

Once again, she saw that strange gleam in his eyes and suddenly she realised what she must do if she were to have any chance of getting out of there. She had no doubt that her aunt would have a search party out looking for her by now but the chances of them finding her here were very remote.

'I . . . I'm sorry, Jasper,' she forced herself to say through her tears. 'I didn't realise we had so much money to give us a start. Perhaps we could make a go of it after all?'

'What? Do you mean it?' His face lit up.

She forced a smile and nodded. 'Yes, I suppose I was just frightened of going so far away from everyone and everything that I know. I am ... er, fond of you. But will you please untie me now? My wrists are so sore.'

'Of course, my darling. And then I shall go straight to the docks and find out when the next ship out of here is leaving. The world is our oyster from now on and when we get wherever we're going we'll be married. Who cares about children, as long as we're together.'

Once more the ties that bound her were undone and she rubbed at her wrists, making them bleed again.

He took her hands in his and stared down at them. 'Oh, my poor love, look what I've done to you.' He lowered his head and she cringed as his lips grazed her sore wrists but somehow, she managed to keep her smile in place. It was clear now that he was unhinged and living on his nerves and she knew that if she were to stand any chance of escaping, she must humour him.

'You get off and find out when we can be on our way,' she said encouragingly. 'In fact, why don't I come with you?'

The suspicion was back on his face now and he frowned. 'No, you wait here. I promise I shan't be gone too long and I'll leave the candle for you so that you're not in the dark.'

He collected the money up into the bag again and tossing the rucksack over his shoulder he headed for the stairs. 'I'll be back before you know it!' Then he climbed the stairs and was gone, but not before she heard him shut the door and place something against it on the other side.

Now that there was at least some light she began to search about the cellar amongst the rubbish strewn everywhere and eventually she found what appeared to be the leg of a broken chair. It was heavy and solid and she quickly hid it beside the bottom of the stairs. Then, heart pounding, all she could do was wait for his return.

At last she heard the sound of something scraping across the floor on the other side of the door and with her heart in her mouth, Emmy quickly blew out the candle and lifted the chair leg, concealing it in the folds of her skirt.

'Emmy . . . where are you and why are you in the dark?' From the faint light that issued from the doorway she could see him descending the stairs.

'I'm down here waiting for you . . . The candle burnt out a while ago.'

She was crouching to one side at the bottom of the stairs and she knew that she must succeed. She was painfully aware that she would only get this one chance and if her plan didn't work, goodness knew what would happen. She tried to stay calm as he continued towards her. The closer he got the worse the stale smell of him became and then he was there at the side of her, just an arm's length away. She knew that his eyes wouldn't have had time to adjust to the light – it was now or never!

'Ah, there you are, darling.' He could just make out her outline and as he stretched his hand towards her, she raised the heavy chair leg and with every ounce of strength she had left she swung it towards his head.

There was a sickening thud as it connected with his ear and for a second he just stood there before dropping like a stone. Emmy had no way of knowing how badly hurt he was or even if she had killed him and she was too panicked and terrified to find out, so lifting her skirts she stumbled up the stairs, sobbing and whimpering with fear.

When she emerged into the large room at the top of the stairs, she saw people lying about, most of them with bottles in their hands. Not one of them so much as glanced at her as she raced for the door and emerged into the filthy alley beyond. She had lost all sense of direction and just stumbled ahead. Every second she expected to feel Jasper's hand on her shoulder and this lent speed to her feet. Then at last she saw the glimmer of street lights in front of her and soon she emerged on to a main road where she almost fell into the path of a hackney cab that was passing.

'P-please, take me to my aunt's house.' She quickly mumbled the address as she flung the door open and fell on to the grimy leather squabs. For a moment she feared that the driver was going to refuse but then thankfully he geed up the horse and they were moving again as she tried to catch her breath and pressed her hand to the stitch in her side.

At last the cab drew up outside the house and as Emmy stumbled down from the carriage she told the driver, 'Wait there and someone will come out to pay you.'

She dragged herself up the steps with the last of her remaining strength and hammered on the door. It was opened almost immediately by Aggie with a grim-faced Jake close behind her. She was sure she had never been so happy to see anyone in her entire life and as she fell into his arms she muttered, 'Can you pay the cabbie?' Then darkness closed about her and she knew no more.

The next time she opened her eyes she was lying on the sofa in her aunt's drawing room with Jake anxiously hovering over her and she managed a shaky smile for him. But as everything rushed back, she began to sob.

Taking her in his arms he tried to soothe her. 'Where have you been? We've been scouring the streets for you along with almost every constable in London!'

Taking a deep breath, she began to tell him everything that had happened, until she got to the bit where she admitted that she'd injured Jasper.

'I . . . I think I might have killed him,' she gabbled. 'But I was too afraid to wait about to find out.'

His jaw set. 'It would be good riddance to bad rubbish if you did,' he ground out. 'But there're are two constables in the hallway. Can you tell them where the warehouse is?'

'I think so.' She heaved herself up on to her elbow as Jake went to fetch the two young officers waiting in the hallway and haltingly, she gave them directions as best she could.

'I think I know where you're talking about, miss,' one of them said when she was finished. 'We'll go there now and try to catch him.' They touched their helmets and left as her aunt appeared, leaning heavily on Aggie's arm.

'That was quite a fright you gave us,' she said shortly and Emmy had to resist the urge to hug her. Trust her aunt to get right to the heart of the matter.

'It gave me quite a fright too,' she answered wryly as Aggie hurried away to fetch her a hot drink. It was then that Emmy noticed the state she was in and she blushed with embarrassment. Her gown was creased and filthy, her hair had escaped its pins and hung in rats' tails about her shoulders and she didn't smell very nice either. But it didn't seem to bother Jake, for the next minute he threw his arms about her, regardless of their aunt, and said chokily, 'Thank goodness you managed to get away . . . I don't know what I would have done if anything had happened to you. If I could get my hands on that no-good brother of mine at this minute, I'd strangle him, I *swear* I would.'

'Oh, Jake . . . I was *so* frightened. I thought I was never going to see you again.' Emmy's hand unconsciously rose to stroke his cheek as it finally began to sink in that she was safe again. But then she realised what she was doing and she quickly withdrew it. It really wouldn't do to let him know how she felt about him. He was her cousin and nothing could change that.

'Right, I'm going to leave you here with Aunt Imogen and Aggie now while I go and get the doctor.'

'But *you're* a doctor,' she reminded him and shamefaced he grinned.

'Yes, I know I am, but I don't think it would be right for me to examine you.'

She opened her mouth to object but he shook his head and smiled at her. 'Those wrists need looking at for a start, and your ankles will too, no doubt. We don't want them getting infected. But don't worry, you're back and you're quite safe now.'

When he'd gone, Imogen moved to sit on the chair beside her.

'So, it's as I thought then.'

'What do you mean?' Emmy raised an eyebrow.

'You and Jake – you're in love!'

Emmy lowered her eyes. 'I-I don't know what you mean.'

'Huh! You'd have to be a blind man on a galloping donkey not to see what's between you,' Imogen retorted. 'I've suspected it for months but tonight just confirmed it.'

Emmy wanted to deny it but her aunt seemed to be able to see into her very soul so she merely shrugged.

'I do have feelings for him,' she admitted miserably. 'Very deep feelings as it happens. But don't worry, I know that nothing can ever come of it so I've never told him. I-I'm sorry.'

Imogen shook her head. 'Don't be,' she said abruptly. 'We can't help who we fall in love with, but perhaps your position isn't quite as bad as you think.'

'And what is that supposed to mean?'

Imogen shrugged. 'Let's just say when I first met my Marcel things weren't straightforward. He was trapped in a loveless marriage but we shamed the devil and moved in together. We were only able to marry when his legal wife died but I wouldn't have cared if we'd lived in sin for the whole of our time together.'

Emmy sighed. 'But you had cut ties with your family by then. Can you imagine what my parents and Aunt Sybil would say if Jake and I were to do that? They would disown us!'

Aggie bustled back in with tea and sandwiches and the conversation was brought to an abrupt end as Emmy tucked into them, ravenous. Once she'd eaten her fill, Aggie took her upstairs and helped her to bathe and get into clean nightclothes, and shortly after Jake returned with the doctor who dressed her wrists and ankles and gave her a thorough examination.

'Apart from the chafing on your ankles and wrists you seem to be fine, young lady,' he assured her. 'Rather shaken up admittedly, but that's nothing that a couple of days' rest won't cure.'

He left as the two young constables returned to tell her that they'd managed to find the warehouse but that there had been no sign of Jasper.

'Are you sure you went to the right one?' Emmy asked.

The younger of the two nodded as he handed her a bonnet. 'We are if this is yours, miss. We found it in the cellar you described. You must have just stunned him and once he came round, he managed to escape. But don't worry, I'm sure he won't try to come near you again. We'll be watching the house and we have officers out scouring the streets for him.'

'Thank you, Constable.' Emmy wasn't sure if she was upset or relieved. After all, as her aunt had pointed out, you couldn't help who you fell in love with and wasn't she as guilty for loving Jake as Jasper was for loving her? Not only that, should the police find him he might well end up dangling at the end of a rope for the murder of his father, and somehow, no matter what he had done, she couldn't wish that on him. She had no doubt that he would leave the country on the first ship that left the dock and she hoped he made it.

The next lot of visitors arrived as the doctor was leaving and when her mother, father and Aunt Sybil were shown into her room, Emmy's eyes almost popped out of her head.

'We got your aunt's letter this morning to say that you were missing and we caught the first train here,' her mother told her with tears in her eyes. 'Jake just told us what happened. Thank God you're safe.'

'I'm fine, Mama, don't get upset.' As her mother cradled her in her arms, she looked over at Jake who was standing in the doorway. Their eyes met and he inclined his head, then quietly left the family to their reunion.

Chapter Forty-Seven

The next unexpected visitor to arrive was Abi the following morning. She had been unaware of what had happened to Emmy and listened aghast as her aunt and mother filled her in.

'But that's quite awful,' she said sadly. 'Is Emmy all right?'

'She will be now,' her mother answered with relief. 'The police called by early this morning to say that they'd still not been able to find Jasper. It seems that three ships sailed from the dock last night, one bound for China, one for Spain and one for France. He could have been on any one of them and I think it's highly unlikely we'll ever see him again. But now tell us all about what you've been up to. We've missed you so much.'

Abi took a deep breath. It was time for the truth; she didn't want to spend the rest of their lives with secrets between them, so slowly and painfully she told her story from the very beginning to the bitter end, omitting nothing.

'S-so I had a granddaughter.' Dorcas looked shocked.

Abi nodded, her eyes bright with unshed tears. 'You certainly did. Her name was Grace Rebecca and she was the most beautiful baby I ever saw.' She waited for the explosion then but it never came.

'But why didn't you tell us? You could have come home to us instead of hiding away at Aunt Imogen's house at the coast.'

'I thought you'd be angry and ashamed of me and I was planning on having the baby adopted when she arrived,' Abi admitted. 'But once she was born and I saw her and held her I knew I couldn't part with her. I didn't know then how poorly she was. Her little heart wasn't strong enough to keep beating.' As tears slid down her cheeks unchecked her mother took her in her arms and clucked sympathetically. This wasn't the reaction Abi had expected at all and she stared at her in confusion.

'I-I thought you wouldn't want anything to do with me once you knew, because I'd let you down,' she gasped between sobs.

Dorcas gave her a wry smile. 'I probably would have disowned you before we lost our home,' she admitted. 'I was such a snob back then. But now I know what's important.' She looked towards Gerald, her eyes shining with love. 'And I suppose now is as good a time as any to share our little secret with you. You see, although I'm in my early forties, your father and I have just discovered that in a few months' time you and Emerald are going to have a little brother or sister. It's ridiculous, I know, at our age, but I hope you won't be too embarrassed about it.'

'Embarrassed! Why, that's lovely news.' Abi looked genuinely pleased as her father flushed like a schoolboy.

'I thought our baby days were far behind us,' he said gruffly. 'But it seems they're about to start again. We're hoping for a boy this time, although we'll be perfectly happy with another girl, of course. And what you've just told us, my love – I want you to try and put it behind you and get on with your life. Everyone makes mistakes – I'm a prime example – but thank God we've all come together again. You'll never forget little Grace, of course, she's a memory you'll hold in your heart for all time, but you have your whole life before you and it's for living, when you decide what you want to do with it.'

'I already know,' Abi admitted, flushing prettily. 'You see Bertie, Mrs M's son, and I . . . Well . . . somewhere along the way we fell in love and he's asked me to marry him. He isn't rich, he's a working man, a carpenter by trade, but he's the loveliest, kindest man I ever met and so . . . Well, when I've had time to come to terms with all that's happened, I'm going to go back and if he still wants me, I shall tell him that I'd be proud to be his wife.'

'But that's *wonderful* news!' Dorcas shocked Abi yet again with her reaction. 'That just leaves us with Emerald to find a happy ending for now but I'm sure it will come in time.'

Aggie came rushing in at that moment to tell them, 'You'd better come quick. It's the missus. She's taken a turn for the worse. It's probably all that's been going on that's brought it on. Will you sit with her while I run for the doctor? Sybil is with her at the moment but she's asking to see you all.'

They all headed for the door at once, almost colliding in their haste and soon they were clustered around Imogen's bed. She looked very pale and frail and her lips were a frightening purple-blue colour but she managed to raise a smile when she opened her eyes and saw them.

'So, all the family back together just as it should be, and about time too! I was beginning to think I was going to have to bang your heads together!' she said in a shaky voice and Dorcas began to cry.

'Now, we'll have none of that,' Imogen rasped. 'It's my time and I'm happy to go. Marcel is waiting for me, there in the corner, look. He's been visiting me for months but I told him, "I can't come yet, not till I've sorted this lot out." And now I have.'

They all turned their heads to stare in the direction she was pointing but they couldn't see anyone.

'My will . . . is in that drawer over there.' She waved a shaky hand towards a drawer in her dressing table.

'Don't try to talk, Aunt Imogen,' Emmy urged. 'Try and save your strength.'

When she took her aunt's hand, Imogen squeezed it gently. A rare show of affection for her. 'Just remember what I told you.' Her breath was becoming more laboured now and as they all looked on, they felt helpless. 'Take love where you find it. True love comes only once in a lifetime and it's precious.'

She turned her head towards the corner and the most beautiful smile lit her face as she raised her hand. Her eyes closed, and as her hand dropped back to the frilly pink counterpane and her breathing stopped, a look of peace and contentment settled across her features.

'God bless her; she's with her Marcel now. May they never be parted again,' Dorcas said brokenly and they all bowed their heads.

The funeral took place the following week and was very well attended. While other members of polite society were there, Abi was relieved that there was no sign of a certain Lord Hugo. She had no interest in him whatsoever now. Her heart was with a certain young man in Lytham St Anne's and once this was all over, she intended to return there and tell him so.

The family had spent the afternoon before telling the vicar who conducted the service all about Imogen's flamboyant style and the exciting life she had led and there were smiles as well as tears as he relayed the memories to the congregation. Then Imogen's coffin was carried with ceremony to the plot in the churchyard where her beloved Marcel was buried and she joined him, together forever now as she would have wished.

At the house Aggie and Cook had provided a feast fit for a king for those mourners who wished to go back and the wine flowed like water as they spoke about how they had each known Imogen and what she had meant to them. It was late afternoon, before the last of the mourners left and then there was only the reading of Imogen's will to be got through, so they solemnly followed the solicitor into the drawing room.

The family sat down and after clearing his throat and offering his condolences, the solicitor took the will from his leather bag and began, 'As you are all aware, we are gathered here today to hear the last will and testament of Mrs Imogen Mary Dubois. If there is anything that any of you don't understand please feel free to question me as we go along.

'First of all, to my loyal friend and maid, Miss Aggie Briggs, I bequeath the sum of two hundred pounds with thanks for all the loyal service she has given me and the same amount to my cook, Mrs Ellen Lowe.'

Shocked, Aggie and the cook began to cry softly and Emmy put her arms about their shoulders and gave them a little hug.

'To my sister, Mrs Dorcas Winter, and my sister-in-law, Mrs Sybil Chetwynd, I bequeath the sum of five hundred pounds each. To my niece, Miss Abigail Winter, I bequeath my house in Lytham St Anne's and all its contents on the proviso that she marries Mr Albert Merryweather, who currently resides at said address.' This brought a delighted gasp from Abi who could hardly believe what she was hearing.

'Finally, to my niece, Miss Emerald Winter, I bequeath this house and all my remaining monies and worldly possessions on the proviso that she and my nephew Mr Jake Chetwynd marry within the next two months. I suggest that they might then adapt part of the house into becoming a poor surgery so that Jake can continue his good work from home.'

There was a shocked gasp from Dorcas, and the colour drained from Emmy's face as she gazed at Jake who also looked shocked.

'B-but that's impossible,' Emmy muttered. 'We've always known we couldn't marry – it would be too dangerous for us to have healthy children.'

Sybil stopped her from saying any more when she said quietly, 'It isn't quite as impossible as you think – but for you to understand, I'm afraid I shall have to start at the beginning.' Taking a deep breath to compose herself she began tentatively, 'A long time ago when I was young and foolish, I gave my heart to a gypsy who came to work on my father's estate.'

At this point Dorcas and Gerald rose saying, 'Perhaps we should leave you to speak to Emerald and Jake in private?' But Sybil waved them back to their seats.

'No, it's time you all knew the truth, please stay.'

Reluctantly they sat back down and Sybil went on, 'As you all know I have never been the prettiest of women so when the gypsy paid me attention I was flattered. Vano was the handsomest man I had ever met with jet-black curly hair and the bluest eyes I ever saw but of course I didn't dare let my parents know there was anything going on between us. Back then they had high hopes that I would make a good marriage. Anyway, all through that summer I was besotted with him, but just before the gypsies were due to leave, I discovered that I was to have a child. When I told Vano, he seemed to take it well and told me that he would make things right. But when I got up the next morning the whole lot of them had gone and I never saw him again.'

She had to stop here to calm herself, before she continued, 'Of course it wasn't something that I could hide for long and when my father discovered I was to have a child he was furious and disgusted with me. Then merely days later he told me that he had found someone who was prepared to marry me. I knew that he must be offering a large dowry, of course. It was never a love match. And so, Bernard and I were married and if anyone noticed that Jake was born within months of us being wed, they all assumed that the child was Bernard's. All but Imogen, that is. When Bernard and I married so quickly Imogen had already guessed that I was pregnant – and it seems she worked out that it couldn't be Bernard's as we had not known each other long enough. She had noticed that I never paid as much attention to my first child as I did to my second and she put two and two together.' She stared at Jake with tears in her eyes. 'That's why I never paid you as much attention as I did Jasper. And for that I am truly sorry. I suppose you were always a constant reminder of the love I had lost. Then when Jasper came along, I rather spoilt him, and look how that ended up! Even so, although I'm appalled at what he did to you and his father, Emmy, I can't help but be relieved to know that he got away from the police. No one wants to see their own flesh and blood being hanged for murder. My punishment will be that I will never see him again and that's something I shall have to live with. But you and Jake . . . do you see now? There is no blood tie whatsoever between you, so when Imogen told me she suspected that you two were in love I knew it would be cruel not to tell you the truth.'

A shocked silence settled on the room, until the solicitor coughed and began to gather his papers hastily together, saying, 'Well, I have nothing more to tell you. I think you all have a lot to talk about, so if you'll excuse me?' He removed his spectacles from the end of his nose and scuttled away like a cat with its tail on fire.

Abi hurried over to kiss her sister's cheek. 'I'm off to start my packing. I shall be leaving for my new home tomorrow to propose to a certain young man there.'

Dorcas, Sybil and Gerald rose too, and with a smile at Emmy her father told her, 'I think you two need a little time alone to chat, my dear. Come along, ladies.'

He ushered the women ahead of him and once the door had closed behind them Emmy flushed.

'Well . . . I suppose we'd better set a date for the wedding then; we don't want you to lose your inheritance, do we?' Jake grinned at her

Emmy bristled. 'Thank you *very* much for the offer but you don't have to worry about *me*!' Her eyes flashed as she spun to face him. 'I promised my father that when and *if* I ever married it would be for love!'

'But just think what a wonderful surgery this room would make,' he teased. 'And the hallway could become the waiting room. We'd have so much more room to see our patients!'

He was really grinning now as he approached her and put his arm about her and she stiffened. They had both known how they felt about each other for such a long time and yet neither of them had ever admitted it to each other.

'And then there's the other reason we should get married,' he whispered, and she stared at him bemused.

'What do you mean?'

'Oh, Emmy, *surely* you know?' He sighed heavily and his smile was gone now as he shook his head. 'I think I've been in love with you ever since you were knee-high to a grasshopper. But the thing is, how do *you* feel about me?'

She gulped deep in her throat as she stared up at him, hardly daring to believe what she was hearing. He was holding her so tightly that she could feel his heartbeat through the fabric of her mourning gown.

'I . . . I love you too,' she whispered, but there was no time to say any more because his lips came down on hers and in that moment all her wildest dreams came true.

Out in the hallway, Aggie removed the glass she had had pressed against the door and gave the assembled family a thumbs up with a twinkle in her eye. 'They've gone really quiet,' she whispered. 'So I reckon you two can start plannin' the weddin'.'

'*Weddings!*' Abi reminded her with a broad grin. 'Perhaps we could have a double one?'

'What a *splendid* idea!' Dorcas and Sybil beamed at each other as arm in arm they headed for the day room to have a celebratory glass of sherry and start planning the big day.

Acknowledgements

As always, a huge thank you to my wonderful team at Bonnier! Kate Parkin, Sarah Bauer, my lovely editor, Katie Meegan, her trusted assistant, Gillian Holmes my marvellous copyeditor, Jane Howard my proofreader and all the rest of the 'Rosie team' who always strive to work with me every step of the way to make each book as good as it can possibly be. Never forgetting my wonderful agent, Sheila Crowley and the lovely Sabhbh Curran at Curtis Brown, always there to encourage and support me.

Of course, there has to be a special thank you to my husband and my family for their patience. And last but never least to you, my wonderful readers for all your wonderful messages.

Thank you all x

Hi everyone,

Spring has sprung at last and it's time for me to bring *A Daughter's Destiny*, my latest offering to you all. I do hope you'll all enjoy meeting the lovely Emerald, with her gorgeous green eyes. I really grew to love her as I wrote this story and hope you will, too. Isn't the book cover just lovely? Once again, my amazing team at Bonnier have excelled themselves. As usual, poor Emerald doesn't have an easy time of it although she starts out in a very privileged background.

I'm very lucky to live close to a small village of Astley in Warwickshire with its pretty little church and the castle, which is steeped in history, and as I was walking there, I was inspired to write a book and *A Daughter's Destiny* was the result. I always have a sense of walking back in time when I enter Astley Church and of course I do give poor Emerald a hard time, but then I think my readers know that none of my characters are going to get off lightly by now.

I'm looking forward to spending more time at the coast this year. What with lockdowns, Covid and moving house, last year passed in a blur and we didn't get away half as much as we would have liked to. It wasn't just the moving that was stressful, we seemed to spend weeks after the move informing everyone of our change of address, insurance, rates, driving licences, etc! Still, we are getting more settled now so hopefully we'll be able to make up for it this year. I'm also looking forward to spending time in my new garden. We've already made quite a few changes to it and so we're busily planning what we want to do with the rest of it. My dogs love their new garden and also now that I have an office downstairs they like to lie in there with me while I am working, which I love.

Of course, I'm now working away on the next book and hope to be able to tell you a little about it very soon, as they say, 'there's no rest for the wicked!' The Precious Stones series has turned out to be such a lovely collection to write and I'm already thinking hard about what I'd like to do next!

In the meantime, I hope you all stay safe and have a wonderful summer. Do keep in touch on the Memory Lane Club page and if you haven't already joined it, please do. On there you can keep up to date with what myself and the other Memory Lane authors are doing, as well as entering some lovely competitions.

I very much look forward to hearing what you all think of *A Daughter's Destiny* and would like to thank you for all your ongoing encouragement and support.

Much love,
Rosie xx

Victorian Picnic Hamper

Emmy and Jake take a picnic to the park to enjoy a fine summer's day, but the day doesn't go as Emmy expected. Victorians simply loved a picnic, and we have to admit that we do too! Follow our top tips below to ensure that your Victorian picnic goes swimmingly.

Serves 4
Four hearty bread rolls
Cheddar cheese, sliced
Punnets of strawberries, blackberries or raspberries
Cold meats, sliced
A small jar of pickles
A small jar of chutney
Cold pork pie
Hard-boiled eggs
Scones with butter and jam
A flask of warm water for tea and coffee
Lemonade
Assorted biscuits

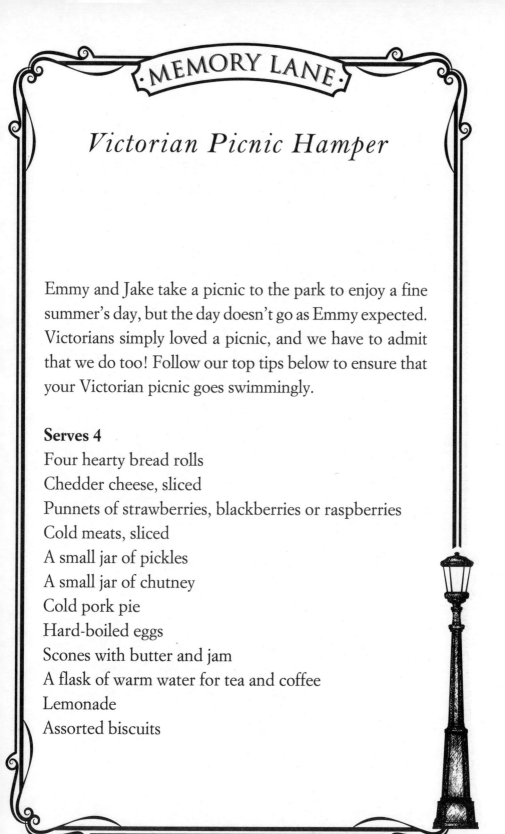

How to Host a Victorian Picnic

Preparation is key: Cook and prepare all your food earlier in the day, or if your excursion is early in the morning, the night before. Slice your cheese and cold meats, boil the eggs and make sure any foods that require oven baking, such as scones and pork pies, have been given ample time to cool down.

Pack your picnic: A good strong basket is crucial to a Victorian picnic. Grape baskets and paper boxes had one advantage as food containers for a Victorian picnic – they did not need to be brought home. They packed each item solidly and wrapped it individually in a napkin or paraffin paper (but nowadays, tinfoil or clingfilm will do).

Don't be precious: There's no need for nice napkins, silver, china cups, or plates, in fact, the breakage or loss of a piece of valued crockery could spoil a perfectly nice afternoon. Wooden or paper plates are a good alternative.

Pick your perfect location: Victorians would often prefer to sit near lakes and rivers. Trees are your best friend, pick a location that has plenty of shelter, you'll be grateful of it come rain or shine!

Enjoy your Victorian feast!

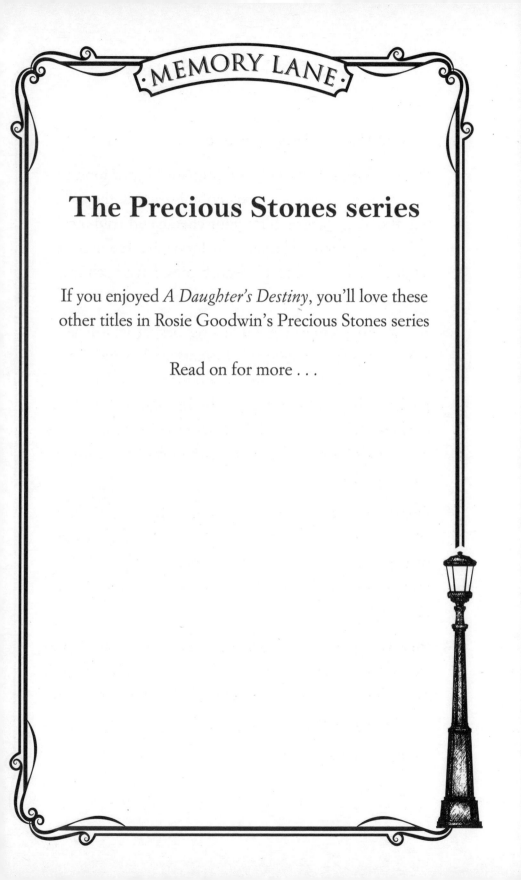

MEMORY LANE

The Precious Stones series

If you enjoyed *A Daughter's Destiny*, you'll love these other titles in Rosie Goodwin's Precious Stones series

Read on for more . . .

The Winter Promise

1850.

When Opal Sharp finds herself and her younger siblings suddenly orphaned and destitute, she thinks things can get no worse. But soon three of them – including Opal – are struck down with the illness that took their father, and her brother Charlie is forced to make an impossible decision. Unable to afford a doctor, he knows the younger children will not survive. So, unbeknownst to Opal, Charlie takes their younger siblings to the workhouse. When she finds out, Opal is heartbroken.

Charlie starts taking risks to try to support what's left of the Sharp family and earn Opal's forgiveness, but he takes it too far and finds himself in trouble with the law.
Soon, he is sent on a convict ship to Australia.

As poor Opal is forced to say goodbye to the final member of her family, she makes a promise to reunite them all one day.

Will she ever see her family again?

An Orphan's Journey

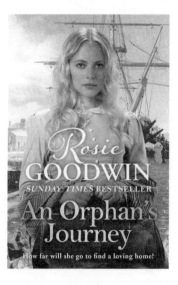

1874.

Growing up in extreme poverty in London, Pearl thinks life can get no worse. But when her parents discover there's yet another baby on the way, they have to tighten the belt even further. Pearl's mother decides to send her and her younger sister Eliza to the workhouse, where they are forced into a new life of hardship and struggle.

Pearl's hopes are raised when the workhouse offers the sisters a new life in Canada and they board an orphan ship transporting unwanted children across the seas. Pearl hopes their luck has finally changed when she and Eliza are hired by the kindly Mrs Forbes to work in her grand house together. But when Pearl meets their mistress's bullying son Monty he reveals he will stop at nothing to make her life a misery.

Will Pearl ever find the home she so craves?

A Simple Wish

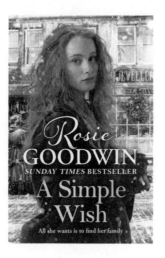

1885.

Life is hard for Ruby Carter. Working at her parents' bakery, her gentle mother protects young Ruby from her cruel father and loves her unconditionally. That is until her mother is stricken with a fatal illness and, from her deathbed, reveals that Ruby was adopted.

Overcome by grief and alone with the violent man she once called her father, Ruby has no choice but to flee. At just fifteen, homeless and alone, she is relieved when a kindly stranger named Mrs Bamber takes pity on her and welcomes poor Ruby into her home.

But soon, Ruby learns Mrs Bamber is not as generous as she first seemed – she forces Ruby into a life of crime as a jewel thief in Birmingham's jewellery quarter. With nothing to her name and nowhere to go, Ruby has no choice but to steal. But Ruby is determined that she will atone for what she's done and be reunited with her birth parents.

Ruby's only wish is to find her family.

The Days of the Week Collection

If you enjoyed *A Daughter's Destiny*, you'll love
Rosie Goodwin's Days of the Week
collection, inspired by the Victorian
'Days of the Week' rhyme.

Turn over to find out more . . .

Mothering Sunday

The child born on the Sabbath Day,
Is bonny and blithe, and good and gay.

1884, Nuneaton.

Fourteen-year-old Sunday has grown up in the cruelty of the Nuneaton workhouse. When she finally strikes out on her own, she is determined to return for those she left behind, and to find the long-lost mother who gave her away. But she's about to discover that the brutal world of the workhouse will not let her go without a fight.

The Little Angel

Monday's child is fair of face.

1896, Nuneaton.

Left on the doorstep of Treetops Children's Home, young Kitty captures the heart of her guardian, Sunday Branning, and grows into a beguiling and favoured young girl – until she is summoned to live with her birth mother. In London, nothing is what it seems, and her old home begins to feel very far away. If Kitty is to have any chance of happiness, this little angel must protect herself from devils in disguise . . . and before it's too late.

A Mother's Grace

Tuesday's child is full of grace.

1910, Nuneaton.

When her father's threatening behaviour grows worse, pious young Grace Kettle escapes her home to train to be a nun. But when she meets the dashing and devout Father Luke, her world is turned upside down. She is driven to make a scandalous choice – one she may well spend the rest of her days seeking forgiveness for.

The Blessed Child

Wednesday's child is full of woe.

1864, Nuneaton.

After Nessie Carson's mother is brutally murdered and her father abandons them, Nessie knows she will do anything to keep her family safe. As her fragile young brother's health deteriorates and she attracts the attention of her lecherous landlord, soon Nessie finds herself in the darkest of times. But there is light and the promise of happiness if only she is brave enough to fight for it.

A Maiden's Voyage

Thursday's child has far to go.

1912, London.

Eighteen-year-old maid Flora Butler has her life turned upside-down when her mistress's father dies in a tragic accident. Her mistress is forced to move to New York to live with her aunt until she comes of age, and begs Flora to go with her. Flora has never left the country before, and now faces a difficult decision – give up her position, or leave her family behind. Soon, Flora and her mistress head for Southampton to board the RMS *Titanic*.

A Precious Gift

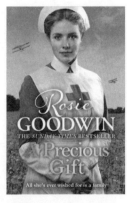

Friday's child is loving and giving.

1911, Nuneaton.

When Holly Farthing's overbearing grandfather tries to force her to marry a widower twice her age, she flees to London, bringing her best friend and maid, Ivy, with her. In the big smoke, Holly begins nurse training in the local hospital. There she meets the dashing Doctor Parkin, everything Holly has ever dreamt of. But soon, she discovers some shocking news that means they can never be together, and her life is suddenly thrown into turmoil. Supporting the war effort, she heads to France and throws herself into volunteering on the front line . . .

Time to Say Goodbye

Saturday's child works hard for their living.

1935, Nuneaton.

Kathy has grown up at Treetops home for children, where Sunday and Tom Branning have always cared for her as one of their own. With her foster sister Livvy at her side, and a future as a nurse ahead of her, she could wish for nothing more. But when Tom dies suddenly in a riding accident, life at Treetops will never be the same again. As their financial difficulties mount, will the women of Treetops be forced to leave their home?

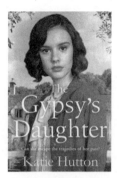

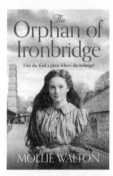
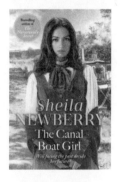
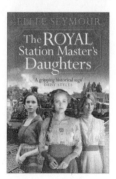

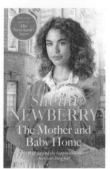

·MEMORY LANE·

Wartime Tales from Memory Lane

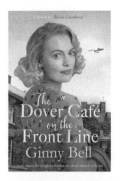

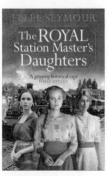

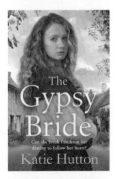

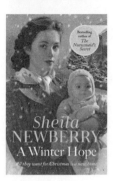

Discover the new stories from the best saga authors

Available now

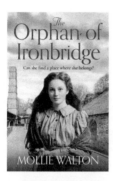
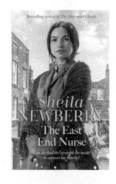

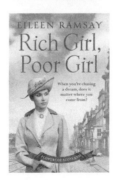

· MEMORY LANE ·

Introducing the place for story lovers – a welcoming home for all readers who love heartwarming tales of wartime, family and romance. Join us to discuss your favourite stories with other readers, plus get book recommendations, book giveaways and behind-the-scenes writing moments from your favourite authors.

· MEMORY LANE ·

www.MemoryLane.Club

f /MemoryLaneClub